PACK DARLING

LOLA ROCK

LOLA
ROCK
REVERSE HAREM

First Published by Lola Rock in 2022

100 Commons Road, Suite 7-303
Dripping Springs, TX 78620
www.thelolarock.com

ISBN 9781955974820

Cover design by Lola

CONTENT WARNING

ONE

LILAH

I'M WRAPPED in weighted blankets, wallowing in home shows and hospital pudding when a knock rattles my self-enforced solitude. "Lilah? It's Doctor Sorensen. There's been another incident."

My pheromones flare in a panicked burst of super-powered sugar, heart beating like I'm taking cover in a trench instead of curled up in my hospital bed.

Because my life is a war-zone.

It's been one week since I woke up at the Wyvern Clinic blind, broken, covered in chemical burns, and scorned by my so-called mates.

One week, three kidnapping attempts, two armed break-ins, and a smoke bomb smuggled in through the laundry.

"We need to move you to a new room. Can I come in?"

"Can you?" My pheromones are a billboard flashing **BREED ME NOW** in screaming neon.

All unmated staff are banned from my floor while my allure's stuck on steal-your-soul levels of temptation that won't turn off thanks to constant threats on my life and hormones possibly permanently screwed because I spent my first heat marinating in a barrel of chemicals.

I'm awakened.

A fully mature omega.

Fucking *fertile*.

And my body's taking revenge for all the years I spent starving, exhausting, and denying myself.

"I'll risk it." Doctor Sorensen cracks the door.

I peek out from my blanket sanctuary even though my instincts scream to nest, hide, call my alphas to protect me.

The reality?

I'm on my own.

I don't have alphas.

And I need to know the latest threat now, so that when the next attack comes, I can protect *myself*. "What happened this time?"

"A nurse tampered with your meds. She was planning to sedate you and smuggle you out." He starts to rub his head but can't, decked out in plague-doctor PPE that reveals nothing but a pair of guilty brown eyes.

The gear smothers his scent, which is the only reason I can handle having a beta in my room when all I want to do is barricade the door and rig a crossbow trap so that no one else can hurt me.

But this isn't my room.

And nowhere's safe when the Redfang Cartel wants me dead or made into their sociopath leader's sex slave.

So, I'm panicky and putting off pheromones strong enough to warp steel, but I force myself to tuck and roll off the bed. Wrapped in a burrito of ten-pound blankets, I shed snack crumbs like a toddler.

And with a stolen scalpel at each hip, I'm ready for whoever comes at me next. "Where to?"

"Room 820." Doctor Sorensen steps back, giving me plenty of space, but the way he braces against the wall, pupils flaring behind his face shield, it couldn't be clearer that my scent is taking prisoners.

Not prisoners I want.

CHAPTER 1   5

The armed guards that pack the hallway jolt when I make my shuffling appearance. One chokes, fingers shaking as he grips his throat.

I tense.

They're decked in Wyvern House's black camo, all mated betas who're supposedly assigned to keep me safe.

But to me, they're just another threat.

It's a beta's fault I'm here.

Fucking Craig.

The doctors think he injected me with some dodgy black market hormone cocktail. I was already so close to my first heat that the chemicals dumped water on a grease fire, and now I'm living the explosion.

If not for him handing the Redfangs the keys to Wyvern Pack's castle, I could've escaped.

Faded away to a new life and kept my hormones stomped down forever.

Even when I first woke up, I thought I had a chance. That I could break free, sneak away, maybe shimmy down the laundry chute, cling to a bumper, and get dragged across the border somewhere with no Wyvern Pack and no record that I ever existed.

Those were the drugs talking.

Now that I'm weaning off the painkillers and sedatives, the truth is, escape is a dead dream.

I'm awakened.

Which means I need alphas.

My body craves them, needs them to survive my heat, and I'm not stupid or suicidal enough to hang up that call a second time.

That pain.

That emptiness.

I can't.

Never-ever-ever-*ever* again.

Thank all the gods and goddesses, I have a few months to plan. The grace period is the last thread of spun sugar holding together the quivering lobes of my crazed omega brain. I'm going to need every blessed second to find a pack that can give me what I want.

Lotsa knots, no attachments.

When I shuffle down the hall, flanked by big, tall bodies, my instincts won't stop screaming.

Hide, alphas, safety, pack, mates, NEED—

I breathe through the hyped-up panic.

Girl.

Nobody's coming to save us.

My new room smells alcohol sterile, and it's just as ridiculous as the first four suites I've used this week.

I double-checked at the desk.

Wyvern Pack is footing the bill, so I don't say no to the luxury. The least my never-mates owe me is a private room.

The suite has a wide, pillow-strewn hospital bed, no windows, and a dimmer switch already dialed down to primordial cave.

First insane priority, I smooth, shift, and stack the sheets and pillows like perfectly arranged linens will save the day. But nesting calms the crazy stream-of-consciousness thoughts hijacking my brain, so I lean into the urge, mushing and moving blankets.

Doctor Sorensen hovers at the doorway, only now he's holding a pink bakery box.

"My alpha sent fudge. Can I tempt you?"

Rumor's out.

I'm awakened, unmated, and a total slut for anything sweet.

I lick my lips, staring down the label of the best bakery in the city. I used to dream about their cakes when I was biding my time at the Omega Cultivation Center, and the other girls came home from the events I skipped loaded with treats from their admirers.

For the first time in my life, I have admirers.

Turns out, I *hate* having admirers.

I'm building my own fan club from the guards and nurses mooning over me like a toffee lollipop they want to lick until there's nothing left but stick.

No thank you.

When Doctor Sorensen was assigned to my case and showed up with the first box of cupcakes, I made the nurses check for poison.

But he holds himself back, not pushing my boundaries or tipping off my well-honed skeez radar.

Even if I'm reading him wrong and the guy's here to assassinate me, if I have to die, I choose death by chocolate. "Thank you."

His eyes crinkle behind his face shield, and he rolls the tray table to my bed, setting down the box. "Jason made this batch just for you."

Did I mention that his alpha *owns* the best bakery in the city?

He's the pastry chef.

I'm not loving this new state of *want-you-for-your-pheromones* attention, but that doesn't mean I say no to free fudge.

"Which flavor would you like?" He pops open the box to reveal a sampler of fudge bites topped with everything from marshmallows to breakfast cereal to edible glitter.

I pluck out a rainbow monstrosity made of food dye and diabetes.

"Unicorn." He *hmms*. "Good choice."

My eyes roll back when the sugar hits my tongue, and I can't keep down a soul-deep moan. "It's so goooood."

"I'll tell Jason how much you liked it." Doctor Sorensen leans away from my elephant-tranquilizing pheromones, gripping his arms. "He said mini cheesecakes tomorrow. Kipp and Rhett want to send gifts too, but I told them to slow down."

I choke mid-bite. "Doctor Sorensen. My debt—"

"Call me Cale," he says. "Your debt's not a problem. Wyvern Pack only owns half the city. Who do you think owns the other half?"

Weird flex, but okay.

I'm definitely not attracted—the man's a Smurf, all blue medical gear, nothing showing but his eyes—but the way he looks at me is nothing how the betas always looked at me when I was growing up at the OCC.

Nothing like Craig's creepery, either.

They watched me like a toy or an asset. A failure or an enemy. Someone they could boss around or treat like trash.

Cale looks at me with *hope*.

It makes me just as sick.

I can't be what his pack or any pack wants—the smiley, happy omega who anchors their bonds—but if he keeps looking at me like *that*, treating me nice, offering to buy my freedom, and feeding me sweets…

I'm gonna wanna take the safety he's offering.

The unspoken promise that his pack would never leave me needing.

Hurting.

"I can't join a pack." My contract with Wyvern Pack voided the second they didn't satisfy my heat, because there's no more textbook way to flush your omega.

Going into rotation—a new pack every heat with zero painful strings like mating bites or pesky bonded souls—is my new life goal.

That's the only way I can guarantee that I don't suffer *and* I'm not lifetime stuck to another pack of dysfunctional fools.

"That's your choice." Cale rubs his arms. "If you're taking pack offers, we're making one. If you're going into rotation, we'll be first in line to bid. I promise not to pressure you. Convince you, yeah, no apologies for that. We'd be honored to have such a sweet omega join our pack."

I snort.

My scent is the only thing about me that's sweet. A smoky caramel that hides my sour personality.

One second-hand whiff of my pheromones that must've clung to Cale's scrubs and his pack wants to lock me down forever.

I'd be more cynical if this were a week ago, but that was before.

Before Wyvern Pack told me I don't belong, then proved it by leaving me alone to suffer.

Before I spent my heat writhing in a barrel.

Before I realized what I actually want.

I want security.

I want safety.

I want an iron-clad, notarized, no-take-backs guarantee from alphas who'll lend me their knots to bounce away the pain, then see themselves to the revolving door so that I can get back to building a life I choose for myself.

I don't know if Sorensen Pack can deliver.

I don't know if *any* pack can deliver.

But Wyvern Pack has proven they can't.

So, I promise myself that no matter how my hormones whine at me to hand over my ass, I'll never mate a pack that can't treat me the way I deserve to be treated.

Because who needs mates?

Screw destiny, fate, and all things meant-to-be.

I take care of myself.

And I'm done hurting.

TWO

LILAH

CALE LEAVES me alone with my fudge, but I'm only halfway through the box when another knock has my hackles popping. Doctor Morgan takes over the room in a wave of alpha female energy that leaves me choking on a bite of cookie dough.

"How are you feeling?" She's masked and decked out in protective gear, but her alpha scent's too strong to stifle.

A warm, cinnamon walnut with a hint of gin.

Boozy aunt energy.

Now that I'm awakened, it doesn't matter that I'm not attracted. Her alpha dominance hits like a punch to the uterus—a sharp reminder of what my body wants and needs.

I shake, take a breath, and remind myself the woman's mated and doesn't have the right equipment to stop the inner ache. "Mostly feeling better. Less pain, but more jittery."

"I think I know the reason for that." She rolls up a stool, and my heart jump-starts at her *this-means-business* arm fold. "Which news do you want first?"

"Is there good news?"

She's silent.

Right. "Just tell me."

"This is your latest bloodwork." Doctor Morgan tugs over a

stand monitor, pulling up a screen full of spiky red graphs you don't need a medical degree to understand. "You have at most a month before your next heat. More likely, it'll hit within the next two weeks."

My pulse rockets to a nasty conclusion.

That's too fast.

Too soon.

Too many decisions I have to make, and I'm not ready to go through that pain.

Not again.

"There's more."

I bite back the desperate whine coiled and ready to spring up my throat. "What else?"

"At this pace, you may be looking at a permanent monthly heat."

Monthly!

A monthly fucking heat!

My last heat was so painful I wanted to die.

"I can't," I croak like an asthmatic frog.

I thought I had time.

Not a lot of time, but at least a couple months to pretend to get my shit together.

"Calm down," she says in a meant-to-be-soothing alpha tone that couldn't be more condescending.

What the fuck is there to be *calm* about?

"We'll find you a pack that can take care of your needs. You have options."

Do I though?

I need alphas NOW.

Instead of months, I have *days* to figure out my life or risk another round of searing pain.

"Your mates—"

"Rejected me."

"I won't pressure you to accept them." She lifts her hands. "But have you contacted your guardian?"

I try not to think about either generation of the Wyvern Pack, even if they're constantly claiming space in my brain.

I remember the guys at my bedside when I first woke up, still bandaged and drugged.

I also remember wanting them gone.

I wasn't ready.

I needed space.

I'm still not ready, but I thought they'd be pounding down my door.

Days later, I'm still alone, and I couldn't be more grateful.

I'm *beyond* grateful they didn't cash the blank check I wrote when I presented myself to their nest, deep in heat and deluded off my ass.

If they'd have bitten me, mated me, *taken* me…

Instead of getting a chance to do this omega thing my way, I'd already be perma-stuck to mates who fail me on every level.

"I'll call the center. I'm going on the rotation roster."

"Excellent." Doctor Morgan nods. "The sooner you can match to heat partners, the better for your hormones. You'll want alphas lined up to ease you through the heat spikes leading up to the big event. Until you have that sense of stability, you'll experience more erratic behavior, moodiness, and intensified nesting instincts."

"*You think?*" I gesture to myself, wrapped like a pig in a blanket and vibrating like a freaking loon.

"Yes. Well." Doctor Morgan stands, brushing her pants. "I can discharge you as soon as you know where you'll land."

"One more thing," I call before she can march to her next crazed omega patient.

"I can't sedate you through your heat, Lilah. It would be too risky after the first—"

"Not that." Clearly, I've asked a few times. "I want birth control."

"For your first—"

"It's not my first." Been there, barely survived, and if that did nothing else, it gave me a hell of a lot of clarity. "I don't care about the side effects. I'm not *breeding*." I scowl the word. "I'm not putting my name out to packs who think that's even an option."

I've grown up seeing the sketchy-ass alphas you attract when your last name says Darling and they read it as *Disposable*.

I'm all about hit it and quit it at this point, but on my own terms. Not some random alpha gangs whose *hit it* would be literal.

What would I even do with a baby?

Teach it to stab the other kids?

I never had a real parent or childhood. I was too busy hiding, biding my time so I could age out of the system and escape my omega fate.

But here I am.

All I can do is walk forward my own way, holding as hard as I can to the version of Lilah I still want to be.

Maybe Doctor Morgan sees the stubborn tension in my jaw, or the *fucking-try-me* look in my grey eyes. She sits down and rattles off my options.

I go with an implant, and in the afternoon, she inserts it into the arm that still sports a semi-healed bullet wound.

That arm throb is my favorite feeling.

It's a reminder.

I can't dodge *all* the bullets, but I can dodge enough.

Truth is, it would be perfect if my mates could be who I needed them to be.

But I didn't end up in that barrel because Wyvern Pack runs like clockwork.

Atlas, Finn, Hunter, and Jett are a hotter mess than a garbage barge in a volcano, and I'm not volunteering for the same hell cruise as Orion.

Even growing up, when all the trainers did was gush over how amazing it would be to bond a pack, it was never what I wanted—never what I thought I could have.

Now that I've seen pack life up close?

Even a dysfunctional one?

I'm good.

And I'm not going to be forced to settle with the Wyverns just because they're convenient. Just because our dovetailed pheromones make us irresistible to each other.

As long as they stay the fuck away, they make it easy to resist.

––––––

IT'S shocking how easy it is to sign away my life.

A few phone calls I never thought I'd make, and I have a move-in appointment with the lead scheduler at Honeymoon Hills—a.k.a. the *heat suites*. It's a huge condo complex, and it's the place to be if you're the kind of omega who'd rather suck on a sugar daddy than be bound with bites.

The little voice inside still screams at me to run away, to hide, but the more practical, still-in-the-hospital part of me knows this is my best option.

Rotation is the only way I keep any kind of freedom.

I'm shuffling to the shower when a commotion kicks up in the hallway.

Heavy steps, raised voices, and dense alpha auras that punch through the door with dominance.

I brace myself, ready for my would-be mates' energies to kick out my kneecaps and turn me into a shuddering puddle, but the gut-punch never comes.

It's not them.

Wondering who the fuck's trying to take me now, I dive behind the sofa, whipping out my scalpels.

"Lilah? Are you—" Max Wyvern pushes open my door with a bearded grin that dies when he chokes on my scent. "Whoa. Wasn't expecting that."

"Move." Tall and red-headed as his son, Kieran pushes past his pack brother. His ice-cold, *I-could-assassinate-you-right-now* gaze snaps to me where I peek from behind the sofa.

When Hikaru and Scorpio step into the room, shutting the door behind them, I'm stewing in so much alpha my eyes water.

I grip my scalpels with shaking fingers.

Half of me wants to smother myself with a pillow so I don't have to keep inhaling the heavy scents that fuck with my iffy omega psyche.

The other half, the horny, just-awakened, needs-sex-yesterday half wonders if they'd let me call *them* daddy.

Oh shit.

I need brain bleach.

Fucking hormones.

They smell like metal, ash, and something musky, sweet, and totally comforting in the most unwelcome way.

"You're safe with us, Lilah." Scorpio steps closer. Tall, dark, and crazy dominant, he reminds me so much of Atlas that I can't meet his gaze.

And *safe?*

Not with them or anyone else. "Security wasn't supposed to let you into my room."

"We called in a favor." Hikaru is as demon-handsome as his son, Jett. Dark hair, expensive suit, and a dark gaze that I can *feel* calculating which levers he has to pull to get what he wants from me.

It's unpleasant, but not the worst.

The worst is seeing the grown-up versions of the mates who can't be bothered to be here themselves.

And yeah.

I'd be even more pissed if they *were* here.

I've earned the right to be psycho.

When Kieran moves to pull me out of my spot behind the couch, I flash back to Finn pulling me out of the barrel.

The heat and the pain and the sorrow.

I yelp, ducking so deep behind the couch he'll have to yank it off the wall to get me. "We can talk from here."

And why the hell are they holding a pack meeting in my hospital room?

They're not my pack.

"We'd like to apologize. Face-to-face." Scorpio's voice is calm, even, and commanding.

I perk up. "Apologize for what?"

There are so many things.

"Because our sons are fucktarts." Max shakes his head. "There aren't words to say sorry for what they did to you."

Okay.

Good start, dads.

I peek from behind the sofa.

They stand shoulder-to-shoulder on the opposite side of the room, giving me plenty of space. I creep out, moving onto the couch with a scalpel in each hand.

Kieran strips off a knife holster and kicks it across the floor. "You need better than that, little wildcat."

I grabby-hand the knives but give him a serrated scowl for that nickname. "I thought this was an apology."

"We're sorry. I'm sorry." Scorpio dips his head, more a nod than a bow.

I lean forward anyway, lapping up their expressions because I can't remember *ever* getting a sincere apology from an alpha.

I wish I could record. "Sorry for…?"

"We shouldn't have forced you into the pack." Max scrubs his beard. "But we thought the boys would fall head over heels and we just want grand—"

Kieran elbows him in the ribs. "We failed you."

I was kicked around the OCC for years before they manhandled me into their sons' pack.

Kinda fucking used to it.

So, I'm glad they admit the truth and all, but their apology isn't the one I need. "Why aren't they here?"

"Because they broke into your suite three times, destroyed a waiting room, and pissed off the clinic's board," Scorpio growls in a disapproving tone I'm glad is for them instead of me. "Then we got a ping on Dominik Redfang's location and sent them to end the bastard."

"And they just…went?"

"They weren't given a choice," Hikaru says.

Thing is, they *had* a choice.

They always have a choice, and they always choose something, somewhere, *someone* else. "Even Orion?"

"He's on house arrest at the compound," Scorpio says. "The Redfangs made another grab for him when he was in the clinic's lobby."

"On house arrest," I repeat, because I can't be hearing him right. "Alone and on house arrest right after his heat. Without his alphas. After a kidnapping attempt."

"For his safety," Hikaru insists.

Yeah.

No.

"You can't leave an omega alone after a traumatic heat. Unless you want him to be crazy?"

"But you're not…" Max frowns.

"Um." Are his eyes working? I'm like a cavewoman after a thaw, brown hair a colony of birds' nests, covered in patchy scabs, melted fudge, and pillow lines. My pheromones need no further introduction. I repeat it for the knuckleheads in the back row. "You can't leave an omega alone after a heat."

"He's fine," Scorpio insists in a stoic *man* way that makes me want to kick his thick shin. "We're here to talk about you."

Here it comes.

"We heard that you attempted to register for heat rotation." Hikaru quirks a brow. "That won't be necessary."

"I didn't *attempt* to register. I registered." And it's more necessary now than fucking ever.

This is textbook Wyvern behavior.

Just wait.

Bet they already have another dodgy contract ready for my forced signature.

I clutch Kieran's knife strap, waiting for them to drop the other shoe. Hope it's a stiletto, because I'll stab them with the heel if they try to tell me what to do.

They can't.

The only reason I ever played along was because I had hope. As long as I was a dud omega, I could escape my fate. Now that I'm awakened, they have zero leverage.

"But they're your mates," Max says weakly.

"That means nothing." Our connection only gives them the superpower to hurt me harder. It makes me weak for them when I need to be strong.

Not points in their favor.

"You need a pack," Kieran insists.

"I need alphas. That doesn't mean I have to mate."

"It wouldn't," Scorpio says, "but we're talking about a scent-matched pack. There's no walking away from that bond."

How 'bout *running* away? "I already made the call."

"Even if not for your bond, Honeymoon Hills isn't an option." Hikaru tries to stare me down, but I refuse to wilt. "Until Dominik's removed, the threat to you can't be underestimated. Better if we keep you under our protection. The manor—"

"No." You'll never catch me in that place again.

When I think of the Wyverns' mansion, I think of the cold basement.

Bodies lumped on the grass.

Dead moths on the kitchen counters.

The garage where Craig injected me and the lawn the Redfangs dragged me across before shoving me into their car.

Worst of all, the stairs.

Crawling up and down in bone-breaking agony.

I'm supposed to walk those halls and feel *safe*?

Nope.

I'd feel safer standing on the corner with a cardboard sign that says **OMEGA NEEDS KNOTS**.

"I'm not going home with them."

Scorpio huffs out a breath. "Lilah. You're not understanding—"

"You're not understanding." I grip my new knives, wondering if the dads can feel my blood boiling, because I'm pretty sure I have teapot nostrils. I'm so angry, so fucking *done,* that it slashes their dominance, letting me hit them with eye contact hard enough to rattle teeth. "I understand the threat. I've always understood what happens to omegas."

A gang leader wants to kidnap and rape me?

Hello?

Knew that could happen since I was five. "My contract with Wyvern Pack is void. Yeah, I still have to pay back my debt, but that's to the OCC. Not to your packs. I have every right to put myself into rotation. You don't get to make my decisions."

"*Fucktarts,*" Max mutters.

Scorpio clears his throat. "We'll have words with them."

They can have all the words in the dictionary.

It has nothing to do with me. "I'm being discharged tomorrow. I'm not going home with them or with you."

"This isn't a negotiation," Scorpio insists. "We'll send an armed escort, but it's taking you to our compound or the OCC. Otherwise, we can't guarantee your safety."

They can't guarantee my safety either way, but I'd rather take the imitation olive branch than keep arguing when it takes everything I have to not roll over and be all *yes, Alpha, whatever you say, Alpha.*

They can and will hammer me into submission, and there's no way I'm stepping a toenail onto their territory.

So, I spit another set of words I never thought I'd say. "I'm going back to the OCC."

THREE

ATLAS

THE ONLY GODDAMNED reason I left Lilah in a hospital bed was the clear-as-day satellite image of Dominik Redfang waiting for death on his private island.

We *finally* had his location locked.

So how the hell did he disappear?

The rabid urge to rip out his throat claws under my skin. But it's weaker than the screaming *need* to see Lilah. To see Orion.

Have to neutralize the threat to our omegas.

Have to finish the goddamned mission my father assigned, so I can get back where I belong.

I keep half my attention on comms, waiting for better news from our teams sweeping the island.

The rest is for Finn, who cackles like a warlock while he chars Dom's island coca field with a flamethrower. He looks like a fire demon, red hair merging with the blaze and smoke.

It's the first time he's not dead-eyed in days, staring me down like he's deciding which organ to skewer. Arson will only keep him high so long, but I can't bring myself to take away his gasoline backpack.

He's losing his sanity.

I'm losing my control.

I'm a weapons-grade idiot.

But this has to be done. We have to burn the Redfangs out at the goddamned root.

Otherwise, how can I look Lilah in the eye and promise I can take care of her?

Broke that promise before it was made.

I failed her.

When I left Lilah with Craig, let her be dragged from our home, and instead of thanking her for saving Orion's life, I sent her to suffer.

Now Dom's making grabs for our omegas from all corners, and there's chatter on a bounty to whoever brings them in alive.

The cartel almost grabbed Orion from the hospital, and I'm still not over the defeated look on his face when I grounded him for safety.

I'm fucking up.

All I am is this job—the leader my father groomed me to be from the moment I could crawl.

Don't want to let Scorpio down.

Lilah.

Orion.

The pack.

Can't let any of them down.

So as hard as my instincts ride me, screaming with the need to bite and claim and *keep* the meant-to-be omega who's the perfect match to the soulmate I already have, I won't run back to Lilah with shallow words.

I need to *prove* the danger's gone.

Get down on my knees and gift her Dom's goddamned head in a sack.

All Lilah has to do is point and I'll destroy, dismember, fucking annihilate anyone who's ever hurt her.

The pack feels the same.

Except, we're the ones who hurt her hardest.

So we're working on destroying ourselves.

"Got a situation," Hunter's voice crackles over the com.

"I have eyes on Finn." I'm hidden in the treeline with my squad, ready to pick off any straggling enemies who think the bare-chested maniac is an easy target.

"Not him. Jett."

"Where?" My throat tightens. Hunter rattles off a location, and I bark a command to the squad leader. *"Don't let Finn out of your sight."*

"Yes, sir!"

Sticking to shadows, I move across the compound. We cleaned out the personnel, freeing the field workers and picking off the cartel's enforcers, but I never stop scanning for enemies and Dom's snake-eyed face.

Gun up, senses primed, I slip into the barn where Hunter's directions lead.

Our men have weapons trained on a row of bound captives, but half the cartel guys are down.

Dead or unconscious, faces pounded, they trickle blood into the packed-dirt floor.

Jett straddles one, blasting him in wet, meat-tenderizing punches and rage-powered dominance. *"Tell me where he is."*

Sometimes, I think Finn's the most unhinged.

Then I remember Jett never had a fucking door.

"He won't stop." Hunter's words are punctuated by pounding flesh.

Shit.

I open the bonds I've been smothering because my self-loathing is heavy enough without piling on my pack brothers' pain.

When the emotional punch hits, I stagger, grabbing Hunter's arm to keep steady.

"Welcome to the party," he mutters.

Inside, Hunter seethes like a banked fire, all tamped-down rage about to burst.

Finn's two flames—one an intense, unwavering blue, the other crazy sparks that flash and flare.

Jett's an inferno.

So much pain.

Instead of pushing the emotions down, I force myself to feel his hurt and fear.

"Help me grab him." Hunter hauls Jett off the guy he's beating to death.

Touch intensifies our bond. When I grab Jett's arm, the dark, toxic mass of his fear settles in my gut like I'm the one who swallowed poison.

We drag Jett out of the barn and haul him against a rusted-out trailer.

"Easy." I press his back to the metal, one hand on his chest while Hunter holds his other side.

Jett's eyes are wild. His long, dark hair flies out of its tie and his ice-carved face is spattered in blood. I ease my dominance over him, trying to reassure him through our bond.

Jett's breathing slows.

But even though his rage fades, fear keeps lashing our bond like the tail of a viper.

"What's this about?" It's not the first time I've asked, but Jett won't share his pain.

His jaw clenches. "It's about destroying the Redfangs."

"We don't have to punch them to death individually," Hunter says. "Shoot the fuckers."

"It's not about that. *Jett*," I add pack leader bite to my words. "You can tell us. Anything." I want to crack open that head and dig out whatever dark secrets made him deny that Lilah belongs to us.

But I don't blame him.

I blame myself.

Again.

Always.

All I want are *answers*.

I want Jett to tell me what's wrong.

I want anyone to tell me what's wrong so that I can finally fucking fix the problem.

It's my job to fix the problem.

Hunter's rage, Finn's distance, and Jett's terror.

Even worse, the numbness in my chest that's Orion.

And the absence where Lilah belongs, but isn't, and might never be.

Our pack bond is stretched to breaking, and when it finally shatters, we won't just lose our omegas.

We'll lose ourselves.

Our brotherhood.

Everything.

"I…" Jett's emotions flicker hot and cold.

"Uhhh…" The last voice I want to hear cuts into my earpiece. "This a bad time?"

"Not now," I snarl, but it's too late. That flare of almost-purged feelings snuffs out and the gate falls behind Jett's eyes.

Nathan coughs softly on the line.

Orion's asshole of a biological brother wheedled himself onto the mission team again. I've yet to understand what my father sees in him. I fully plan on booting him from Wyvern House the second I take the reins from Scorpio.

"Team three has a higher-up in custody. You want?"

"Where?"

"Main house," Nathan answers.

"Bring Finn."

"I don't want to get torched. Can't you—"

"*Bring. Finn.*" My bark rattles over comms.

Let Finn roast him.

I'll gladly fill out that paperwork.

"Can you handle this?" I fix Jett with a stare, trying to get back in his head, but the security gate's down with every lock bolted tight.

"He's *mine*," Jett hisses.

"Let's go."

We run to the big beachside mansion.

Our team has the prisoner zip-tied to a chair. Light-skinned, in a white linen suit and boaters, he looks like he stepped off a yacht.

One of the cartel's deputies.

Jett circles him like a wolf.

"Sweep the house again?" Hunter asks.

Before I can answer, Finn kicks through the front door, not giving a shit that the rest of us are here.

He shoulders past Jett and presses the red-hot muzzle of his flamethrower to our prisoner's chest. "The fuck did you do to my Star?"

There's a sizzle and a scream but no answer.

Yet.

"Find out the bounty and where Dominik's hiding."

Jett and Finn make a killer team.

Not good cop, bad cop but the cold sociopath and the crazy sociopath. They'll get the info.

Hunter and I sweep each luxe room of Dom's beachfront mansion. The breezy halls are lined with omega nudes that I rip from the walls, not because I'm looking for hiding spots but because they're creepy as hell.

Finn can have them for a bonfire.

Other than reams of sketchy art, there's nothing suspect. Everything's clean. No drugs, hidden safes, or weapon caches. No human skulls decorating the massive wall tanks of exotic fish and strange-colored lobsters.

Hunter and I reconvene in the office. It's filled with floor-to-ceiling beach views and faux leather-bound books that his decorator probably shipped in to match his evil island lair aesthetic.

While Hunter digs into the desktop computer, I tap the shelves and pull out books, looking for mechanisms. There has to be a panic room. A bunker.

Dominik's plane is in the hangar, his boat's in the harbor, and the satellite picked up zero outgoing traffic.

"Anything?" I ask Hunter.

"Enough pics to get the monster a few more life sentences, but nothing about his business." Hunter scratches his scalp. "I'd call Nathan, but..."

"Wait for Jett." He's almost as good with the tech, and no matter how frayed our bond, he's still the brother I trust.

I want to tear out my hair.

Where did he fucking go?

If this is a trap, it's pretty goddamned shoddy, given the haze of smoke that proves how much bank Finn's torching just cost the Redfangs.

I'm about to call HQ to report when Scorpio's number rings on my sat phone.

I answer on video.

My father's face scowls from the screen, a familiar tightness pulling at his dark eyes.

It's the look he always wore when he stripped off his belt before a beating or called me to the training field with a whistle and a plan to run me to death.

This time's worse because there's no lecture. His disapproval is crystallized in his silence, leaving me to play *guess the fuck up.*

"How's Lilah?" I ask, first priority.

"If you asked yesterday, I'd have a different answer."

My fists bunch so tight my knuckles pop.

I swear to all that's holy.

If the dads do anything to hurt her worse, I'll—

Hunter clasps my shoulder, grounding me before I can loose the nasty growl rumbling in my chest. "What's the news, sir?"

"Mission report," Scorpio says, always business.

Make war, not love.

I don't even know my mother's name.

Doubt he does, either.

"No sight of Dom. We have the team working a prisoner."

"Stay with it. Need him brought in. The Patricks are pressuring us to get this tied off. Government's going to get involved if we don't move."

Fuck the Patricks.

Those politicians are the ones who hired us to assassinate Dom's brother and started this epic clusterfuck. Wanted a drug-war win they could show off during campaign season. Now we have a body count, and it's not ending before Dom's death.

"We'll bring him in if he's here," I concede, "but if he's not, we're on a plane back to Lilah."

"How is she?" Hunter presses.

"How are they?" I add.

"We have it under control."

Not long ago, I wouldn't have questioned. *Things are changing.* "Have what under control? Are they safe?"

"As safe as we can make them." Scorpio gives a subtle, but out-of-character lip twitch that raises my alarms.

"What's Lilah's status? Is she still in the hospital?"

"She's being discharged tomorrow."

"The hell?" Hunter grabs my wrist, tilting the phone screen. "We need to be there."

"Agreed." Shit. All I wanted was to keep her safe. Eliminate the threat.

We shouldn't have left.

"She's going to the OCC," Scorpio says. "She put herself on the rotation roster. Don't worry. We'll have her name removed."

Hunter draws a sharp breath that's double loud in the empty silence after my heart stops beating.

"We're not forcing her to do shit," he snarls.

"We'll stall until you can finish out the mission and get back."

Finish out the fucking mission?

I can't fathom why she'd do that to herself, and a feral creature snarls inside me at the thought of our mate running to another pack.

"Why was she in such a rush?" I thought we had months to nurse her back to health and prove that we deserve to be with her.

Time to prove we're not total fuckups.

I was counting on it, otherwise, even when Lilah banned us from her room, I wouldn't have agreed to put our pack on a plane.

We're supposed to have time.

"Her heat schedule's off because—well, you know why. Med report says her heat's due in two to four weeks. You need to claim her now."

Hunter and I freeze.

Two weeks.

Two weeks to apologize.

Two weeks to win Lilah back.

I growl like a rabid tiger, blood boiling, my heart churning with whitewater rapids.

"Find Dominik," Scorpio insists. "We'll hold her until—"

"Fuck that." Hunter hurls my phone. It shatters against the breezy tile.

"We're going back," I grit.

"No shit," Hunter spits. "Then what?"

"Whatever's best for Lilah."

"At. We're not following whatever bullshit plan the dads—"

"I know. I know. But we can't have her in rotation either. She deserves so much better."

Better than me.

I haven't begun to figure out how to apologize to her.

Hunter's eyes flash. "Lilah deserves to do whatever the fuck she wants to do."

Tension builds between us, only cutting when Finn stalks into the office, red dots blending with the spray of freckles across his nose.

Jett follows, hair in a frantic tangle and his natural cedar drowned by the scent of blood. "What was the call?"

Hunter pushes. "We have to—"

"*Enough.*" I force Hunter into submission. "We don't have time to argue." Have to get to Lilah, have to speak to her before she checks into the OCC. Then we'll need special permission just to see her face. "Did the guy tell you anything we can use?"

"Five million to kill either omega," Jett says. "Ten and a bite into the Redfang pack if they're alive. Offer's not just to his people. Anyone who delivers gets the cash, pack membership, and a stake in the cartel."

Hunter curses. "A nun would jump on that shit."

"And Dom?"

Jett shakes his head. "Guy didn't see him leave."

Fuck.

There has to be a bunker.

But there's not enough time to dig, and now we have the double worry of needing to keep the omegas safe from every underworld alpha on the continent.

We need to get back.

I need to talk to her before she can sign herself away.

That's as far as I can think.

Get to Lilah. Make sure she's safe. Make sure she's eating and sleeping and well. Put her and Orion in the safest, coziest nest and lock them in together.

"We're out." I bark orders like the commander I can still be when I'm not so fucking focused on all the ways I'm failing. "Finn, get Hunter to the runway. Hunter, need you to get our wheels up. Jett, transfer mission control to Nathan. Let him clean up the rest of this shit. I'll have the teams keep sweeping."

They jump.

Not to obey, because they're all seething at me for their own special fucked up reasons.

They jump because the faster they move, the faster we see Lilah.

FOUR

LILAH

THE MORNING of my discharge drags through final checkups with nurses who lick their lips while they rattle off my care instructions.

If my scent hits betas this hard, I'm dreading alphas.

Or not?

I shouldn't dread.

I should *want* to attract as many alphas as possible and give myself as many options as I can.

But just because I *need* alphas doesn't mean I have to like them, love them, or want them around after my heats.

I'm bracing for impact when my escort finally arrives. Trainer Evgenia marches ahead of a file of armed guards, strutting into my suite like the majorette in a holiday parade. She wears a brunette ballerina bun and a silk brocade robe that's way too extra for the clinic, let alone my plans to stealthily crawl back to the last place I ever wanted to return.

But better her than any of the other trainers.

They're going to be *insufferable*.

"My god, your pheromones." She presses a handkerchief to her nose.

"That bad?" I mean, I can smell myself, but it's freaking me out how strongly everyone keeps reacting.

"You're going to make a sensation."

Just what I never wanted.

"Come dance for me before you let a new pack sweep you away."

"I won't have time to play." There are only so many days until my heat, and I need to jump into every social event I can with both feet and my best fake smile.

"Nonsense." Evgenia dismisses me with a wave. "Schedule one pole showcase and you'll be *drowning* in knots."

There's another thing I should want to do. Be the sexy center of attention and dance my way to a pile of horny heat partners.

The thought makes my stomach bubble.

It would be more awkward than alluring because instead of learning how to smile and flirt, I learned how to scowl and threaten—and that's not a part of myself I want to change.

I would've been flattened every day of my life if I showed up soft.

I have to show up snarling if I'm going to survive.

"Omega on deck," Evgenia calls to the guards before gesturing to the door. "Let's get you home."

I refuse to call the OCC home, but at least there, I know the dangers. Plus, it has high fences, tons of security, and if the Redfangs or the Wyverns come for me again, I'll be on my turf.

I know all the hiding places.

Trying to hold my head high, I brush off my hospital pajamas and enter the gauntlet. The guards are Wyvern House agents decked in that delicious black camo, and their pheromones hit me like a food truck.

Somebody smells like peanut butter, and my body's all *he could be the one*.

My inner muscles clench while I breathe through the insanity.

Well-trained, the guards cut off their snarls, but it's too late, the sounds already rattling through my brain like the threat that they'll take me right here in the hallway. The flare of lust dies in full-on panic, and I grab for Kieran's knife strap, shaking.

"They're here to protect you," Evgenia says as softly as I've ever heard her speak.

Maybe they'll protect me from the Redfangs.

But who protects me from them?

Who protects me from *me*?

My head's a mess, instincts torn between wanting to lick the sweat off Mr. Nut Butter's thick neck, and wanting to run, run, run, because now that I'm awakened, I'm the goat at the dinosaur park.

Two big betas ride the elevator down with us. I keep a hand on my weapon, but when we step onto the ground floor, my stomach bubbles pop and fizz. Wyvern House has the clinic's lobby blocked off, two columns of agents forming an aisle like they're greeting their mob boss.

When I pass, you can follow my path like tipping dominos.

The alphas shudder, rumble, jerk, every single one reacting to the bite-me-now pheromones so dire that de-scenters don't make a dent.

Not that I can touch de-scenters.

My skin's still patchy pink and tender, and when I tested a bottle of lotion, the memories sparked by the cursed chemical scent had me sweating and popping hives.

So, the spotlight is all mine.

But I refuse to let myself shrink from the unwanted attention.

I won't show my fear.

Or my madness.

Because the lobes of my crazed omega brain keep slap-fighting.

It's an insane tug-of-war between licking my lips at alpha bulges and wondering what the fuck is wrong with me.

I feel like a little kid who'd happily hop in the creeper van for the promise of candy.

Except the candy is dick, and I fucking pray the Wyverns

aren't behind the wheel, because if this is how I react to randos, I don't know how I can keep myself away from *them*.

I scurry across the lobby before I can act on the bad decisions my instincts are already co-signing.

A convoy of black SUVs waits in front of the clinic. Evgenia and I hop in, and I don't realize how loudly my heart is pounding until a beta slams the door, and the frantic *thrum-thrum-thrum* is the only sound filling the back seat.

When the car starts, I remember the last time I was behind the wheel, and my head spins in a dizzy wave of dread.

Screaming metal.

Blood and shattered glass.

"Lilah?" Evgenia's voice cuts through the flashback. "What's wrong?"

"I'm fine." I hug my arms to ribs, sucking in my crazy, just breathing until I don't feel like I'm spinning out. Evgenia's perfume—the bottled kind—blots over her beta scent, and the familiar floral grounds me back to reality.

I take a few deep breaths.

What happened, happened.

I saved myself then, and I'll save myself now.

Not sure I'll ever drive again, but I can handle being a passenger for the quick ride to the OCC.

When we roll up to the iron-tipped gates, I can't decide if I should celebrate or scream.

I never wanted to come back.

I wanted to disappear.

But now that I can't go five minutes without some kind of freak-out, I know this is where I need to be. Away from the kidnapping attempts, recent nightmares, and alphas that hack my reproductive system.

With enough guards for a parade and drones zooming over the high-fenced perimeter, OCC security is much thicker than before.

Thiccer too.

Tons of towering alphas patrol the outer grounds, and my newly awakened self has a brand-new appreciation for a thicc set of thighs.

Our convoy pulls around the fountain in front of the admin building. I hop out as soon as the car stops, wanting to get to my room or *any* room that I can make my own space. Somewhere dark and safe, where I can lock the door and be alone without nurses checking in, alphas staring at my throat, or random staff members drugging my dinner.

I just want to stop feeling like I'm under attack.

I can taste the sweet, sweet solitude when tires screech down the drive.

Guards stomp into motion, shielding me from the attack. I'm about to snatch one of their guns and take cover under the SUV.

Then I feel them.

That tug in my gut.

It's like I was drifting without strings, but now that Wyvern Pack is finally here, all my cut pieces strain to reconnect.

It's the best feeling.

It's the worst feeling.

Because I'm not a fucking puppet.

I don't need these strings, these ties that bind me, dragging me to a fate I never wanted.

When the car screeches to a stop, some deep inner part of me whispers, *you're safe.*

I want to scream.

Safe?

Are my instincts fucking high?

Finn leaps out of the driver's seat, not even putting the thing in park. He's shirtless. Scarred skin and red hair streaked with ash.

"*Star.*" He sprints to me, calling in a raw, ragged voice that crackles in my chest cavity.

Finn bulldozes guards to get to me, staring not at my neck or my body, but *me*, in a way that turns the air to syrup.

And when his scent hits, blood oranges spiced with cream and smoke, Finn has me.

For just one second, I crack.

Logic melts out my ears, because I *know* deep in my soul that if I let him wrap me in his arms, Finn will never let me go.

Then Wyvern Pack will have me too.

Forever.

The same part of me that insists I'm safe, that everything is fine and my mates are here for my rescue, gives a girlish squee that's as sharp as a 4 a.m. wake-up call.

Thankfully, my brain restarts before I can act on that running leap into their arms.

"Lilah." Hunter's a step behind Finn, and he looks twice as wrecked with stubble over his square jaw, and the long top part of his dark hair looking like he crawled through a typhoon.

He dives into the battle line with Finn, more and more guards pouring from the building to keep the guys away from me.

"*Stand down!*" Atlas roars.

I can't catch his scent in the chaos, the shouting and fighting, but his pack leader dominance rolls over me like he's pulling me to rest against his warm chest.

Comforting.

Suffocating.

"Orders, sir!" a guard shouts. "We protect the omega."

Guards blot out my view in the shuffle, but I catch flashes of Atlas through the gaps between their bodies. He stares straight at me, golden-brown eyes so intense, I flinch.

Then I spot Jett.

He's not fighting. He stands at the edge of the fray, gripping his shirt over his heart with claw fingers, and I'm sickly satisfied how he looks like total hell. Skin sallow, dark eyes sunk.

At least they weren't on vacation.

But neither was I.

Now they want to roll up like they own me, start stupid fights, and what? Drag me back to their cave? Chain me up next to Orion so they can get back to their regularly scheduled black ops?

It takes me a solid few seconds to shake off the testosterone and crashing waves of alpha dominance, but when I finally find my voice, I fucking belt. "STOP!"

It's like I hit the universal pause button.

An instant stop-motion that couldn't have gone faster if I'd alpha-commanded them.

Maybe this is what it's like to be a real omega.

The crowd parts, giving me a clear view of Wyvern Pack, and the guys drink me in just as hard as the guards.

This is *power*.

I stare Atlas down. "What are you doing here?"

"We came for you." Atlas pushes through the guards, voice raspy, rough, and desperate. "You're ours, Lilah. We want to take you home."

My stomach clenches and not in the fluttery first date kind of way. More like a rock dropped in a lava pit. "Your omega's home alone and probably tearing out his hair. That's where you should be. Not here."

"You're ours," Finn growls. "*Mine.*"

His growling purr rattles my backbone, and a ticklish thread of warmth starts to melt my stubbornness.

But grab the freeze cannon, because I'm not going soft over one little purr. "*I'm* not even mine. Go take care of Orion. Then you can book an appointment to see me like the other alphas."

"You don't need other alphas," Atlas growls. "Let us take care of you."

"You can't even take care of yourselves!" I wave at them, fighting their own men, making a fucking scene *now* after leaving me alone for days.

My gaze slips to Hunter.

He rubs the back of his head, opens and closes his mouth. Whatever he wants to say, I'm not waiting for him to find his voice.

I whirl around, ready to stomp inside the building but an ice-choked whisper stops my steps. "Lila—"

Jett.

I can hear my heart cracking.

But I'll staple that shit right back together.

They don't ever have to know that I'm this weak.

How hard the mate ties want to tie and strangle me. *If Jett was about to say what I think he was?*

I shudder. "Don't call me that name."

Jett makes a choking noise, and I kind of wish he'd choke instead of coming at me with all that broken heart energy when he's the one who could've saved me a lifetime ago.

"We had a mission," Atlas insists. "We had to—"

"You didn't have to. You *chose* to. Shocking concept, but you chose to leave me and you chose to leave Orion." I push a breath through my teeth. I'm not listening to their words, their *pity-me* eyes, or their crazy fucking pheromones.

I'm listening to their actions.

All that other shit lies.

Actions don't.

"Lilah—" Hunter starts.

Too freaking late.

"Learn to take care of the omega you already have."

"We're sorry." Atlas rumbles. "Don't do this to us."

I let the words wash over me, but they're just noise.

Vibrations in the air.

Atlas doesn't get it.

They don't get it.

"You're not sorry." Not when the apology comes on the same breath as the accusation that I'm doing something wrong.

I'm doing this to *them*?

All I'm doing is looking out for myself.

Because they sure as hell won't.

"You want to see me? Back of the line." I stride into the building.

Hope my scent sticks in their noses *forever*.

FIVE

ORION

I PACE a path through the carpet, sweaty, exhausted, and fucking jittering with the need to see Lilah.

I haven't slept.

Haven't eaten.

All I've had are energy drinks. Half-crushed cans scatter the sofas and monitor-choked tables in the living room of our Wyvern Compound condo unit while fizz burns my stomach, filling me with bile.

My alphas are who-the-fuck-knows-where.

I wish we could trade roles.

Make me and Lilah the alphas.

Maybe Wyvern Pack would finally run right.

Run *at all*.

I've been watching Lilah on the security feeds for days.

Only watching, because I'm not allowed to help.

Fucking degenerate Redfang minions keep hitting the clinic. They failed to snag me when I insisted on waiting for Lilah in the lobby.

Now they're making passes at my future mate.

I need to see her.

Need to hold her.

Apologize.

Fuck.

She needs to be held even more than I do.

I rub my arms, feeling the lack of my alphas even though all I want to do is dick-kick them into a snake pit.

They call it a mission.

I call it running away.

Meanwhile, I'm locked up with nowhere to vent, and all I can do is follow Lilah's route through city traffic cams, making sure she's safe.

One glance at the street grid, and it's clear she's heading back to the OCC. All I can do is wait for her to reach campus so I can catch one last glimpse of her on the perimeter cams. Once she's in, I lose access unless I hack the military-grade system.

Or if Hikaru gives me clearance.

Both equally unlikely.

I'm so desperate, I'd call Nathan and suffer through his smug poison to borrow his black hat powers, but guess fucking what?

My brother's with my mates.

I chug another energy drink.

My hormones are more level after my heat, so I'm only half as crazy as I've been the past months, even though my blood is fifty-fifty taurine and caffeine.

I'm finally seeing clearly.

If this were before, I'd be curled up in a whiny-ass ball, pitying myself that my mates left me because I'll never be the omega they deserve.

Lilah changed everything.

The pressure I thought would crush me? The inadequacy, just knowing I'd *never* be good enough?

It's gone.

Lilah can be their everything.

I only need her to be *mine.*

So I'm not pitying myself.

Now I'm just fucking pissed at my alphas.

Lilah deserves better.

I deserve better.

I wish I'd cracked the whip years ago, but I was so deep in self-loathing, I didn't know I could.

Always thought they'd drop me the second I complained. They might still drop me, but whatever my instincts cry, the Wyverns aren't who I'm most afraid of losing.

Motion on screen drags me back to the banks of monitors crowding our mission control living room.

At the OCC, a convoy of bulletproof SUVs pulls around the manicured entry circle.

I zoom forward, ready to drink in the smallest sip of my omega.

The picture isn't great—CCTV bullshit—but it doesn't need to be movie quality to show the guards preening like they're shooting a muscle calendar, angling toward the central car. They puff out their chests when the door opens.

Lilah slides out of the SUV in hospital pajamas. She's so short she has to hop to reach the ground.

I touch her image on the screen, and my chest rumbles.

Mine.

I'm not an alpha.

Can't really even mark her.

What we have is more than chemistry. I don't need Lilah the way the alphas do, just because her biology calls to theirs.

I need Lilah because she's the only one who's ever understood.

Not that I don't want *her*—she's hotter than a fucking scotch bonnet—but I need her next to me. Falling asleep to stupid movies. Sharing blankets, playing the games I'll program just for her, and laughing while we battle to see who can handle the hottest Buffalo wing.

The guards watch Lilah like a fawn.

I hate that she's back to that place.

Still alone.

She's almost to the steps when a Humvee rockets down the driveway.

Finn dives out, dashing to her and the others follow close.

Claws rake my chest.

I don't care that they went to her first.

Fuck knows I'd be with her if I weren't under armed guard.

What bothers me?

I'm not second on their list, because I'm not on their list at all. I'm just the houseboy who'll be here whenever they show, ready with a smile and their fuzzy fucking slippers.

Not anymore.

They rush to her, ready to rip through every guard to get to their meant-to-be mate.

Finn's a battering ram, but there's at least a sliver of conscience left in him, because nobody pulls weapons on the rent-a-cops.

Yet.

Shit.

My mates need an ass-blasting, but I don't want them dead.

"Stop!" Lilah's voice rings out, clear, sweet, and full of righteous fucking fury.

And shit do they stop.

They freeze. The guards. The guys.

Every male, like his heart just stopped pumping and obeyed because Lilah Darling said so.

Hot.

But then no one moves for so long, I have to bang the monitor, worried the signal dropped.

Lilah makes a frustrated noise. "What are you doing here?"

"We came for you. You're ours, Lilah." Atlas's voice drips pain that aches in my chest, our strained bond twinging from miles away. "We want to take you home."

"Your omega's home alone and probably tearing out his hair. That's where you should be. Not here."

It's like the sky opens, turning Lilah gold with angel-blessed sunlight.

Somewhere, a heavenly choir bursts into song.

Fucking when has one of my mates ever stood up for me?

Lilah should loathe me.

If I hadn't been drugged, if I could've gotten my shit together for five fucking seconds to explain to the guys what was going on, then she wouldn't have had to spend what should've been a sweet first heat floating in a barrel.

They would've bitten her, and she and I would still be snuggled up in the same nest instead of locked in separate prison cells.

Finn growls something, but all I hear is Lilah's answer.

"*I'm* not even mine. Go take care of Orion. Then you can book an appointment to see me like all the other alphas."

"You don't need other alphas," Atlas growls. "Let us take care of you."

"You can't even take care of yourselves!"

It's official.

Love her.

Want her forever.

"Lila—" Jett sounds like his soul's falling out, but I have zero sympathy when it's at least fifty percent his fault how things played out.

"Don't call me that name."

"We had a mission," Atlas insists. "We had to—"

"You didn't have to. You *chose* to. Shocking concept, but you chose to leave me and you chose to leave Orion."

"Lilah." Hunter has that look like he's about to drop an insight bomb, but he should've been the one to start this intervention instead of coming in on the clean-up crew.

"Learn to take care of the omega you already have."

"We're sorry." Atlas rumbles. "Don't do this to us."

Fuuuuuuuuuuuuuck.

Way to make it selfish, asshole.

I know what Lilah's going to do before she twitches. "You're not sorry. You want to see me? Back of the line."

She struts into the sunset, shaking her ass and leaving total fucking devastation in her wake.

Do I scream?

Give her a one-man standing O?

Long after she's gone, the zombified guys finally drift back to the car. Hunter drags a dead-eyed Finn, shoving him into the back seat.

I pace.

Pace some more.

Chug more caffeinated poison and keep pacing.

Whenever they leave me for days or weeks, then skulk back bloody and apologetic, I always smile.

Comfort them.

Anything to earn their touch.

Knowing they're on the way back, my insides quake, instinctively eager to see, feel, and scent my mates.

Omega instincts?

Crazy powerful.

Shitty at decision-making.

Every time I give myself a *what-the-fuck* pep talk and plan an epic speech, they walk in and my inner psycho overwrites my logic.

I know the same shit'll happen again.

They'll pout in, hearts juiced under Lilah's pointe shoes, and I'll want to hug it out.

Let them play down their mistakes.

Not this time.

Not this fucking time.

It's a while before I hear footsteps in the hall. There's a low rumble of conversation as they greet the guards. Then the front door opens, letting in a sexy, sultry caramel sharper than a kick in the groin.

Their alpha scents tangle with Lilah's sugar.

Leathery musk, smoky honey, bubbly orange, and sweet cedar.

The springs rattle inside me like a jack-in-the-box about to punch through my chest.

Go to them go-to-them gotothem!

I focus on the caramel, crème brûlée sweetness instead of their dominance, and my feet stick, rooted to the carpet.

"Orion." Atlas drops his gear bag. He's dirt-streaked with sagging eyes that say he hasn't slept.

Join the fucking club.

"Yo." I stand my ground, giving my mate a two-fingered salute as the rest of the pack schlumps in behind him.

Dirty, thin, and raggedy, they look like they lost a trench war.

But, the way they're going, they're gonna lose a lot more.

Jett moves like a half-animated corpse, and Finn gives off grim reaper vibes—not just dead, but ready to drag the rest of us to hell.

Hunter hauls them in like luggage.

His thick lashes and brown eyes are usually soft and smiling. Now he's shooting flames, nostrils flared and knuckles white.

Haven't seen that since—

I don't want to think about it.

Hunter's eyes widen, anger slipping when he catches sight of me. "Holy shit, O. You good?"

"Fine." I'm in sweatpants and a tee, haven't showered in days, and probably soaked the room in stress pheromones. *Lap it up, fuckers.* "How is she?"

Hunter's jaw clenches. "She's on the rotation schedule."

My heart jutters. "And we're making an offer?"

"Shouldn't have to," Finn mutters from the seventh circle. "She's ours."

Hunter shoves Finn onto the sofa, putting him in time-out. "Yeah, well we fucked that up. Now we're at the back of the line."

Jett drops into a chair, staring into space, and he's never been a golden retriever, but I've also never seen him look this fucking lost.

Atlas moves to me, but I step back, avoiding the magnetic pull to go to him, to forgive and forget and submit. "So? What's the plan?"

"We get her back." Atlas is so focused he doesn't notice me distancing myself. "She can't go on that list. We only have two weeks."

"Why two weeks?" I glance to Hunter, whose square jaw tics.

"Because her heat cycle got screwed and that's when the doctors think she'll pop."

"Two weeks?" It feels like we were just pulling her out of that barrel, and she's supposed to go through that again?

How?

And how do they think they can fix shit in two weeks?

We'd be fucked if we had four months.

Four years.

And fuck knows when *I'll* get to see Lilah. Nobody's going to let a bonded male omega court her.

"Shower." Atlas clicks into mission mode, dishing out orders without seeing how any of us react. "We stop in the office and run through Lilah's security plan. Then we'll deal with her name on that list."

"At. No." Hunter grits his teeth. "We can't—"

"She's not going into fucking rotation," Atlas snarls. "Not when Redfangs have a multi-million bounty on her skin. We're the only ones who can keep her safe."

He barrels from the room, leaving us to shake off the dominance he just dished.

"Fuck." Hunter frees himself first, wandering out to follow the boss's orders. As Finn and Jett start to react, they move around me, but I'm underwater.

Everything's swimmy and blurred.

Safe.

I get where Atlas is coming from.

I do.

You love someone, you don't want them hurt, let alone gang kidnapped.

But that doesn't mean you strangle them with bubble wrap, jam them in a vault, and chain it shut. That doesn't mean we get to tell Lilah what to do.

She's going to hate their plan.

And if they piss her off even more?

I need to distance myself.

Because if I have to choose between the pack or her…

I choose Lilah.

Every time.

SIX

LILAH

I'M ten feet onto campus and still seething when I hit my next Wyvern speed bump.

Hikaru. A designer-suited iceberg with eyebrows sharp enough to cut paper.

Should've known the dads wouldn't give up trying to lasso me.

"Can I help you?" I glance for a way to pick him off, but Evgenia is long gone and my guards would rather stare at their boots than meet the eyes of the OCC's absentee director.

"Come with me." He heel-turns on his expensive loafers, used to being followed.

Only, I don't play that game anymore. "I'm going to my room."

"Your room was reassigned."

I blink. "You're making a paying customer live in my laundry closet?"

Hikaru stops walking. "Your *what*?"

"There's no way you reassigned my teeny tiny cell to one of your omega princesses, so this is obviously some bullshit excuse to—"

"*Come with me*," he barks a command I can't refuse.

Alpha-whipped, I'm dragged on the march to his office.

I grind my molars.

I'll bite myself hard enough to bleed if that's what it takes to shake off the next command he tries.

When we enter the ritzy lobby attached to the important office suites, Hikaru's secretary, Stacey, pops up with a file folder and a grin smeared in fresh red lipstick.

Then she spots me, and her kiss-ass expression falters. "Director Wyvern, she—"

He yanks the folder from her grip. "Don't move until I call for you."

She goes statue mode.

I thought I was whipped.

Guess he was holding back.

Hikaru's office is sedate and mostly empty. No photos or personal touches. Just a dark wood desk, functional cabinets, and a scent more dust than his alpha gunpowder. Clearly he's not around much.

"Sit." He takes the big chair and spreads the folder he just yanked. "Your room's listed as a suite in the A dormitory."

"Then someone's seriously screwing with your books, because I've been living in A dorm's former laundry nook for like fifteen years." And *holy shit.* "Were you charging me for a suite this whole time? I want receipts."

If they try to bill me for perks I never saw, I'll take the OCC, Wyvern House, and every one of their businesses down on fraud.

Hikaru hits his intercom. "*Stacey.*"

His half-whispered bark is an icicle to the ribs.

The sound isn't for me, but just in case, I scoot my chair out of murdering distance.

"Yes, Director?" Stacey flies in, pale and oh-so-totally guilty, wringing her hands in her blouse and filling the room with anxious, peachy musk.

"Where does Lilah Darling live?"

"In the A dormitory…"

Funny thing.

Stacey?

She's been to my closet home. Personally handed me a punishment slip or twenty over the years.

"Is that so? Why is she telling me she's housed in a laundry room?" When Hikaru pushes the file across the desk to flash the evidence, I glimpse the upside-down lies.

"What the—" I snatch the folder.

And *holy shit motherfucking biscuit.*

I mean, I had zero expectations management would do me any favors, but this.

This!

My records are a dictionary-thick list of disciplinary actions.

Fights.

Punishments.

More fights.

And if you believe the hype, I've started every fight in the history of time.

Threatened Juniper with scissors. One day suspension.

How about, I defended myself with the scissors Juniper used to cut off my *entire GD head of hair*, then got pulled out of class for *a week*, most of which I spent in the basement solitary cell the trainers keep open for me.

Every entry is the same.

I started an unprovoked fight and was given a super reasonable, above-board punishment. The footnotes lament bullshit like, "doesn't respond to discipline," and "Uncooperative. Omega identity suspect."

My chest falls, heavy with the unexpected sense of betrayal. I thought I had no hope left, but as always, the OCC finds another floor in my heart to demolish.

I shove the folder. "None of this is right."

"Don't lie to the director." Stacey huffs. "You—"

"Show me which entries are wrong." Ignoring her, Hikaru pulls his chair around the desk to me.

"You have all afternoon?"

"As long as it takes."

"You asked." Whether or not he'll believe me?

Don't care.

I have to say the truth.

Remind myself what really happened.

They don't get to erase what I survived.

I run Hikaru through the dossier line by line, from the kitchen receipt that says I have the biggest meal plan—I absolutely switched it to the smallest one to save cash—to the actual punishments the trainers dished out for all the fights I never started.

Hikaru takes notes while Stacey shakes in her pantsuit.

"You were caned." He speaks dangerously low. "Starved and punished with isolation. Is that how we discipline omegas?"

"It's...not," Stacey stammers, "b-but, Lilah. She—"

"You'll have to excuse me." Hikaru unfolds from his chair. "I'm calling a campus meeting. Cancel classes and call all faculty and staff to the auditorium. Ten minutes for anyone who wants a chance at keeping their job."

Stacey flies out of the office.

"Talking to them won't change anything." This place is too rotten.

"If it's that corrupt, I'll burn it to ashes."

"If you say so." I don't care if there was a conspiracy because that doesn't change shit about my past.

It won't undo the fights, the beatings, and growing up watching every supposed adult in my life fail to step in and do the right thing.

Including Hikaru.

I mean, yeah, make those assholes suffer.

Love to see it.

But if he expects me to bat my lashes and call him my hero, he should've stepped in *before* I had to learn how to save myself.

"I want names. Which trainers are responsible?"

"The worst? Marc, Renee, Tasha, Noah, Michelle." It would be easier to list the ones who aren't evil.

He pulls out a thick sheet of paper, scrawls a few lines, and finishes with the flourish of a signature. "I put you in one of the VIP bungalows. We have the most secure perimeter on that side of campus. I'll have your scheduler wait for you there. It's not safe for you to leave campus."

I take the paper, shocked he's not flat-out canceling my meeting. I was ready to bite my lip in half to shake his next alpha command. "You suddenly care?"

"It's not sudden."

I snort. "Where've you been since I was four?"

"Managing dozens of other businesses. If I'd known…"

"Known what?"

"That you were their mate."

My stomach roils. *Hate this topic.* "You knew."

"I didn't know a thing until your dance showcase. Then I saw the way they watched you on that stage. That's when we remembered Jett's friendship with you."

"*He* knew." And that's the root of it.

Jett knew and he left, just like everyone else leaves.

"No. It's not possible to recognize a mate bond that young. If he'd so much as mentioned your name in the decade afterward, then I would've followed up."

"Then why did you bother putting me with the pack? They already have Orion."

"Because they're stubborn pups and proximity was the only way to knock them out of their funk. My packmates and I believed your relationship would resolve itself with your heat."

Let's not revisit my heat. "Well that worked out fantastic. I'm ready to move on unless you have more schemes? More shady contracts?"

"No more schemes." Hikaru exhales. "Your fingerprints are coded to the door for Bungalow Six. Don't go anywhere else until we can formalize your security plan."

I take his words as the dismissal they are and scurry past Stacey's empty desk, back out to the campus green.

Feels like I never left.

The OCC is all manicured lawns, flower-lined brick paths, and herds of baby omegas who got kicked out of class just in time to witness my walk of shame.

Ah, the memories.

Like, look over there!

The copse of stately willows where I used to hide from Noelle and her posse between combat and etiquette.

And there, the memorial bench by the pond where Marisol and I first teamed up to kick the older girls' asses.

Because they were bigger, but we were scrappier.

I miss her.

Or maybe I just miss the feeling of having someone on my team.

Been a while since anyone had my back.

A flash of pity may have given Hikaru a moment of conscience, but I have zero doubt he and the dads will come back with some bullshit once it's clear I'm looking for anyone but Wyvern Pack's second generation to take care of my heat-related needs.

Wanting away from the kicked-anthill crowds, I sneak onto the side path that skirts the pond. The bungalows are for adult omegas who visit campus to lecture or take short courses.

Security's good all over, but the bungalows are an extra step in the maximum-security direction. The perimeter features blade-tipped, double-wide fences and tons of mounted cameras that actually set me at ease.

The only way inside is through a guard house.

The beta on duty smells like cucumbers. I catch his nostrils flaring at my perfume, but he's professional, letting me press my own finger to the scan pad without touching me. "Your afternoon appointment is waiting for you on the porch, Miss Lilah."

"Oh. Thanks?" It's super weird for a staff member to not go instant douche-mode on me, but the staff here don't work the main campus, so they must not know my story.

The bungalows are their own world.

Each one is a stand-alone cabin, isolated by lush landscaping. It gives the illusion of a jungle resort instead of an institution.

I follow the signs to number six, where a woman in a vintage skirt and cat-eye glasses kicks her feet, waiting for me on the porch swing.

"Lilah?" She hops to her feet. "I'm Catherine from Honeymoon Hills. So pleased to finally meet you in person. Hope you don't mind that I came early—there was some debate whether I'd be allowed on campus to see you."

Her omega scent is a warm banana bread.

I tense.

I don't have the best history with omegas, and my newly awakened instincts are a total wildcard.

But either because Catherine's thirty years older, her intentions are pure, or I'm just too freaking exhausted to be territorial, I don't get swept up in any *stab-the-intruder* urges.

I press my fingerprint to the keypad and wave her inside my latest temporary hidey hole. "Thanks for coming. I just... I need all the help."

"The things you've been through. Promise. I'll do everything in my power to get you happily settled." Catherine pats my shoulder, and instead of flinching, my reflex is to lean into her motherly warmth.

I pull back blushing the second I realize.

Am I that desperate for touch?

Thankfully, weighted blankets are a thing.

My bungalow's kitchen and living room are one big space, all gleaming white and cozy-but-sterile, bleached to remove the scents of anyone who's ever spent the night.

Catherine seats herself on the cream sofa, tipping the contents of her cherry-print tote onto the coffee table. "We're so excited to have you on our roster. "

Yes. *The sex roster.* Just like I always dreamed. "My timeline is—"

"Tight." She nods. "It's not a problem. Our alphas will be delighted to meet a new omega. You can jump right into all the pre-scheduled socials on campus starting tomorrow." She slips me a stack of calendars and event invites. "If you're wanting individual dates, those will take a little longer to vet and schedule. The real sad thing is we can't throw you a proper debutante party. I—"

"No. No party." My last one ended with a gunshot wound. "Just normal socials."

"Love a woman who knows what she wants." Catherine taps my feedback into her phone. "Are you wanting unchaperoned dates?"

"No." The answer pops out with zero thought. "Only chaperoned." I need to meet alphas, but I want to meet them in public and take official offers.

Not off-book sexcapades.

"Noted. There's a bonus for your first heat with us, so even with your higher debt to the center, you'll be clear within a few years."

"It's not…*technically* my first." I wiggle on the sofa.

"I heard, but… You were alone throughout?"

I dry-swallow. "Yes."

"Oh, Lilah." She pats my hand. Just two warm taps that are gone before I can pull back. "That'll never happen again. Even if your heat hits suddenly, we have trained, on-call alphas ready to ease you until your pack of choice can arrive."

It says how far I've fallen that on-call sex sounds so comforting. "Will I have much choice in alphas?"

"You'll have a buffet." Her smile flashes two deep dimples. "Why choose one pack when you can sample all the flavors? Rugged. Refined. Wild. Athletic. Academic. After the first few heats, you'll stop craving a mating bite and start enjoying the adventure."

"You make it sound so…"

"Liberating?" Catherine crosses her legs. "Rotation gets a bad reputation. But, you tell me. You've spent more time than most with all the princesses pining over forever packs. What happens when they choose wrong?"

I don't need to think of any omega but myself.

Look at me and Wyvern Pack.

Biology would tell you we're perfect for each other. I shake my head. "It's a fucking mess."

"Exactly. Never choose and you'll never choose wrong." Catherine pushes the tablet across the table to me. "Now. Let's get your name on this schedule and find you some alphas who'll be begging for your attention."

I want to believe.

I don't, because whatever she says, I'm still a Darling.

I've been at the edges of too many tea parties, casino nights, and awkward social situations where I get more leers than greetings, and all I want to do is steal some lunch and get the fuck away from the shady-ass alphas staring with too many teeth.

But, I'm hoping I can be happy in rotation.

I'll have a sleek condo instead of living my cottagecore dreams, but I can get my accounting certification, build a business, and do whatever the fuck I want in between the unavoidable heats. I'll build a life for myself, all by myself, and all the while, I'll be safe in the heat suites' housing tower instead of tossed out as gang bait.

I'm just hoping the "buffet" she's pitching actually shows and I'm not knot-blocked and stuck with a hot line full of Wyvern kebabs.

With plenty of brochures and visual aids, Catherine walks me through the upcoming on-campus events. I agree to an ice cream social, a brunch, and a speed-dating event, not because any of those sound fun (except for the ice cream) but because they're the soonest.

Clock's ticking.

Heat's coming.

I want contracts and consent forms signed and a pack of vetted, well-hung alphas waiting for me with their pants down.

"There's a mixer tonight," Catherine admits. "I can put your name on the guest list last-minute, but we missed the window to hype your attendance the way we should've."

"I'll go." Without the hype.

"Fantastic." She claps, businesslike. "The dress code is cocktail attire."

"Fantastic," I echo.

We spend a while filling my calendar before Catherine has to rush to another appointment. After locking the door behind her, I fall onto the sofa, smacked in the face with the leftover piles of glossy brochures.

I want to crawl under the coffee table and sleep for twelve hours, but I resist the siren call of coma sleep and stumble to find the shower.

Old Lilah would hide.

New Lilah goes to the party.

But Lilah past, present, and forever *always* packs her knives.

SEVEN

LILAH

WRAPPED IN A POST-SHOWER TOWEL, I stumble into my latest problem.

The only outfit I have to change into is the OCC tracksuit that came in my bungalow's closet.

It's grape soda purple and says **OMEGA** across the ass.

I think fucking not.

If this were a normal social, I could cope long enough to steal a plate of mini quiche and bounce before anyone noticed.

But this is my debut.

My desperate, *only* grab at landing a decent pack for my heat.

So, I make the move of pure desperation.

Changing back into my hospital pajamas, I hug my arms against the chill and the guards' stares and head across campus.

I *could* contact Wyvern Pack and ask them to return my shit. But my tablet's still in their basement, so I have no way to call, even if I wanted to.

I'd rather wear the tracksuit.

I need to cut ties with them so cleanly, their names don't dirty my mental doorstep ever again.

Least of all, when I can solve this teeny problem myself.

I skirt the performing arts center, skipping past the grand glass entryway for the fire door in back near the dumpsters. A few shady maneuvers bring me to the dance studios just in time for the last lesson before dinner.

Every classroom is rocking, so there's no one to spot my scurry to the storage room. It's not locked.

I throw the bolt behind me, then sag against the door. In the dark, windowless vault, I take what feels like my first breath in *hours*.

I'm tempted to curl up, this time in a pile of taffeta tutus, but I can't give into the urge. If I let myself take fetal position, I won't get up for days.

I rummage jam-packed racks of old performance outfits until I find a black leotard halter and a matching skirt bottom. They're sleek enough to get me in the party's door, but not so attention-grabbing that I'll be uncomfortable.

My goal is to show up, meet alphas, and then get gone—not be the star of the social season.

I grab a pair of nude ballet flats, then unbolt the door. Before I can escape, a too-familiar nightmare voice freezes me in the cracked doorway.

"Hurry. We're late for makeup." Rachel hustles ahead of her dance team posse, dark curls pulled into a ballerina bun, with a dance bag over one arm and both thumbs texting fast enough to start a fire.

"You think *she's* coming to the cocktail?" asks Jovie, ever the loyal minion.

"Who?"

"The *Darling*."

Rachel sneers. "I have her handled."

Fan-tickity-tastic.

I'm so past the point of petty teen girl drama. My life is not a game, and if they try to fuck with me, I'll fuck with them harder.

When the halls are finally empty, I make my escape, sneaking toward the side door to avoid the lobby.

The route forces me past Evgenia's office. I duck my head and hurry past.

Just a student, strolling by.

"Darling Lilah."

Ugh. *Spotted.*

Evgenia pops into the hall with a scowl for the balled-up clothes in my arms. "My entire storage room at your disposal, and *that's* what you take?"

"I'm in a hurry."

"Not that much of a hurry. Come. Let me fix you."

I sigh and follow her to storage.

Evgenia hums as she flicks through the racks, thrilled to finally have me as her doll. "There's a performing arts showcase in a couple days. I can save you a slot. Help you throw together a routine that'll leave the alphas panting."

"I have socials scheduled every night."

She scoffs. "Nonsense. Dance. The alphas will come to you."

"That's what I'm afraid of."

"Time to stop being afraid." She pushes a blue poof at me. "This. It'll bring out your eyes. And show off your throat."

I consider not taking it, but the puffier skirt will make it easier to hide my knives. "Grand."

"And for your makeup—"

"No. Thanks for the dress, but no."

She tries to wheedle me, but I skip away and duck in a bathroom to change.

I hate how perfect the dress is.

The drape of the satiny, navy fabric is lingerie for my throat, sparkling with silver and gold embroidery. With the puffy petticoat, you'd believe I have hips.

I *aspire* to have hips.

I look less emaciated after all the hospital meals, IV drips, and fudge treats, but my full-time address is still in anxiety city, so I haven't been keeping up with my meals.

One good thing about the OCC?

The catering is amazing.

So, even if tonight is a wreck, I can stuff myself with bacon-wrapped dates and lava cakes.

When I pin my long, brown hair into a soft updo, leaving my neck long and bare, I look textbook *omega on the prowl* even if I feel more *omega-upset-stomach*.

The cocktail's held at the on-campus lounge. I've seen it decorated for luaus, under the sea, and magic shows.

Tonight's theme is casual elegance.

A red carpet leads to the doors, and it's roped off so that every alpha who arrives in a sleek supercar gets ushered inside like an old money tycoon.

Alpha packs enter in dark suits, and their dominance gut-punches me even though I'm far from the action, hiding behind a hedge.

The omegas enter in small, giggly groups, looking like designer cream puffs.

All bright and smiley.

Meanwhile, I crouch in the landscaping, pretending I don't taste stomach acid at the thought of walking in there all alone.

I don't belong.

But I don't have a choice.

In a second, I'll go.

I promise.

When it's been more than five minutes since the last late arrival, and I'm officially half an hour behind schedule, I finally brush the wood chips from my skirt and walk the red carpet.

A red-headed beta in a uniform vest greets me with a happy smile. "Good evening. Can I check you— *Oh.*" Her customer service voice chokes. She pinches her nose. "Miss. I have some de-scenter here if you—"

"I'm allergic." I wave off her spray bottle, but before I can step back, I catch the chemical tang of my nightmares.

Slosh, slosh, gasp.

My mind goes dark, spots fuzzing my vision.

I can't.

My skin still needs prescription salve, and even if I were fully healed, pretty sure I'd black out from one spritz.

Don't want to follow the memories down that sinkhole.

"Your scent is…" The woman's eyes glaze. "Uh…your name, please?"

"Lilah Darling."

"Yes!" She shakes herself, going cross-eyed as she tries to do her job. "Um. Our VIP. You're our only Honeymoon Hills omega, so you have your own section. So many alphas have asked about you."

That's good.

But the bile rising in my throat says *maybe not.*

I swallow hard.

Have to do this.

Have to walk inside, or my future's going to be just as bleak as my past.

The beta leads me through a security checkpoint, and I'm happy to find armed guards posted at every wall.

The lounge is super dim. It's perfect nest ambiance, with candles on white tablecloths and the chandeliers lit just bright enough to glitter.

But scents are stronger in the dark.

So strong, I stagger.

A fucking alpha buffet, just like Catherine promised.

They smell like soap and wind and grass.

Rich wine and even freaking barbecue.

My mouth waters, my belly tightens, and I pinch my wrist to keep from being swept away by pheromones.

My everyday scent is apocalyptic.

If I get any more turned on, I'll spark a fucking riot.

The omegas each have their own table, and they do *not* like when their alphas turn to watch the piece of meat that just wandered into their territory.

They track me like hunters following a fat deer.

I stroke the knife hidden in my skirt, but I don't let myself hunch.

Let 'em look.

Let 'em tell their rich alpha friends there's a new omega on the market.

"Here you are." The beta leads me to a dim corner booth loaded with snacks on gilded plates and crystal glasses. Makes me paranoid that I'll break something and get it added to my bill, but I need to stop worrying how much everything costs.

I have bigger problems.

Like how isolated I am in this corner.

How anyone could try anything, and the guards would be too far away to help.

And not the worst, but definitely the most annoying, the goblet of shrimp cocktail. I push it to the opposite side of the table before I catch its fishy stink.

"I'm Alice if you need anything. A drink?"

"Soda water?" I don't dare touch alcohol when I'm on my own. Just hope the bubbles will keep me alert.

"Right away." As soon as she disappears, the dog whistle sounds.

I can't hear it, but I feel the aftermath in my bones.

Alphas descend.

Two packs crash my table at the same time.

Four big alphas each.

Eight pairs of burning gazes, throats that work and choke, hit with the hammer of my sugared perfume.

I brace, hands on my knife, prepared for the worst.

But instead of diving on me, they smash into each other.

"She's *ours*," snarls one hulking pack leader.

"Saw her first." The other puffs out his chest.

My heart pitter-patters, lashed by their growling vibrations. While they throw out dominance, trying to crush each other, I end up crushed to my seat, waiting to see who wins.

They jostle rugby-style. I'm not impressed, but my hormones are happy to watch thick alphas muscle each other around.

They're busy pushing and posturing when a solo alpha presses through their barricade.

"This seat taken?" He's blond, blue-eyed, and weirdly familiar from the straight line of his nose to the bow of his upper lip.

Do I know this guy?

I'm so thrown, I miss my chance to answer. He pulls out the chair, ignoring the curses from the line he just hopped.

"Lilah Darling." There's something weasley in his smile. Too much grease. It's the way I've seen a hundred betas smile at an omega when they're sucking up.

"You are?"

"Nathan," he says with a flourish, waiting for me to respond. Like I should know the name.

He smells like fruit gum—the kind that loses its flavor after two chews—and even though he's putting out alpha in buckets, I'm no more attracted to him than I am to Doctor Morgan.

"Okay." I grab a wafer cookie and wait for him to leave.

"They didn't mention me?"

I munch while keeping an eye on the dominance battle. One pack almost has the other pushed back, and they'll evict this guy as soon as they're free. "Who?"

"Wyvern Pack."

I choke. Thankfully, Alice appears with my drink. I drown the cookie crumbles in bubbles. "I don't talk to them."

"That's not what I hear." He smiles again, and it hits me.

The light blond lashes. The wave in his soft hair.

Nathan's a little bulkier, more wrestler than swimmer, but their eye color is so similar–that crisp, gem blue–I gasp. "Orion."

"That's my little bro. What does a pretty piece like you want with a pack that already has a mate?" Nathan slides from his chair into my booth. *Too close.* "You can do so much better."

"Like you?" I slide away.

"Smart." His grin is so smug it flips my switch—just not the *fuck-me, nest-me, make-me-yours* switch he meant to pull with his greasy palms.

It's the same switch that told me to stay the fuck away from Craig.

Just what I need. Another Grade A creeper.

"Did they send you?" I look for the guards, but the dim corner is fulfilling its ominous promise. Between the dominance battle and the candlelight, nobody can see what Nathan's doing in my booth.

"I came on my own. If you want revenge, there's no better alpha." Nathan licks his lips. "Let me have your heat, *Darling*. They'll die with jealousy."

It's the perfect offer.

I bet my three-figure fortune that Nathan's telling the truth.

There's no alpha who could torture them more, and they'd agonize knowing what they lost.

Only one problem.

"I have standards." I'd pick a random alpha off the street before I chose one so oily he probably stained the booth's upholstery.

I mean, I'm petty, but I'm not stupid enough to screw myself over just to make the Wyverns suffer.

They don't need to suffer—they need to stay away.

Nathan's lazy smile sharpens, but before he can toss his next barb, the winning pack leader struts to my table.

He and his three guys move in-sync like a football team busting through a banner. None of their scents make me want to roll over, but someone is a smoky bacon that fries Nathan's gummy scent out of my nostrils.

I'd at least say *hi* for that.

"You've had your time." The leader straightens his tie, flexing broad shoulders. He pushes out a wave of dominance, and I expect Nathan to pack it up.

Instead, he leans back, giving a lazy stretch that moves his suit jacket. "Relax, bubba."

"You relax, you f—" The pack leader chokes, then jumps back. "My mistake. We'll get out of your way."

My jaw hits the tablecloth as the big, muscular alphas I was counting on for an assist scuttle away, leaving me alone with Nathan and a whole lot of questions.

"Why…"

Nathan flashes his lapel, showing off his pin—a stylized black-gold **WH** with a dragon tail. "Wyvern House. I'm an agent. Who's going to stop me?"

Hah.

I will.

But I hope it doesn't come to that. "Now we've met. Go mingle with the other omegas."

"I already found the best one." He slides closer again. I jump out of the booth before our thighs touch, pulling my knife and making sure he sees the blade.

Nathan smiles wider. "Feisty."

Barf.

I'd hate Nathan for being himself, but I hate him twice as much for acting like a shit wearing Orion's face. "We're done."

"I'm just getting started."

It's either stab him or walk, and I don't have time to go to jail. Freed from the alpha barricade, I bolt.

My arms shake. I hide the knife in the puff of my skirt, but now that it's out, it's staying out.

We're off to a fun start.

I head for the bathroom.

I'll splash my face and reset, then come back ready to smile my best plastic smile.

There has to be at least one pack worth meeting.

Maybe that alpha who smells like brisket?

Before I get anywhere, an alpha in gangster-chic pinstripes steps into my path.

I dodge, then curse, coming face-to-face with the season's top mean girl, seated at her table like the prom queen.

"Lilah. So good to see you." Rachel lowers her glass. "I've been dying to introduce you to one of my favorite packs." With her dark curls pinned up, and a murder-red, off-the-shoulder gown, she smirks like she just issued a kill order.

It's worse.

There's a way a man looks at you when he thinks he can buy you.

It's this half-lidded gaze, part smugness, part contempt.

The alpha who blocks my path hits me with a leer like he already paid his cash.

His round jaw is shadowed with stubble, and thick, sour cigar smoke hides his alpha scent.

Danger.

"This is Artur Braun and the Braun pack."

Artur closes his eyes, giving me a sniff so deep it's violating. Then his scent spikes over the cigar smoke.

Limp boiled hot dogs.

So much danger.

I edge away.

"She's perfect." Artur rubs a thumb along his stubbled jaw. "Send my thanks to your sister."

"Enjoy getting to know each other," Rachel says sweetly. "You have so much to plan before her heat."

I duck, but the Brauns surround me.

Trapped.

My breathing picks up.

Six.

I can't fight six alphas at once.

Have to run.

They herd me toward the side door. When I try to push between their thick bodies, Artur grabs my arm so hard I yelp.

"Be good," he barks, his dominance smashing my resistance.

But it's the wrong fucking command.

I can't be good unless I'm far, far away from this pack.

I widen my eyes, faking docile, and he relaxes his grip with a sickening chuckle. "You smell like sugar, Darling. Me and my boys are gonna take a lick."

Nope.

No.

Never gonna happen.

I drop to the floor.

The unexpected move gives me the second I need to bulldoze through their calves.

I bear-crawl under the closest table, pushing through legs, ignoring the screeches of riled omegas. When I finally pop out, three tables separate me from the Brauns.

Frantic, I look for security, then dash for the closest guy in uniform.

The middle-aged beta reaches for me like he's going to help. Then his gaze slips past my shoulder. "Mister Braun…"

"*Stop her!*" Artur barks.

"You'd better cooperate." He grabs for me again, only this time, it's to help the gangster. "It'll be easier on you."

Some fucking security.

I slash him.

The beta howls, too busy trying to keep what's left of his thumb to stop me from running.

Everyone watches.

No one helps.

When I hit the exit, Alice waves me past, holding her phone. "I'm calling for backup. Go!"

How nice.

One pure soul left on campus.

But even if help is on the way, they won't get here in time. Artur will drag me into a dark corner, and—

I run.

All I wanted was a lava cake.

All I want is to be left alone.

EIGHT

JETT

I'M NOT sure how much time has passed since we left Lilah. Hours? Days?

Reality is hazy thanks to bourbon and my falling barricades.

The only thing that's clear is the wall of security monitors I'm manning.

My father patched us into the OCC's network, so I can follow Lilah everywhere. In clinic pajamas, she moves from her bungalow to the performing arts center.

When I click to follow, pulling up the interior cams, the long hallways of bulletin boards and crepe paper spark the movie reel of buried memories that I can barely still pretend happened to someone else.

My high, cold walls are breaking.

My head throbs.

Pain I deserve.

"Where is she?" Orion leans over my shoulder. I flinch at the brush of his warm skin, jumping from my chair.

It's not him I fear.

It's touch.

Touch will shatter my last support column.

Orion's apple-scented stress pheromones remind me how close I am to collapse.

They'll be happier when I disappear.

"Jett." Orion grabs the chair and rolls it back to the monitors. "You need fucking help, dude."

"Yes."

I agree.

But do I deserve it?

"Where's Lilah?" He takes the mouse, and I step back, calves bumping the coffee table. The others are at HQ, tracking leads on Dominik. Just one afternoon and we already busted a gang planning a full-scale infiltration to get to her.

My phone buzzes in my jacket pocket.

Hikaru: OCC office. Now.

I shudder.

If I step on that land, I'll shatter.

"What now?" Orion snags my phone. I tuck my hands away, hiding the shake in my fingers.

"Asshole texted everyone but me. I'm going with you." Orion rises from his chair.

I'm alpha.

It shouldn't take effort to resist his challenge.

But I'm the one who looks away.

I'm the one who submits.

Weak.

So weak, I hear the voices.

Her voice.

Not Lilah's.

The demon and her nightmare minions.

"You can't keep me away from Lilah." Orion quivers, ready to fight.

I'm not here enough to argue, and I wouldn't argue with him. *I've hurt Orion enough.* "You can drive."

He lets out a tight breath. "I'll grab the keys."

I drift behind, trying to stay lucid, but I'm fraying. The threads that make me *me*, the sticky web of lies that holds my past together—it's all unraveling.

Maybe tonight's the night I finally face my truth.

Too soon we're pulling onto campus.

Every time I'm here is death.

I follow Orion like a ghost, drifting to the admin building. My father's secretary is gone, but familiar voices argue in the office.

The pack is here.

I reach for my bond, banking on that last thread to keep me from falling apart, but as soon as I cross the threshold, Lilah's scent slices everything away.

It's burnt sugar, sweet and perfect.

Pain stabs behind my eyes.

Hikaru dishes his usual acid, sour that Orion followed, and my pack brothers argue, but their voices echo through a lead pipe.

I move to my father's bar cart, pour a shot of something amber, and knock it back.

"You may as well pour another glass." Hikaru's eyes pinch.

Atlas looms over my father's desk. "Is she hurt?"

"Not at the moment."

Finn hefts a crystal paperweight like he's testing if it's strong enough to crush bone. "You'd better get real chatty, *Uncle*."

I refill my glass, then pour one for my father, never once feeling my fingers.

He takes a swig, then rubs his temples. "I spent the day firing half the staff. I'd fire them all, but we'd have to shut down and send the omegas home."

"What's the deal?" Hunter eyes my father's desk.

Following his gaze, I finally notice the thick folder half-hidden under my father's elbows.

"Read it." Hikaru offers the folder.

Hunter takes the offer first.

Silence hangs.

Drags.

The papers tremble in Hunter's hands. "Holy…"

Atlas grabs it before it drops to the floor, and Orion reads over his shoulder. Atlas's dominance rises with anger that smokes in my chest.

He punches the desk so hard his fingers crack. "God fucking damn it."

"How?" Orion falls into a chair. "Oh, God."

Finn is next.

He's quiet.

With eyes dark and dangerous as hell pits, he absorbs the report. When he's had enough, he sets it on the desk and starts counting his knives, muttering. "Didn't bring enough."

The chill in his voice is so absolute, it rattles me in the half-here space where I've been drifting.

"Read it," Hikaru insists.

"I've seen her file." I read every page when the girl I thought was gone suddenly resurrected into my life.

"You read the whitewashed version. This is Lilah's version of events."

I'm slow to pick up the folder, clinging to my last shred of sanity.

But I already know.

This is when I break.

The printed pages are all familiar. When the dads placed Lilah in our pack, I did my due diligence.

Every word confirmed the lies I'd built like a glass castle.

Lilah was a troublemaker.

Lilah did things she shouldn't.

Went places and saw things that weren't for her eyes.

Lilah had become a female just like *them*.

The pure girl I'd loved was long gone.

Lies.

Page one, line one.

Lilah bit a student. Was sent home without dinner.

Hikaru's compact notes reveal the truth in stinging red ink.

Attacked by three, bit one in self-defense, and was punished with no food for 48 hours. Six years old.

Broke a window with a baseball bat becomes *broke out of the classroom she was locked into overnight.*

Not "threatened Trainer Isaiah," but *warned off a staff member who was later fired and jailed as a predator.*

The lies fall away.

Falling.

Falling.

Crash.

Metal collides and pieces shatter in my brain. But the memories that surge to the surface aren't the ones buried so deep they warp who and what I am.

They're memories of the Lilah who ran until her feet bled.

The Lilah who ran to my office in a T-shirt, ready to defend Orion.

The Lilah who looked at me, *needed* me, and made me remember the first time she walked in on what she wasn't supposed to see.

Then, the buried memories boil, and I remember why I hate omegas.

Why I *had to* hate Lilah.

Because the person I hate most?

Me.

The worst alpha.

The one who can never live up to my father's expectations.

The weakest link in the pack.

That's all fine. That's all true.

Where I really fucked up was believing Lilah changed.

That the sweet, special girl who drew me in like starlight grew up to be an evil omega bitch.

That she was just like the others.

That my *Lilac*, the one pure relic of my childhood, was dead, gone, disappeared, and that Lilah Darling was an entirely different creature.

They're not different.

Lilah was always my Lilac.

Pure and perfect and good.

But I didn't split them into two people for no reason.

The reason is the memory that comes with a stabbing, ice-pick pain that sends me sloshing bourbon over shaking fingers.

It's too deep.

Too toxic.

But I *need* to know.

Need to know why I am this way, why I hurt her, and whether I deserve death by injection or something much, *much* more painful.

I grit my teeth.

There's a room that smells like paint.

Thick perfume.

Hands on my skin.

And then Lilah—

Molten pain and the ping of a phone drag me back to reality before I can finish tearing the scab.

Hikaru pulls out his cell. "Shit. Warned her not to go out."

"*What?*" Atlas snarls.

"911," my father says. "Lilah's being hassled at an event. The Braun Pack."

"*Where?*" Hunter's bark is jumper-cables—sharp and so dominant, it sizzles away my shadows.

"Lounge. Front of campus."

My feet are already moving.

I don't hope to bond Lilah.

Never deserved her and never will. I can't be an alpha. Can't protect or nurture or love.

But I finally found a target for my hate.

Braun Pack.

They're not Redfangs, but they do business with the cartel.

I have a whole dossier on Artur.

I'll have his liver if he *looks* at Lilah.

Because I may be weak. Useless. A wretched fucking *monster*. But I can at least be the monster who protects *her*.

We dash through the door.

Atlas stutter-steps in the hall. "Orion, stay—"

"Fuck off." Orion's first out the building. "And catch up."

He's our fastest sprinter, but I'm not far behind.

I need to run so fast my demons can't follow.

Blurring through the night, we bull through the guard check-point. We're close to the lounge.

But when we hit the location, the pale-faced hostess points into the night. "They chased her that way!"

We rush through the landscaping, and in the distance, movement flashes.

Lilah darting through a patch of bushes.

She's a shooting star, her dark dress glittering in the moonlight.

Chased.

I spot four alphas, the rest hidden in trees.

"Keep one alive," Atlas snarls.

I'm good at keeping them alive.

I'll keep them alive for a very, *very* long time and make them suffer for profaning her.

I spot my target.

A slow, bulky alpha at the back of the pack.

Going to destroy him, Artur, all of them.

Then, when Lilac is safe, when she dishes out the punishment I so deeply deserve, it'll be my turn to be destroyed.

NINE

LILAH

THE WOLVES ARE CHASING.

Panting, I dart through the landscaping, ducking between ornamental trees.

If I cut across the open grass, I can reach the gate to the inner campus, but I turn in the opposite direction.

Can't trust security.

The way tonight's going, they probably already cashed the Brauns' check.

I run for the pond.

Water's the only place I'm safe.

Because maybe I can't outrun them, but there's no way they can fish me out of that murky pond water. I'll drown them like a freaking kelpie.

Footfalls pound closer. I squeeze my knife, ready to stab someone in the fucking jugular.

They won't take me alive.

The alpha's so close I choke on his scent.

A nasty combo of mint and banana.

I throw myself into running 'til my lungs burn, but my stamina's not as good since the heat and the hospital.

The alpha lunges, slamming me to the dirt.

I slap the ground and roll before he can grab me, tapping into years of self-preservation practice to jump up and stumble away.

"You're ours," he rumbles, low and nauseating. "*Submit.*"

The bark sends me staggering, and that's the utter bullshit of being an awakened omega.

Any alpha's word is law.

The guy's wrist hooks my shoulder, wrenching me around. My muscles lock, not cooperating, but the idiot just gave me all the momentum I need.

He doesn't see the knife.

I twist my wrist and let his yank smash our bodies together.

My blade slips into his belly.

He chokes.

He falls.

I run.

"*Stop!*" Artur roars, and his fucking pack leader bark knocks me again. It takes everything I have to throw it off, including seconds I don't have.

Two Brauns bookend me, each grabbing an arm.

"*Submit!*" A rubber-smelling motherfucker barks in my ear, and my body shuts down.

I go limp.

"Get her to the car," Artur grits. "Someone grab Tommy."

No. No car.

I feel like I'm replaying my nightmares. But I survived that time.

I'll survive this one too.

I bite my cheek until copper and pain shake away the alpha command. Then I land a dancer's heel-kick in the guy's balls.

He howls and drops my arm.

"Bitch!" The second guy snags me in a bear hug, and all I can do is thrash, kicking at his knees while he smashes my waist to his sweaty chest.

"Have it your way." He crushes my ribs, choking me out. It

hurts so bad I'm afraid the bones'll crack. I go limp again, only this time with a better plan.

Hold my breath.

Let him think I'm unconscious.

I thrash a few more seconds, then play possum, praying he can't feel the drumbeat of my heart.

He lifts me into his arms, treating me to a face full of rubber and stale cigarettes. I fight to not react to the scent, peeking through my lashes and waiting for the right moment to bail.

"Shit. *Omega*." He inhales me so hard his stubble beard-burns my throat.

Screw playing possum.

I'm about to blind him dead with my fingernails.

Then a voice pierces the night, clear and sharp as raw crystal. "*Lilah!*"

Orion's golden curls catch the moonlight, and he brings me back to life.

His face is flushed with anger. With terror.

All the emotions swirl through his night-blue eyes as he runs down the alpha who's trying to spirit me away.

Am I hallucinating?

Can't be.

I was ready for the escape plan where I slathered myself in pond mud and breathed through a bamboo straw like a cartoon mouse. I was even ready for the worst-case plan—the one where I take myself out to stop myself from being taken.

I'd put my money on an airplane-toilet meteor crushing the Brauns' skulls before I ever made a plan that relied on a rescue.

It doesn't happen.

It's *never* happened.

I either save myself or I don't get saved.

But Orion's here.

He moves like an action hero, judo throwing one alpha, kicking the one I stabbed, running like a shot.

I quit playing dead, using Orion's distraction to palm-strike Mr. Stubble in the nose.

The crunch of bone stings but sounds so sweet.

I struggle out of his roaring reach. The guy snags me, coughing tears and blood. Orion kicks him away, giving me the chance to scramble free.

I stumble a few steps, hands and knees scraping the mulch of a landscaped island. We're at the far edge of campus.

All I want to do is keep running.

But a roar cuts the night.

Every hair on my body lifts in salute, a ticklish, terrible chill rocking my spine.

It wasn't wolves chasing.

It was Wyverns.

Atlas, Hunter, Finn, and Jett.

They fucking rip into the Brauns.

I've seen them train.

I've seen them spar in those teeny tiny shorts.

But I've never seen the real thing.

It's not a fight.

It's a combat clinic, and I suddenly understand why a lapel pin is enough to send a whole pack running scared.

Finn's first lunge sparks a yelp so pained, it sounds like a field castration. Atlas turns Artur into a rag doll, Hunter knocks out alphas hard enough to scatter molars, and Jett stands on a man's throat, grinding him into the ground.

His eyes are on me.

They're full of a wild desperation that's so unlike his usual ice, I swear I glimpse his younger self.

Feelings I don't want crush my chest until I'm breathing through that cartoon straw.

Run.

"Lilah, stop!" Orion's pleading voice makes me miss a step.

Can't stop.

Wyvern Pack just saved my ass, and I don't want to be

anywhere near their heart-twisting pheromones when my adrenaline fades.

Because then my hormones will take the wheel, and those deluded bitches will steer me straight into their claws.

I'd rather wear the tracksuit.

I'd rather throw myself into the sea.

I turn to sprint, to flee, but I'm ended by a freaking ceramic toad.

I stub my toe hard enough to see the deities.

When the Brauns chased me, I didn't scream. When they carried me away, I didn't cry.

But one stupid landscape ornament and my pathetic whimper-shriek silences the fight.

The roars and punches cut so completely, a confused cricket starts to sing.

I hop, holding my possibly disintegrated toe.

Ballet flats were a stupid choice.

I'm going to the next social in running sneakers.

Shit.

I have to go to another one.

I'm not sure I can walk, let alone run. Orion swoops in before I can find out.

He scoops me into his arms.

I wish I could say I flinched.

That I hesitated for even one second, thinking he was a threat.

But my body knows him.

His scent wraps me, and crisp, cinnamony apple burns off the lingering alpha stink.

"I've got you," he purrs.

So soft.

His voice. His hands. Even his freaking sweater.

I loop my hands around his neck and nuzzle the fabric so I can scrub away the feel of that alpha's nasty stubble.

While I pant like I'm still on the run, Orion shields my eyes and carries me away. He cuts through the bushes, popping out next to a bench at the campus pond.

When he sets me down, my arms go rogue, refusing to let go. Then I realize what the hell I'm doing and bail, scrambling onto the seat.

"Ow." I flinch. My ribs ache, my skin's scraped and bruised, and blood seeps through the toe of my slipper.

Pretty sure it needs amputating.

"Where are you hurt?" Orion drops between my knees, and my heart seizes. Then he takes my foot and softly strokes my ankle. "You're bleeding."

"I'm fine," I say from the high altitude where his touch sends me. Need climbing poles, the air's so thin.

He cups my calf, examining the scrapes on my knees with the same focus he gives a screen full of code.

The same dedication.

That's what knocks me back to earth.

I kick free of his warm palms.

I can't.

I'm not ready.

Haven't really talked to Orion since the heat. I don't need to flash back because tonight almost ended the same.

The sprint through the woods. The kidnapping. I would've hit the trifecta if the Brauns shoved me in their car.

That time I saved Orion.

Now I don't know what to say.

If he should apologize.

If I should apologize.

Or if I should jump into his arms and hug out his soul because he protected me, and I missed him, and I've been so fucking alone.

Before I can decide, Wyvern Pack busts through the bushes.

I grip the bench, bracing for the hit, and the wind gods deliver their worst, wafting the Wyverns' scents straight into my soul.

Atlas's tonka and leather hugs me tight.

I throw out my hands before any of them can try to do the same, already spinning from smoke, cedar, and blood orange.

They stutter to a stop, focused one-hundred percent on me until Orion rises. The motion's just as heart-piercing as the oncoming wave of alpha dominance.

Orion steps in front of me.

It screams his position.

He just shielded me from his own pack.

My throat goes so gummy, I think I swallowed chalk.

In black camo, with quads and shoulders thick enough to deadlift a private plane, Atlas looks like he was mail-ordered from a mercenary brochure. He twitches at Orion's stand, and a thread of doubt sneaks into his businesslike question. "What happened?"

I duck behind Orion.

I need a second.

A week.

An eternity.

I'll never be ready to face them.

It's too hard with their scents in my nose and their dominance draping me like a weighted blanket. Every psycho omega instinct says I should already be in their arms.

Or riding their—

Shit.

If they purr, I'll have to bail into the pond so they can't scent me.

"Lilah, baby. How hurt are you?" Hunter peeks around Orion. His hair's a mess after the fight, all dark and rumpled, and the smoky honey of his scent soaks into his sweet voice.

"I'm fine. Not a baby." I'm going to break into the nurse's office and steal the good painkillers, but as far as Wyverns need to know, I'm peachy.

Hunter starts to crouch. "Let me—"

"No thanks." I cross my legs, ignoring the throb of my toe to keep my feet out of his reach.

He may have forgotten the time he bandaged my road-rash,

but I can't, and it makes me twitchy that he wants to repeat his caretaking performance.

I learned my lesson.

None of them can be in touching distance or I swoon.

Except, apparently, Orion is whitelisted.

But damn it.

I need *some* comfort.

Without him blocking, I'd already be swept away.

"*Star*." Finn's soft, toxic whisper seeps into my ear, and I jump high enough to catch air.

Finn snuck past Orion's barricade, circling behind the bench while I was worrying about other alphas.

Should've remembered who's the most trouble.

Finn's green eyes are black in the darkness, and his freckles shine stark against his pale, moonlit skin. His blood orange scent has me twisting just as hard as the single-minded insanity in his gaze.

Watching me the same way I watch lava cakes, Finn offers me a shard of green pottery. "Killed it for you."

"What…" I suck in a breath because *holy shit*.

The toe-breaking toad is dead.

The perfect gift.

He pushes it into my palm before I can react.

"*Finn*." Hunter puts a thousand words in that name, including an unspoken command to back up.

Finn *tsks*. "Make me."

"*I'll* make you." I wave the piece of shattered toad like a blade.

"*Yes*." Finn bares his throat, eyes lighting like lanterns. "Make me, Star."

I dry swallow.

Big mistake.

"Finn. *Back up*," Atlas barks, spitting out the growl he's been chewing.

Finn's jaw clicks when he grits his teeth, trying to fight the command, but he's as vulnerable to his pack leader's bark as I am to any alpha's.

Bullshit omega genes.

When Finn falls into line, I finally catch sight of the shadow who couldn't stand farther away.

Jett flinches when our gazes bump.

The breeze sweeps his long hair, and he yanks out his hair tie, letting wind-whipped hair shield his face. The moonlight gives them all an otherworldly charm, but it turns Jett into a demonic prince.

Jett is not a prince.

He's the king of mixed fucking signals.

I shake myself.

Whether the Wyverns love me or hate me, they want to heal me or send me away, I'm no longer accepting transmissions. "You're not supposed to be on campus."

"*Lilah,*" Atlas grits out my name in a way I wish I hated more. "What. Happened?"

I turn my shudder into a shrug. "The same thing that always happens."

"It shouldn't," Hunter says softly. "It won't again."

Promises, promises.

Easy to make.

"I'm fine, okay? If you want to help, hide the bodies. I'm gonna go swim and—"

"You are *not* swimming," Atlas snarls.

I fume, but before I can hit back, Orion growls. "Don't fucking use that tone with her."

Atlas rocks like he just took a punch. "Shit. I didn't mean... Her cuts..." He struggles with the words, and an eensy weensy hint of sympathy flutters in my chest. Then he squares his shoulders and reads me my rights. "We're taking you to the clinic. Then we're taking you home. You're not safe here. Not with the bounty."

"The *what*?"

"Shit," Hunter murmurs.

Atlas ignores him. "Dominik put a price on you. Now all he has to do is wait for someone to cash in."

"He wants me dead?" I ask hopefully.

"Alive."

My stomach hits the grass.

Atlas must mistake my fallen expression for throwing him a bone because he keeps rolling. "We can protect you until your heat. There are too many ways to get to you as long as you're at the OCC. If you come with us—"

"No." I stand, pretending I don't feel every ache. Pretending I don't see them tense when I wobble. I steady myself, then step past Orion's body-shield. "Doesn't he want me because of you? If I choose another pack, he'll choose another target."

Finn's chest rumble has me wobbling again. "Too late to walk, Star."

"She's right," Jett croaks. We whip our heads toward the shadows. "She should—"

"Say one more word." Finn pulls a knife, and the air goes liquid.

"*Enough*!" Atlas's bark knocks me into Orion's waiting arms.

Shit.

Artur's bark was strong enough to stop me dead.

Atlas isn't even commanding me, but some part of me wants to roll over and submit, so he'll know how well-behaved I am.

Just in case he wants to order me to do something fun later.

Stupid pheromones.

"*We're going.*" Atlas's power rocks my knees and solidifies my need to punch him in the ribs the second he lowers his guard. "Nothing's more important than your safety, Lilah. Even if you hate me, I'll keep you safe."

"I'm not leaving campus." I can't emphasize that enough.

If I walk away with Wyvern Pack, I'll lose the sliver of freedom I have left. I won't have a choice of packs. I'll have to go back to their cursed mansion, where Orion and I can sit around waiting for our next abduction.

I'm not going to fuck with my safety either, but *come on*.

Go back with them?

In what world is that safe? "Just help me find a trustworthy bodyguard. I'll pay you back when I get my heat check."

They flinch, and I'm petty enough to enjoy four out of five of their twisted faces.

Orion's is the only one that feels sour.

"Lilah…" He touches my fingers.

I'm not expecting the jolt when our knuckles bump.

The electric-eel flutters when he holds his skin against mine.

My belly kickflips and I don't know if it's happiness or pure fucking dread.

Because I can resist the Wyvern Pack's alphas.

I can grit my teeth and shut them out forever.

But Orion slips under my defenses like they never applied.

Orion can crack my heart like an egg and trick me into loving getting fucking fried.

And our chemistry's so wild, I'm not the only one with yolk oozing out my ears. Orion's scent spikes, all cider and apple-soaked *need*.

"This is the plan." Atlas squares his feet, vein pulsing in his neck. "We—"

"*Stop*." Hunter breaks formation.

Then he marches forward and majorly violates *Alpha 101*.

Don't step between an alpha and his omega.

Atlas vibrates. "The hell are you doing?"

"What I should've done a long time ago." Hunter pushes out a breath that flips the whole fucking table. "I'm challenging you for pack leader."

TEN

HUNTER

WRONGNESS BUZZES THROUGH MY VEINS.

The unraveling of our pack bond.

The sad-sack state of my brothers.

And boiling fucking rage after watching Lilah being chased. The blood on her knees and the fingerprint bruises on her pale arms.

I'll rip down the motherfucking sun to keep this from happening again.

Atlas squares up, ready to go full wrecking ball. "*Get in line.*"

It's not my first rodeo with Atlas.

I've been dealing with the bull since I could crawl and gotten the horns in my cheeks more than once because I opened my mouth.

That's how it works.

Tell him he's being a dick, get barked into submission.

I always let it go, because Atlas is a good general.

He's the one who takes the fall for our fuck-ups, fights for our interests with the dads, and stays up late, planning and back-up planning, making sure we come back from every insane mission alive.

He's pulled me out of hell.

But I can't keep watching him stumble.

Atlas glares, nostrils flaring like I waved a red flag, but instead of rage, frustration, fear, our bond only sends me muted noise.

Jett's self-hatred, Finn's emptiness, and Orion's inadequacy.

What should be crazy powerful emotions are dull bursts of static.

Our bond is that weak.

Years of not talking, not fixing problems, letting things fucking go because we had missions and enemies and more important shit to worry about.

"Hunter. We can talk, but not now. We're taking Lilah. Now *move*." Atlas throws the dominance hammer, ready to maintain the status quo forever.

But the second he barks, there's a ripping, tearing, *hell-no* resistance in my chest, because I *know* his plan is going to make Lilah hate us even worse.

We all spilled this bucket of shit.

The dads. My brothers.

Group fucking effort.

But I'm the only one who knows how to mop, and...

Just *fuck*.

Fuck me and fuck them, because I see only one way to make things better, and that means making them hella worse.

This pack isn't a remodel.

It's a tear-down.

So, I fight Atlas's command, refusing to click my heels and play soldier boy.

"We're taking—"

"*No*."

Atlas rears. He hasn't heard my full bark in years.

"*Submit*." His will pounds my temples.

"*No*." My knees wobble, my vision wavers, and I taste iron filings in my throat, but I cannot submit to his well-meaning but deluded bullshit.

Not now.

Not ever again.

"Hunter." He presses, and at the deepest level, I *want* to obey my pack leader. I want to shut my mouth, give in, go on, and let him eat the responsibility.

But I can't.

"We're going to lose her." I glance at the girl in question. Lilah stands with Orion, grey eyes sparkling. Probably wants a bowl of fucking caramel corn while she watches our pack melt down. She can have it. She can have anything as long as she stays right there. "Yield, At."

His jaw clenches.

Yield isn't in his word bank.

Atlas grew up with *fall in line* and *follow the leader*. Scorpio had us military march behind him to kindergarten.

This time, I can't let him lead us deeper in the shit.

When Atlas hits back, I don't bend.

Instead, I feel something ripping.

A scraping in my chest.

Rusted steel sawing a red-hot line from my throat to my heart.

I should cave, but I grit it out.

Eat the pain.

Rip it all to the ground.

The rope that binds us is so fucking raggedy, it can't take the tug-of-war.

Deeper than flesh, it tears.

Flash.

Bang.

And our bond fries in a blaze of lightning.

My ears roar.

Atlas bellows.

The guys give the gasp of a kidney punch.

I brace to feel their pain, but there's nothing.

Nothing.

The only pain I feel is my own.

Atlas. Finn. Jett. Orion.

All gone.

I swallow three times before my voice comes out in a ragged rasp. "I broke the bond."

High and drifting, I'm a balloon, cut free.

"What did you do?" Jett grips his chest.

Orion goes down, but Lilah catches him, hauling him onto the bench.

Atlas is adrift in space.

Fucking Finn just cackles.

He's free from our orders to slow down and stop trying to kidnap Lilah. I glance to Atlas, waiting for him to step in with the command.

Only he doesn't.

Shit.

I broke him too.

I snag Finn before he can sink teeth into Lilah's throat. "No biting."

He gives me the look he gets right before he breaks a bottle over the bar and starts a fight with twenty bikers.

"*Chill.*" I flex my dominance.

Finn pushes back. His alpha energy looms, wilder and colder than Atlas's, but without that pack leader yoke pulling me down, Finn can't beat me unless I submit.

And I'm not fucking submitting.

I fight until he sucks in a breath, not giving in, but pulling off.

A truce.

"Since when are you the dom?" he mutters.

"Be good or I'll put you in a harness."

"Lilah can put me in a harness."

"*Finn.*" I make a noise at the back of my throat. "Go tie up the Brauns and grab some revenge for our girl. *Don't* kill them," I shout as he skips off.

"Buzzkill," he calls back.

One psycho off my hands, I triage the rest of the squad.

Atlas and Jett are both in statue mode, staring into the void.

Orion's worst off, shaking while Lilah keeps him from falling off the bench.

I drop in front of them, bracing Orion's knees. "How bad is it?"

He rubs his neck. "Itchy. Shit. Needed a warning."

The way he trembles looks more like withdrawal than an itch, but I let him have that lie. I ruffle his hair the way I used to before everything got so complicated. "Feels free."

"Yeah." Orion lets out a shaky breath. "I think… it's good."

"Right?"

A fresh start.

Our last chance to fix our fuckups.

"Killer." Lilah jerks when I call her nickname. "Need your help."

"With what?" Her voice drips with well-deserved suspicion, but her poker face is cracked; she's still smoothing Orion's shaking back.

I swallow.

Her emotions are so high, her scent hits like a caramel club. I want to sweep her into my lap and purr until she's calm and safe.

I want to fucking devour her.

But I have to be patient.

Have to make shit right and prove I'm worthy of her trust before I earn a taste of that crème brûlée.

"Orion." His scent's just as sharp, just as sweet, but the apple doesn't warp my brain at the same level. "Do you want to stay with us or with Lilah?"

"Lilah," he says with zero thought.

Perfect answer. "Can you help him enroll in classes?"

"*Here?*" Lilah's snub nose wrinkles.

So fucking cute.

"Adult classes." Orion's still shaky but he shoots the easy layup I just passed. "I can get my shit together and be your bodyguard."

"I'll show you around, but this doesn't change my plan. I'm going to keep meeting packs."

Atlas clicks back online, instinctively rumbling his displeasure. *Time to get the omegas out.* "We won't get in your way. Just hold our spot at the back of the line."

"If you say so." Lilah probably wants to argue, but she and Orion are wrecked.

"Stick together tonight. I'll send the new security plan in the morning."

"If by morning you mean noon." She stands, offering Orion a hand.

Together, they shuffle to the security gate. My instincts hate letting them out of sight, but we have to play the smart game. Orion catches my eye, giving me the nod.

Fucking finally, we're on the same page.

At least some of us are.

I watch until they disappear.

Then it's time to deal with the two butt ends of this idiot sandwich.

Atlas is on his knees.

I kick him in his muscular ass, knocking him onto his elbows.

Falling restarts his brain.

Jett's still mid-lobotomy. He stares shell-shocked at the moon and flinches when I grab him.

I drag both their stubborn asses to the bench.

It's time for a talk.

I expect Atlas to fight because he always fights, and he doesn't disappoint. "We have to—"

"Bro." There's a burr in my throat. That always-there fear that what I say will only fuck things up worse.

But I just imploded the pack, so we're already at bedrock, and nothing's worse than watching my brothers keep shambling through their pain.

So even if I'm not a leader, even if I ruin every fucking thing, I have to step up. "You're a kickass team leader, and there's no one

I trust more to have my back on a mission. But when it comes to the pack, you have the emotional intelligence of a fucking gummy bear."

"Damn it, Hunter." He puts his head between his knees, and his voice tears. It costs him everything to keep speaking. "If you can fix the pack, you can have it. I'll stand down. Just...tell me how to stop hurting everyone."

What I want to do is puke in the bushes.

But I pulled the trigger, so I have to clean the splattered brains.

When I clap Jett's shoulder, he flinches again.

I don't know what he went through, but I know it's dark, and if he doesn't get help, the past'll keep eating him until there's nothing left but bones.

"Jett. Do you trust me?" I offer my hand, asking him to jump on the carpet and go for a magic ride.

His eyebrows furrow—must not've seen the movie—but I keep going. "Are you ready to get help, or do you wanna keep fighting alone?"

"I..." He reaches out, and his fingers shake. Then he makes a fist. "I want to make things right."

His jaw firms with determination, and with the passion flashing in his eyes, he's like before-Jett—the one who smiled and laughed, who I pray we can still resurrect.

Fucking pumped, fucking terrified at the way they both look to *me* like the only life raft at sea, I straighten my shoulders. "This is the plan."

ELEVEN

LILAH

ORION and I stagger across campus. Pretty sure we're recycling the same thought.

Can't believe the pack broke.

Orion's lucky the backlash only has him stumbling. I've read case studies where omegas died from a severed mate bond.

Rare, but it happens.

Was their bond that fragile?

Wyvern Pack was never at the top of my heat list, but they were at least a footnote. A backup, last-resort, better-them-than-another-heat-alone option that I was keeping open in the way-back of my psyche.

Now they're broken and basically off the table, and I'm equal parts relieved and terrified.

I also have one less day to find a pack thanks to that total bust of a social.

And if I'm going to survive the next one, I need better than makeshift shivs and borrowed knives.

So, I take Orion on a side trip to the indoor range.

The building's locked this time of night, but I paw through a potted plant to find the bent paper clips I left the last time I broke in.

"Is this your dorm?" Orion asks while I fiddle.

"Nope." The lock clicks, and I lead him downstairs. The actual armory's a fortress with a keypad and bomb-proof hinges I couldn't crack with a blowtorch, let alone office supplies.

But wouldn't you know?

I memorized the code, and the lazy trainers haven't changed it in years.

"Take whatever you want." I help myself to handguns and magazines until I'm armed for a fucking siege.

Orion picks through the weapon racks. "We won't get in trouble?"

"Worth it." I feel so much better knowing I won't have to run again. Now all I need is an ice pack and a full night of REM sleep.

I'm leading us back to the bungalows when it clicks that it's too late to register Orion. He'll have to sleep over at my place.

That should go well.

I'm still hoping for that territorial twinge to kick in, needling me to go claws-out against any omega in my territory.

The rules never apply to Orion.

I let him in the bungalow with zero problems.

Zero problems, except for the way his scent's going to soak every inch of fabric and drive me to hump the pillows.

"You can have the couch." I hurry to grab sheets. The linen closet has ten spare sets.

I load a pile so high I can't see where I'm going, but before I can get back, Orion snatches the bundle. "Don't. You're hurt."

I rub my palms against my bodice, itching to get out of the torn-up costume and away from the attentive Orion who makes me question everything. "Need anything else before I crash?"

He dumps the linens on the coffee table, then clutches his throat with shaky fingers. "Stay with me?"

My heart gives a pathetic squeeze.

Bite scars still loop his neck in a silver collar, but they'll fade as the mystical mating magic dissolves and shows his freedom on his skin.

I cannot give into his fallen prince vibes, but the pull is real.

So, I panic, and my mouth goes for the nuclear option that must've been stewing in my subconscious all along. "You didn't stay with me."

The distant, drifty quality he's had since losing his anchor snaps with that slap in the face. His blue eyes focus on me and *only* me, and suddenly I'm the one adrift.

"Lilah." He takes a step forward.

I step back.

Forward, back, forward, back, until my legs bump the couch, and I fall into the seat.

Orion drops to his knees.

"I'm sorry about your heat." He crawls until I have to spread my legs to make room, my thighs parting like we're opening the gates to his very own castle. I breathe so high and shallow, his words sound like they're drifting down from a cloud. "I'm so, so sorry. That wasn't supposed to happen. Everything the guys said to you. *Fuck*. I know you hate me, but I hate myself more."

Gripping the couch cushion, he kneels between my wide-spread thighs. We don't touch, but his body heat soaks through my skin and my suddenly scratchy throat begs for a sip of apple cider.

My fingers twitch.

His hair's too long, that stupid blond piece hanging over his forehead.

I want to push it back. Cup his cheek.

But if I touch him, I'll forgive him.

And if I forgive Orion, I'll bobsled right down the slippery slope toward forgiving *them*.

I'm not ready.

I might never be ready. "You're not the one who needs to apologize."

"I do." His honeyed breath feathers my inner thigh.

Too close.

I press the hem of my skirt, trying to block his heat *and* mine.

"It already happened. You should be focusing on getting your pack back together."

"No." He pouts, sticking out a bottom lip that's ten times more lush than legal.

I can't.

I can't have him crawling into me, practically begging me without melting like soft serve. "You belong with them. I don't."

"The fuck I do." Orion rumbles so rough, the couch cushion vibrates. "You know what pisses me off? If I hadn't taken their shit for so many years, that night never would've happened."

I squeeze my eyes against the memory.

Orion was so drugged he was slurring when I dragged him to his nest. Pheromones at nuclear, he was drunk on a long, *long* overdue heat.

He had no idea what was happening.

But even if he did?

"It's not like you could've claimed me. I shouldn't have gone upstairs." It feels even stupider now, the hope that they'd be all, *come on in, join the fuckfest, intruder omega we never wanted.*

I blame the pain.

It corroded my brain.

Now I know exactly where I stand.

By myself.

"I'd claim you if I could." His hands slip to the outsides of my knees, warm and gentle, careful not to touch my scrapes.

"The guys—"

"You can fucking take 'em. As long as I get to keep you."

My heart gives a giddy flop. "That's not how this works. They're your mates."

"Not anymore." His fingers tense.

I flinch at the pain in his voice. "Orion…"

"The only thing I ever wanted was to be good enough for them. Then I awakened and everything got so twisted. Felt like I owed it to them to be the perfect omega, but I was never built for that. Still don't know what the hell I'm doing. I'm glad the pack broke. Now they can't keep me away from you."

"Can you…?" I wave at the couch, hoping he'll move so we can have this very serious conversation at a level that doesn't make me want to scoot my hips into his face.

"I'm good." Orion hooks his elbows over my thighs, using me like a prayer bench.

My throat makes motions, but I can't pretend I want him to move.

He's warm.

Hard and soft, and the only person in the world whose touch just feels right. He soothes the primal panic after another night of running for my life.

"Do you have a first aid kit?" He blows gently over a scrape on my thigh.

I tense my quads to hide my shudder. "No idea."

He goes to rummage through the bathroom, returning with bandages and spray. When he starts to clean my knees, the sting of antiseptic restarts my critical thinking skills. "What are you doing?"

"Taking care of you."

My temperature rises. "I can't do this."

"Do what? Me?" He fucking smirks.

I push his hands, and Orion lets me retreat to the other side of the couch. I still don't know how I'm this attracted to an omega, but it's impossible to deny when he barely touches me and I swear my thighs are slick.

I try to take a breath, but instead of centering myself, I'm stuck in the center of an apple cider donut. I rub my arms. "Your pack doesn't want me."

"That's because my pack is deadass stupid." Orion sighs. "And it's me they don't want."

"Not true."

Orion gives a sad smile. "When you showed up, I was terrified you'd replace me. You'd straight up take my spot or make me second place."

"I—"

"I'm not blaming you," he says quickly. "I know the dads forced you. I just realized I was ready to throw down with you over a position I never wanted. If we weren't all so wrapped up in our own bullshit, we would've seen how much we needed you."

I feel warm inside, but not cozy warm.

Like my internal organs just went *sploosh*.

Melted.

"You have two weeks," he says as if I need the reminder. "They don't understand how fast they can lose you."

"They're going to find out."

"I know. And if you want to go into rotation, I get it. I get it more than they ever could. Just, please. *Please*, don't shut me out because of them. I can't take losing you too."

His voice is so raw.

When his shoulders hunch and he bites his lip, I shatter.

What willpower?

I open my arms.

Orion dives, rolling me like a seal until I'm lying on top of him, squeezed so tight I realize I've never been held before.

My face slips into the hollow of his neck.

Perfect fucking fit.

"I don't want to be alone," he whispers, fingers in my hair.

"I feel like I can only be alone." His warmth fills up my empty spaces, but this soul-soothing touch is only temporary.

He'll be as helpless as I am when my heat hits.

He can't stop the pain.

Orion rubs his nose against my scalp, breathing me in, and I know he feels every little shiver I can't stop. "I can't bite you, but that doesn't mean I'm letting you go. I want you on my team."

I groan into the scent-soaked fabric of his shirt. "I don't like your teammates."

"Former teammates. Have to see if they can get back on the squad."

"You think they can change?"

"They will for you."

I make a disgusted noise. "I'll believe it when I see it."

Either way, I'm not waiting on them.

Don't have time.

While I try to build my case for leaving the couch, Orion nuzzles my scalp. His thumb traces the sensitive hollow of my hip.

I morph into pudding, sinking deeper and deeper into his tall body until I can't ignore the hard ridge in his jeans.

His apple scent thickens.

So does he.

And my traitor body, confused as fuck over this comfy omega pillow, unleashes the flood.

Now I don't just think I'm dripping.

I know.

Slick.

Heat spike.

"*Lilah*," Orion rasps. "You should maybe…"

I tuck and roll, dart into my bedroom and slam the door, panting as I sink into a crouch.

I'm sweating.

Steaming.

And my pussy twerks, announcing that it *wants* an alpha's knot, but it's happy to give Orion a test-drive first.

If I had alphas I could trust, I'd be dialing 911.

It's called *easing*.

Foreplay and orgasms to smooth out the high hormones leading up to the main event.

All the touch and snuggling set the mood for an on-the-way heat, so you know you'll be absolutely taken care of during your time of need.

Guess who's going to ease *me*?

The new-in-box silicone alpha that came in my nightstand.

All ten speeds of him.

Toys work for now, but the closer I get to heat, the more it'll hurt to be alone.

You need your alpha's body heat.

That comforting purr.

The swelling knot that fills you up like a promise and says *I'm here and I'm never letting go.*

The hormones aren't strong enough to blot out my anxiety. The jangle behind my ribs says I'm going to end up hurt.

Again.

I have to find a pack that's not broken.

Soon.

Tomorrow.

Please.

Until then, I grab my vibrator and settle in for a long solo night.

TWELVE

LILAH

I'M dead asleep when my blankets rustle. In a blink, my hand's under the pillow, grabbing my stashed gun.

I'm already flicking the safety when citrus clogs my windpipe. Blood orange.

Spicy, sexy sweetness mixed with a dangerous hit of gunpowder and whipped cream.

"*Finn?*" I yelp, scrambling until my head cracks the headboard.

"Ouch." He cups the spot I just banged, not even a little bit worried that the position wedges my loaded gun against his abs.

"*Ouch?*" I can taste his breath. His hot fingers tangle in my hair. "You show up now and *ouch*? You can't be here." I pull the gun from between our bodies, and he oozes into the freed-up space.

"But I am." He rubs my scalp in gentle circles, and he's so fucking alpha, my pheromones go on parade. I sweat, saliva pooling in my mouth and other things pooling other places I'm not ready to handle.

I push him away. "*Why* are you here?"

"Because you're here."

I make a frustrated noise, pulling my blankets tight around my hips, hoping the fabric masks my scent. "Last time we had a heart-to-heart, you said I don't belong."

"I said you belong to me."

I grip the sheets to fight a shudder. "Didn't happen."

"Did. You were asleep."

"Not your first time sneaking into my bedroom?"

"Not my last." He licks his lips, staring at my neck. "You smell like Orion." He moves so slowly I could stop him, but my nervous system locks down when he softly takes my wrist. "And hot fucking caramel sauce."

Finn licks the fingers I used to fuck myself.

His tongue is soft, wet, and hot as the fucking sun.

I scramble away, rattled at how easily I melt for him.

For all these Wyvern motherfuckers.

Finn closes his eyes and sucks his lips, savoring my flavor. "More."

"No more." I can't handle any more.

"Why?"

"Because your pack isn't right for me. I can't have a pack." For exactly this reason.

Show up when you want, all licky, and smoky, and tempting.

Leave me alone when it counts.

I'd rather go all-in on solitude except for pre-scheduled sexcapades with the knotted gigolos who write *me* the checks.

"Perfect. I don't have a pack."

"Finn. *Come on.*" The Wyverns chose the wrong guy if they sent him as peace ambassador. He's like the honey badger who mauled the dove and used its olive branch as a toothpick. "Shouldn't you be with them? Figuring out how to rebuild?"

"That's Hunter's thing. My future's right here."

Red card on the field.

That shit is so illegal.

"Get out of my room."

Finn accepts the command, all docile, nodding with that glint in his green eyes that promises he'll be back in my sheets the second I fall back asleep. "I'm serious. Next time you climb into my bed, I'm pulling the trigger. Got it, Trouble?"

For a moment, Finn is silent.

Flat.

That gaze like his father's, where you don't know if he's meditating or mentally slitting your throat.

Then he smiles.

It's not his shit-stirring smile or his instigating and watching shit pop off smile. Not even his burn-this-motherfucker-to-the-ground smile.

I've seen those before.

Walked away still breathing.

This is a smile that should be banned after dark.

A boyish fucking grin that makes his freckles pop and his eyes light up and hits the soft, gooey part of my heart in a spray of honey-soaked bullets.

"*Star*," he says huskily, all melted butter and smoked brown sugar. "You used my nickname."

My nipples perk, saluting the alpha they very much still want to recognize as *theirs*, and I churn out pheromones like a caramel bomb at an ice cream factory.

"*Out!*" I sprint to the bathroom.

Bolt the door.

Been doing a lot of that.

I'm sweaty, throat parched, with a phantom pain in my hollow place that Finn could fill so, *so* well if only I'd ask.

But I won't.

I swear.

I won't.

Unless I have to, but otherwise, I'm a nun.

Ugh. Wyverns.

Flicking the tap to cold, I scrub off Finn's raunchy, brain-altering orange. When I'm so icy my teeth chatter, my hormones finally leave me alone.

It's not like I didn't know they'd test me.

Fated, scent-matched mates aren't easy to resist.

I have to be stronger.

When I peek into the bedroom, Finn's gone, but he left me a gift. The ratty duffel I abandoned in the Wyverns' basement looks like a hobo satchel against the puffy white cloud of my comforter.

It holds my equally ratty possessions. Threadbare sweats, my falling-apart shoes, and even my cracked-screen tablet.

Plus a bonus.

Finn stuffed in his own clothes.

Sweats, T-shirts, and two pairs of boxers that I push off the bed with the corner of a tax law textbook before I can scent whether or not he pre-wore them for me.

Gunpowder and orange seeps into everything I own.

I don't want to spend the day wearing Finn Wyvern, but it's that or the tracksuit.

You know my thoughts.

I slip into my own sweatpants and Finn's tall, hooded sweat-shirt that hangs to my knees.

It's big and comfy, and instead of driving me crazy, the spiced citrus hits like a second-hand hug. When I indulge and press my face to the cloth, the constant anxious hum in my ribs drops from a twelve to a six.

I totally just cracked the code.

Steal Wyvern Pack's clothes and stuff them 'til they're man-shaped.

Pillow mates will never disappoint me.

I accessorize with knives and my new guns, then brace myself to open the door. Good thing, because I face-plant in Finn's chest.

"Star." Something dangerously obsessive shimmers in the dark pits of his eyes. "You look so fucking good when you look like you're mine."

"Not yours." I push past him, swallowing another shiver.

This is not sustainable.

Orion sits at the marble breakfast bar in the same jeans and soft sweater from last night.

"You let this in?" I jerk my head toward our intruder.

Orion sets down his phone. "Hunter texted. Finn's officially on bodyguard duty."

"You're joking."

Finn yanks a lanyard from his pocket and flashes a glossy OCC ID badge that says PRIVATE GUARD.

There goes my plan to rat him out to campus security.

I take a cleansing breath. "Breakfast. Then I'll show you where to register, and you can still make morning classes."

"Hold that thought." Orion lifts his phone. Finn peers over his shoulder. "This one?"

"Ooh. This one." Finn taps the screen.

My anxiety ratchets back up to eight. It's french toast stick day, and I'm not missing my chance now that I'm freed from the need to starve *and* hooked up with an unlimited meal plan. Also not going to wait around to play tour guide.

They can download a campus map.

"Meet you there." I head for the door.

"Wait. Just ordering clothes."

"Don't let me stop you." Must be easier to buy new when you're heirs to a multinational conglomerate.

"And a phone," Orion says. "What color?"

"Does it matter?"

"It's for you."

"No, it's not. Don't need a phone." Wyvern gifts come with tangly Wyvern strings.

"You could've called us last night instead of running."

"Can't afford it." The phone *or* the call. I have a feeling Wyverns would want the kind of interest I'm not willing to give.

"Pack card," Orion pushes. "Just spend their money."

"Her tablet's cracked." Finn rubs his cheek on Orion, scent-marking him just to screw with me.

"Already in the cart. What else do you need?" Orion shifts on the barstool but isn't half as distracted as I am, flashing back to the two of them together during the only peek of his heat I care to remember. The way Orion tipped his head back, blissing out while Finn bobbed up and down on his—

"Nothing." *Another cold shower.*

Orion's judgy gaze flicks to my duct-taped shower sandals. "Uh huh."

"Gotta go to breakfast." I keep walking. "I have a big day."

French toast sticks. Ice cream. Maybe a gun battle.

"Wait." Orion's call holds me back. "Today's socials were canceled."

"*What?* Why?"

"Event security shortage. Hunter and Jett fired everyone on staff last night."

Shit.

"Lend me a phone?"

Finn hands me his so fast, I want to pet him and call him a good boy. If he were this obedient all the time, maybe I could keep him around.

But that thought is the exact reason he's so dangerous.

Finn's a trap.

All of them, traps.

I find Catherine's business card halfway under the living room couch and call, praying Orion's info is wrong.

"Catherine speaking."

"It's Lilah Darling. Was today's schedule canceled?"

"Unfortunately. I'm so sorry for what happened, Lilah." The words spill out in a rush, tight and so unlike her calm confidence yesterday. "We canceled today's events as a precaution. Don't worry. We're rescheduling the ice cream social for tomorrow. And we're working with the OCC to hire a more reliable private security contractor. They'll make everything safe for you."

"Which private security contractor?"

"Wyvern House."

"Right." *Who could've possibly guessed.*

"I promise," she assures me, "We have such a great lineup of alphas waiting for you. One more day won't hurt your prospects."

I agree, because what the hell else can I do? "Call me if anything else changes."

I am so boned.

And not in the good way.

————

I DROWN my frustration in a soup bowl full of maple syrup. Sitting with Orion and Finn is a brand new experience in being thrown omega dagger-eyes, but I forgive them a little because they take turns mounding my plate with hot French toast sticks.

Reminding myself I can't get used to this treatment, I take Orion to the registrar. I pawn him off on a moon-eyed secretary and hang around just long enough to make sure he picks the classes he needs most.

I'm dying for a swim.

I need to do a thousand laps, replace these Wyvern scents with the burn of chlorine, and stay under 'til my whirling thoughts go dark.

"You're not coming to class?" Orion asks when I start shadily edging out of the office. "I thought we'd have the day together."

Just one class.

Then it'll be just one kiss.

Just one eensy, weensy, itty bitty mating bite from his once-and-future pack leader.

It's a slippery fucking slope covered in black ice and barbed wire. "What class do you have first?"

"Omega physiology."

"With Trainer Eleanor?"

"That one."

I bite my cheek to keep from smiling. I'm not sitting in, but this will be priceless. "I'll walk you."

I can navigate the OCC's halls in the dark. I know every escape route, every side door, and every cranny that'll hold a balled-up omega girl gripping her shaking knees.

I've skulked these halls my whole life.

I've never strutted them.

But with Orion at my side and Finn at my back, I can ignore the stares and bad memories.

It's powerful.

I thought the betas would be all over me when they caught my scent. I'm half right.

It is pure art when Trainer Bethany lifts her nose, catches a whiff, and turns with a sycophant look pre-plastered, only to realize she's sniffing *me*—her least favorite student in history. Her fishy lips pout, then fall open at the sight of my rabid red-headed shadow, whose mercenary smile dares her to fucking try.

I can't help grinning as she flees.

"See someone you know?" Orion asks.

"Someone I hate." Bethany always smacked my knuckles with her baton in music class. With most classes, I faked being an idiot to avoid attention.

Piano, I failed naturally.

It's nice to get a teeny slice of revenge.

I make a grand gesture when we finally reach Orion's class. "Tell Eleanor I said hi."

Orion peeks into the stadium classroom. The seats are more than half full, and curious omegas size us up with their stares.

Trainer Eleanor breaks into a toothless grin when the blond Apollo walks through her door. "My new student. Come and get your goodie bag."

I don't know Eleanor's exact age, but if she said 120, I wouldn't ask for ID. Her omega scent's long faded, and she's so shrunken, she makes *me* feel like a giant.

When Orion glances at me for confirmation, I shoo him toward the nice old lady. "Have fun."

Eleanor pats Orion's abs, and he shoots me a look of deep betrayal. Finn leans his chin on my head while I'm distracted with the show.

The "goodie bag" is the tote full of sex ed supplies given to every new soon-to-awaken or adult omega. I never got one, but oh have I seen what's inside.

Pulling no punches, Eleanor whips out a dark, flesh-toned dildo.

It's one of the fancy models with a pulsing jelly bulb at the base to mimic an alpha's knot. Then she takes out the beads, and the plugs, and the double-thick lube.

"Why aren't we taking this class?" Finn's chin moves against my scalp.

"Already took it." I've been to all these lectures. Sat through pretty much every course the OCC has to offer, because I overstayed my welcome a long time ago.

I have no interest in reliving the years I sat at the back, hunching my shoulders, staying quiet, and lying about who I really am. Not even if I get to watch Orion's cute blush. "Come on."

My feet start toward the pool, but I change my mind and take the brick path to performing arts.

I want to swim, but I need a backup plan first. With today's social already scratched, I can't bet my future on the next one being a win. I need to play to my strengths instead of waiting for the right alphas to fall into my lap.

Morning classes just started, so campus is empty until we enter the bright dance studios. Evgenia runs a ballet warm-up in the biggest classroom.

I was going to wait and talk to her after class, but I forgot that Rachel takes first period ballet.

In knee socks and a pink leotard, she stretches lazily at the barre, looking way too at ease after selling me up the fucking river.

I bust in, slamming the door so hard it rattles the walls.

Evgenia's snitty look flashes to a bright smile, growing even wider when she spots my escort. "My little Darling. What brings you to my lair this morning?"

I'm still facing Evgenia, but I hold eye contact with Rachel through the wall mirror. "I'll do a pole routine if you let me have the main slot at the weekend showcase."

"Finally!" Evgenia claps. "You'll be drowning in kno—" Finn's rabid growl cuts her off, but Evgenia is a slick bitch. "You'll be drowning in praise. I have the most luscious choreography for you."

Rachel's nose scrunches, wrenching her face into a gargoyle mask.

"Perfect." I skip off to claim a corner in the pole studio and start practicing my routine.

I'm five steps down the hall before Rachel rages after me.

"Bitch! How dare you—"

Finn flashes between us, shielding me behind his broad back.

A sinister warning rattles in his chest, but it's only a warning for *her*.

To me, it's omega uppers.

My could-be mate, protecting me with his body.

Defending my honor.

Swoon.

Damn it.

Rachel's lip trembles. She breaks out big, brown doe eyes, all glassy and fake innocent. "Finn…"

"*You don't say his name.*" The words whip out my traitor mouth.

Finn's rumble sweetens, good as stroking between my thighs, but this time, I'm pissed enough to not get sucked in by the sound.

"How can you be so mean?" Rachel says in a baby voice that makes me twitch. She glances up at Finn through damp lashes, coy and begging for help.

The *audacity* of playing the pity card.

The girl took a baseball bat to my skull and sent me to be raped with a clear conscience. Let alone all the other violent, shady shit she's pulled.

I'm done being her victim.

I cock back, flatten my palm, and blindside her with the slap I've been charging for fucking *years*.

Her head wrenches to the side, and the impact's so loud, it drowns out her pathetic mousey squeak.

Rachel collapses in a heap.

I planned a speech.

A truly epic monologue calling her out for her abuse.

But it won't change anything. Rachel's rotten beyond redemption, and she doesn't deserve my words.

Just one last, real-talk warning. "I'm filing a police report."

She pales, but quickly regains her old-money confidence. "All I did was introduce you to a pack that's a better fit for your status. It's not my fault your charm makes men want to—"

"Can I kill her?" Finn's hand hovers at his hip, a half-second away from drawing a blade, he could've already pulled if he weren't waiting for my permission.

Good boy.

"I'll tell you when." I pull him down the hall, loving the way he rumbles under my fingers.

I have to laminate this memory so it never fades.

Finn's sweet protection is just as good as walking away after leaving my nemesis in a pathetic pile.

But once I save the image, I have to put it in a box and stash it deep, deep at the back of my mental closet.

Rachel will hit back, and Finn…

I need to know I'm not a game.

Problem is, everything's a game to Finn.

He's fun in the crazy way.

Not reliable.

I mean, just his scent and I can *guarantee* he'd have me orgasming until my eyes crossed, but that's not the promise I need.

I need a sure thing when Finn is fucking chaos.

If I had a whole deck of alphas, I wouldn't mind one wildcard.

But can't risk myself on jokers.

I need kings.

THIRTEEN

FINN

I THOUGHT the universe was fucking huge, all dark ooze and evil motherfuckers. No reason to keep kicking around except to take a few more with me before I go.

Newsflash. The universe is tiny.

Just one star.

Five feet balanced on pretty pearly toes.

When Lilah dances, I find all the colors I forgot.

I don't give a shit about the pack, the Redfangs, and these ballerina bitches. All they have to do is die.

Easy.

Then I get forever with my star.

She's not just my reason to stay.

She's my reason to *exist*.

Lilah only does a few twirls. A few shakes of that cute little ass on the pole.

Not enough.

The minutes roll too fast. The hours disappear.

I spend every second watching her, and I'm never going to stop.

Bodyguarding Lilah Darling is the career path they never told me about at the academy.

I would've gone to class.

I text Hunter. *Don't come. I'm going full-time.*

He leaves me on read.

Ass.

After dinner, Lilah stops me from following into her nest. "Not happening. I have work, and then I'm going to sleep. Don't let me catch you sneaking in again."

"Okay." *You won't catch me.*

She shuts the door in my face, and when the lock clicks, the giddy high that's been carrying me cuts like a fucking guillotine.

Color gone.

Purpose lost.

Habit has me checking in with the mofos who used to live in my chest, but the bond that pretended to be my conscience is all ripped out.

I stand at Lilah's door, sucking her candy-sweet scent and waiting for her to fall asleep so I can sneak between her sheets.

She can shoot me, stab me, bite me.

It'll all be good if it's Lilah.

Without her, I don't feel at all.

I stare at the door for hours. The floorboards squeak when she pads over the carpet. The water runs when she brushes her teeth.

There's a soft *shik* when she slides between her sheets, and then I'm counting her breaths. Waiting for them to slow.

I'm sure she's asleep, but before I can pick the lock, Hunter rocks up in babysitter mode.

"*Hands in your pockets,*" he orders in that riff that forces me to obey.

"Dirty move."

"You're giving me white hair." Hunter drags me to the living room, nudging me onto the couch next to Orion.

Hands in pockets, I log-fall onto the cushions and press my nose to a spot that smells like caramel.

"How'd we do?" Hunter ruffles Orion's hair. "You liking class?"

"I don't know if *like* is the word for getting a butt plug lecture from a ninety-year-old, but yeah. Should've gone to learn this shit years ago."

"And Lilah?" Hunter asks.

I pop up. "Who's that bitch Rachel and why did she introduce our girl to the fucking Brauns?"

"Wait. Rachel did that?" Orion frowns. "She's Noelle Patrick's sister."

"What did the Brauns say?" Jett must've flayed them.

If he didn't, I'm free.

"Same as the other attackers. They're after the bounty. But it's sus as hell. Someone got paid to vet them for a campus visit." Hunter unbuttons his collar. He's in a suit. No tie, but looking all gangbanger with his dark hair slicked back and ink spilling over his cuffs.

"You have a job interview with the mob?"

"Went to the bank. House has a cash buyer. Lilah can have the check tomorrow."

I lick my lips over the promise of drama. Dads are gonna be epic when they realize we liquidated our shit to set Lilah free.

"What about Jett's part of the plan?" Orion asks before his voice lifts an octave. "And Atlas?"

They're fucking idiots with the push and the pull.

You love each other and the sex is bananas.

Get over yourselves.

"Jett's gathering info and taking out threats in-between therapy sessions," Hunter says. "You're with him tomorrow, Finn."

"Nice." The torturing. Not the therapy.

My pack brothers are like those broken bowls you can glue back together with gold.

I'm powder.

Nothing but crushed-up dust so wrecked that all the king's horses and all the king's men couldn't put me the fuck together again.

"He's actually going to his sessions?" Orion asks.

"I drove him," Hunter answers. "He's serious. And so is Atlas. I took his phone and put him on admin leave. He'll be in full-time tutoring twenty-four-seven unless he has a guard shift."

"Redfangs?"

"Same shit." Hunter rolls his cuffs, flashing ink. "More plots to grab you and Lilah. Mostly Lilah. No new pings on Dom's location."

My hands are still in my pockets—*thanks, Daddy Hunter*—but I have knives in there, so I grip one of the hilts, mapping how I'm going to peel Dominik Redfang's skin.

Fucker probably has snake scales.

I'll pop them off one-by-one and use 'em to make Lilah a little clutch. She needs somewhere to keep my leash.

"What else did you find out about Lilah?" Hunter asks.

"She's obsessed with French toast." Orion smiles like he has a secret, but fuck that.

I'm watching her harder. "My Star hates piano. And put Trainer Bethany on our list. You know she did some shady shit."

"Done." Hunter sends a text. "Come help me grab her gifts."

"Not leaving." Lilah's the only thing holding me together. Fucking hate having her out of sight, and I don't know what happens if I go farther away.

"You can do donuts in the golf cart."

"Fine."

Hunter and I haul presents into the cart. I zoom past two security gates and a tripled guard staff.

Love me a golf cart.

I'd tip it, but I can't hurt Lilah's gifts.

We ordered everything she needs. After a ton of trips, box towers fill her living room. I start digging as soon as they're inside.

The knives I chose aren't here yet, but my other picks are just as sexy.

Vivid orange lingerie for her and spiked collars for her to put on me.

"*Finn*," Hunter makes that strained, *the-fuck-are-you-doing-now* voice that I love. "Way too soon."

"When?" I want to buy Lilah so much shit.

Give her everything.

Feels so good, I'm adding online shopping to my list.

Things that keep Finnegan Wyvern from cliff-diving into the abyss:

- Lilah
- Saunas
- Mating Lilah
- Shopping for Lilah
- Saunas with Lilah?
- Bar fights

"How you holding on without the pack bond?" Hunter peers all up in my eyes, but what the fuck does he expect to find in there?

It's like an empty well in my head.

The tie to the pack used to be my only rope.

But soon there'll be a better line keeping me from free-falling. A stronger one made of moonbeams and pink sugar.

Have to bite her soon.

Need her too much.

Crave her light.

"She's my reason."

"Good. But you have to get Lilah's trust before you start giving her kinky shit. Otherwise, she'll run."

"How?"

"Prove you can be the alpha she needs. We have zero street cred, so we have to show her we're ride or die or she'll never want to build a life with us."

Silence roars between my ears.

"Think about it." Hunter claps my shoulder. "And also, get the fuck out. It's my turn to take care of her."

I don't want to take turns.

I need my Star full-time, all-the-time.

But I'm not too far gone to understand what he's saying.

I hop on my bike and tear out.

The roar of the engine echoes, but everything's so dark without Lilah, I can't even tell if my headlight works.

I'm driving downtown, scraping the pit of my head for answers when I skid and flip a U-turn, roaring to a stop at Hunter's favorite place on earth.

Tat Brat.

I've sat in on Hunter's sessions, but I never wanted ink.

Probably would've liked the pain, just that nothing spoke to me.

I like my scars. *The memories.*

Didn't want them covered with stupid shit.

Now I know what I want.

Ernie is a middle-aged goth pixie, and she quakes in her pleather stilettos when my entrance dings the shop bell. "You got an empty chair?"

"Where's Hunter?"

"Busy. I want a chest piece. Big. Lots of colors. Probably a few sessions."

"Seriously? What kind of design?" She clack-walks to the counter, pulling binders as I describe my dream tat.

"Lilah in huge letters. With stars and butterflies and caramel syrup."

"Syrup?" Her pierced eyebrows pinch.

"I'll start the sketch."

Ernie hands me stencil paper and goes to clear her station.

I draw **LILAH** in big, big letters. Galaxies of stars, flowers, and balisong knives with butterfly wings.

All the deadly sweet and beautiful things.

Prove I can be a good alpha?

I can't wait to headshot every asshole who looks at Lilah, even *thinks* of Lilah, but that doesn't make me good for her.

I'm empty except for a borrowed thread of starlight that I have to figure out how to lock down and keep in a pretty jar.

With air holes.

And, like, purple Easter grass and little cookie snacks in there.

What I offer is a shittton of nothing.

So Lilah can have me.

The whole fucking nightmare package.

I'll put her name on my chest so she knows she owns me. Then I'll dig in so far, she can't breathe without sniffing oranges.

Gonna keep my Star forever.

And she's gonna have to keep me.

FOURTEEN

LILAH

IT WAS torture falling asleep with the ghost of Finn's citrus and cream clinging to my sheets, but I didn't spike another heat.

It *will* happen.

And soon.

That's why I jump out of bed early, ready—if not excited for—the ice cream social and more pole practice.

I can pretend to smile.

I shower, then change into my hoodie and the clean pair of sweats held up by a triple-knotted cord. I expect to step out to Finn stalking my door frame again, but instead I find an invasion of box towers and a burning smell.

Whichever unwanted roommate turned my bungalow into a storage locker also left an aisle. I creep to the kitchen to find Hunter and Orion huddled over the stove.

"It's burnt." Orion pokes a suspicious black lump on the griddle pan.

"It's melted chocolate," Hunter insists.

"It's charcoal, dude." Orion tips the pan into the trash.

"What are you doing?"

They jump.

"Making French toast." Hunter side steps, switching my view

of the blackened pan for one of him in a hooded sweatshirt with cut-off arms and unfairly tight workout pants.

Trying to avoid staring at the canvas of ink and muscle, I focus on the bridge of his nose, but his hypnotizing dark features don't cut my ovaries a break. "Why is it you?"

"The guys are trading guard duty." Wearing a temptingly soft sweater, Orion dredges a fresh piece of bread that sizzles and pops when it hits the way-too-hot pan. "One will be with you at all times."

He's way more concerned about the griddle than the consequences of pawning off his former alphas, but there's not a whiff of jealousy in his vibe.

I was expecting him to be ragged, or at least a little bit rattled after severing his bond.

But no.

He and Hunter seem…loose.

They're lighter than before. When their arms casually brush, there's no tension. It doesn't feel like an alpha and his omega, or even two guys wrecked by loss.

They look all shiny, fresh, and new.

The shift makes my belly swirl, and I don't want to examine why. "What's the deal with the boxes?"

Hunter walks toward me.

He watches me with thick-lashed, dark brown eyes, and a bamboo cane knocks out my knees when I realize what changed.

Hunter's focus.

He used to see everything and do nothing.

Now he's only looking at me, and I don't think I want to know what he's about to do.

I'm not sure what *I'll* do because that single-minded Hunter focus is as good as a belly rub to the needy, whiny creature inside me.

She wants to roll over.

The boxes are the new MVPs, stopping him from coming any closer.

"We ordered you some things."

"*Some?*"

"Just basic stuff you need. Here." He grabs a stack of clothes carefully arranged on a box tower. "Workout gear. Figured we'll hit the gym when Orion goes to class. I want to see what you can really do." There's a smirking challenge in his eye.

Like, seriously?

Did someone give him a map of my buttons?

Hunter knows exactly where to push and just how hard.

If he ever gets his hands on me, I'll fucking combust.

But so might the kitchen.

Orion coughs over the stove as the room fills with smoke, so I take the easy out and hurry to change before he sets off the alarm.

Hunter's stack has everything. A pair of thick, expensive leggings with cutout stripes, a fitted tank, a cute long sleeve, and perfectly sized underwear, sports bras, and socks.

When I slip them on, my shriveled omega heart expands two sizes and gives a squee that I fight to muffle.

I know I said Wyvern gifts come with twisty Wyvern strings, *buuuuut…*

The leggings make my ass look fantastic and the matching galaxy-print top has thumb holes.

The on-purpose kind.

Not the ones you get when your sleeves fall off from old age. I give my threadbare sweats a last salute before tossing them in the trash.

Goodbye integrity, hello athleisure.

I don't forget to keep myself in check.

Hunter's the one who took care of me from the beginning. He bandaged my feet and made sure I got fed, but he was only doing the minimum you'd do for a stray dog.

Give them a bowl and a place to curl up in the basement.

So, yeah, I have to deal with the constant urge to lick his tattoos, but he was the one Wyvern who could've done better.

Now if he wants to watch, have at it.

He can watch my legging-lifted ass disappear.

––––––

AFTER WALKING ORION TO CLASS, Hunter and I hit the sports complex. The halls are weirdly empty. We enter a silent training room filled with mats and punching bags, and unless someone changed the schedule, there should be a self-defense class in full swing. "Did you rent the room?"

"Fired the trainer."

"Barb? Way to take out the trash." She used to use me as her test dummy for judo throws.

"We're going to protect you, Lilah."

I'm not so oblivious I can't see Hunter making an effort.

But, I also see the bloodstain ingrained in the corner carpet. From when I was maybe ten?

I'd just gotten off a punishment for fighting, and I was starving, but Trainer Barb forced me to class. When she demonstrated punches and made me hold the bag, my arms couldn't match her strength.

The bag cracked my face, giving me a nosebleed and a split lip. *Protect me?*

I shake my head. "Little too late."

Going rigid, Hunter takes a hard breath through his nose. "Let's warm up."

I jog and stretch while he punches the ever-loving shit out of a bag. When he comes back, he's burned off that flare of rage, trading it for a full-lipped smirk that clenches my thighs. "You going to go all-out for me this time?"

"If you can handle it." The last time we sparred I didn't so much phone it in as refuse the call.

I didn't want him to see the real me.

"Come at me, Killer." His cocky grin is oil in my veins.

I drop into my stance, circling. Hunter's posture is easy, but his muscle isn't just for show–even if the show is good enough to be pay-per-view. His knees stay loose and he angles his hips as I move, not giving me any easy openings.

I dart in, throwing a test punch.

He dodges with a *tsk*. "Still holding back?"

"I'm better at defense. More practice."

Hunter's nostrils flare. "Follow my lead."

He tosses me a few softball jabs, testing my form. His smile blooms as I match each one, proving my skills and how deeply I've been hiding.

Then he really starts to move.

Hunter's a Muay Thai god, with fast hands and faster feet, and I've never fought such quick, lethal kicks. "I thought big guys were slow."

A hint of feral fire lights his smile. "I'd be dead if I were slow."

"Same." I dodge a shoulder chop.

"Knew you could fight." Sweat drips from his forehead to the corners of his smug smile. "You move like a street fighter."

"Mostly taught myself." My style's a mish-mash. When I wasn't the instructor's dummy, I stayed in the back of combat lessons and absorbed it all to practice in the OCC's after-hours halls.

Punch, dodge, sidestep, kick.

Sparring with Hunter is the same as dancing with a partner who's a perfect match, and it feels so freaking good to work my body.

I lose track of time, lost in the rush of the back-and-forth, and a little bit hypnotized by the smoky-sweet scent of Hunter's sweat. He offers gentle posture corrections, and a stream of easy compliments that melt me down.

"Nice."

"Perfect."

"So good, Lilah."

Help.

Finally starting to wear out, I miss a block on a punch to the ribs, but Hunter hits like he's wearing mittens.

He's not trying to hurt me.

Just like I'm not trying to hurt him.

Only a monster would deliberately harm their meant-to-be mate.

But just because Hunter *could* be my mate, doesn't mean I'm pulling punches. When he eases back, wanting to make sure he didn't add to my bruises, I hook his ankle and score a sweet takedown.

I've used the move a thousand times, so I instinctively follow him to the mat.

One problem.

I'm always fighting omegas, so my muscle memory sets me up for betrayal. I pin my full weight on Hunter's hips. He grunts when our bodies slam.

I want to say I gasp, but *nooooo*.

When my spread legs bump his package, I make this soft, kitteny moan, and I don't know which of us goes more stiff.

I want to disappear.

But my traitor body warms, and my instincts scream to take him for a ride.

Hunter's eyes heat, liquid chocolate. My hands land on the firm shoulders that heave with his ragged breaths as I stare down at him in shock.

And then, the most intrusive of thoughts.

I like to be on top.

Hunter's eyes glint like he's reading my mind. He's so dominant he makes my insides pulse, but it's not the bossy kind.

It's worse.

It's a dominance so confident, he's happy to lie there and let me do whatever the fuck I want.

He knows who's in control.

My gulp echoes.

I think if I asked for bossy dominant, Hunter would give that to me too.

I scramble off, breaking the moment.

And *maaaaybe*, I grind down on him when I swing my legs off his body. Because if I have to suffer, so should he.

This time, I clamp the breathy reflex sound when my over-heated ass drags across his length and the wide, hard bundle of his knot.

While I crawl away with zero dignity, Hunter rolls onto his stomach and groans into the mat. "Lesson postponed. You win."

Do I?

As I hurry to the showers, feeling him follow, but not daring to sneak a second peek at that bulge, I'm fucking *dripping*.

While I quickly and silently get myself off in the shower stall, letting the scent evidence spiral down the drain, it's a small comfort that he has to stand guard at what felt like full mast.

I palm my forehead.

I'm playing with fire, scissors, and fucking C4 every time I get close to a heated-up Wyvern.

I keep my distance as we grab lunch, then go back to the bungalow to change for the social. Hunter goes directly to shower, and my dirty mind follows.

I can't help picturing water slicking all those tattoos, his thick palm stroking what felt like an equally thick—

Bad Lilah.

But it's hard to think about anything else when my body's convinced Hunter already belongs to us, and I'm wasting natural resources by not taking him for a test hump.

I splash my face, do some deep breathing, and refocus. When I'm less horny, there's plenty of anxiety to keep me busy.

I dig through the boxes of clothes and quickly find one filled with dresses wrapped in tissue.

It's too expensive and too much.

According to my omega nature, I should adore getting gifts, but my nurture got so twisted, it's not that simple.

I'm always waiting for the bill to come.

With interest.

In the end, I take a dress because I need something to wear, but I don't accept whatever feelings are attached because if I don't draw some line, the Wyverns will be the ones who take *me*.

The line blurs once again when I zip into a navy slip dress that fits so perfectly it must've been tailored. And shit. How does Wyvern Pack just know my measurements? Do they have their own sweatshop?

I know Jett can sew.

He patched a hole in my sweatshirt once, when he still spoke to me.

I'm crossing my fingers he doesn't have a guard shift. It makes my internal battle that much harder when we have all the twisty history.

I do my hair but not my makeup, then dig a pair of cute white sneakers from my loot pile. From now on, I only wear shoes I can run in.

All dressed up, I look *good*.

There's more color in my cheeks and meat on my bones thanks to regular-ish meals and sleep. In a new bra, I even have boobs.

Still working on the hips, but I'll get there.

Goals.

It's just nice to look in the mirror and not see my past reflected in hollow cheeks and thready clothes. I look like a normal omega, who's pampered instead of kicked around.

I hope the alphas at the social pick up the vibe and treat me with respect.

But the bar is low, and the skirt also hides my gun.

I stay in my room until the last minute, and hiding was the right decision, because Hunter dressed up.

He'd look sexy in a onesie with fluffy ears and a tail, so in a tailored James Bond suit that highlights his body-builder lines, with his hair styled back, and his all-seeing gaze seeing only *me…*

I swallow and walk past.

Zen.

"Lilah." The soft way he says my name glues my feet to the carpet.

"Before you go..." He offers me an envelope. "There's one more thing. From all of us."

What now?

A contract?

A heart-felt written apology I'll have to pretend doesn't affect me?

I open the flap to find a check, and when I read the number, my heart roars in my ears.

"We paid your outstanding OCC debt. I had the accounting team calculate and credit everything you were overcharged. This is what's left."

As I stare at the zeroes, the paper trembles in my fingers. "No."

"You can't actually give it back." Hunter lifts his hands. "The check is symbolic. The money's already been deposited."

A dizzy wave crashes.

This debt has been hounding me since I was old enough to count.

I was a charity case.

An omega raised for sale to the highest bidder.

A girl whose mother sold her for a check just like this.

The debt's half the reason I suppressed my awakening. Because I knew what's happening now would happen then—I'd have shitty choices on the mate marketplace because alphas treat a girl differently when they're buying her wholesale.

I built my life around a plan to run and pay back the debt in installments from an offshore account.

Or just run.

Now the noose is gone.

The check folds in my clenching palm. "So, you own me now?"

"Lilah, no." Hunter reaches, but I skip away. It's the weirdest feeling. The more pissed I am, the more I shake, the more his scent calls to me, begging me to sink into his arms—the poison and the cure.

"You can't buy me. This—"

"*No*. Let me explain. Please." There's a frantic tone in his voice that I've never heard before—he's always so smooth and too cool for drama. "It's not a transaction. It's what we owe you, okay? Take it as compensation or damages or just what we owe you for putting you through hell."

I look at the zeroes again.

This changes fucking everything.

The clock's still ticking on my heat, but I don't have to wait around for a pack willing to shell out whatever crazy price is set as the base bid.

I can pick anyone I want.

I'm free.

"Take it," Hunter says softly.

I'm torn between giddy and bitter, numb at the same time I'm freaking the fuck out.

But then, because Hunter Wyvern gets off on exploding my brain, he goes down on one knee. He clasps my hands in his warm palms, instantly stopping my shakes. "I'm sorry."

I suck honey-soaked air through my teeth.

Don't give in.

Do not give in.

"This doesn't change my mind." A wisp of breathiness sneaks into my voice. I clear my throat, knocking out the nettles. "I can't join your pack. You don't even have a pack."

"I know." Hunter squeezes my fingers. "All you have to do is follow your dreams. It's our job to convince you we're part of them."

His words are vines, little tendrils drawing me closer and tighter. Making me question. Making me doubt.

I tear away from his demon-hot hands and bolt.

But the check's still clutched in my palm.

Fuck.

FIFTEEN

LILAH

THE ICE CREAM social is in the same atrium where the OCC throws high teas. I've snuck into so many events to steal food, but this is the first time I'm attending when my name's on the list *and* I comply with the dress code.

I'm more composed after a brisk walk across campus. While I wait to be seated, I avoid looking at the bodyguard who outshines every other alpha in the crowd.

I tucked his check into my bra with my spare shiv.

I never asked for happily-ever-after, but with the money, I have a chance at *this is okay*.

That's more than I ever hoped.

I also don't expect to find a pack that sears the Wyverns out of my nervous system—it's not fucking possible with them wormed down to my cell nuclei—but that's not what I'm here for either.

All I need is one decent pack willing to lend me a long weekend.

I say a silent prayer as I stand at the entrance, waiting to be seated.

There has to be one.

"Lilah?" A voice cracks through my anxiety.

I whirl to find a beta backed by three alphas in tailored suits.

Familiar voice. Really familiar brown eyes.

But the rest of him is new—in a suit and tie instead of hospital scrubs.

"Doctor—uh, Cale?"

"I was afraid you'd be mated off before we had a chance to speak with you." He glances warily at Hunter, who hovers like a tatted Ken doll. "May we join you?"

"Yes! Are these your alphas?" I'm curious about the pack he claims owns half the city. I take a step closer, but Cale doesn't answer.

He breathes hard, while the alphas quiver, the first full-on hit of my scent lighting a fire that has them adjusting their ties and biting off growls.

I expect to get hit just as hard, but I don't feel the same fireworks.

The alphas smell like blueberry muffin, buttered popcorn, and cherry amaretto.

The fourth, softer scent is Cale's crushed graham cracker.

All scents I like just fine.

They're the frozen yogurt of alpha energy.

Like, it's good, but it's not ice cream.

Not that have-to-have-it, lick-up-all-the-drops, get-inside-me-now sexual napalm that the Wyverns blast me with every time they strut into my space.

They're perfect.

I don't need more brain poison.

"Sorry." Cale shakes himself. "I'd love to introduce you. This is Jason, Kipp, and Rhett Sorensen. Guys, this is Lilah."

Jason is the muffin man. He's probably mid-thirties with a hint of eye crinkles that give him distinguished professor vibes.

Next is Kipp, a blond who smells like movie theater butter and has bright green eyes that *almost* remind me of Finn's.

Only Finn would never wag his tail like a golden retriever trying to catch my attention. He'd hand me a Molotov cocktail with a smirk and tell me where to throw.

Kipp vibrates with pure smiles.

Last is Rhett.

He's the obvious pack leader, with the densest energy, and he smells like almond-spiked maraschino. With dark, neatly combed hair, glasses and a fancy tie, he looks like he works at a bank.

Probably *owns* a freaking bank, and his gaze volleys between Hunter and me. "Cale told us all about you. But he didn't mention your friend…?"

"My bodyguard," I say quickly.

"Wyvern? Hunter, right?" Cale asks. "I think I saw you briefly at the hospital?"

"Kind of his fault I was there," I say, drawing the attention away from my GQ shadow. "Don't mind him."

I catch Hunter's jaw clenching before a chipper voice flips my attention back around.

"Miss Lilah," says Alice the red-headed beta. "I'm so glad you're okay."

"I thought everyone got fired?"

"Everyone else," she chirps. "I got a raise. Let me show you to your table. You're right in the center today."

I'm not sure if the center's what I want, but it's safer than being put in another shady corner.

The dining area is gorgeous with pink tablecloths and unfurled peonies, bright and widely spaced so that alphas don't have to crowd to get to the omegas they're courting. Alice seats me near a picture window where crystal water goblets sparkle in the sun.

I'd squee over the ambiance, but I'm happiest about the super-sharp bread knives.

I brought my own from home, but every time I stab a guy, I lose the blade. More knives is always better.

The calligraphied place card reads LILAH DARLING. Subtitle: Honeymoon Hills.

Rhett reaches to pull out my chair, but Hunter beats him.

"You're not serious." I sit instead of making a scene, but I'm eyeing the bread knives hard.

Ignoring me, Hunter unfolds my napkin and carefully spreads it over my lap. "Won't get in your way, but I'll be close. You're safe."

I shoo him with a disgusted noise to clear my heart flutter. Hunter takes a post with his back to the wall, scanning the crowd. I'd be lying if I said I didn't feel safer having him as backup, but that doesn't mean he gets to claim me in public.

Rhett smooths the aggro expression he was just trading with Hunter. "Let us make you some dishes. We'll be right back."

Huddled up and sneaking glances I pretend I don't see, the four-man pack heads to the buffet table piled with ice creams and glass bowls of candy toppings.

Alphas have to offer you a bowl if they want to sit at your table and chat. I ignore the sneers of omegas in couture, waiting to see what flavors Sorensens will bring.

If they come at me with maple nut, this is over.

Pretty soon, they're back with their offerings. It's not their fault the bowls are tiny—maybe two bites each. You'd be sick if every alpha brought you a full serving.

Still sad.

They made me two dishes of chocolate and two of vanilla, all with basic fudge and cookie crumbles.

I'd rather make my own bowl.

But I'm not driving away the only pack that meets my criteria over their failure to choose the chocolate-covered honeycomb.

"Thank you." I pick up a teeny spoon and dig in.

It's *gooooood* ice cream—the expensive kind that's cream and sugar and none of the chemicals.

My eyes roll back, and another one of my unstoppable moans slips free.

The guys' chairs squeak.

"Wow." Kipp leans elbows on the table, half ready to vault the centerpiece. "Not to be the crude one, but I *am* the crude one. Your perfume—"

"Don't be rude." Jason elbows his packmate.

Cale clears his throat. "How've you been feeling, Lilah?"

"Fine. Just rushed. I'll be happy when I can move out on my own."

"No packs have caught your attention?" Rhett flicks his gaze to Hunter.

"Still looking."

"That being the case…" Cale starts.

"We're serious about putting in an offer for your heat," Rhett says. "If you're interested, we'd like to book a private date and get to know each other a bit better."

Wow. He's totally making a sex arrangement sound like an appointment to do my taxes.

"We have a permanent box at the opera," Jason offers. "We'd love to take you."

Oh no.

They're *opera* people.

I mean, I'm not a total lowbrow scrub—I'd take ballet tickets any day—but *opera*?

I don't do music unless it has a bass line.

Especially vocals that give me flashbacks of the OCC's voice coach smirking while she made me sing solo after tone deaf solo for the enjoyment of the class.

Luckily, I have a more solid built-in reason than *helllll no.* "Thanks, but I shouldn't leave campus."

"Are you still being targeted?" Cale frowns.

"It'll stop after my heat." I'm positive Dominik will back off when he sees me choose anyone but Wyvern Pack. If I'm not involved with them, I can't be used to hurt them, so I'm not worth the cash and prizes.

"Dinner, then?" Jason suggests. "I think we can rent the kitchen here. I'd love to cook for you. How do you feel about lamb?"

Like it belongs in a pasture?

But who knows? "I've never tried it."

"Ah. I'll be your first." Jason brightens.

If this were any other pack, I'd take that the creepy, suggestive way, but Jason doesn't ping my sixth sense.

I think he's just a pure, innocent muffin man, which is weird. He's a decade older, but I'm the one who's been run through the sausage grinder.

"When can we see you again?" Kipp asks just as brightly.

"I'm on call tomorrow," Cale says. "But the night after?"

I shake my head. "I have a dance performance."

"Really?" Kipp straightens so fast he shakes the table. "We'll be there. Front row."

"It's a pole performance."

The Sorensens trade looks.

They might be opera guys, but they're still *guys*.

Rhett straightens his glasses. "I've heard aerial pole can be very athletic."

I turn my snort into a cough.

"It can be." I also could've done an emotional contemporary routine in a flowy onesie.

Instead, I'm laying down a thirst trap.

I need knots. Not a fairytale.

"We'll be there," Rhett says.

"So, dance, huh? What else do you do for fun?" Kipp asks with his too-happy smile.

We chat until my ice cream's gone. They tell me about their charity work and hobbies.

All the Sorensens golf.

I limit my hobby list to reading and dancing because I don't think they'll be impressed with my ability to craft shivs from household objects.

Thankfully, they don't ask for my booklist. I'd have to lie and pretend I read anything other than tax law and shifter smut.

When Rhett's cell rings, he checks the number and gets a tic in his cheek. "Office. I'll have to take this. Anyway, we've taken too much of your time."

"Thanks for sitting with me." I don't think we're compatible, but that's why they just shot to the top of my list.

They're decent.

I won't catch feelings and neither should they if it's clear upfront that none of us are looking for permanent.

"We'll see you at your showcase." Jason smiles with eye crinkles. "I'll bring cheesecake."

"Front row." Kipp waves.

"See you soon, Lilah." Cale ducks away, following his alphas as they trade excited whispers.

I take a few deep breaths.

I think I did okay?

Nobody tried to kidnap me, I didn't get shot, and I wasn't too awkward.

It's my most successful event ever.

After a beta clears the empty dishes, I drum my toes against the carpet, waiting for the next pack.

I sip water, eye the ice cream bar, and keep waiting.

No one comes.

The room's filled with small talk and laughter as alphas mingle. Spoons clink, and a lucky few alphas hand-feed their chosen omega. Tables are crowded, and packs hover at the edges of the room, waiting for space to open.

My table's the only one without a line.

It doesn't make sense.

I have zero expectations that a pack of princes will take my empty chairs, but Darling plus Honeymoon Hills should at least score some sleazy curiosity.

The same alphas who've always approached me at these things. Stubble, shifty eyes, and smirks that send me running to hide in the bathroom.

When a dreadlocked pack leader walks toward me with his boys, I straighten, thinking I'm finally getting customers. But instead of a dish of ice cream, they offer me respectful nods before striding past.

The pack leader shakes hands with Hunter.

I deflate.

Okay. Maybe they're friends.

When he leaves, a three-pack of blond surfer alphas approaches, and one smells so much like watermelon, I could totally get behind it.

They go straight to Hunter.

When the surfers peace out, I glance at my shadow. To his credit, Hunter's not doing anything obvious to warn off interest.

Just standing, casing the room for threats.

But all Hunter Wyvern has to do is stand.

Between his size, his dominance, his position behind my shoulder, and the fact that no other omega has a personal guard who's a well-known gillionaire heir…

Every alpha here must think Wyvern Pack already has a claim.

Which is bullshit.

Why would I go through socials and risk the embarrassment if I already had Wyvern Pack locked down?

I wouldn't.

I'd be snuggled in my nest with all five of them wrapped around me and—*holy shit did that take a quick turn.*

I shake myself.

I wait a few more minutes, but there's a Wyvern-shaped force-field blocking my table.

Nobody has the balls to bust through.

Fine.

I met a decent pack, scored a date, and didn't have to flee in my new sneakers.

I'm calling it a win.

And I'm getting my own freaking ice cream made just the way I want it.

Alphas ooze out of my way when I step to the ice cream buffet. I do a lap, but my flavor isn't on the bar.

Scoffing, I head for the kitchen.

Hunter's forcefield works even harder on betas, so none of the catering staff says a word when I push past them to the walk-in freezer.

I find an industrial tub of almond cake ice cream wedged way in the back and haul it to an empty counter like a leopardess securing her kill.

Wielding a scooper like a trowel, I start to dish the spoils. Only, I'm too short to get leverage, and the ice cream's so rock hard I can only scrape the top layer.

I'm so frustrated I almost betray myself with a whine, but Hunter tugs away the scoop. Finally using all those muscles for good instead of evil, he digs in, scooping, scooping, scooping, until my bowl overflows with sweet, almondy deliciousness that I can't even pretend I'm going to reject.

I snatch the ice cream and start to shovel. "Thought you said you wouldn't get in the way."

"I didn't."

"Then why does every alpha think I belong to Wyvern Pack?"

His eyes glow.

Because I do belong to them.

I take my bowl and walk.

I know what they're doing, using the threat against me as a reason to slide into my life.

But why?

When I'm not being swept away by the hormones and the unholy heat, I genuinely think the Wyverns are setting me up for another fall.

My mom pawned me.

My best friend disappeared.

My teachers proved every day that not all omegas are created equal.

And after Wyvern Pack said *nah* to my first heat, I'd have to be an idiot not to spot the trend.

So, I'll enjoy the gifts and the temporary sweetness just

because they like the way my pheromones tickle—I like theirs too
—but in the end, I'm so much better off alone.

I douse my ice cream in caramel sauce and honeycomb and
treat Hunter to a chorus of mouth orgasms on our walk to the
pole studio.

I'm going to eat every.

Fucking.

Bite.

Then I'll hit the pole, spin until my brain falls out, and choreo-
graph a routine so demonically sexy, every alpha in the building
will be begging for a taste.

SIXTEEN

ATLAS

I'M USED to being looked at for the big decisions. When it's life or death, and the guys turn to me, it's heavy, but it's my responsibility.

Scorpio raised me to be that strong.

What I can't handle?

My ancient tutor Celeste sucking her gums at me like she's watching her great-great-grandson try to fit the square block into the round hole.

When I get too frustrated, hating that I'm not in control, I remember why I'm trying.

Lilah.

Orion.

Lilah *and* Orion.

The pack. Back together in a better, stronger form, all according to Hunter's—not my—master plan.

Chanting their names keeps me from falling over the edge and saying *fuck this* to the emergency course that has me locked in a hotel conference room instead of hunting and scalping Redfangs.

Instead of taking charge.

Lost that privilege.

"Soothe your omega," Celeste croons, ignoring my slow internal meltdown. "Stroke its back and say something sweet."

My "omega" is a demented life-sized sock doll spritzed with synthetic pheromones.

So not only do I have this creepy fucking scarecrow hugged to my chest in a room full of alphas wearing my same *how-did-we-get-here* stare, but my dick's also raging hard and ready to breed a dummy full of mutant polyester spawn.

"Remember. Omegas thrive on praise and reassurance. Offer a compliment."

I flinch at the doll's drawn-on face.

The only compliment that comes to mind is *thank you for not coming to life and chasing me through a cornfield.*

"Picture *your* omega." Celeste pats my arm. "You don't have to say anything deeply emotional. Just a soft, gentle praise, and bonus points if you can bring out your purr."

I bite back a frustrated growl.

This is a fucking nightmare, but it's one I deserve.

This is the best alpha/omega crash course anywhere, and Celeste Beaurivage is so in demand, she's tutored every world leader for the last five decades.

I need to learn, and I am—I'm memorizing the textbooks, doing the extra homework, and studying full-time, even though every second is a struggle not to rage out and rush back to tracking Dominik.

Rush to see Lilah.

It's not that I don't trust Hunter and his plan.

I'd give Hunter a kidney. An eye. Even part of my heart if he asked.

But giving him control?

Being here instead of taking the lead?

I'm spiraling.

Because how can I be so goddamned dense?

I have to take a class for something that should be easy as breathing, and I lost my pack because I don't even know how to interact with an omega without sending them straight into rage-quit.

So I have to trust Hunter. He and Wyvern House can run an investigation without my micromanagement.

Even if every instinct screams I should be able to hold up the sky, I can't do it all.

My vision for the future keeps me from ripping the doll in half. I stroke its back, but my voice comes out more gravelly than soothing. "Good omega."

"Remember your omega's scent," Celeste presses. "Try to bring in more softness."

I close my eyes and inhale, imagining the caramel apple swirl that I've only tasted in my dreams.

Lilah straddling one of my legs, Orion balanced on the other, both of them safe and smiling in my arms.

Now, instead of cloth, I feel Lilah's silky hair under my fingertips. I remember how strong she is. How noble and fucking delicate. How she's so much more than I deserve, and I want to wrap her in diamonds and silk and tuck her away so she never feels pain again.

"*Good girl,*" I say huskily.

Celeste hums. "Now that's how you set the mood. What else can you compliment?"

"So perfect." I stroke the doll's head, imagining Lilah's precious smile—the smile I wipe from her face every time I open my alphahole mouth.

I wince, but stick with it, tagging in Orion instead.

That smirk he wears when he unbuckles my belt. His soft lips and his breathy sighs that feather my neck on the rare mornings I'm not out the door at four a.m. and we can wake up curled together. "So good for me. Wanna bite you. Make you mine again."

"Why, Mister Wyvern. Look at all that sweetness you've hidden away." Celeste fans herself, and her swoon snaps me back to my public audience where I'm dry-humping a dummy and purring like a pregnant cat.

I cough. "Was that right?"

"Did it feel right?"

It felt fucking creepy.

But I get the gist of where I've been going wrong. Too much hammering. Whipping everyone with my bark instead of just being present and asking what they need.

Communication.

It's a new concept.

Because when Scorpio shouted, I fell in line or else. He ran the house like a regiment, and that's how I learned to run my teams.

He trained me to give orders, not take care of a family.

But I can learn.

Finally, Celeste lets us put away the creepy dolls so we can break for lunch. I inhale a cardboard sandwich and pace the lobby.

Hunter took my phone.

I'm so desperate for intel, I put out a raging dominance force field that keeps the other alphas twenty feet away.

It's a relief to go back in session. I devour the afternoon workshop on heat cycles and soothing techniques.

I'm glad I'm learning, but the lecture tosses more guilt boulders onto my sagging shoulders.

I've been doing everything wrong.

Not enough touch, affection, reassurance.

Turns out, I have to *say* what I feel.

But I attack the books the same way I attacked learning combat. If I can learn, I can do better.

I'll eat every slice of humble pie with a side of crow pudding.

At the end of the day, I haul ass to my truck, needing to see Lilah and Orion with a desperation that turns my veins to frayed electric wires.

I'm halfway across the parking lot when I spot the man leaning against my door, spotlighted under a pole light. I don't need to see his features to know what's waiting.

I haven't crossed paths with my father since shit went down. Hunter broke the news to the dads.

He didn't update me afterward, but I don't need the minutes.

Breaking the pack is the same as shattering their legacy.

It must've been a shitshow.

Scorpio's dominance makes me feel ten years old again, caught playing with Orion's video games instead of studying wilderness survival.

The light catches the silver threads in his dark cropped hair, casting his hard-ass face in deep shadows. "You took leave."

"I lost my pack bond and my mate. I need a few days." Weeks, years. It takes how long it takes to fix my mess.

Scorpio straightens, a shadow in black camo. "Need you back at the ranch. We're negotiating—"

"No."

"No isn't an option." Scorpio quirks a *don't-test-me* brow. "Unless you want your leave to be permanent."

There's a sick roar in my stomach or maybe in my ears. It's the rush of everything I built collapsing. "I thought you wanted me to mate Lilah."

"Of course. She'll be a fine mother to our next generation." Behind his words is a clatter, more bullshit falling away.

Lilah isn't here for us to *breed*.

She's our salvation. "This is where I need to be."

He makes a noise in his throat. "You can mate without abandoning your work. You'll be off duty for her heat. Once the four of you fix your bond, you're boots on the ground. We have too many fires to put out. Can't leave our best team on the bench."

The sound in my ears reminds me of being dropped in the woods with a map and a mission to find my way home. After a rough night in the worst downpour, a patch of forest overturned. All these big, ancient trees groaning and splintering in a haunting roar as their trunks fell and their roots overturned.

Scorpio's words are just as devastating.

Already lost my mate, my pack, my role.

Now I'm losing my father—or at least my respect for him and it's the same goddamned thing.

"There's five of us." I shake off his dominance and hit him with my own.

Scorpio jerks. "Excuse me?"

"Six counting Lilah. Four alphas, two omegas."

"Drop the farce with Orion. Keep him on the side if it makes you happy, but not in your bond. It's his fault the pack was weak."

"It's *my* fault," I grit out.

"Noble of you to take responsibility." Scorpio bears down with a hit of authority that's lead in my gut. "But this is the chance we've been waiting for. Assert your dominance, reclaim leadership, and rebuild. You four will be stronger once the girl's claimed."

"No."

Goddamn fucking shit.

Is this what I sound like to Hunter?

To Lilah and Orion?

No wonder I fucked it all up.

Hammering, hammering, hammering.

No compassion, just blind, single-minded dominance.

Scorpio draws himself up. "If you test me—"

"I resign." The words taste like ash but they're right.

His tone is deadly flat, his dominance pressing. "You'd leave Hunter to run your pack? Your teams? Throw away your career?"

He's handing me the strap, and this time I'm more than willing to give myself the beating. "Hunter's the better leader."

He shakes his head. "We wanted better for our sons. *I* wanted better for you. A better life."

"Dad. I have two omegas. What could be better?"

He rocks like I announced I'm mating the goddamned scarecrow dummy. "I'm putting you on indefinite leave."

"All I care about is OCC bodyguard duty."

"Hope that boy's worth it. You'll lose everything."

"They *are* everything."

Scorpio climbs into his car and guns out of the parking lot. I stand, vibrating, processing what the fuck I just did.

Feels like I ripped a Band-Aid that was connected to my spine.

But I have to walk away from Scorpio's vision of the future and finally fucking start claiming mine.

I haul ass to the OCC and flash my new bodyguard badge at each well-manned gate. Hikaru must've put the fear of god in the board over Lilah's abuse. Now the staff is mostly guys I recognize, contracted from Wyvern House.

Better, but the only people I trust with Lilah are my former-future pack brothers.

I jog to the bungalow.

Need to see her.

Feel so fucking unspooled, I wonder if this is what it's like for Finn all the time.

No one answers my knock, and the lights are off.

The crème brûlée perfume that reminds me I still have a purpose soaks the porch. Her sweet, lickable scent is even stronger without the pack bond rooting me to the earth.

A rumble works my chest, pure instinct.

Need.

Orion's cider-sweetness isn't as thick—he's nowhere near his heat—but it hits me just as hard.

Goddamn.

I need to talk to them.

Practice these communication skills Celeste has been telling me about.

My senses are so honed to Lilah's scent, it only takes a few steps to pick up her trail. Or maybe it's a new sixth sense. I follow the signal to the dance studios, tracking her through the lobby, down a long hall.

Dozens of omega perfumes sour in my throat.

None of them are *mine.*

I want caramel sugar sweetness.

I want crisp apple on my tongue.

I find both scents in a dim back studio blasting a low, pulsing beat that stirs my veins.

When I open the door, it's over.

The room's choked in Lilah's syrupy scent, and if the bass weren't enough to blow out my brains, the way she moves would kill me fucking dead.

She spins high on a pole in nothing but ass shorts and a belly-baring sports bra.

So high, I'm terrified she'll fall. My muscles torque ready to dart in for a rescue catch.

Then Lilah dips, arching her back and sliding to the floor in a controlled drop, and my knot inflates like a fucking bowling ball.

Lilah Darling will be the death of me.

And I can't wait to suffer.

SEVENTEEN

LILAH

INVERTED, clinging to the pole, I spin and spin, trying to purge myself after another day of Wyvern antics.

Hunter and Orion lean against the mirror wall, but I'm not performing for them.

I'm performing to stop them from taking over my brain.

My latest loss is caving to Orion's unrefusable, puppy-dog-eyed request to stay at my bungalow instead of the one he was assigned because he "wants help with his homework."

Uh huh.

Planning my routine is the only way I'm staying sane. I test tracks, trying to find a song that balances powerful sexy and slutty sexy.

Like, let me ride, but I'll end you if you try shit.

That's why I picked pole instead of another style.

Tap won't get me knotted.

I tool around with floor work and spins, flipping through songs.

After fifty false starts, I finally find THE song.

All raunchy and bassy and sexy attitude.

I crank the volume and hit the pole to work out the kinks on a few spins and inversions.

It feels *so good* to spin.

To twirl in the air, hair flying out.

I dissolve into the music, adrift in a world where I do what I want, when I want, and nobody—including my *own* body—gets to force me into anything.

Then the door opens, casting an unwelcome sliver of light into my dim oasis and letting in a tall, thick figure.

Hunter's dominance makes me dizzy and a casual smile from Orion turns my world upside down, but when Atlas brings that bow-down, big knot energy, I dissolve into a primal mess.

My knees go so weak, I skid down the pole.

I catch myself with a thigh squeeze, and still spinning, somehow lock his gaze.

The clang casts fucking sparks.

Shuddering, I break the eye contact that rattles me so hard my rib bones clack.

I still feel his stare.

It touches every part of me, settling the jittery inner omega with the absolute reassurance that *alpha is here*.

THE alpha.

But I'm THE omega, and all that noise can take a hike in poison ivy.

There's a different look I want to see on Atlas Wyvern's face.

Not awe, not lust, but pure regret. Some kind of remorse or bitterness instead of that über-confident, I'm in-charge-here look that he wears like a mask.

I want to see him cracked the way they keep cracking me.

With my song blaring, I'm invincible.

I arch my back, point my toes, and give him a show to fucking remember.

When the bridge hits, I slide to the floor, pole between my legs, running my hands up my body from my thighs to my throat.

My skin's hot, my scent fills the studio, and I smooth the collar of my neck in long, luxurious drags, rubbing the unbroken skin in the ultimate alpha tease.

When the song finally fades, my back's on the floor, my legs are bent, and I'm spread out and panting like I just survived the orgasm of my life.

The guys stand shoulder-to-shoulder, only there's none of the devastation I wanted.

Atlas shakes, and not because he's trembling.

He's holding himself back.

Orion licks his lips and Hunter crosses himself.

Golden, brown, and blue. All three pairs of eyes glow because they want to fucking *eat* me.

I turn my shiver into a stretch, pretending I'm not affected, but I'd have to be scent blind and stupid not to taste their pheromones. The studio's a smoky, musky, apple-scented sweat box.

Gonna be another *looooong* night with my silicone helper.

Orion shakes back to reality first.

I tense when he walks to me.

Because maybe seeing Atlas stare at me like a lickable caramel ice cream pop is what finally switches his dial back to normal omega behavior. He smells like apple-soaked sin, with that same piece of hair falling over his forehead.

All he does is hand me a towel. "Every pack there is gonna make an offer if you dance like that."

"That's the idea." I wipe my neck, then grab my water and chug while they watch, mesmerized, by the motion of my throat.

"You done for the night?" Orion asks a little breathily.

"Think so. You?"

"Yeah. I've got homework."

"Right." I grab the dress and sneakers I tossed in the corner after borrowing a spandex outfit for pole. "Ready?"

"Wait. You'll freeze." Orion strips off his hoodie and drapes it over my shoulders. Then he pulls my arms through the sleeves, making sure I'm all tucked in before he zips me up.

I stand like a doll, letting him fuss because being smothered in his scent gives me the good shivers.

I forget I should be pushing him away until he lifts the hood, covering my eyes. "I'm still sweating."

"I know." Orion yanks both hood cords with a smirk, narrowing my vision to a tiny hole. Then he ties a bow while I try to smack him with the ends of his too-long sleeves. "Have to seal you off. You smell too good."

"Shit." Hunter's low curse shatters the moment, his sudden, serious tone instantly killing the mood.

I shake free of Orion's trap.

"Have to run." Hunter jams his phone in his pocket. "Your schedule for tomorrow just got canceled."

"Why? What now?"

"Bomb threat. I'll text you if I have more info."

"I don't have a phone."

"You do," Orion says. "I'll set it up for you."

"Sure," I agree, still stuck on *bomb*.

Am I seriously worth this much fuss?

"Yes," the three of them answer at the same time.

Great. I've officially reached the level of Wyvern brain-fry where I start speaking my thoughts aloud.

Hunter disappears to handle the latest threat to my life, and then it's just the three of us in the stuffy studio. Orion and I stand on one side, Atlas on the other.

Not the team distribution you'd expect.

Orion tugs the end of the sleeve that hangs well past my fingertips. "Go home?"

"Yeah."

The tension in my sleeve tightens when we pass Atlas. Maybe Orion subconsciously tugging harder.

Caving the way I always cave for him, I stick out my hand and give him a squeeze.

He takes the chance to twine our fingers together, stealing my whole arm.

I don't fight.

I need his touch because I'm busy worrying where this ends.

A bomb is too much escalation.

What next? Redfangs kidnap me in a helicopter?

Is there an upper limit to what they'll do?

I don't get it.

I'm not Wyvern Pack's mate.

Well…*technically*…but we're not bound. I'm actively on the rotation list, open to bids, and searching for heat partners.

Is this really about me?

I shiver in the night.

"Lilah?" Orion uses our joined hands to tug me to a stop. "You okay?"

I blink. We're halfway back to the bungalow, standing under a light pole, like an island in the dark. Atlas hovers behind us.

He hasn't said a fucking word.

To either of us.

He meets my eye with a complicated look I can't read, and I finally have a target for all my jittery, frustrated fear. "Is there anything you want to say?"

When Atlas steps under the light, Orion pulls me tighter. It's the same little motion he made when he stood between me and his pack.

That shook me hard.

But seeing him stand against Atlas?

My heart flutters.

He's choosing me.

Over his mate.

Over his lover.

Atlas sees and he makes the same conclusion. When his mouth opens, I think I'm ready for anything.

So wrong.

"I resigned from Wyvern House."

The words echo, met by silence until Orion hisses. "You fucking *what*?"

"Scorpio wanted me to drop you, then claim and breed Lilah."

"Un-fucking-believable." Orion shakes his head.

"Believable." I knew the score from day one. I'm the original breeder the dads put on reserve.

"True." Orion tugs my arm against his belly, and the tremor under his skin matches the one moving under mine. I cling to his fingers, and it's like a closed circuit, giving us both the energy to bleed out all the poison we've been carrying. "So what? You think I'll pack my shit? Think you can just claim Lilah after everything you put her through? No, Atlas. Fucking *no*."

"I know. That's why I walked. I'm out. No more work. No more bullshit. All I'm doing now is taking classes so I don't turn into the exact same asshole as my father. Or at least reverse the damage. All I want to do is take care of you."

Atlas shakes. His voice. His fingertips.

The giant in black camo looks so fucking vulnerable, my voice comes out scratchy. "Can you?"

He flinches. "I'm learning."

"Learn faster," Orion mutters, pulling me away. "Come on. Wanna get you home."

It's a thousand kinds of uncomfortable to show our backs to the big bad alpha, but when Orion and I let out a deep, coordinated breath, we share a secret smile.

Feels so fucking good to not roll over.

Also exhausting.

But maybe that's just today.

I'm ready to collapse, but when we get back to the box tower bungalow, the piles have multiplied. The place is officially a fire hazard and at the rate the guys burn food, that's a problem.

The clutter's bad enough, but the idea of people I don't know hauling things into my space when I'm not here makes me feel omega violated.

Unsafe.

I rub my forehead.

I don't have the energy to clean, but I'm not sure I'll be able to sleep if I let it go.

Even Orion twitches. "Eleanor was saying how mess increases

anxiety. It's nice knowing there's a scientific reason we're so fucking crazy all the time."

"*All* the time."

"I'll take care of it." Atlas grabs the closest box.

Orion and I lift our brows in unison, but I quickly twist the expression into a scowl. We're getting waaaaay too much on the same wavelength.

"Rest," Atlas insists, already stacking. "No one gets through that door while I'm here."

With Atlas on a new mission to bulldoze the enemy boxes, I take pity and tug Orion into my room, shutting the door behind us.

"Wow." He whistles at the bed. "Better than the couch."

The room *is* pretty much a bed. A big, big cloud of a bed that's the most comfortable place I've ever slept.

The ceiling is almost low enough for him to scrape his head, and it's hung with dark fabric to muffle sounds. Like my own escape pod.

Only now there's a hijacker, and I'm slowly giving up resisting.

I fall onto the comforter.

Finn's scent is faded. Now I'm swimming in Orion's sweatshirt, but there's a lingering whiff of Atlas that snuck onto my skin.

"Shit." Orion collapses next to me, rubbing his arms, where soft blond hairs stand on end. "Wasn't expecting a head-to-head with the pack leader. Ex-pack leader?"

"Wasn't expecting that *or* a fucking bomb threat."

"If we're both…" Orion holds up a shaking hand.

"Jittery as fuck?"

"That. You think it would help to nest? I know I'm not—"

I smush his lips under my palm. "Can we snuggle and not talk about it?"

I want the comfort, not the implications.

"Hell yes." Orion snags a blanket and gathers it around us. We prop ourselves with pillows, burrowing deep.

Then he drags me against him, gluing us chest to ankle, and I let out the most cleansing sigh.

I need this.

Probably needed it my whole fucking life.

Orion's the only one in the world who can offer me a safe snuggle, and with both of us so shaky, it's anyone's fucking guess which of us needs the touch the most.

I stroke his arm. "Will you take them back?"

"I don't know." He breathes. "Will you?"

"Never had them."

"But you could. Especially now. If they mated you instead—"

"*No.*" We're gonna shut that talk right down. "I don't want mates."

"Everything's different now." Orion strokes my back.

I snort against his chest. "You think?"

He chuckles like warm honey.

I relax into him, loving this more than I'll ever admit. I can still hear Atlas thumping around moving boxes, and that's another plus. My jitters need the reassurance that no one's breaking in tonight.

Orion keeps stroking me, trying to turn me to Lilah jelly, and it's good, but even this magic moment can't keep out my fear.

Another day, another busted social. "Can I borrow your phone?"

He pulls it out and hands it to me unlocked. I memorized Catherine's number, so I send a quick text.

Did Sorensens put in an offer?

Her dots pop up and I chew my lip, waiting.

No offers yet. But we're messaging the entire client list about your showcase. They'll come rolling in!

I hand back the phone, but my belly cramps with phantom dread.

My heat's another day closer and I don't have any guarantees.

I could ask the Wyverns, and I know they'd say yes, but then I remember being at the top of the stairs, too terrified to speak up, and already being denied.

My vision of the future is just as vivid.

Another heat where I'm sitting in some frou-frou nest in the heat suites in fetal position, waiting, waiting, fucking waiting for mates who never come.

I whine.

I don't slip that sound very often, but when I do…

Something clangs outside.

Atlas dropped a box.

"Hey. You'll find where you belong." Orion wraps me tight.

I should push him away.

I should run.

But I can't.

Omegas are *supposed* to be clingy.

Touchy.

Affectionate.

I swear I'm none of those.

I'm also a fucking liar.

I hug back, arms twining his shoulders, soaking up his scent, his breath, his warmth.

Even his affection.

I want to burrow inside him and just for a minute, pretend I belong in the world where I'm held and safe instead of tossed around like a kite with its strings cut.

"You said you'd help me with my homework." Orion's voice is soft as feathers.

"Now?" I ask too sharply.

"Grounding techniques." He smooths my hair from my neck and runs his thumb along my collarbone. "For soothing omegas. Been learning the omega half. But I can practice the alpha part on you. If you want to be soothed."

"You can try." But I've read the books, and with my heart hammering its bars like a prisoner with a tin cup, I don't think his tricks are gonna work.

Until Orion nips my throat.

A sharp, ticklish jolt that drags me out of my doomsday thoughts, straight back into my needy, just-got-electrocuted body.

He kisses the bite.

Soft lips.

Gentle heat.

I melt.

Liquid fucking jelly.

Then he bites me again.

And again.

Soft nips, just hard enough to tug my skin between his teeth. He moves lower, lower on my neck, each bite followed by a dizzying stroke of his tongue until he's teasing the sweet spot where my neck and shoulder join and I'm jackknifing in his lap.

My body doesn't give a shit that Orion's not alpha.

"*Sweet girl,*" he purrs against my neck, tugging my hair just hard enough to tip back my throat. "Such a perfect omega."

Oh fuck.

I'm not being grounded.

I'm being set on fire.

Slowly.

And the way he licks my neck…

Bring on the burn.

"So precious." Orion bites my collarbone.

I wind my fingers in his hair and he tilts his head, his face suddenly so close that all I can breathe are his apple-soaked pheromones rising to meet my need.

Orion nips my lower lip.

The tug shatters the last chain holding back my heart.

When his lips meet mine, they're slow and soft and sweet.

His kiss is more cinnamon than apple.

He's all I can taste.

Soft, soft, so fucking soft, he cradles my head, thumbs stroking my ears, and I surrender.

All I can do is surrender because it feels too fucking good

being held, and just this once, just for now, I know I can trust Orion to be what I need.

One of us groans.

I straddle his thighs, fingers tangling in his curls.

His tongue parts my lips, claiming me as hard as any alpha. With a squeeze of my waist, he pulls me tighter. When I bump his hips, wanting to get so close I'm in his skin, my center grinds against his hard omega cock.

"Lilah…" he breathes my name.

The hint of reverence finally shakes me free of his spell.

I scramble off him, kicking out of the blanket fort to press a hand to my thundering heart. "I think you'll get an A."

Leaning back, smug as fuck with his hands folded behind his head, Orion laughs.

Too cute. Must be stopped.

I put a pillow over his face.

He uses it to swat me.

So of course I hit him back.

It devolves into a pillow fight, and I laugh until my sides ache.

Another box crashes.

Maybe I'm steering toward a disaster, but it gets exhausting keeping my walls so high.

Just once, I want to let myself play.

Just once, I want to take what Orion's offering without calculating the cost.

EIGHTEEN

LILAH

WHEN ORION and I roll out in the morning, rumpled and slathered in each other's scents, the first thing Atlas does is drop a plate. It shatters on the tile.

"Breakfast," he says in a super-satisfying choked robot voice.

With the box towers that were giving me hives arranged in neat soldierly lines, pushed back and stacked high, I have an easy path to the kitchen. I creep over to check the food.

"*Shoes!*" Atlas barks, freezing me short of the kitchen. Then he clears his throat, and I can walk again. "I mean, careful. Your toes." While he goes to find a broom, Orion lifts me onto the kitchen barstool.

I tense when he drops to the floor, gently putting my feet into socks and sneakers. The view of his golden head between my thighs is so unfair.

So is the way he keeps treating me like a doll and the way I keep wanting to return the favor.

"How long are you going to keep doing that?" I ask shakily.

"As long as you want me to."

I'll never admit how good it feels to be pampered. Orion even ties my shoelaces. By the time he joins me at the counter, Atlas has swept up his mess.

"Ordered bagels. French toast. Onion." Atlas pushes us plates, looking red-eyed and raggedy.

"Good sleep?" I ask sweetly. Atlas definitely heard us doing more than snuggling. Small payback for the times I had to listen to their sex moans.

Atlas grunts. He wears a dark T-shirt tucked into his belt with its stupid huge buckle and those deadly mercenary pants they all use as a form of torture. They hug his rugby thighs.

Atlas also cut up fruit salad, and he offers Orion a coffee that must be made exactly how he likes it because Orion bites his plush lip, hiding a smug omega smile.

I don't bother hiding my smile when I push the mug away from his outstretched fingers. "No coffee."

"I'll make you your own—"

"No. You haven't started nutrition yet. But omegas and caffeine? You think that's a good idea?"

"What?" Orion pales.

I pat his shoulder. "Cocoa?"

"I'll make it." Atlas dumps the coffee with a low growl and zero mercy. "I didn't realize."

"Shit. My energy drinks?"

"Toxic." I *tsk*, having way too much fun.

Groaning, Orion mashes his head on the counter.

I laugh into a fucking fantastically crunchy French toast bagel while Atlas mixes hot cocoa with the intensity of general at war. He reads the cocoa package like he's going to be tested, measuring milk, powder, and temperature to exact fractions of a unit.

He looks like he could solo overthrow a government, and between his size and his dominance, he takes up my whole kitchen.

It's honestly…cute the way he's so focused. Atlas sloshes and mutters, but eventually presents us with two steaming mugs of cocoa.

"Thanks." I sip and it's decent, if missing whipped cream. Guess the packet didn't say to add it.

But I bet he'd follow the instructions if I gave my own recipe…

Atlas watches me drink with primal satisfaction.

The way he watches me is the same way Orion stares at Atlas's coffee. "Fuck my omega life."

"Wait until you hear the other news. Pork rinds? Still not a food group. You're going to have to eat a vegetable."

"You are *killing* me," Orion moans.

I hide another smile in my cup, but Atlas catches this one, and I swear his golden-brown eyes shimmer.

So we're not doing jealousy? I thought he'd be pissed I keep flirting with his mate. Or pissed Orion keeps flirting with me.

He's the opposite of pissed.

An expression I want to call…*fond*?

I turn away before I can read any deeper. I'm already way too fucking deep.

"What's your plan for the day?" Atlas busies himself, mopping up the cocoa powder he spilled.

"I need to go to the dance studio to finalize my routine and grab my costume, but I don't need to be there all day."

"Come to class?" Orion nudges me. "We should mostly stick together, given…"

The kidnappings. The bomb threats. *The usual.*

"I'll sit with you, but I have work."

"Speaking of…" Orion ducks to the shopping bag that was tucked under the breakfast bar. "New phone and laptop. They're all set up for you."

It's past the point where I can fight their gifts.

I'm so tired of doing spreadsheets without a keyboard. I hug the laptop box to my chest. "Thank you."

Orion grins. "Can't wait to teach you more code."

We break to shower and then head to Orion's morning physiology lesson where Atlas posts up next to the door and draws a classroom of thirsty looks.

Maybe including mine, but he's not the kind of alpha you see on every street corner. No other alpha comes close to his breath-stopping dominance.

I force myself to tune out the mountain Adonis by playing with my new laptop. I catch up on the emails I've been ignoring and dig into the overdue bookkeeping for my back-alley roster of strip clubs, titty bars, and shady business fronts.

It's so weird being back in the classroom.

I always sat by myself.

I always wanted to *be* alone, because after Marisol disappeared, I was the universal omega target.

Now I'm sharing a desk with a male who hooks his ankle in the legs of my chair and drags me so close our shoulders bump.

Orion's scent, heat, and touch are a triple-threat, worming into my brain and making me question everything. Especially when he sneaks on a pair of gold-framed reading glasses that match his golden hair.

It's pure sexual blackmail.

And last night…

It makes me doubt.

If it feels this good being with *him*, then having a pack—

No.

I can enjoy the moment.

I can even admit how weak I am for the omega spun from sunshine.

What I can't do is trick myself into thinking this ends in the fairytale. Because even if Wyvern Pack pulls off a miracle and totally handles their shit, I'll still be what I am—the lone wolf who wants to disappear into a forest cave, only returning to civilization to get heat-treated.

We don't part ways until after lunch. Orion has afternoon classes, and I need to dance. I already have the song and the moves, but I need to chain them into something magic enough to lock down the promised alpha buffet.

I hit the studio with good intentions, but Atlas's gaze follows me everywhere.

I feel him in the mirror, when I spin, and every blessed second, boring into my skin.

The part of me that recognizes Atlas as *mate* hasn't stopped wanting him since I climbed those gazebo steps and got hit with a face full of the all-encompassing scent that knocked my life plan off its axis.

That part of me says to give him a private show.

The rest of me is freaking annoyed. "Do you have to keep watching like that?"

"I'm your bodyguard."

"There's only one door. Bodyguard from the hall."

He rumbles. "I need to keep you in my sight."

"Redfangs aren't going to crawl through the ducts." But as soon as I think it, my gaze flicks to the ceiling. The grates *are* pretty big…

"If they do, I'm here," Atlas says so matter-of-factly, it takes the air from my lungs.

"You'd take a bullet for me now?"

"Without hesitating."

I shiver. "If you say so."

"I won't ask you to trust me," Atlas says. "I want you to *watch* me. Watch how I change for you. Watch me just as hard as I'm watching you."

He's super intense, so I have to fight for it, but I wave him off. "That's the problem. You're watching me *a lot*. Can you tone down the dominance? The air's like soup."

"Soup?" Atlas tilts his head, and the low studio lights make his dark skin glow.

"Chowder." I run my fingers through the too-thick air. "It's like dancing with sandbags."

"I'll try to rein it in?" His plump lips press, suspiciously close to smiling.

"Are you allowed to smile at me?"

"Why wouldn't I be?"

"Orion…"

"We'll both smile a lot more if we have you."

Not touching that with rubber gloves, but I'm honestly curious where he thinks this is going. "You can't mate us both."

"Why?"

I sigh. "Your pack wouldn't agree."

"My pack would cut off their sacs if you asked, Lilah."

"Forgetting Jett?" I never forget the fifth Wyvern, no matter how I try.

"Even him."

"Doubtful."

"You'd be surprised what Jett's willing to do for you."

"I'd be surprised if Jett gave me a stick of gum." He's made his hatred clear. "He knew we were mates."

"None of us knew," Atlas insists. "Even the dads were just guessing to stir shit. We had no reason to believe anything they said with their shitty record of throwing people at our pack. They picked fucking *Craig* for us."

Ugh. Craig. "Fine. But Jett knew when we were kids."

"Did he? Did you know then?"

"I…" I *liked* Jett—or the JJ he used to be. But I would've liked anyone who showed me the smallest kindness. Either way, we were both too young to have a personal scent.

"*You* knew and you never told us we were meant to be." Atlas grips his chest. "If I'd known, I—"

"You still wouldn't have believed. You thought I was another omega trying to scheme my way into your money."

"We're assholes. I'm just saying. You went to such extremes to hide from us. Give us a chance to go to the same extremes for you now that we believe the truth."

I pretend his ask doesn't knock out my knees, hopping onto the pole and spinning. "Do your best."

"I am."

Atlas keeps watching me practice.

He doesn't blink.

NINETEEN

JETT

"I WOULDN'T RECOMMEND GOING BACK to the location." A deep wrinkle forms between Doctor Jakob's brows. It's the same expression my therapist has donned every time I've darkened his office. "If the trauma has affected your memories, it's most likely a form of self-protection. Digging at those wounds could—"

"I have to." The more I fray, the more I realize how fucked I am.

Maybe therapy could help in the long-term.

In the short-term, the best therapy for me isn't these sessions, but what I do between them, ticking down the list of trainers who hurt Lilah.

Marc. Isaiah. Barb. Bethany.

They've paid for what they did.

Punishment in equal measure to their crimes. An eye for an eye, a beating for a beating.

I put my name at the top of the list in bold block letters.

JETT.

The worst offender.

Doctor Jakob suspects that trauma has warped the way I remember my abuse.

That's why I *want* to pick the scab.

I need to know the truth so I know how final a punishment I deserve.

"I'll go to my bodyguard shift as planned." I give the doctor a look so dead-eyed, even Finn might flinch.

He and I are more alike than the others know.

I'm just better at hiding.

Or maybe I've done a better job clinging to the image of who I was meant to be. I'm jealous how easily he cast his old self away. How easily he found outlets for his pain.

"Mister Wyvern—"

"*I'll go.*" Even if my promise to be at Lilah's side forces me to go back where everything happened.

So, whether or not I should pick the scabs of my past, they're about to be exposed.

Doctor Jakob and I talk through the morning.

Therapy makes me feel worse.

Talking makes me *remember*.

There are so many memories I fought to forget. And every one that resurfaces threatens to pull me under.

The doctor gives a grateful sigh when he finally trades me off to Hunter in the office waiting room. They share a silent glance, as if I'm a hound that needs to be put down.

That's fine.

If Lilah wants it, that's what we'll arrange.

"How'd you do, J?" Hunter asks in the elevator.

"It's over."

"That bad?"

"It seems…" I need to answer enough to keep him off my back without revealing the depth of the fucked-up rabbit hole in my soul. "I had undergone some trauma. Doctor Jakob suspects I don't remember events strictly as they happened."

"Which events?"

My vision whitens.

There's a maze of a storage room behind the OCC's theater.

It smells like old fabric and set paint, with a fraying orange couch tucked in a back corner, surrounded by racks of costumes.

I'd come to work and learn with my father—the OCC was one of so many offices—but, overwhelmed by the omegas and the crowds, I ducked away to hide somewhere quiet.

I found the prop room.

So did Lilah.

She was kicked out of a tea party for wearing the wrong clothes. She huddled on the couch, hugging her bony knees, watching me like a feral cat. Big grey eyes and ready claws.

"Who are you?"

"Je-j…." How was I supposed to react to the delicate creature who clutched a sharpened pencil in self-defense?

"JJ?" She loosened her grip, deciding not to fill me with lead.

After she relaxed and I coaxed out the story, it was the easiest thing to solve her problems with a dress from the rack. Her sad, prickly wariness melted into the soft smile that exploded the trajectory of my childhood.

Suddenly, I *wanted* to go to work with my father. I looked for Lilah every chance, bringing her treats, and finding spots to hide on campus where it was just the two of us in our own world.

Once, she brushed my hair.

She loved my hair.

I keep it long, just in case she ever thinks to brush it again.

That prop room was my happy place, tucked away from my father's expectations of perfection. I was to have the best grades. The best performance.

With Lilah, I could just *be*.

But then Renee.

The prop room.

The orange couch.

Not just once.

Not even just one omega.

There are more voices in my head as the barriers fall away—voices I'd forgotten and worked so hard to erase.

And, then the part of the memory that makes pain ice pick my skull.

I remember Lilah peeking through the door. Her face twisted with disgust. Contempt.

While Renee—

And then Lilah *knows*.

She knows I'm not a real alpha.

She knows my shame.

She didn't touch me, but she's in the room with them, and that makes her one of them, and everything is broken.

Broken.

Broken.

"Dude." Hunter grips my arm. "You are not okay right now."

"I'm fine." My voice is dry as ash.

"Play the stoic card all day, but you're not with Lilah if you're not one-hundred percent. There was a fucking bomb, J. And we caught another guy trying to scale the fence. These fucks are relentless."

"He's in custody?" The thought brings me back to the present—walking to Hunter's Jeep, and the constant danger to the mate I never once deserved.

"We moved him to the compound. You can have him when you get back."

"Perfect." I slip into the car as if nothing's wrong, but I can feel Hunter watching.

He's the hardest to fool.

We're halfway to the place I'm dreading when he speaks. "If you need to talk, I'm here. The pack needs you if we're going to be whole."

"Does it?"

"You fucking kidding?" Hunter smacks the wheel. "We've never given you a role you couldn't own. You do combat, strategy, intel, tech. Anything the team needs."

"I betrayed the team."

"How?"

"Lilah."

"Look. Maybe you knew what Lilah was to us and maybe you didn't. We all twisted the knife. Any one of us could've acted differently and called you out."

"I told her she doesn't belong." Recent events have made it obvious I was speaking about myself.

I'm the one who never belonged.

"And I fully fucking failed to go check on her. Every one of us forced her into that barrel."

"It's different."

"So what? You want to be punished?"

"*Yes.*"

Hunter's silent.

I'm less and less able to keep up my act.

My control.

It was all doomed to be shattered the second Lilah returned to my life, and I'm oddly looking forward to the moment she puts me in my place.

I want Lilah to pull the trigger.

Too soon, and we're at the OCC's gates.

I shudder.

Hunter drives us through the checkpoints to the performing arts center. "If you don't want to—"

"I'm going."

Hunter levels me with a look that drips in his newfound dominance. "You swear on your life you're good to watch her?"

I *tsk.*

Swear on something with value.

"I swear on her life."

"Call if you need anything."

When I step out of the car, gravity is denser. Feels like my soles are sinking into the sidewalk, my lungs are being crushed under the pressure. Omega scents whirl, growing thicker and thicker as I travel deep into the belly of my nightmare beast.

I take careful steps to her location, passing through a manned metal detector, and trying to stay present as today bleeds into all the days rotting my memory.

A full year of memories.

A year I clung to my Lilac and pretended nothing else was going on. A year it took to find evidence on Renee—to build a case against her that had nothing to do with my truth.

Luckily, she wasn't just an abuser. She stole to feed her habits. Drugs. Alcohol.

Her "friends" even paid her to use—

Forcing out a shredding breath, I tear myself back to what I think is reality.

Lilah dances center stage in the main auditorium. Her teacher coaches her through a routine.

I'd braced to watch her dance again, but I wasn't expecting the pole.

No one warned me about the pole.

But Atlas is proof that a warning wouldn't have helped.

He stares at her like he's seeing his future, and every day, I doubt more and more it's a future that includes my body in their pack.

I can't look at Lilah and breathe.

I give her my back so I can give Atlas my report.

"What'd Hunter say?"

"Another climber." I rub sweating palms against my slacks. "I'll handle him tomorrow."

If there's a tomorrow.

Maybe Atlas hears the edge-of-a-cliff tone in my voice. "How was therapy?"

"Therapeutic."

He hits me with the full force of his dominance, and even without the pack bond, that in-charge energy quiets the loudest volleys in my internal civil war. "Why don't I believe you, Jett?"

"Don't you have night classes? You'll be late."

He gives Lilah a wistful glance, but not wanting to disturb her time with her teacher, he silently slips away.

The music and her sensual movements try to draw me in, but I don't allow myself to watch. Instead, I scan the auditorium.

The smell of the red velvet seats makes acidic memories boil inside, but I keep them at bay minute by minute.

Finally, her teacher claps. "You're going to slay. But what are we doing about your costume?"

"I'll grab something from the racks." Lilah's voice is deadpan, but it's enough to rattle my bones.

"The theater department got a shipment of showgirl—"

"Hard no."

I'm surviving their conversation until Evgenia's words strike like a cattle prod. "Fine, fine, but check the prop room. I have veto rights if you pick another boring frock."

"I'll pick something good. It's my night too, you know."

"*Finally*. You deserve to shine."

When Evgenia leaves, Lilah finally deigns to give me the attention I don't deserve.

"Shadow Number Four," she mumbles.

"I won't get in your way." I keep my gaze down.

Don't deserve to look her in the eye.

"That's what Number Two said." Lilah whirls, parting the curtains to walk backstage.

I follow until I realize where she's heading. The long hallway to the prop room.

Oh fuck no.

I follow in stop-motion, losing time with each step.

Lilah goes through the door.

I—*can't.*

The ice pick gauges between my eyes, and the memories slam back so vividly, I scent mocha and almost fucking wretch.

I'm not sure how long I stand, I just know I don't have the courage to move.

Then there's a crash.

Lilah yelps.

The sound whips me, because I need to make sure she's okay —even if these last steps end me.

I rush in.

Lilah sprawls in a heap of gowns at the bottom of the ladder she just slid down. She's already brushing herself off.

Relieved, I move to her.

Then freeze.

The couch.

"Thought I could reach." Lilah tosses the masks she spilled into a busted box, but her motion is as hazy as a ghost's.

I'm on a different timeline, sucked deep into the past, seeing other faces, hearing other voices that force me to submit.

I'm vaguely aware of Lilah's attention, shifting to where I'm staring into space. Her voice drops to a tone I can't read. "So you didn't forget?"

"Forget…what?"

I'm about to collapse.

"Us." Lilah hugs her ribs. "I tried to make myself forget you. I kept waiting for you to come back, but you never did."

"Did you see?"

"Did I see what?"

"Renee."

"Trainer Renee?" Lilah frowns. "Haven't seen her in years. Thank fuck. She's the reason— Jett?"

My gaze drifts to the side door.

Lilah was there. "Did you see what she did?"

Lilah goes so still. "What did she do?"

"Something she shouldn't have."

"She was the first trainer who hit me. Made it a trend." Lilah speaks carefully. "Did she…hit you?"

"I wasn't beaten."

"Then…"

The full-color memory blazes through my head, lighting my skull on fire.

It started with Renee.

Then her friends. Other trainers.

They liked having a pet alpha who couldn't do anything but submit.

I point to the side door.

I remember.

Lilah's sweet pink upper lip twisted in the ugliest sneer. Grey eyes that were supposed to be filled with stars were suddenly thunderstorms.

I disgust her.

She's just like them.

Bad, cruel, painful omegas.

Because Lilah saw and she knew that I was broken. A failed alpha, long before my awakening. "You were there. You saw."

"No. The last time I saw you, you gave me a muffin." She speaks so carefully, pronouncing every word. "Jett... What do you think I saw?"

"Renee," I repeat.

What I'm saying finally hits home.

Horror widens Lilah Darling's eyes.

Finally.

Now we can end this clean.

TWENTY

LILAH

A SINKHOLE OPENS in my stomach. It's big, and it's dank, and I think this one's so deep, I'm never escaping.

Because *holy fuck*.

The first time I saw grown-up JJ, I thought *demon*.

He was so achingly gorgeous and so full of hate. It took me a while to match him to the dark-haired boy in my memories who fed me treats and smiled so sweet.

Tonight's Jett is just a shell.

His shoulders are a little too pinched and his scent a little too weak, like he's fading to nothing.

And I'm ill, because I finally understand why.

All the pieces that never made sense connect in a sickening click.

Most OCC trainers are betas. The rare omegas are old birds like Eleanor who've already raised families and have knowledge to share.

Except Renee. She just wanted attention.

A captive audience of fawning betas and free access to alphas at campus events.

She taught electives on mating and pack dynamics, and the

other girls loved her. I was the only one who saw the darkness in her smile when she had to play polite.

I saw her real face when she kept me after class.

She was the trainer who introduced corporal punishment because "traditional discipline" wasn't keeping me out of fights.

Turns out, I wasn't the only one Renee made suffer.

Jett.

I thought my heart was done beating for him.

He's like a spooked horse, rigid with this wary, tense energy, but it's worse because he's not even that present. His dark eyes are so haunted, he's tissue-paper under his collared shirt.

Like he's already ripped into a thousand shreds.

The sinkhole keeps yawning, growing the queasy feeling in my gut. "What did she do?"

"What did you see?" He asks from a million miles away.

"Nothing." I shiver. "Nothing. If I'd seen her hurt you… Shit. You're the only one I—" The only person I cared about.

For a long time.

Jett stares into space like he's staring through time.

And the hole inside me grows too big, seeing him this broken.

I want to touch him, to tug him away, but I don't dare. He's too fragile.

"Follow me." I stride out of the room, heading for fresh air.

His papery complexion regains some life when we walk into the night. I keep walking down the sidewalk to the line of ornamental boulders on the grass.

"Sit."

Jett obeys.

The motion's so instant, it gives me chills.

Feels like I could tell him to do anything, and he wouldn't say a word. I perch next to him, leaving a huge gap between our bodies. Then I pull out the phone Orion gave me.

It only has a few contacts. I pick Hunter's from the list and send a message. *Jett needs help.*

You okay? He responds before I can put the phone away. *We're on the way.*

No one's hurt, I answer just as fast. "Hunter's coming."

"That's for the best. I won't bother you again." The resignation in his voice rings every one of my alarms.

"What do you mean?"

"I owe you more than an apology." Jett straightens his shoulders, like he's finally coming back online, only it's not the same program running as before. "The best thing I can do for you is disappear. You have no reason to avoid the others if I'm gone."

My heart drags down my chest, growing heavier and heavier. "Disappear where?"

"Away." He stares into the distance. "Not yet. First, I'll finish dealing with the trainers who hurt you. Then Renee and—" he chokes off, swallowing. "And then I'll go."

"Why?"

"Because everything is my fault. That you were targeted. That you were hurt. That you couldn't bond with your rightful pack." Jett's scent is as faint as his voice, but even that tiny whiff of cedar proves he's mine to claim.

But Jett always wants to walk away.

Rejecting me again and again and again.

Rejecting *himself*. "You're part of my rightful pack."

"I could never be your alpha." His soft resignation hits me dead in the spleen, another *oof* I didn't see coming.

Suddenly, all my sympathy, all the sick sorrow over what he's been through pivots on a fucking *dime* and that quavering rejection boils into rage.

"*Jett*," I drag out his name like silk. "*Fuck. You.*"

His head snaps, and a hint of fire kindles in the dark pits of his eyes.

Maybe he's finally waking up.

"You want to disappear. *Again.*"

"Because I don't deserve—"

"*Stop.* All I ever needed was your friendship. I just needed one person willing to be at my side. You were my person until you disappeared. And I get it. You were going through hell. But then I got dropped into your pack and you pretended not to know. Now you 'owe me more than an apology?' There *was* no apology, and you think disappearing is the fix? No. You don't get to check out. You have to stay and fucking work for it."

I pant, surprised at all the words that just poured out like poison.

I'm sweating.

Feels good to let out so much that I've been holding back so long.

"I'm broken," he whispers.

"Have you met me?" Like I'm the poster child for healthy, normal omega-dom? I could teach a class on self-destruction. "Have you even met your pack brothers? What standard are you after?"

"Perfection. You deserve the perfect alpha."

My head hurts.

I think my logic center is finally fried. "You realize what packs are after me? My main criteria is no kidnapping."

"You deserve so much better."

"We all deserve better. So where's my apology?"

"Lilah." He closes his eyes.

I brace for more bullshit, although I have to admit, I'd rather yell at Jett forever than watch him slowly disappear.

He takes a deep breath.

When his eyes pop open, I reel.

He doesn't just drop to his knees.

He drops to his elbows and puts his forehead on the ground. "I'm sorry."

I hesitate, not sure what to do with this fragile, crazy boy who I've loved and I've hated and I don't forgive. But I also don't want to watch him die or sacrifice himself or whatever the fuck he's planning when he's crying out so desperately.

I know what it's like at the edge of that abyss, when it would be so much easier to just give in.

I don't want that for anyone.

Especially for my JJ.

So, carefully, watching his smallest movement to make sure I'm not pushing him the wrong way over the cliff, I lift Jett's chin with my toe. "You're going to stay with me. You're not allowed to go away."

When his gaze meets mine, a jagged arrow punches the center of my chest.

There's not just a spark in his eyes.

There's a fucking bonfire.

Jett *likes* to submit.

And just like that, another Wyvern ruins me because the feeling of controlling an alpha is everything I never knew to dream.

Before I can follow the white rabbit, Hunter's Jeep tears down the drive.

Jett kisses my shoe. "If you want to keep me, I'm yours."

———

HUNTER TAKES JETT HOME, leaving me with Finn and a massive headache. Ignoring his and Orion's attempts to get my attention, I stumble into my room and lock my door, intending to pass out.

All I do is toss and turn.

I'd bet my new leggings that Renee's the one who started tampering with my files.

She marks the spot where Jett and I were both ruined. But I can't fix his past any more than I can fix mine.

All I can do is make sure Renee suffers.

And shit.

I keep picturing Jett on his knees.

Those vulnerable eyes.

It felt like he was ready to hand me some part of his heart that I'm not capable of handling. I can't have nice things. Don't want them. I don't like strings, and Jett was watching me like a whole net, ready to fucking *bind*.

He looked like the world started and ended with me, and it doesn't matter if he's on his knees, offering me his tattered soul, or if he's knotted deep inside me—that's not a feeling an omega can resist.

That's the dream.

Supposedly.

To be your alpha's everything.

Nothing could freak me out more.

I don't want to give anyone anything. Because anything I give will be taken away.

What more proof do I need than Jett's latest commitment to disappearing?

I spend the night bricking over the walls in my heart that crumble every freaking time a Wyvern gives me googly eyes.

When my alarm goes off, I kick off the covers. Even though I'm exhausted and mostly unslept, I promise I'm going to own today, my performance, and all the days that follow.

It's like Hunter said.

All I have to do is follow my dreams.

They're the ones who have to prove themselves.

Digging through Evgenia's treasure trove, I find a spandexy skirt and halter with peekaboo panels, and these butterfly-wing streamers that attach to my arms and flow out when I spin.

I spend the afternoon practicing how not to get tangled in the extra cloth, and when I nail the motions, I soar.

Night finds me fast.

Soon, the auditorium's filling and other dancers are every-where, doing their makeup, warming up, and filling backstage with their excited chatter. Alphas' voices hum behind the curtain, and their pheromones have me sweating.

It's the first time in my dance career that I'm waiting for my curtain call instead of hiding in the bathroom. I'm nervous as ever but for totally new reasons.

I need offers.

And to get them, I have to show the real Lilah Darling.

No sweat suits, no knives, no hiding.

Just me on the stage, baring my soul.

And a little bit of my ass.

Rachel and the dance team perform right before me. With her hair in a tight ponytail and smoky eyes, Rachel's scowl is textbook mean girl.

I whirl away to stretch.

No time for stink eye.

I stretch and bounce until a round of roaring applause follows the dance team's strut off stage.

Evgenia pats my back. "They're waiting for you."

I tense. "Who?"

"*Everyone.*"

"Oh, good. No pressure then." I take a deep breath and walk between the curtains.

The lights are down, but I don't have to see the crowd to feel the alphas.

Their scents whirl like a vortex.

My palms sweat. I rub them against my skirt while double-checking the pole on the off chance that Rachel lubed it with butter.

There's no grease. No sabotage.

I take position, arched back pressed hard to the metal, and listen to my heart beat while I wait for the music to start.

The crowd's energy is static, feathering my skin, lifting the hairs on my arms.

I can feel the Wyverns in the dark.

Their energy's that much thicker and more compelling than any other alpha pack's.

It's worse than the first night I performed for them, when we hadn't met, and I didn't know what they were.

Even if I never accept our connection, I can't deny it's there.

It's always there.

The music starts with a low rumble like a purr.

I drag my arm up my body until it's pointed over my head, spotlight silhouetting my slow, sensual movement. I snake my hips, and as the beat speeds up, I start to climb.

I lift and split my legs.

I'm upside down, clinging to the pole by my thighs, arms outstretched and the butterfly wings fluttering when I catch sight of all five Wyverns in their box, deadly as ever in dark suits.

They're on their feet, leaning over the rail.

Hunter has his arm hooked in Finn's, stopping him from jumping off the balcony.

My heart speeds, and I can't help but smirk.

Enjoy, boys.

Another rotation, another inversion, and I spot the Sorensens. I hold eye contact with Rhett, and his pupils dilate behind his glasses.

Again and again.

Every time I pick a pack leader out of the crowd, I meet his gaze and hold it in challenge until the spin takes me away.

Still don't know how to flirt.

But a dominance battle bordering on eye-fuck?

I can throw that down.

I finally slide to the ground to finish the song on the floor.

On my knees, I throw myself into the music until they can see everything I am.

I writhe until the crowd growls. The vibrations light me up, lifting my temperature.

And when I finish, spread out on the floor, there's a moment of silence before a cascading cheer and so many wolf whistles, I blush.

Eat that, Wyverns.

I glance at the balcony.

My smugness slips at the fire in their eyes.

The desire.

The heat.

The way their knuckles clench the rail.

It sparks that flip in my belly, and something deeper that I never want to name.

I give my bow before running off the stage.

In the crowded backstage dressing room, I shrug into a robe and collapse. My station's a powder-covered mess, like someone dug out their bronzer to screw with me.

I brush off the dust, sneezing and semi-shocked they didn't go all-out and graffiti my mirror in lipstick.

Missed opportunity.

But backstage is packed with parents, family members, and guards, so nobody can come at me unless their family is in on the conspiracy.

Omegas laugh and unwind, fixing their hair and makeup for the afterparty.

I try not to shoot envious looks at the omega in the next chair, whose mom and sister congratulate her performance, gushing over pack so-and-so until they're all giggling.

Evgenia is the closest I've ever had to a mother figure, and post-show, she's already occupied with a vodka soda and a beta guard twenty years younger.

Good for her.

I just have myself.

Probably should've asked Orion to be here with me, but I wanted the Wyverns watching from the crowd.

I'm scraping off stage makeup when I catch the familiar strain of laughter that makes me flash back to being locked in a closet.

Noelle.

She looks so much like Rachel. The perfect dark wavy hair and big beautiful eyes that flash venom as soon as she spots me.

With a fanged smile, she whispers to her sister. Then they're both gliding over, swans on the attack.

I'm not playing this game.

I grab the dress I hung on the back of my chair and bolt.

They can choke on their own poison.

TWENTY-ONE
LILAH

MY COCKTAIL DRESS is red and black, sparkles with crystals, and gives me the confidence of an evil queen. Whichever Wyvern picked it out paired it with these red-bottomed platform pumps that would've matched *soooo* good.

Instead, I go with my gut and a pair of black running sneakers. *Safety over style.*

Hair combed, makeup done, knives and smiles sharpened to points, I strut into the afterparty.

The last time I went to a post-recital reception, I signed myself away to Wyvern Pack.

I'm hoping tonight ends with a better offer.

There's no fanfare at my entrance, but heads turn. Awareness prickles my skin where alpha stares linger. And one spot between my shoulder blades prickles harder than the rest.

"Star." Finn looms, electric orange and vibrating with a sinful purr. "Only dance like that for me."

"Did you like the show?" I slip from his reach. If Finn catches me now, he won't let go.

I have packs to fake charm.

He prowls after me, stance dropping dangerously low. "I want a private dance. Book me for seventy—no, eighty years."

"Can't. There's a line." I wave to the table with my name card. For the first time in my life, alphas are waiting and none of them have gang tattoos.

Well, visible ones.

Finn's glimmer fades to dark. "Not if I remove the line."

"Sorry, buddy. Guard duty." Hunter snags him before he murders my wannabe suitors. "Got your back, Killer. You're safe."

I let out a breath.

There are *a lot* of alphas tonight.

A lot of men who could make a grab for me.

Hunter and Finn join Atlas and Jett, loosely surrounding my table, looking deadly in their suits. Their casual, crushing dominance keeps the crowd from surging.

I'll never admit how comforting it feels to know they're holding the line.

Even if their stares prickle hardest of all.

The tables are clustered into seating areas, one per omega, and mine's directly under the central chandelier. Glamorous, but I can't help glancing up.

Hope nobody cuts the chain.

Rachel—voted most likely to pull that stunt—sits on the opposite side of the room, happily fluttering lashes at alphas. Her sister, Noelle, Senator Charlie Patrick, and the other politico-mates mingle around Rachel's table. All's good as long as they stay in their lane.

I grab champagne from my ice bucket. Keyed up from my dance and the humming energy of the party, I'm gonna need bubbles to get through this night.

I'm trying to figure out the cork when Orion steals the bottle, trading me for a massive bouquet. "You were amazing."

"Thank you." I go gooey over the big rainbow flowers, which I've never thought to want before. Clearly I should've. *So pretty.* I sniff them, but all I catch is Orion's crisp apple. "What are they?"

"Gerbera daisies. I didn't know what kind you liked."

"Neither did I." Never gotten flowers, or anything really. Last time I was at this party, I didn't even get a tablecloth.

The glow up is real.

I try to sniff one more time, then sneeze.

Still have crumbled makeup dust in my nose thanks to catty omegas who can't let me breathe.

"Let me stay?" Orion uncorks the champagne with a satisfying *pop*, pouring me the first glass. "I want to meet these packs."

I don't want to use Orion as a crutch, but my insides twist when my gaze slips to the riot of bodies and scents.

It's a lot of alpha for just one girl. "You can stay."

"I won't leave your side." He pulls out my chair, and I'm not going to get used to the treatment, but I can enjoy it.

Just for one more night.

"Thanks." I have enough time for a deep breath, a rub of my itchy nose, and a sip of champagne.

Then the circus rolls into town.

The first pack is four alphas in their early thirties. They bring me roses, smell like iron, and ask straight out the gate, "Can he come to your heat?"

Orion throws a protective arm over my shoulders. "I'll come wherever she wants me."

The alphas rumble in a metallic lust spike that has me screaming *next*!

When they leave, promising to put in an offer anyway, I shrug off Orion's arm. "Don't be a tease."

"I wasn't," he says innocently.

"You'll come wherever I want?"

"I mean…" He bites the corner of his lip. "I'm not offering anything I won't follow through on. Whatever pack you choose for your heat, I'll be there. To participate. To chaperone. Anything you want or need, I'm yours."

I try to breathe through the sudden hitch in my throat. "Just don't scare away my offers."

"Your offers are creaming themselves." Orion presses so close his breath feathers my throat. "See?"

Alphas give us their growliest attention, and packs huddle, whispering and watching our every move.

Wyvern Pack is the worst.

Hunter keeps barking at Finn to focus and put away his knives while Jett hits me with a black hole stare.

Not sure if he wants to devour me, or let me devour *him*.

Atlas is torqued, gaze flicking from alpha pack to alpha pack, seeking threats, but every time he lands on me and the omega glued to my side, his jaw does that satisfying, tooth-cracking clench.

I smile into my champagne. "Love watching them squirm."

"Right?" Orion grins sunshine and mischief. I've never seen him so light. So unbothered.

Losing his bond really was for the best.

Now Orion's a billboard for why I never want to mate.

Free and easy is so much more fun than bound and neglected.

Drawn in by my dancing or Orion's continued touches that I never ask him to stop, more packs rotate through my table. They heap me with flowers and gifts until Orion has a side-hustle taking care of the pile.

Hope the Wyverns are taking notes.

I chat and give my best smiles, but with each pack, the stares and scents are more overwhelming.

My body warms, wondering why we aren't sampling the menu now that we finally found our way to the buffet.

I try to pace my breathing, and find myself gripping Orion's arm to stay grounded. Having him at my side keeps me from giving in to proudly slutty stray thoughts like how *would* Hunter's tattoos taste?

Like smoke?

Or more honey?

The most calming are the verbal heat offers.

Almost every pack that sits claims they'll be in touch to schedule a private date or toss in a bid.

I finally, *finally* have options, and thanks to the Wyvern-supplied funds in my account, I have a real, honest *choice*.

Orion's tempting me with chocolate-covered strawberries, and I'm fighting the urge to tease his fingers with my tongue when a familiar voice calls my name.

"Lilah."

Rhett Sorensen's pack steps into the hot seat. His eyes tighten behind his glasses, and his cherry scent spikes more almond with lust when Orion pulls a half-bitten strawberry from my lips.

I lick leftover chocolate.

Jason, Kipp, and Cale zero in on my tongue flick.

"For you." Suddenly breathy, Jason offers a lace-wrapped bouquet of red roses and a bakery box for my growing present pile.

And Cale gives Orion a more-than-friendly smile. "Orion Wyvern?"

"Just Orion."

Kipp bounces. "You two smell so good together. Like whoa with the caramel apple. Are you together? Do you want to be?"

I chew on my answer. I don't know what to say, and no matter the response, I'm not impressed with the fetishy interest in both of us together as omegas instead of either one of us as people.

"We're friends." Orion gives me a cute side-eye, like he's waiting for me to approve the label.

I warm, lips curving. "Friends."

"Like heat buddies though?" Kipp asks. "Because—"

"Enough," Rhett cuts him off with a baby bark that doesn't spark a flutter.

Total froyo.

"What did you think of the dance?" I ask.

"It was an experience." Cale straightens his tie. He's a little too buttoned up, so I can't tell if he's into it or uncomfortable, but he's for sure casting flirty glances at *my* omega.

I scoot in my seat, blocking his sight line to Orion.

"Mmm," Jason agrees. "I'm glad we have dinner on your calendar. You're very popular."

"Is that tomorrow?" I have to check with Catherine. I'd kind of forgotten, and now the room's starting to blur.

Jason keeps talking.

The tickle in my throat climbs to my sinuses. I sip champagne, then choke.

Suddenly, my head hurts.

"What's wrong?" Orion smooths my back, warm hand on the bare skin of my spine, and the contact jolts me.

"Nothing." I rub my neck, gaze drifting.

Maybe I'm hallucinating, but I spot Noelle surrounded by her mates, and I swear she wears the witchiest smirk.

Sweat prickles under the tie of my halter.

I feel stuffy.

Hot.

Then, an all-too-familiar cramp wracks me, and I go rigor mortis rigid. My perfume spikes hard and high in a crème brûlée explosion that scatters shards of sugared shrapnel.

Orion's hand freezes. "Lilah. You…"

One-by-one, conversations die.

Every alpha turns, eyes on the prize.

I'm spiking.

Here.

Now.

Shit.

Please be a spike. If I go into full heat—

Orion wraps me in his arms, trying to hide my body and my scent, but it's way too late to pretend this isn't going down.

The first alpha growl makes my skin crawl.

The second makes me shake.

Then I lose count, because this party just turned into a fucking jungle full of panthers tensing to rip me apart.

I pull out a knife, checking the exits.

The crowd ripples.

Some packs are confused, but others came with an evil master plan, because they know exactly whose job it is to seal the doors.

Someone knew I'd spike.

Someone planned another grab, and this time, I'm so outnumbered, I think they have a shot.

"Come with me." A pack leader steps to my table, rocking the stubble and tattoos of my typical kidnapper. Five bulky alphas stand behind him in the same shady uniform.

Too many to fight on my own.

"Malcolm? What are you doing?" Rhett folds his napkin when he needs to be pulling a weapon, but he probably doesn't carry one. Maybe doesn't know how to use one.

"Collecting." The alpha jerks his head. "Grab them."

His packmates fan out, ready to drag us from the table.

I reach for my gun.

Orion reaches to pull me behind him.

But before either of us can fight, Wyvern Pack descends.

The other pack has six guys.

They should've brought twenty.

Finn and Jett fucking dismantle them in bones-broken, pounded-into-the-floor, brutal efficiency that leaves the room holding its breath.

Not me.

I'm gasping, squeezing my thighs together because apparently, I get wet over Wyverns who maim in my defense.

Not even ten seconds and the pack's groaning on the carpet.

"Wait!" Cale hurries to kneel next to the guy whose arms are no longer in their sockets thanks to the Jett-Finn combo play that deserves its own highlight on gangbanger ESPN. "There's no need for this. We'll call the police."

"*Sit. Down,*" Jett unleashes a snarl so vicious, Cale staggers.

There's nothing submissive about Jett when he grinds his heel into Pack Leader Malcolm's ribcage. But before he can juice the guy's spine, he frowns, pressing his earpiece. "More incoming. Need to get Lilah out."

Hunter and Atlas trade glances.

"You want to…" Hunter starts.

"No." Atlas cases the room, a solid wall at my side. "You're in charge. Tell me what we need."

"Shit." Hunter turns to me, trying to be reassuring, but I'm sweating and already so hot. Wish he wouldn't look at me at all if he's not going to offer up his knot. "We'll get you out of here and take you somewhere quiet, okay Lilah? Finn?"

"Gotcha." Finn scoops me up. I *oof* into his arms, face-bumping the button of the dress shirt I could totally unpop with my tongue.

Shit, I'm horny.

"Rub her back," Orion says. "Purr. Keep her soothed."

"Mmm." Finn cradles me, and I start to calm, feeling his low rumble body-to-body.

Then he licks my jugular.

Electric-shocked, I jerk. "Not soothing!"

"So good," Finn mumbles. "Hold on tight, Starbear."

Hunter and Jett punch a hole through the crowd, Finn huddles me like a touchdown football, and Orion and Atlas move behind us, systematically taking down any asshole who makes a lunge.

Their formation is tight, their speed is bumping, and for half a second, I think we might actually walk out.

Ha.

More alphas unfold from the crowd.

And there are my gang tattoos.

Red-scaled ink flashes at their wrists.

Redfangs.

It's a full-on invasion, and if I survive the night, I'm going to make it my personal mission to make sure every person working OCC security is lifetime-banned from the profession.

"Let me down." I wiggle.

My omega instincts might be happy to let our crazed mate-candidates tote us around like a useless bump, but I'm too jaded.

Have to be ready to fight.

Have to be ready to run, to hide, and protect myself from the attackers.

Also have to deal with the insane urges that bubble every time a Wyvern kidney-punches a guy in my defense.

And the urge to beg Finn to tear into my itchy fucking neck while he sinks his knot into my empty, aching core.

The thirst is real and super unaffected by the life-or-death situation.

"I got you. *Stay*," Finn slathers on that raspy alpha bark, and I'm in no condition to disobey.

Hunter and Jett picked up knives. Their hair's messy and I can smell their sweat. Mezcal and cedar. They must've taken down twenty guys and they're not slowing.

I can't see Orion and Atlas, but I hear them close behind, grunting and punching.

If the Wyverns weren't here, I'd already be zip-tied on Dominik Redfang's floor.

But I can't just watch. Can't just rely on them to carry me to safety.

"I can fight," I insist. "I can—"

Finn bites my neck.

He doesn't break skin—just breaks my ability to think anything but *Finn. Teeth. Bite.*

Fuck.

"Know you can fight. Star only has to bask." Finn nips my ear.

I go limp, maybe dead.

Panties fucking soaked.

When my head lolls, I catch sight of the Sorensens, gaping from the table where we left them.

Call the police.

What a weird, normal response that'd get me worse than killed.

"Move!" Atlas roars.

The last few alphas dumb enough to be in our way fall back, clobbered by his overwhelming dominance.

Jett reaches the doors first, pulling out the metal rod that had them barricaded. Then, agents in black Wyvern House camo pour into the reception hall, running down every single alpha who made a move.

I'd relax now that the danger's mostly past, but I'm busy clenching my thighs. I can barely resist humping Finn to stop the growing, empty ache.

Please be a spike.

"Keys!" Hunter shouts as we hit open air.

An agent tosses him a set for the SUV idling on the curb with its doors open. Finn hoists me into the back seat, the guys pile in, and then we're hauling ass.

"Hospital," I grit.

"Spike or heat?" Orion climbs over the middle seat to get to me.

"Spike."

I hope.

Please, please be a spike.

Otherwise, I won't survive the ride without earning some binding new jewelry—a full collar of their bites.

TWENTY-TWO

LILAH

I'M BEING *COOKED.*

Suffocated in a Wyvern hotbox.

With shaking fingers, I push the window button, but night air can't cure the toxic pheromones that beg me to beg *them.*

Wyvern Pack could ease me into oblivion.

If I ask, if I whine, if I so much as make heavy eye contact, I'm afraid that's the end.

Oranges and apples clog my throat with Finn and Orion crowding me in the third-row seat.

Finn clutches me like his dragon treasure, while Orion's half in our laps, smoothing up and down my calf and whispering reassurances I can't process while I'm sweating to death.

It's the same push and pull.

I want to crawl inside them just as much as I want to jump out the window.

I'm stubborn enough to keep resisting.

But for how much longer?

I'm *cracking.*

Brittle with heat.

"Almost there." Hunter watches the rearview mirror more than he watches the road we're tearing down.

"Hurry." I cradle my belly.

Atlas grips the bar in the front seat. Their eyes are wild and their jaws are tight, because the more I need, the more my scent calls them to answer.

I'm terrified they'll listen to my pheromones instead of my words. "Please. Just don't…"

"*Never.*" Jett sits in the middle row. His hair fell out during the fight. With blood on his cuffs and a crooked tie, he's a delicious mess. His voice softens to the one I haven't heard since JJ disappeared. "We'll never do anything you don't want."

I shiver.

"Of course we won't," Orion murmurs.

Finn rumbles. "Tell me what you need."

Their care wears me down.

Sandpaper, grinding away layer after Lilah layer.

I'm weak in Finn's arms, but it'll be worse if I let go. "Just hold on."

"Forever." His rumble against my skin cools the heat.

When we hit Wyvern Clinic, Doctor Morgan waits in front of the ER with a team of masked-up nurses.

"*Get her in a room,*" she barks.

The nurses reach for me, but Finn snaps at a beta's hand.

"For the love—" Doctor Morgan growls. "Then carry her. Hurry."

Finn hauls me into a room, and nurses flurry, taking my vitals and my blood. All the while, I'm sweating, trying to ignore the ache made worse by hovering Wyverns.

I can *taste* them.

After long enough to sweat through my dress, Doctor Morgan has a verdict. "It's just a spike. Let's get you transferred to one of the nesting suites. You'll feel more comfortable if you're eased, but at this level, you should still be able to ride out the symptoms."

The fluttering cramps make me ill.

It's not pain, but the *memory* of pain that has me shaking.

Can't do it again.

Nurses wheel me to an omega comfort suite.

The small, dark nesting room has a big bed, a low ceiling, and an attached bathroom. It's calmingly quiet until five big-shouldered shadows stalk inside.

Doctor Morgan pushes past the Wyverns. "Say the word and they're gone."

"Give me a few minutes?" I pray they'll leave without a fight.

"We'll be outside." Hunter tugs Finn, glancing at the others. "Guys?"

Slowly, giving me plenty of lingering stares and chances to suck in their keyed-up scents, the Wyverns file out.

When the door shuts, and I'm alone with Doctor Morgan, a whine finally slips.

I grip my throat.

I'm sweat-soaked, slick as fuck, and feverish for a knot.

There's a second of panic as I wait for the pain to hit.

The death cramps.

But my pussy's all flutters and ache.

Another pre-game event.

I'm not ready for the main show.

The doctor pulls a drawer-cart to my bedside. "It might feel good to take a bath. Or we have a wide selection of easing aids. The spike should pass within a few hours."

"You're sure it's not my heat?"

"It's not." She pats my knee. "You have a few more days."

I sag against scratchy pillows. Without the guys' scents blowing up my nose, everything smells medicinal. The opposite of what I need if I'm going to feel at ease.

And there's one more thing I need to ask—one more thing I don't want them to know. "Can you run a drug test? This doesn't feel like a natural spike."

"I'll have your blood sent for panels." She leans in, checking my eyes. "There's definitely some irritation. Any other symptoms?"

"Itchy nose and throat." I've been scratching them all night.

"I'm on it. Hit the button if you need anything. In the mean-time, try to relax."

I want to resign myself to a night of hospital sex toys, but the light's wrong, and the blankets are wrong, and I think I'll finally shatter if I force myself to keep doing this alone.

That doesn't make it any easier to ask. "Can you…"

"I can have your alphas attend to you if—"

"They're not mine. Orion. Can you ask if he'll come in?"

"Of course. Rest, Lilah. You're going to be just fine."

Her reassurance does *not* reassure, and when the door shuts, I shake, rocked by the old fear that Orion'll ghost.

It hurts to admit I need *anyone*.

I'm still floored that Wyvern Pack protected me.

"Lilah? What do you need?" Orion's soft hair glows burnished gold in the dim light. I smell the guys on him, but he rockets to me like they don't exist.

He stops short of the bed.

Afraid to touch.

Afraid to move.

I'm just as terrified, but heat overrides my fear.

I need *someone* to make the bad memories disappear.

If I want to try pretending I can still trust, then Orion's the one. "Need you. Sit with me?"

"I'm here." He cups my face, fingertips trembling.

Letting out a shaky breath, I pat the bed.

"Wait, wait, wait. I have notes for this." He strips off his suit jacket, pulling out a notebook and the devil's reading glasses. He sits and perches them on the bridge of his straight nose.

Must want me to lick his face.

I edge closer until our hips bump.

His forearms flex as he flips pages, and he swallows hard when I burrow into him, drawn to the coolness that's the only cure for my ache.

"For a spike, it says…" he trails, finger on the passage.

I know what it says. "I need to come."

He keeps reading, voice strained. "Then you need a nest. And snuggles."

"Need more than that."

"You're supposed to stay hydrated. I'll grab water and then get everything set up so you can…"

He darts to the bathroom, and the faucet rushes.

Without him, the heat rages. I sweat and cradle my belly.

Orion trips on the carpet, sloshing water as he sets down a cup. "What else do you need? Snacks? Heating pad? I always want a heating pad when I'm close to my heat. Doctor Morgan said there were toys…"

Digging in the wheelie cart, he pulls out a row of knotted toys and vibrators. Then he lines up lube and tissues, and somehow finds a pack of crackers. "In case you get hungry."

My belly flutters.

"That should be everything. I'll get out of your way. If you want, I can come back in after you, uh, finish…"

Fuck him, his cute rambling, his glasses, and his blush.

Orion Wyvern is a poison apple.

You know it's toxic, you know it'll hurt, but it's so pretty and juicy. *Who can say no?*

Not me.

Not when my body aches and my vision wavers and he offers to walk away, even though I can *taste* his cinnamon-spiked lust.

He's almost to the door when the word stuck in my throat finally pops. "Wait."

Orion whirls, blue eyes bright. "What do you need?"

So many things.

I need to be independently wealthy, have an unlimited supply of chocolate cake, and a harem of knotted manservants who fuck me and then disappear.

Maybe what I need most is a lobotomy.

Because when I look at Orion standing in the doorway, the thing I want the most is the courage to ask for what I *actually* want.

I want him to stay.

I don't want to do everything myself.

Not all the time.

"Would you…" I swallow hard.

My belly's not so much flutters as a wasp nest hum because omegas aren't built to be rejected, and just risking it makes me choke up bile.

It's the hormones that make me this fragile.

I swear I'll survive if he says no.

Just vibe another one out, alone.

But it's not that easy.

If Orion tells me no, just walks away while I'm mid-spike, and leaves me here to hurt…

That's the end.

Maybe my scent tells how hard I'm begging in my head. Maybe it's the way I twist under another phantom cramp.

Orion comes back.

He kneels on the bed and sets the gentlest hand on my neck. "Do you want me to help?"

It's easier when he asks, when all I have to do is breathe out the word waiting on my lips. "*Yes.*"

He kisses my nose.

That's when I know I'm fucked.

If he jumped me, just pure lust and hormones, I could pretend this is all about need.

Biology.

But nose kisses. Soft and feathery. Those aren't instincts talking.

His eyes are liquid sapphire, his voice as ticklish as velvet. "I'll take such good care of you."

"No sex," I blurt. Because if we go that far, I might as well stamp his name on my ass.

But I need him.

Need him or I'll *burn*.

"I've got you." He hugs me close, lifting my face.

My gasp has a hint of a whine.

"*Shh*," he whispers against my lips.

Orion cups my chin, his soft touch lighting up my spine. Sweat drips down my neck. Molten ache roars between my thighs.

It's so fucking *hot*.

Then Orion Wyvern kisses me.

Slowly, tasting like cool, sweet cider, he teases my mouth with his clever tongue.

I open.

I *submit*.

He gently bites, then licks my lower lip, slipping inside my mouth like melted sugar.

When he pulls back, rumbling with a gentle omega purr, my face drops to the hollow of his throat. I nestle into his fading mate bites and the sweet smell of his skin.

"You're safe," Orion purrs, pulling me against him. "I've got you."

My ass settles between his hips, back to his shirt. He holds me body to body, wrapping me in his arms and cradling me in his scent.

Snaking a hand under my skirt, he flattens a warm palm against my belly.

Orion's touch is more comforting than a heating pad.

Or maybe it's his low voice, the rough whisper that crawls into my ear. "I'll take such good care of you."

He rests one hand over my heart. The other drifts south, making me twist in his arms.

He rubs from my belly button to the top of my mound, but when my legs kick out and my thighs part for him, he doesn't press down.

"Is this okay?" he asks in a throaty whisper, dragging his teeth down my ear.

"*Yesss*." I *like* teeth.

Almost as much as I like the way his cock teases my ass.

My dress rucks around my thighs. The only thing underneath is a pair of panties with a growing wet spot.

Orion rests his hand on my pussy, lighting up every nerve. The slight pressure of his longest finger almost, *almost*, presses between my lips.

I'm goo for him.

"Tell me, Lilah." He cups me harder. "Tell me what feels good. I won't do anything you don't want."

"More." My hips jerk, trying to grind against his finger.

I've touched myself and played with all the toys until I know exactly what speed and thickness I like, but this…

Orion's breath in my ear.

The caramel scent I hate twists with his luscious apple, blending into something more perfect than either of us alone.

His hard body, his gentle hands.

I was lost the second I asked him in the door.

"Orion… Please."

His groan vibrates my temple. "You're so perfect, Lilah. You're so good. Fuck. Want to eat you." He shifts us, sinking his teeth into my neck as his gentle fingers slip into my panties.

I gasp.

The bite's just hard enough to leave me arching into it, wishing he could claim me.

He rubs my pussy up and down, first with broad strokes, then in slow, clit-teasing circles. He's not even inside me, and I'm dripping for him, slick soaking his fingers.

"So wet. So beautiful."

His other hand rubs my chest, casually teasing my razor blade nipples, and he must feel my heart beating so fast I'm about to launch into the air.

But solid arms lock me down, keeping me grounded.

He presses that long, single finger into my heat, then drags it forward to my clit. When he pulls back, breaking contact, I almost riot, afraid he's finally going to run.

Instead, Orion lifts the coated finger to his lips, sucking it by my ear.

"Holy fuck." His hips jerk against my ass. "I've never…" He pushes under my panties and scoops another taste that leaves him panting into my throat.

"Are you easing me or eating me?" I complain.

I'm *dying* for his touch.

"Both."

Fuck it. "Then hurry."

Orion lifts me onto the pillows, propping extras under my head and hips. Then he kisses my forehead. My nose. My cheeks.

The corners of my lips.

He kisses me everywhere, sliding down my body until I'm melting, melting, *gone.*

"Orion…" I lift my hips, but he pushes them back down so he can spread my thighs.

I open wide.

No resistance.

No more fear.

Just *need.*

Kneeling between my knees, Orion pushes my skirt out of the way to kiss the soft curve of my belly.

I've never felt anything like his lips against my skin. The warm, wet touches travel deep inside me, stroking every instinct. My inner muscles clench, not in pain, but in anticipation.

Wish he were alpha.

Want his bite.

Want *him.*

Orion drags down my panties and tosses them, chaining kisses up my inner thigh. "Do you know how beautiful you are?"

He kisses my smooth mound the same way he kisses the tip of my nose. A soft, sweet peck, and every touch makes it that much more obvious how I'm melting.

Slick glistens on my thighs.

Flowing.

More than I've ever seen before.

When I touched myself.

Even when I touched myself imagining *them*, I was never this turned on or desperate.

He spreads me with gentle fingers, and takes a long lick, circling my entrance before flat-tongue lapping up to my clit.

My hips jerk, but he slides up my body, hooking his arms around my thighs. "Don't tease."

I just need…

I just need!

Orion kisses my belly button. "I'm going to lick you 'til your voice gives out, fill you with my fingers. Then I'm going to clean you and snuggle you so fucking tight. And when you wake up, I'll still have you in my arms. Because that's where you belong. To me, Lilah. Not to the alphas. No matter where you go, what you need to do, always come back to me. I'll never let you down again."

I whimper.

Fucking whimper.

I want his mouth.

I want everything he's promising.

"Please. *Orion.*"

Giving me exactly what I need, he licks a luscious figure-eight around my clit, then sucks the sensitive nub into his mouth. The heat of him. The wetness. Even what he does with his nose, adding more sensation with his pressing, urgent touch.

The warm slide of his tongue and his open mouth turns my brain to frantic fuzz. My belly shakes. My thighs tighten. Something unspools inside, probably forever, and I cry out, wetting his face with slick.

"Caramel fucking syrup," he moans, the soft purr in his chest vibrating me before I can come down from the sudden orgasm. He laps my slick like he's eating ice cream, licking every single melted drop.

"More." The ache inside me isn't going away. It's getting hotter, begging for more than his tongue.

"This?" He presses a finger to my entrance. "Or a toy?"

"You." I wiggle my hips, desperate. I want to feel his skin, not silicone.

"Tell me if it hurts."

"It won't hurt. Please."

He slips a long finger inside, then groans when my muscles clench, sucking him deeper. My body wants more. It'll pull in his whole fucking arm if he doesn't give me what I want.

He sinks in a second finger, dipping to suck my clit.

I gush.

So wet. So ready to take so much more.

"Look at you." He strokes in and out, and then I need a third finger. My hips buck, his tongue works, and his fingers pump. My body tightens, one hand yanking his curls, the other digging into a pillow as my spine rocks.

When I finally shatter, they must hear my moan on the roof.

Holy fuck.

I pant, eyes glazed, my abs still twitching.

"Such a good fucking girl." Orion stares over my glistening body with so much possession my heart punches my throat.

Still, he works me, drawing out another aftershock with a thumb on my clit and a palm nestled between my legs.

"Never letting you go," he says huskily.

My defenses are melted.

I can't argue. Can't protest.

All I can do is watch him through fluttering lashes while he follows through on every single thing he promised.

He wipes me with a warm washcloth, finger-combs my hair, and then spoons me against him before wrapping us in blankets and pillows in a perfect cozy nest.

I'm safe for the first time I can remember, with his soft breath tickling my ear. "Sleep. No one can hurt you while I'm here."

Orion asked for nothing.

Gave me everything.

And I don't think I'm ever going to recover.

TWENTY-THREE

LILAH

I WAKE TO A NEW WORLD.

I'm snuggled into Orion's warm chest, my arms locked around his neck, and my legs hugging his hips.

Orion smooths my hair and I'm floating in pure heaven until my memories kickstart.

I go rigid.

"It's okay." He keeps stroking, voice soft. "Still got you."

That's what I'm worried about.

I don't regret a thing.

I want to do it all again. *And more.*

But we should've talked before my hormones hijacked the conversation. "The pack—"

"It's just you and me, koala bear."

"Koala?" *Ugh.* Those things are creepy—with those little weird beak snouts.

Orion sits up, pulling me with him. When he lets go of my back, I don't slip because I'm clinging to him like I'm climbing a phone pole.

He bites my nose. "Koala."

My flush has nothing to do with heat.

This swimmy, dizzy, delicious feeling?

Pretty sure it's happiness.

But it sours when I remember what I have to say. "This doesn't mean anything for the pack."

He lets out a shuddering breath, then squeezes me tight. "Shit. Don't say it like that. I thought you meant this doesn't mean anything."

"This is…" *Everything.*

"Just us. Wyverns are on their fucking own. But we do have to get up. The nurses keep knocking."

Right.

Because I'm in the hospital again. "Did the guys say anything?"

"No idea. I wasn't going to leave you."

My heart clenches.

Ruined.

I am so, so permanently ruined because now I know what it's like to wake up warm and snuggled, and I won't be able to stop myself from wanting more.

"Are you on my team or their team?" I keep my eyes on his chest and the peek-a-boo shadow of his nipple through his dress shirt.

How did he ease me so good and stay fully dressed?

"Yours."

I ignore the belly flutters. "Then you don't mind if I screw with them?"

"Mind?" Orion's laugh bubbles. "That's my love language."

"Good. I'm not showering."

"They're going to fucking flip," he says gleefully.

"Let them in?" I straighten my dress and cover my legs with rumpled blankets that smell like omega sex and caramel apples.

"On it." The second Orion slides open the door, they bull through in a wave of dizzying testosterone.

"Lilah, are you—" Hunter chokes.

Atlas's jaw clicks. He bites back the primal struggle to pounce us as Orion slips between the sheets to spoon me on the bed.

While Jett takes a sentry post, Finn zooms to my tossed panties like a freaking bloodhound, snapping them up and into his pocket.

Right. I wanted to rub my scent in their faces just a little bit, but I forgot Finn's not fuck-with-able.

He's fuckery in its purest form, and he shoots me a pointed grin that says he knows my ass is bare under these blankets.

"Feeling better?" Hunter's brown eyes are bleary, and his shirt's rumpled, with rolled-up sleeves that flash the tattoos I still haven't given a good lick—I mean *look.*

"Much better." I lean into Orion, enjoying how the little motion makes the alphas stiffen. Orion grins into my hair.

Before we can have any fun, Doctor Morgan rolls in to check my vitals. "Looking stable this morning."

"I am. What's the news?"

She shakes her head. "Toxicology showed you were exposed to a hormone stimulant. Did you eat or drink anything that could've been tampered with?"

"Who fucking *dared.*" Atlas's growl is all kinds of stroking, but I feel like I just got shot into space.

Drugged.

How? When?

I shudder at the sense of violation. "All I had was champagne. Orion opened the bottle. A few bites of strawberries."

"Everything was sealed." Orion hugs me close.

Doctor Morgan frowns. "Did anyone have access to your clothes? Perhaps you were exposed to an aerosol? Any strange smells?"

"Nothing. I—" Then I remember. "There was dust all over my dressing room table. I thought it was makeup. A petty prank." Must've left the OCC too long if my danger radar is that rusty.

Should've known.

"I'm sending a team to swab for prints and chemicals." Hunter punches orders into his phone hard enough to crack the screen. "We'll get answers."

"I don't have proof, but let's not waste time. It was Noelle Patrick and her sister, Rachel."

Noelle's been gunning for me since forever and she wasn't subtle with her smirks. Guess she doesn't care if I know she's guilty.

She doesn't think of me as a threat.

She's wrong.

Finn glares at Hunter. "They're already on the list. Just let me fucking ki—"

"*They're mine,*" Jett's voice is barely a mutter, but the fucking *ice.*

I shiver while Doctor Morgan pales.

"Share," Finn agrees happily, rubbing his palms.

"I'm filing a police report," I say before Doctor Morgan calls for backup. Maybe a few police reports, including the one I still owe Rachel for the Brauns.

Let's see how Noelle's smarmy mates run for reelection when she's sucked into an assault scandal.

"Let me run a few more tests, and then you can be on your way." Doctor Morgan edges away from Finn and Jett, making her escape.

I pat my dress, before remembering it doesn't have pockets. "Has anyone seen my—"

"Panties? Mine now."

"They'll look great on you." I lift the blanket, doing my best to ignore Finn's bait. "My phone?"

"Here." Orion hands it to me.

"Thanks." I'm still ragged and reeling, but I have business to take care of. I dial Catherine. "How did I do last night?"

"Fantastic! Oh, my goodness. I've never seen such offers."

Maybe more omegas should pole dance. "Email me the pack info?"

"Already in your inbox. You have a dozen formal offers on the books. A wonderful variety, and more to come! Are we scheduling private dates? You have a raft of requests."

The Wyverns make no effort to hide their eavesdropping, and I don't bother hiding what I have to say. "No. I don't want to schedule anything else."

I'm done.

I'm done playing chatty, pretending to smile, and putting myself out there for alphas who aren't worth the risk. I suck at it, it's awkward, and I desperately need to get back to my regularly scheduled sweatpants, shifter novels, and hermitdom.

Plus, I'm more than done making myself a juicy Redfang target. "Cancel everything. I'll pick heat partners out of the offers I already have."

"Your entire schedule?" Catherine gasps. "Even your date with the Sorensen Pack?"

"Oh… Um. Postpone that one? I'll call you back." They're not off my list entirely—because being disposable is firmly in the pro column—but I'm seriously put off by last night's performance.

Sorensens can't handle my lifestyle.

I can't fucking handle my lifestyle.

"If that's what you want, consider it done. And you're feeling alright? Just say the word if you need our easing team. I'll send Juan Pablo. His touch is *divine*," her purr vibrates the phone.

And the alphas vibrate my room with unhappy growls.

I bite back a smile. "I'll let you know."

"Who the fuck is Juan Pablo?" Finn flicks out a knife.

Orion sets his chin on my shoulder, all lit up with mischief. "Aren't I your easing team?"

"Mmm." I run fingers through his hair, stroking him until his eyes roll back and the alphas twitch. *Fun.* "You're my team."

Orion butterfly-kisses my shoulder, and the air thickens, my breath bottoming out.

Better stop before I'm twitching too.

I clear my throat, fooling no one when the room smells like simmering caramel, then turn to Atlas and Hunter. I'd go straight to the pack leader, but they've been doing some weird power trade-off that shifts their dynamic. "I can't go back to the OCC."

"Right," Atlas rumbles. "Not safe."

"Where do you want to go, Killer?" Hunter leans against the wall, playing casual.

"I thought Honeymoon Hills, but—"

"Abysmal security," Jett offers, giving off murder vibes that have Finn licking his lips and me praying for inner peace.

Stop being attracted to psychos.

I sigh.

Grim reaper energy or not, Jett is right.

The heat suites are just condos. They're *nice* condos—the brochures brag about the spa and pizzeria—but the OCC has ten times their security, and we know how that's been going.

Packs are vetted for OCC events.

I've always doubted how well, but still.

Last night, a scary amount of alphas threw away their respectability to cash in a chance at underworld power.

That would've been enough to make me change my game plan.

But then they had to drug me too.

Makes my stomach churn.

If I'd gone into heat—

I swallow sour bile. "I need a safe place to crash."

"If you're willing to go with us—" Hunter starts.

"I'm not going back to the manor."

The guys trade weird looks.

"About that." Hunter scratches the shaved back of his head. "We sold the manor. In like two hours, by the way. Real estate is fucking crazy. Got twice what the dads originally paid for the place."

"Sold? But that's your home." I was ready to die on this hill.

Turns out, the Wyverns already bulldozed it.

Orion grumbles against my back. "That was never our home. The pack started falling apart the second we moved in."

"After what happened…" Atlas's deep voice softens. "All we had were bad memories. We want a fresh start."

"And we needed cash," Finn adds. "Stars are expensive."

"That's where you got the check?" Doubting Finn on principle, I glance to Hunter to confirm.

He nods.

Something swoops in my belly.

I'm grateful because I have a binder full of offers that never would've come without their help.

Then again, it's messed up that my future was going to come down to that.

I frown. "If you sold the mansion, then where've you been living?"

"We have a condo on the Wyvern compound," Orion chews his plush lip. "But we can't bring Lilah there. It's…"

"A pit?" I lift my brows. The manor was so squidgy, I shudder to imagine how bachelor chic their condo would be. Probably carpeted in chip bags and crushed cans.

"Not the condo." Hunter breaks eye contact. "I may have already reserved you a unit in the family complex."

Wow. That doesn't sound like a setup.

My shoulders start to rise, but Orion gives them a calming rub. "Mated agents live there with their families. Omegas, too. It's mostly underground, so security's rock solid."

Underground sounds good in theory, but I glance from alpha to alpha. "No one will try to lock me in when my heat hits?"

They rush to make sounds of denial.

Jett's farthest away, an ice block sentinel guarding the door, but I hear his hissed whisper like his lips are at my ear. "*Never.*"

Hunter's voice rises over their sounds. "We want you to do whatever you want to do. Hell, invite Juan Pablo."

"All we care about is keeping you safe." Atlas flanks Jett like there's a sniper waiting to ambush—and given how things are going, he's not wrong to be ready. "If there were anywhere more secure than the compound, that's where we'd take you."

"I want to help tracking Dominik." I was trying to play ostrich, focusing on my heat problem and hoping he'd fade away, but that snaky motherfucker made this a you-or-me situation.

And he's the one going down.

"Anything you want," Hunter quickly agrees.

Finally.

This is how it should've been since the beginning.

––––––

ONCE THE DECISION IS MADE, everything moves fast. After a few more tests, I'm discharged and the guys escort me to the police station.

When we move from the car to the building, the five of them surround me in a solid wall that's even more intimidating while they're rocking what's left of last night's rumpled, blood-spattered suits.

Jackets missing, ties lost, and way too many buttons undone on those dress shirts.

Hunter tugs me just before we hit the doors. He rubs my hand with a thick thumb, and everything but him disappears. "I want you to report Noelle, but I also want you to know this doesn't end in court. Blood for blood. She can't touch you and walk."

I thought Hunter was the softie, but there's so much dark conviction in his promise, I want to roll over and let him take care of *everything.*

Possibly forever.

But then Finn presses behind me, dropping an equally dark whisper into my ticklish ear. "Say the word, Starfighter. I'll turn those bitches into people leather."

A shudder rolls down to my toes, but I hide it with a swat. "We're at the police station."

Hunter, Atlas, and Orion give co-signing shrugs.

Jett nods. "Leather-bound book."

"Bro." Finn fist-bumps him, beaming.

When the hell did they become best murder buddies?

"Let's get you inside." Hunter steers my shoulders, and I let him lead.

Not sure my brain is working anymore.

Atlas steps up when we approach the desk in the center of the big entrance foyer. The other guys circle, shielding me from passing looks.

"Mister Wyvern!" A middle-aged alpha flies out, bypassing the secretary so he can be the first to shake Atlas's hand. "How can I help you?"

"Chief." Atlas returns the shake. "My… Lilah's here to make a report."

"Anything you need. Come straight to my office."

Who knew you could be a VIP with the police?

The chief, a detective, and a social worker all crowd into the guy's corner office suite with Wyvern Pack, ready to solemnly listen to my statement.

If I'd come alone, I'd probably still be standing at the front desk trying to explain my story to another authority figure who won't listen to the truth.

With Wyvern Pack's blessing, I'm automatically legit. I'll take it, but I ink the moment onto my things-to-change-about-the-world list.

Everyone who's been hurt deserves to be believed.

"Can you tell us what happened?" The detective asks, notepad ready.

He's going to need the whole pad for this story.

I spill.

Last night's drugging. The beatings. The bullying. Two sisters' crimes over years and years.

The Wyverns make angry beehive rumbles and choked growls. Atlas snaps the handle off his coffee mug, and whatever Finn's muttering has the social worker turning green.

Jett's reaction surprises me the most.

He scratches his arm until it bleeds.

When the police step out to discuss my case, leaving the tension thick as the Wyverns plot revenge murders I'll happily watch them commit, I steal the gray silk tie poking out of Jett's pocket.

"You're not allowed to hurt yourself." I rope his wrist to his chair.

"I deserve to hurt. What they did to you—"

"Neither of us deserves to hurt." I pull the knot hard. "I'll punish you if you need to be punished."

The second those cursed fucking words spill out, my thoughts catch up with my mouth. *Shit.* "Not that you need to be... I didn't mean—"

"Punish *me*." Finn offers me his wrists and a pair of freaking police handcuffs he lifted.

I bat him away.

But Jett.

"I understand." He fingers the tie with a gravity-crushing gaze that makes me shiver down to my soul.

Understand what?

I don't even understand. "I just don't want to see you hurting yourself. Okay?"

"Yes." His head tips up, and those *eyes*—

Dark, glittering *need*.

My breath hitches.

I swear I said no strings.

No ties or bonds or promises.

But Jett cuffed himself to me without permission, and when he strokes the knotted silk around his wrist, my heart gives a fluttering quiver.

I think I just walked myself into his snare.

TWENTY-FOUR

LILAH

THE OFFICERS FINISH TAKING my statement, and I feel so much lighter after the truth is free. Now I don't have to hide or suffer, and hypothetically, Noelle's going down.

Or being made into a series of encyclopedias.

Don't care as long as she pays.

The lightness only lasts until we hit Wyvern House HQ.

Pulling up to the gates, there's no way to mistake the place as anything but a military compound.

Cameras and K-9 units.

Fences and barbed wire.

When we pull through the parking gate, muscle men in tight Wyvern camo use mirrors to check under our car for bombs.

Atlas is right.

If I'm not safe here, I'm not safe anywhere.

All I want is a few days of peace and no attempted kidnappings so I can pick my heat partners and chill down my hard-ridden hormones.

We drop the car in an underground garage, then head through an access door with metal detectors. Hunter set me up with a guest pass featuring an obnoxiously large omega symbol.

As if I need ID. The guards' eyes bulge the second they catch my scent.

Wyverns collapse to shield me, Orion at my side, and a box of alphas surrounding us. Now I can't see or smell anything but Jett's tight shoulders, cedar, and his snarl. "*Eyes down.*"

I shouldn't like their protection.

It should feel suffocating.

Restricting.

But the tighter they close me in, the more I feel like I can finally breathe.

Way to logic, Omega.

When the guys swipe their badges, an angry beep sounds a few times before a guard hesitantly speaks. "Sir… Your access was voided."

"Run it again," Atlas says through his teeth.

Beep.

Beep.

Beeeeeeep.

"I can call my superior…" The guard trembles.

"*Shit.*" I'm the only one who hears Orion's soft mutter. I offer him my hand, and he tugs it into his pocket, squeezing my fingers.

"I'll apply for a family pass. Shouldn't take longer than a few hours." Atlas claps Hunter's shoulder. "You're in charge. Get them home safe."

"Fucking Scorpio." Hunter shakes his head. "Say the word and we'll sneak you back on the compound."

"I can handle it. You have more important things to take care of." He moves to us, and I still.

I never forget how big Atlas is, but it's not 'til he's standing right in front of me that I feel so fucking *tiny*. Orion's grip tightens.

I don't know what I'm expecting Atlas to do. Maybe bark at us to obey Hunter?

Instead, he puts one palm on my head, the other on Orion's.

He pats us.

Gentle. Like you'd pet a soft bunny.

My spinal cord loses tension. My knees give.

Because *holy shit*, do I love being petted.

Orion reacts the same quivering way.

Least I'm not the only silly rabbit.

"Be careful," Atlas whispers. "I'll come back to you as soon as I can."

The heat of his palm lingers on my head long after he's gone.

Orion blinks. "Wha—*what*?"

I shudder. "Same."

"Let's go, team," Hunter calls, shaking us back to reality.

I swat a few stomach butterflies and keep moving.

Hormones.

My reactions are just hormones.

Now that Orion has my hand, he keeps it as we cross the compound. It's split into clearer areas than the OCC's campus, with walls and razor wire marking zones to avoid.

I have zero plans to explore.

I'm just here to hide.

We collect a few curious looks, but anyone in Wyvern gear who spots my escort salutes, flinches, or whips the hell around and jogs in the opposite direction.

Finn licks his lips. "They've missed us."

Jett nods. "No one will bother Lilah."

After a lifetime of experience, I'm gonna hit the doubt button on that, but I'm glad the guys inspire so much fear.

They make a great shield.

Hunter takes us to a block of clustered residences with a court-yard in the middle. He swipes us in, then leads into an elevator.

It goes down until my ears pop.

When the bell dings, Hunter waves us out. "Floor seventeen's all yours, Killer."

I'm expecting a bunker. Like steel walls, exposed pipes, and buckets of emergency rations.

So when Hunter opens another set of doors with a retinal scan, my jaw hits the softly carpeted floor.

We walk into a sunken living room decorated from a home show. It has a huge cloud of a sectional sofa, fuzzy rugs, and blankets and pillows by the basketful. Everything's gold and white and so comfy cozy, I have to bite back a gleeful omega moan.

No windows.

Instead, ceiling-mounted light strips beam out soft, mock sunlight.

I've never felt so at home.

Anywhere.

Ever.

The living room opens to a huge marble kitchen with god-tier appliances and a cute breakfast nook. I have to remind myself it's just a hideout and not my dream home.

"There's a nest and a ton of empty bedrooms," Hunter says. "Take whichever you like. We're having your stuff shipped."

"Send mine too." Orion gives my hand a last squeeze before letting it free. "I'm grabbing a room. You mind?"

"Go ahead." I don't plan to be here that long, so if anything, I'm the one who should be asking him to borrow a bed.

The Wyverns post up in the living room while I creep around.

There's one long hallway that pulls me like I'm being summoned—basically a tunnel, only it's carpeted with the softest fabric that's ever touched my feet.

When I reach the end, it feels like crossing onto a private island. Not a sound reaches this far, and the silence wraps me like a hug.

I hesitate to open the door.

If this nest is as freaking perfect as the rest of the place…

But I can't help myself.

I have to look.

And *why*?

Why do they have to do this to me?

Three steps lead up to a huge mattress platform too massive to be called a bed. I flick on the light, and the ceiling twinkles with LEDs embedded like stars. When I hit the controller, they flash in rainbow colors.

In case anyone wants to disco fuck.

A little alcove has a mini-fridge, and a pass-through to a bathroom with a deep, deep soaking tub and an orgy shower.

I squish down every omega instinct jellified by the perfection.

But if you gave me a blank piece of paper and told me to sketch my dream nest—

Bam!

Here it is.

When Orion enters it's worse.

I can feel that tingle at the back of my neck. I'd claw the shit out of anyone who invaded the territory my body instantly recognizes as *mine*.

Bigger problem?

I recognize *Orion* as mine.

So when he leans his chin on my shoulder, all I want to do is yank him up the steps, swan-dive into a pillow mountain, and snuggle 'til we both pass out.

"Kind of perfect, right?" There's a wistful note in his voice.

"Too perfect." I heel-turn and get the fuck out before my brain writes the alphas into the snuggle fantasy.

I choose the closest bedroom, which turns out to be the master suite. I'm itching to get out of my dress, so I peek into the closet, hoping someone left a stray pair of sweats.

The walk-in's so huge it has a chandelier and one of those sitty puffs in the middle.

It's *overflowing* with clothes.

I tug a sleeve with tags—a sweater, maybe cashmere if that's the material that feels this soft?—and wince at the zeroes.

It has no scent. So no owner. New.

I march to the living room. Jett disappeared and Orion's still poking around, so I'm left with the unholy duo. "What's with the clothes?"

"They're yours." Hunter won't meet my gaze.

"Why?"

"Because online shopping," Finn chirps. "Star. Wait until you see what I—"

Hunter puts him in a headlock. "Want a tour of the common areas?"

"Is there a pool?" I ask, slowly losing my mind.

"Olympic size."

Thank the chlorine gods.

I need a deep spiritual cleansing.

I'm dizzy with rescues and gifts and perfect cave homes that make me start thinking I can keep things that'll never be mine.

I duck back into my room, where my fully-stocked closet has a lifetime supply of expensive yoga gear and swimsuits. I change into a navy one-piece, throw on comfy yoga clothes, and then bump into Orion in the hall.

"Lunch? You must be hungry."

"Sure." I'm not, thanks to stress and hormones, but that's exactly why I need to eat.

"Where'd Jett go?" I ask as Finn and Hunter escort us back up the elevator.

"Talking to prisoners from last night," Hunter says.

"*Talking.*" I lift a brow.

Finn *hmms*. "I get to talk with what's left of them."

Orion pats my arm. "Jett will get answers."

"I bet." I should probably feel worse about the torture thing, but stop trying to kidnap omegas, and you'll be fine.

The guys show me around the upper floors of the bunker building. There's a grocery store, coffee shop, spa, and even playgrounds where kids run and parents cluster together, laughing.

So happy.

It's like the childhood you wish you had.

Can't relate.

Female omegas go glitter-eyed with gossip when they spot me

surrounded by Wyverns, but nobody dares to come into their protective triangle.

"You can move around the public levels," Hunter says. "We'll be in and out while we hunt Dominik, but one of us will be with you at all times."

"As long as I can help with the hunt." After all the attempts to spirit me away, I'm all about the extra protection.

We walk into the cafeteria as a pack, and Finn grabs a black plastic tray. "What are you eating, Star?"

"Everything," I sigh, smelling something fried.

The place looks more like a fancy mall food court than a mess hall, with vendors at the edges of the room and groups of booth seats in the middle.

Spotting someone with a milkshake, I beeline to the burger stand, but when I pick up a tray, Hunter snatches it from my fingertips. "Let me."

"I can carry it."

"Why?" Finn leans on me, soaking me in oranges and gunpowder.

"Because I have hands?"

Nobody listens.

When it's our turn, I order a cookies n' cream milkshake.

Orion *tsks*. "You want to lecture me about nutrition?"

"All you ordered was onion rings."

"You told me to eat a vegetable."

I'm grabbing for my milkshake with greedy hands when Hunter and Finn snap, blocking me from the alpha that just appeared at our backs.

"Who's this?" The alpha smiles, unfazed by Finn's warning growl. I peek around Hunter.

Guy's cute. Dark, dreamy eyes and spiky hair, wet from a shower. I hum in appreciation, drawing his gaze and a wicked smile.

Hunter blocks my view again. "Fuck off, Razer."

"Don't upset our omega." Orion munches an onion ring, casually selling himself out.

"But you're—"

"Some of us were blessed with two," Hunter cuts him off.

The guy scoffs. "I don't see a bite. What's your name, pretty omega?"

"Lilah," I answer, just to hear them snarl. "What's yours?"

"Eason Razer. Razer Pack. And, Beautiful, if the Wyverns don't treat you right—"

Hunter rips a chainsaw growl. "You wanna meet me on grudge night, E?"

I shiver—totally because my milkshake's cold.

Totally.

"No, no, no, no, no! Y'all enjoy your lunch." Eason scampers into the crowd.

But the second he's out of sight, Eason ceases to exist. I secretly love the way the three of them go back to grabbing me fries, heaping the trays they're carrying for me.

French fries.

That's how easy I am.

Every freaking time.

We stop at the pizza, curry, and salad stations, but every time I grab a plate, one of them takes it away.

I walk empty-handed to a booth. After a quick scuffle, Finn and Orion snag the seats at my side. Hunter pouts an unfairly fat lower lip on his own side of the table.

I make a power move, snatching all the fries to horde. "*Mine.*"

"It's all yours, Starfry." Finn pushes over his ketchup.

Orion gives me his spicy ranch.

I wish Atlas and Jett were here, because this is how things need to be run.

When I'm stuffed thanks to three table-mates who keep refilling my plate, they continue the tour, taking me down past the gloriously huge pool to the weight and training gyms.

Hunter leads us into a huge practice room with a padded floor and agent teams sparring. It's soaked with sweat and old pheromones. So many alphas, I have to plug my nose.

"I planned a formal training routine for you," Hunter says, showing me to a corner with punching bags. "We can start tomorrow."

I glance around the room, watching alphas watching me. Not stalkery yet, but I'm in no place to relax. "And if they come after me?"

"Won't happen. Everyone here's a full agent. Remember the team that came at you when you visited the training center?"

"Vaguely."

"They're still on punishment."

"When are the dads getting their punishment?" *When are the rest of you?*

Hunter's easy smile hardens. "Been thinking about that."

"Invite me to the beating. Better yet, train me so I can beat you all myself."

"Nothing would make me happier. Want to practice a few moves?"

"Sure." I always feel better when I can move, and I'm at least sure the guys won't let anyone screw with me while they're here.

Plus, I have knives in my bathing suit.

Hunter walks me through some easy punches and ways to break grabs. When I can easily throw off his hand on my shoulder, flipping him onto the mats, I tag off to grab water while Finn and Orion rotate into the mix.

It's insanely fun watching them trade punches. Finn and Orion are just as fast as Hunter. I tag back in, and with their long reaches, I have to work to stay out of their hands.

It's *less* fun when a sweat-drenched Hunter strips off his T-shirt, hitting me with a face full of salty-sweet mezcal and wicked tattoos.

I've been sweating, but now I sweat pheromone *bullets*.

Orion and Finn's scents, plus all the other alphas' wrap around me and my blood starts to simmer.

Hotter and hotter.

Shit.

Shit.

"Lilah," Orion's whisper comes out hoarse. "You're spiking."

"No I'm not," I yelp, tearing away from his hands and arms and eyes.

"Please don't lie." He clutches his chest. "Tell us when you need us and we'll never let you down again."

"I just need to swim."

"Lilah. I can help—"

"I have it under control."

That's what I tell myself as I fall back into my favorite habit, running the fuck away from the trio of males who crawl inside my brain like poison.

I need to swim.

Run.

Dance.

Scream into a jar.

Do something to burn off this energy that doesn't involve letting them four-way fuck whatever's left of my common sense.

I haven't even looked at the packets Catherine emailed. I'm tooling around, playing house while the clock ticks on my heat.

Stupid.

The Wyverns' scents cling to me like a freaky fruit salad—apples, oranges, and honey—and I dodge alphas, sprinting to the pool like that water's my only salvation.

It's been way, waaaay too long.

The pool's dim and totally empty. I strip off my clothes on a jog.

Someone's behind me, but I sense it's one of them, otherwise my instincts wouldn't be shouting to jump into their arms instead of the water.

I cannonball.

The water splashes, and I hug my knees, sinking, sinking, sinking until I hit bottom.

The water swallows me.

I'm waiting for the release. That cozy, suffocating nothing feeling that'll blot out the Wyverns and the threats and the cursed fucking heat rushing through my veins.

My heart doesn't slow.

My temperature doesn't cool.

Because instead of zoning out, I flash back to the last time I was underwater.

In the fucking barrel.

Wet.

Hot.

Pain.

TWENTY-FIVE

FINN

LILAH EXPLODES INTO THE WATER.

I start counting seconds.

The seconds until she comes up. The seconds until I can show her my surprise. The seconds until I can make her mine.

That's why I notice the exact second Lilah jerks.

Angry bubbles froth to the surface, and she kicks but goes nowhere.

More bubbles.

My heart gnaws at my ribs.

Fuck waiting another second.

I dive deep into the gray.

Lilah's blush lips are dark, almost purple, and she grips her throat, flailing instead of swimming.

I snag her and kick off, rocketing us to the surface.

When we punch through, my Star takes a wracking, gasping breath.

She shakes.

Trembling.

Too cold.

Her skin's all pebbles, and I don't know what the fuck to do to make it better.

"Finn." She throws her arms around my neck.

So cold.

"Got you." I walk us out of the water, holding her hips. Hate the way she shakes but I love the way she clings.

Fucking needs me.

But shit. She can't be this cold.

"Gonna warm you up." I rub her back.

"Don't let go," she whispers into my collar bone. "Just for a little…"

"Never letting go." I carry her into the sauna.

It's empty.

Careful not to jostle my treasure, I flick on the dim light. Hit the dial. Toss water onto the stones and let them *hisssss.*

The heat and the steam bring me back to life when everything is dark and broken.

They'll work for Lilah too.

I carry her to the corner bench and seat her on my lap.

She nuzzles into me.

So sweet.

"What happened?" I rub her back, stroking the silk of her wet hair.

"Flashback."

"Of?" *Someone new to kill?*

"Barrel."

Fuck.

Well, I'm not killing myself.

Should, but I can't lose Lilah. "You're here and you're mine." A rumble-purr kicks up, so natural.

I'm a nurturing *beast.*

Her candy-flavored breath puffs against my Adam's apple.

Minutes drag. Her breathing never slows, but it changes from a ragged panic that scissor-kicks my brainstem to a desperate fucking pant that juices my knot.

Don't think she feels it yet, but she will.

Her hips are right fucking there.

I keep purring, and her fingers drift. They freeze at my neck. She brushes the edge of a dark line that spills above my shirt. "You got a tattoo."

"You want to see it, Starshine?" Been dying to show her, to get her alone. That's why I snarled until they hung back in the gym.

Can't let those other fuckers see.

They'll copy.

This shit is my intellectual property.

Lilah leans back to watch.

Wish she'd always be watching me.

Her cheeks are flushed.

Pink.

So pretty. Love her little nose. The wrinkle it gets when she's all *the hell is he doing now*.

You don't even know, Star.

I yank the hem of my tee and whip it off.

Lilah's little rosebud lips part. "You…"

I have more sessions before the colored parts are finished, but letters are done.

L I L A H.

Dreams come true when she traces the L of her name, satin fingers running over my skin. "Why?"

"Because I'm yours." My body, this whole fucking shell.

All hers.

She brushes a butterfly wing, following its morph into a knife blade. All the pretty, sharp, Lilah things. "This is real ink? Permanent?"

"Forever."

She makes a fist. "You're trying to break me."

"*Never*," I purr. "I want to keep you. My mate."

Lilah's perfume spikes. "You can't say shit like that and not follow through."

"That's why I'm saying it."

"*Fuck*."

My purr hitches. Love that word on her lips. I wanna find out what other sweet, filthy things I can drag out of that mouth.

Lilah grabs my neck and squeezes.

Both hands.

My dick goes so fucking hard.

"Finn." She leans until our foreheads touch, peering deep, deep into the empty well. "Are you serious?"

"Serious about you." Nothing else can hold my attention, but when Lilah stares into my eyes, her breath and heat are mine and my world's alive.

Chubby-ass baby angels break into song.

"Don't move." She squeezes my throat.

No one on this frigid fucking planet can tell me what to do.

But Lilah.

She could tell me to walk in traffic.

Which lane, baby girl?

So when she tells me not to move, I'm stillness. That moment before I pull the trigger, when everything stops.

Including time.

Lilah takes the lips that already belong to her.

Her sweet mouth is softer than marshmallows, and her breath is all vodka and brown sugar.

Addictive.

Better than ten shots and a base jump.

She puts color in my veins, stirring my heart, my cock, and my primal instinct to stake a fucking claim.

I'm not good at being good, but I *obey*.

I hold still when I want to flip her, fuck her, and scare the bad things away. Sweep her tongue into my mouth and play until she's gasping.

Lilah's choked moan makes it too hard to hold back.

The sauna's steam holds us in our own little hot pocket. Her pale skin glistens with sweat, and every lickable drop drenches me in torched-sugar pheromones.

Straddling my lap, Lilah starts to work her hips. It's jerky. Clumsy.

So fucking sexy cute.

She grinds on my cock, and the heat of the sauna's nothing compared to the molten hot steam of her perfect cunt.

Her perfume blooms 'til syrup chokes my throat.

Lilah uses me like a toy, rubbing a broken rhythm over my diamond-hard cock.

Best shit ever.

I purr and growl. Anything to make her keep going.

"Not enough…" Lilah pants against my lips. "Need… Need…"

"Use me."

"Can't… If you knot me, I'll… We can't. But it hurts. *Finn*. It hurts."

A panicky fire blooms inside me, electric and crazed. I never panic.

Until now.

Need to help. Need to make her feel better. "No knot. Let me taste you, Starfire. You take what you need."

I dive on the bench and haul her by her thighs until she straddles my face with her heat hovering just above my chin.

She stares down at me with parted lips.

Dazed and sweaty.

Fuck.

There's a slick spot at her center, darker than the damp fabric of her bathing suit.

Smells like caramel syrup heaven.

"Use me, Starshine." I don't touch her, just lick my lips and lie back, waiting for her to choose.

"I shouldn't." She lets out a jagged breath.

But when Lilah locks my gaze, her eyes are sex and brimstone.

She needs me.

"You're an omega, little Star. You do whatever the fuck you want."

"Is that how it works?"

"From now on."

Her shoulders shake, then firm.

She pushes aside the crotch of her suit, baring the smooth, slick skin that's everything I dreamed. "Show me."

Then Lilah motherfucking Darling mounts my face.

Best day of my life.

TWENTY-SIX
LILAH

HOVERING OVER FINN'S MOUTH, I don't know what hits harder.

His scent, his purr, or his massive fucking chest piece that says **LILAH** like he tattooed it there to save me a seat.

I'm so sweaty.

And panic attack?

What panic attack?

Finn purred it out, then set me on fire.

He grips my thighs so good they dimple.

I hiss, keeping my center just out of reach, even though he lifts, trying to sneak a taste.

Want him so bad.

Instead of giving in, I squeeze his head between my knees. "I'm using you. So don't think—"

"Star." His raggedy voice is brain-meltingly hot, his breath puffing against my swollen, exposed wetness. "Use me however the fuck you want."

If I'm honest, I've been thinking about Finn like this for a long time. Then last night, when he carried me to safety…

I'm only human.

Only omega.

I might have willpower for days, but not even I can resist

when my body's on fire and he has the cure—not when Finn inks my name on his skin and says he wants to keep me forever.

I sink onto his mouth.

Finn moans into my body, his soft hum zinging straight to my clit.

He darts his tongue inside.

I quake.

Kneeling over him, I should feel exposed, but between the sauna's steam and my own heat, we're in a fuzzy world of our own.

"So slick for me, Starshine. So fucking good." He mutters into my heat, then starts to move his tongue.

Finn laps at my entrance.

I don't know what to do with my hands except brace against the wall. When Finn grips my hips, pulling me tighter, I grab hold of his arms.

We're connected.

I tremble.

Too good.

His heat and his touch are everything I didn't know I needed.

"Ride me. Like this." Finn rocks my hips back and forth, helping me find the right rhythm.

It feels so good, I tip forward, shaking. My ass goes up and my elbows hit the bench.

He growls at the change of angle, delving deeper, pulling me down. My walls flutter, craving something thicker than his tongue.

But then he licks up to my clit and starts to suck.

My thighs shake, my belly tightens, and a sudden climax rolls until I'm twitching against his face. The rush of slick has me crying out and him sucking glossy lips.

"I didn't mean to—"

"*Again.*" Finn's eyes are green fire. He laps up the slick like he's starving and yanks my hips down for another taste.

He's already licked me halfway to a second orgasm when the

sauna door flies open.

"Lilah. Are you—" Hunter freezes.

"Lilah?" Orion pushes past, then curses, quickly pulling Hunter in and slamming the door.

Their scents whirl into the steam.

Spiked cider and smoky mezcal.

Finn couldn't give a shit, fully booked tongue-flicking my clit, his juicy purr vibrating me better than a rabbit.

I'm shaking, panting. "*Can't stop.*"

"Don't stop," Hunter rasps, low and sultry.

Orion moves to my side. Kisses my ear. "Do you want us to leave, koala bear?"

Oh, fuck.

This is everything I didn't want.

Everything I feared.

Everything I fucking need.

The way they watch me like no one else exists. Soft touches and voices and care.

It'll kill me when it doesn't last.

But I've come this far. Might as well see how much fucking farther I can fall. "*Stay.*"

Orion climbs over Finn, then he and Hunter both lift me up, one supporting either hip, helping me find the best angle to grind Finn's face.

"Is he making you feel better?" Hunter whispers in my ear. I don't know why, but the stroke of his thumb on my hip is just as sweet as the sweep of Finn's tongue.

My voice breaks. "Ye-ess."

"You're so beautiful, Lilah." Orion kisses my neck. "Look at you, getting off on our alpha. He's so lucky you're letting him take care of you."

"I—*Unh.*" Something's wrong with what he just said, but I can't make words. Can't speak. Can't think with the three of them touching me, purring until every inch of me is loose and vibrating.

Someone teases my entrance with a finger just as Finn gives my clit a toothy nip.

I scream.

Arch.

Try to lift off because it feels too good, too intense, but they hold me in place, letting Finn milk every last twist of my body.

Every last whimper.

I come so hard, I'd fall off the bench if there weren't three sets of hands waiting, fighting to be the one to catch me.

Hunter wins the war while I go semi-comatose.

He drags me into his lap so he can rub my belly while Finn licks my thighs clean.

Orion works his fingers through the tangles in my wet hair, only stopping to twist Finn's head, yanking him to the spot he missed high on my inner thigh.

"This isn't real." The steam cooked my brain and created a fever dream.

"It's real." Hunter kisses my neck, and I can't help hoping he's reserving his spot. "It's what you deserve."

"But—"

Orion covers my mouth. "You don't have to trust us forever, but at least trust us to take care of you. Look how good we can be."

My only response is a panicked baby goat noise.

"Go get her a towel." Hunter nudges Finn.

They swaddle me in ten layers of fabric before carrying me out of the sauna. Between the steam, their stroking touches, and the best orgasms of my life, I'm so tapped out my eyelids droop.

"*Rest*," Hunter makes the softest bark.

I'm out of options.

Places to run.

Places to hide.

Just finally fucking out of willpower to resist.

All I can do is give in.

TWENTY-SEVEN

LILAH

I WAKE to a full-face view of my name on Finn's chest, three bodies in my bed, and the realization that I've let this go way too fucking far.

Finn and Hunter have me alpha-sandwiched, and Orion tangles in our legs, face nested in my belly.

It's warm.

It's safe.

It's much too fucking perfect.

So, naturally I panic, kicking my way out of the cuddle pile.

There's a yelp and a flash of pain that says I just kneed somebody in the face.

"What's wrong?" Hunter untangles from my sheets.

I dive out of bed, putting my back in the corner so I can reorient my whole entire worldview.

We're in the bedroom I chose yesterday, in the perfect cozy cave home. I wear my bathing suit and a sheet while three sexy, disheveled men with my scent rubbed all over their skin watch me like the candy they haven't finished sucking.

Shit.

Before I can decide whether to bolt, or maybe dive under the big bed, my stomach rumbles.

"You need food." Orion puts a hand on his taut bare abs. "Oh. *We* need food."

Hunter stretches his arms above his head, and the shoulder flex makes me choke. "I'll go—"

"I'll cook!" Any excuse to escape this room and their pheromones and the traitorous, happy warmth in my soul.

I grab the robe that's mine now, hung on the back of the bathroom door and dash out, hoping to finally catch my breath.

Atlas and Jett sit on the sofa like two kids in time out. Stacks of flattened cardboard pile by the door from whatever they spent the morning moving in.

They snap to life when I careen past, shooting into the kitchen.

Atlas jumps to his feet in those stupid pants that hug his thick thighs. "What happened?"

"Nothing!" I say, too high-pitched. "Just hungry. Gonna cock. I mean *cock*. I mean *cook*!"

I dive headfirst into the fridge, pretending to rummage while I deep-freeze my shame.

My heat spike's soothed, and my panic attack worked itself out, but my baseline is so wrecked. I take a few calming breaths while holding heavy eye contact with the cow on the milk jug.

I'm going to be okay.

This is fine.

I'll erase all memories of face-sitting orgasms, and go back to living a peaceful, quiet life, just me and my vibrators, alone in the woods.

Shit.

Is that even what I want anymore?

The heifer gives me serious side-eye.

I know, I know.

I liked being with them just as much as I liked waking up next to them, and I need a fucking minute.

So I take a few minutes, head in the fridge, hitting the button every time the appliance chirps.

Eventually, my neck cools and the silence behind me thickens, gazes burning my shoulders. I have to peek.

The five of them lean at the kitchen island like action figures.

Watching.

Judging?

But no. They can't read my mind.

Yet.

Although Jett stares so intensely with those dark, dark eyes, maybe he spent the night practicing.

"We'll help cook," Atlas starts. "I've been learning."

"I'll help *cock*." Finn licks his lips.

Hunter smacks him.

"No, no. I've got it. Sit." They had my fridge stocked like they planned to visit anyway.

I fish out eggs, bacon and sausages, and these super-soft English muffins, then focus on the food so I can ignore the wall of alpha.

I've trained for this.

So, so many home ec classes on how to prepare a nutritious, loving meal for your pack.

Who knew I'd get to put my skills to use?

I'll *show* them how Lilah Darling's love tastes.

Pawing through the cupboards for seasoning, I find a box of sauces and spices that are clearly Orion's work. One called NEMESIS comes in a teeny eye-dropper marked with warnings in three languages.

I stealthily add a few drops to my scrambled eggs. While I flip meats, I reluctantly let Orion man the toaster, but he's on a burn notice.

When the eggs are done, he catches me sprinkling on more chili flakes.

With zero reaction, Orion grabs the shaker of chili salt and gives the plate a hearty sprinkle.

That's when I know he's my fucking soulmate.

Orion's blue eyes twinkle—I'm sure mine do *not*—as we serve the platters in the breakfast nook.

I sit at the spot they saved me at the head of the table, but before I can make myself a plate, Atlas hands me the heaping one he already made for me.

He hands the second plate to Orion.

He's being so sweet, I'm almost sorry for what he's about to experience.

Then again…*nah*.

The unsuspecting alphas dig into Lilah Darling's fire eggs.

Jett chokes first.

"Did I forget to put water on the table? My bad."

Hunter goes down next, thumping his chest. He turns to me with red, tearing eyes of betrayal.

Now they know something's wrong, but they're big manly alphas, so they say nothing.

Atlas turns to Orion, maybe hoping to get a lifeline.

"Delicious." My partner in crime shovels eggs like nothing's wrong. There's a hint of forehead sweat, but otherwise, his poker face is immaculate.

I take a bite. The eggs are so magma hot they give third-degree lip burns. I smile as my tongue goes numb. "What do you think?"

Atlas takes a bite. His eyes widen, and he swallows hard. "Guh-good."

Finn choke-laughs. "This is how you want to play it, Starfire?"

I make eye contact, asserting dominance as I shake more chili flakes onto my plate, then take another bite. I love the burn that warms me all the way through. "What? I like spicy."

Atlas, brave soldier, keeps lifting his fork and chewing. But every time he blinks, it's like he's seeing the devil.

Jett sighs and helps himself to another scoop. His skin flames angry red. Instead of his killer, clean complexion, he looks like he did ten shots of tequila and a marathon.

"*Liiiiiilaaaah*." Hunter dabs teary eyes with his napkin. "*Why?*"

I can't help it.

I lose my shit, gripping my belly and giggling like an idiot. Orion collapses, cackling into my shoulder.

Payback is sweet *and* ongoing.

They eat everything, and then I make them do the dishes.

I move to Jett, who's loading rinsed plates into the dishwasher. "Did you get any good info after you talked with the guys from the afterparty?"

He stills, maybe surprised I'm talking to him.

Half the time, I want to give him an exorcism, but I also can't look away. Someone needs to watch him.

And if I keep watching, I keep hoping I'll catch a glimpse of my JJ.

Jett straightens, drying his long fingers on a dish towel. "They knew you were going to be drugged."

Shit. "Is the Patrick Pack working with the Redfangs?"

"Unlikely," Jett says. "They're the ones who hired us to assassinate Erik Redfang. Dominik knows and wants them dead."

"So Rachel and Noelle just want to screw with me and they're not above calling in the underworld." I shouldn't be surprised, but I am.

Because why bother? I'm not a threat.

They'd never have to see me again if they stopped coming at me just because they can.

Busy scrubbing the bacon pan, Atlas rumbles. "Noelle's being brought in for questioning today."

Hunter nods. "Plus our guys pulled her prints off your station. She's fucked."

"Pays to know the chief."

"He owes us some favors," Atlas says, still scrubbing.

I hope that when I crack this whole Redfang thing open, the Wyverns owe *me* some favors too. "Do you have the Redfangs' financials?"

Hunter rubs his thick neck. "Bunch of files from Dom's island and the other sites we've hit. Teams have been sifting through the paper trail."

"Let me see."

"J, when's your appointment?" Hunter asks.

"Afternoon."

"Good. Bring Lilah into the office and grab everything. At, you going to class?"

"After this." Atlas scrubs that pan the same single-minded focus he'd use to clean a rifle. "Be back tonight."

"Then, Finn, Orion, help move the rest of Lilah's boxes. And unpack the liquor. I have a meeting with the dads."

"How many boxes?" My voice lifts. "I'm not doing that hoarder thing again. Not in here." Not in my perfect, cozy cave home that I only get to enjoy for a limited time.

"I got you." Orion rubs my ear. "It'll be out of sight before you get back." His gesture's so familiar, I don't react until he's already out of the kitchen, dragging Finn to work.

Then I have to ball my fists to keep my fingertips from shaking. I'm getting too used to their casual touches.

I duck away to shower and change. As soon as the Wyverns' scents wash down the drain, a tremor bubbles under my skin.

I force myself into three tight layers of shirts, then a hoodie. Being swaddled takes the edge off my nerves, but I don't need to be a psychic to see where this is going.

I'm moving closer to the edge.

Closer to my heat and the inevitable decision.

Jett stands when I come back into the living room. "Ready?"

"Let's go." I'm glad I get to spend time with him alone.

His ice should mellow out my insanity.

Jett's scent is more subtle than the other guys' and it's much harder to read, but I've always found cedar so comforting.

My mom had a big cedar chest I'd climb inside to nap. That's the best memory I have of the woman who gave me away.

Jett's scent is the same. Sweet, fleeting memory, and then an epic falling apart.

Now I know his reasons.

They're good reasons.

But I'm still mad, still heartbroken over losing one of the three people I ever considered mine.

Evgenia. Marisol. JJ.

The end.

The only ones who ever cared.

And Evgenia's only halfway on the list. An auntie figure I can only count on half the time.

I peek at Jett as we ride the elevator up. He wears a black T-shirt tucked into belted pants, looking lithe and deadly, leaning against the wall. Or maybe the deadly thing is his man-bun. All that thick, dark hair bound in a knot, showing his high, pretty forehead that's still red from chili overdose.

Jett doesn't take me to the surface. Instead, he swipes us into a tunnel, and we take an underground passage to another building.

We pass armed guards, entering the non-civilian area. Unless there's a full-scale, civil-war level infiltration, no outsider's going to pull me off this compound.

The knowledge calms the squeaky wheel inside. That ever-present meerkat urge to pop up, wary of danger. Or maybe it's walking beside Jett.

He doesn't make a sound.

I'd say like a cat, but he's more predatory.

A snow leopard.

We enter a surprisingly normal office building, even though we're still underground. Whenever an office worker spots Jett, they do a hard one-eighty.

"So popular," I murmur.

"I have…a reputation."

"I bet." We round a corner and a pretty beta dodges us so fast she sloshes coffee all over her blouse.

Jett—for all his awkward, serial killer charm—is seriously fucking hot. Like K-pop idol, fallen angel, should have his own fan café attractive. His cut cheekbones deserve their own poster.

But the way the woman spins away, fingers shaking…

That's not how you avoid someone you dislike.

She avoids him out of pure, eye-widening fear.

"I thought Finn was the crazy one."

"He is." Jett's lips twitch. "This way."

He's leading me into a room before I can decide if he just smiled. Squinting at his pressed lips, I miss the tall blond body coming at me like a missile.

Jett grabs me before I headbutt the walking piece of fruit gum who looks way too much like my Orion.

"Lilah." Nathan grins. "Knew I'd see you again."

"Did you?" *Is he delusional?*

Jett steps between us with a salty growl. "Walk away, Nathan."

"*Chiiiiiill.* Just saying hello to my favorite omega."

If I were Nathan, I would back the fuck up from the menacing hitch in Jett's snarl.

But Nathan lives in a different reality.

And since I'm Lilah, the sound is pure catnip. A glittering ribbon twirling down my spine.

"Me and a few of my boys got together to put in a bid for you. Ready any time you are, Darling."

"*Walk. Away.*" Jett's satin bark twines every one of my vertebrae, soft and tight.

I don't think I've heard that bark before, and I don't want to again. It's much too deadly smooth.

Nathan's smile flattens. Maybe he does sense danger. "Going, going. See you soon, Darling girl."

"*Ugh.*" I want to scrape out my ears. "How can they be related?"

"Why do you know him?" When Jett watches Nathan leave, I don't have to imagine where he got his "reputation." That look is so chilling, I can almost see the bloodred numbers of his body count painted on his forehead.

"He came to my first social. Not a fan. Why?"

"Stay away from him."

"Planning on it."

Him and every other male in this godforsaken compound.

Jett leads me into the office suite, and a file storage room full of paper Redfang records. While he loads boxes onto a handcart to haul back, I crack open a lid and flip through.

The box is filled with receipts and invoices. Shipping manifests and a mess of loose papers choked with numbers that make my heart sing.

Want me to stay away from Nathan?

I'll one-up you.

I'll never talk to anyone again.

Give me twenty boxes of raw data, a padlock on my bedroom door, and one night without a heat spike, and I'll finally be a happy girl.

Just have to ignore the whisper growing inside from the same cursed place that has me watching Jett's shirt tighten across his toned back every time he lifts a box.

Just have to ignore the more and more undeniable reality.

Wyverns are my favorite kind of poison.

TWENTY-EIGHT

ORION

I SPEND the day unpacking for Lilah, carefully tucking away every little thing that belongs to her in what I already consider our home.

Every time she touches me, looks at me, fuck, probably every time she thinks of me, it burns off another wisp of the toxic smoke that's been fucking with my head for so long I forgot who I even am.

She's the purpose I was missing, and the reminder I needed that I don't have to earn Wyvern Pack's approval.

I'm the omega.

They have to earn *me*.

And honestly, I couldn't give a shit.

Without the bond jerking me, I'm aware of Finn moving boxes beside me, but that's it. There's no tension. No drive to win his approval or his touch.

All I have left of him and the pack is the itch of their fading bites.

Maybe because I'm so recently past my heat, or maybe because omega was never what I wanted to be, I'm not missing what I lost.

Isn't that the mindfuck?

All that time I spent terrified I'd lose them, and it's the best fucking thing that's ever happened.

I'm free.

But as I haul another box of gifts into the closets that are all hers, I catch a whiff of the musky leather scent that still socks me in the ass.

Atlas.

We haven't talked.

Need to, but Lilah needs me more.

I *like* being needed.

And the thing I like the most is that they can alphahole around all fucking day.

I'll always be the one who understands Lilah best.

I want to learn everything about being an omega so that I can anticipate what she needs and be the first one to give it to her.

Must be learning something, because I feel the shift in the air the second before Lilah walks in the door.

I drop Atlas's box and go to her.

She leads Jett, who's surprisingly docile, directing him to push a stacked handcart into her bedroom.

"Need help?" I ask.

"If you want to carry. All the boxes go in my room."

Finn appears, and the three of us tear down the pile, taking turns not letting her lift a thing.

Lilah huffs, not used to things being done for her.

Get used to it, Koala.

I should want things done for me too, but having Lilah is the ultimate brain hack. She scratches the itch. There's no grasping, needing, clinging omega bullshit as long as she keeps her eyes on me.

As long as Lilah lets me stay.

But she shoos us out of the bedroom when everything's unloaded. "I'm not coming out until I've read every page."

"Shout if you need anything."

"Sure." She nods, hearing but not listening. Lilah wouldn't ask for a sandwich, let alone actual help.

When she shuts us out, the lock click hits like a bullet. Finn, Jett, and I stare at the place where she was just standing.

Then I feel that stinging pull, the rise of the old Orion in the grasping need to be with her.

I'm like a duckling that changed its imprint.

At least this time, I'm not the only one.

I'm not even the worst.

Without Lilah, Jett and Finn go empty behind their eyes— nothing but chilling shadows and creepy fucking mist that does a shitty job hiding the demons Lilah doesn't need coming out to play.

"Don't bother her." I tug them to the living room.

The bond might be gone, but we still have years of brother-hood and history, so they tolerate my touch.

If I were anyone else, they'd rip off my fucking arms.

"Need her." Finn pulls against me.

"We all need her, but give her space. Last night freaked her out."

I died when we walked into the cloud of her sex-drenched caramel. Went to heaven when she let us join and I got to spend the whole night in her arms. And her legs.

That's the future I want.

For all of us.

Feels so good to let go of the fucking burden, being the only omega who could make that dream come true for the pack.

A cracking sound cuts off my future fantasies.

I open my mouth, ready to tell Finn to stop whatever the fuck he's doing now, but all he's doing is smiling in thin-lipped, weirdly dark delight.

Jett's bleeding.

His phone's shattered in his hand.

He doesn't twitch.

Don't think he notices, even though blood drips onto the rug.

"Jett."

He takes a sharp breath, looks down, then frowns at the mess. "Oh."

"*Oh?* You need stitches."

"No, he doesn't." Finn snatches the mangled phone, lobs it, and hits a three-pointer in the kitchen trash. Grinning his toothiest serial killer smile, he pulls Jett to the door. "He finally gets it."

"Gets what?" I've spent years of my life with Finn, mated him, fucked him, and still never know what the hell goes through his head.

I thought I had a better handle on Jett.

Wrong.

"How much I need her." Jett stares through the walls to Lilah like she's the North Pole to his broken moral compass. He's icy as ever, but there's something new inside the freeze. Something dark and crazed that vibrates on a frequency only Finn can fathom.

"Right?" Finn bounces. "Let's go fuck up those guys from last night. Then we can go shopping for Star. I'll show you the best shit."

"Good." Jett nods, brushes off his shirt, leaving a blood streak down his chest. "Let's go."

Total fucking psychos.

I'd pity whoever's in our cells, only they're getting the torture they deserve for coming after Lilah.

I shake my head.

Whatever's going on, it's nice to see them looking alive. Finn and Jett always felt like lead in my chest.

If we're ever bonded again—if Lilah can let us in and be the center I never wanted to be—all of us will be different men.

If she can't…

That's the thought that steals my air and pops the bubble on this new freedom.

I want to fucking yak.

Can't lose her.

I'll turn right the fuck back into that needy gremlin if I can't keep Lilah in my life. Not that I won't need alphas when my heat rolls through—I just need Lilah *more*.

I spend the rest of the day unpacking boxes of clothes, lotions, knives, and every other thing she could possibly want or need, keeping an ear cocked just in case she calls.

I'm deciding what to bring her for dinner when the main door clicks. Atlas shoulders in, carrying a huge plastic container.

I don't relax, but I stop reaching for my gun.

He's in his casuals, a black tee and pants.

I've spent a lot of time staring at Atlas, but he always bowls me over, even now. His broad shoulders, thick torso, and solid, sky-holding aura.

His gaze snaps to me, and suddenly I'm just a needy omega again, because he's *my* alpha. Atlas is the one I wanted even when I thought I'd be alpha too.

"Did you eat?" He sets the container on the kitchen counter, then moves to my side.

He smooths up my arm, wrist to neck, then tugs the back of my head, pulling me in for the most unexpected kiss.

It's just a quick peck, but my lips burn.

His thick fingers twine in my hair, and his eyes are just as hot as my skin.

A soul-shaking shiver rocks my gut. "*Huh*?"

Dragging his palm to the top of my head, Atlas gives me that wide-palmed head pat that makes my knees shake and my cock go iron.

"Dinner?"

I blink. "Ye—Yes?"

What the fuck are they teaching him in these classes?

Atlas pulls out a stool for me. I sit at the island while he whips out a bunch of smaller lidded containers. "I cooked. Spicy sweet potato gnocchi."

It smells like cream and spices, and I'm still not processing as he stabs one and offers it to my lips.

I reach for the fork.

Atlas pulls back, lifting his brows.

Playful.

The fuck?

Atlas never does the touchy-feely omega shit. His foreplay and aftercare are solid A's, but outside the bedroom, he almost never stakes a claim.

Thought he wasn't interested.

Did he just not know how?

I gape at the fully-loaded fork. "You're seriously going to feed me?"

Atlas smirks.

Smirks. "You want airplane noises?"

Oh, fuck no.

I jerk forward to bite the pasta like a snapping turtle. I don't know how to react to any of this until the flavor hits. Cream and sage and melt-in-your-mouth sweet potato. "Wait. You cooked? *This?*"

He stabs another bite for me. "Celeste helped. It's nutritionally balanced. Root vegetables are good for omegas. And there's cauliflower in the cream sauce."

I for sure need to make up nutrition class.

Still praying Lilah's lying about the coffee.

But the taste of cream sours on my lips. "You shouldn't give this to me. Give it to her."

He mounts the other barstool, sliding to trap my knees between his legs. "Orion—"

"We need to give Lilah a plate. She hasn't eaten. She'll—"

"*Orion*," he says with that rasp that sends me into deep freeze.

I've been waiting to have THE TALK.

I know he's going to cut me loose.

I'll be fine. I have Lilah, and I can find an alpha for my next heat.

Hunter, Finn, and Jett aren't going to mate me again, and I don't want them to, but they'll be there for me if I need.

Especially if Lilah wants to watch. Or join.

So it's fine if Atlas wants to officially hack away the last spiderweb thread of our bond. "At—"

He stuffs another gnocchi in my mouth.

While I'm forced to chew, he grips my shoulders, trapping me with a mouth full of cream sauce. "Orion."

I swallow the sludgy mouthful. *Here it comes.* "Yeah."

"Do you want to watch a movie with me?"

"Do I…"

Fucking, what?

Who the hell is Celeste and what kind of mushrooms is she feeding him? "A movie? Now?"

Atlas nods.

I glance at Lilah's hallway. "I thought you'd want to focus on—"

"Is she safe?"

"Of course. She's working."

Atlas hands me one of the plastic-lidded containers. "Give this to her? I'll make popcorn."

It takes me a second to kick back into motion, floored that he doesn't want to deliver the meal himself.

He should want to take credit because he's learning to cook, and learning to take care of our omega. I thought he'd fucking tackle me out of the way to deliver the plate he made.

I was ready to get booted off the island and eat my final rejection.

So why is he being…*sweet*?

To me and not to her?

Reeling, I set the dish in front of Lilah's door and give a soft tap. "Lilah? Dinner."

I walk away, taking loud steps so she knows I'm gone, then wait around the corner until I hear her crack the door and grab the dish.

Glad she's staying in.

If Atlas and I need to fight a civil war, she won't ever need to know there was a battle.

But while I'm tense and ready for the throw-down that'll shake my soul, Atlas is popping popcorn.

I sit on the sofa, mannequin style.

When he comes in juggling the popcorn bowl, he pulls me between his thighs and wraps us in a blanket.

My iffy omega instincts crackle back online.

His body heat thaws parts I didn't know were cold, and the leather, sex-god scent of him sinks into my flesh like a three-hour massage and a fifth of whiskey.

Fuuuuck his touch is good.

Solid pack leader vibes.

Atlas drapes his arms over my shoulders. "Is this alright?"

His heart beats against my ribs. His breath ghosts my neck, and my throat fucking burns in the half-moons where his bite used to mark my flesh.

Is it alright?

His touch is fucking magic.

Only, I wonder if it's real or an illusion. "Did you get brain surgery?"

"I got a wake-up call."

"About fucking time."

He offers a piece of popcorn to my lips and I take it. He slathered it in Cajun seasoning that I love but know he hates. I swallow and feel the bite go down in a lump. "I thought we were going to talk."

"Do you want to?"

"Not really." This fantasy moment's too good to ruin with reality. "Just feels like we should."

"I want to be your alpha." He rubs my neck, thumbing the fading scar of his bite with electric fingers. "This spot right here? I'll earn it back."

I tighten. "Lilah—"

"Want to be her alpha."

"You sure?" I ask, torn between longing and killer doubt. "This is your chance. Just bite Lilah and let me go—"

"*You're mine,*" Atlas growls, digging thick fingers into my hips. "I'm gonna bite you. Bite Lilah. Make all of us a pack. A *family*."

Fuck.

Lilah can give us kids.

I knew that before—thought about it all the time when I thought she was coming to steal my spot—but I kept picturing her with my alphas.

Me out in the rain.

Now I see a different future.

The kids we'd raise together.

Mine, Atlas's, Hunter's, even Finn and Jett's demon spawn.

Bunch of squishy omega babies who look just like *her*.

I want it for us so bad I'll mourn if we can't make it be. "If you say that shit, then go hurt her again—"

"You can both stab me." Atlas moves my hand, pressing it over his thumping heart. "Right here."

"Atlas…" He always makes me soft, but this time, I can't cave. "I want us to fix the pack, but I *need* Lilah. For the first fucking time in years, I don't feel insane. She's the only thing that makes sense, and if she goes to another pack, I—"

"It's okay," he purrs. "I trust you to take care of her. Tell me if I'm not doing a good job. Tell me if I'm fucking up. There's nothing I won't throw away to keep my omegas safe."

I'd call bullshit, but he's walking the walk. He literally resigned. Scorpio revoked his access. He's letting Hunter take control and hanging back instead of barking orders. "You're changing."

"So are you." He strokes my hair.

"For the better?"

"All of us are. We need to be. For her."

"She's so sweet, Atlas. So good. I'm fucking terrified she'll walk."

"Even if she does, I won't give up. Will you?"

"Never."

"Tell me about her." He sinks his chin onto the crown of my

head and his bass voice rumbles into my brain. "What have you learned?"

"She loves flowers." A surprising amount. "French fries are a must."

"What else?"

"Likes to be fed but won't admit it. Have to coax her a little." Which I can't wait to fucking do, every day for the rest of my life. "You should be feeding her, not me. I don't need the cute shit."

"You need *some* cute shit." Atlas's breath puffs against my scalp, making me twitch in his lap.

"I don't. Just wanna give all the good things to her. It feels better."

"Tell me." He rubs my stomach and purrs.

I share all the Lilah intel.

What she likes and dislikes. Every time I caught her trying to hide a smile.

We sit, twined together, plotting how to win Lilah over while the movie plays. Every so often, Atlas strokes my hair or feeds me a handful of popcorn.

This is *almost* everything I ever wanted.

Just need Lilah here with us and it'll be perfection.

TWENTY-NINE

LILAH

I WAKE DRENCHED in the thick, sticky, panicked sweat of another heat spike.

Gripping my belly, I stumble into the bathroom to splash my reddened face.

It's not the full heat.

Not yet.

But the insistent ache ramps harder every time this happens. *Which is every day.*

The pain gets a little bit worse. A little less horny and a little more...*hungry.*

I'm running out of time, and I can't keep running.

Have to finalize my plan and stop screwing around.

When I drift back to the bedroom, reaching for my vibrator, my outstretched fingers freeze.

It's hard to go back to plastic after riding your mate's tongue. Plus, knowing all my would-be alphas are so close...

I don't want to lock myself away and suffer.

It's addictive being held.

Body heat. Purr. *Connection.*

Even when Orion holds my hand, it's more touch than I've ever had, and the more I feel, the more I *want.*

Panting, I stumble into the hall.

Need Orion.

Maybe need all of them, but I can't be alone with the alphas, or I'll be begging them for much more than a touch.

I hear voices.

One lighter, one bass.

Atlas is here.

My heart kicks when I peek into the living room.

Atlas and Orion lie tangled on the couch. They snuggle under a blanket, so glued together there's no room for anyone else.

I must make a sound.

Their heads snap.

Then the blanket flies, and they're dashing to me before I can swallow the hard bubble stuck in my throat.

I dodge Orion's reach. "No. I won't interrupt you, I—"

Atlas purrs.

The sound's so deep it reminds me of being underwater, cradled by the crushing pressure. The solid, all-over, hug of the water and the lick of the current teasing my skin.

The pack leader's purr is pure safety. And just because he's not pack leader anymore, doesn't mean that's changed.

"Tell me what you need, sweet girl," he rumbles like a promise. Then he fucking *kneels*, slipping his hands behind my trembling knees, and dragging me across the carpet.

Atlas nuzzles my belly.

The cramps disappear.

Instead, there's a crazy fucking flutter.

One hard, breathless clench, like my downstairs real estate just did a fitting for his knot.

Surprise.

We have the perfect spot.

Right here, next to the last oozy bits of my heart.

Let me just sweep up those shards.

What are they?

Oh, my willpower?

Great.

Make yourself at home.

"You're spiking, baby bear." Orion strokes my hair. *Must ban ridiculous pet names.* "Let's get you to bed."

Atlas is still camping in my belly button, still gripping my thighs, still soaking me in that dense pack leader dominance that makes me feel like the moon can fall and the sky can burn and as long as I'm in his arms, none of it can ever hurt me.

Dangerous.

I try to pull away from his quicksand hands. "This doesn't work. I can't come between you. I—"

"Why?" Orion caresses down to that sweet, sweet spot between my neck and shoulder. "We want you between us."

Atlas's approval puffs against my stomach.

I'd collapse from shaking knees, but he's already holding me up.

"You know what I mean." My heart aches, but this is the truth. "You're mates. You'll bond again, reform the pack, and I'll be—"

"At our side," Atlas mumbles into my skin.

"No."

"Why not?" Orion thumbs my neck, so soft.

"Because." I try to swallow, but my throat's too dry, and the raw, ugly reality finally claws its way out. "You won't keep me."

Atlas lunges.

Suddenly, I'm high off the ground, crushed to the broadest chest I've ever touched, and it's nothing like being underwater.

I have no reference.

Nothing feels this good.

Atlas is firm and soft. Solid and yielding. His purr strokes my insides, his arms hold me tight, and with the scent of soft, cozy leather and a spine-melting caress, he silences all the crazy, whiny, heat-soaked bullshit that has me doubting my sanity on a minute-by-minute clock.

I'm limp omega mush.

If Dominik Redfang busted in with a rocket launcher, I wouldn't even turn my head.

Atlas wouldn't let him touch me.

Hurt me.

See me.

I'm that sheltered in his arms.

Orion presses against my back, an extra layer of warmth and protection. "What kind of fucking idiots wouldn't want to keep you?"

"Don't answer that," Atlas mumbles into my hair.

"I know five," I say, but I'm slipping into an alpha coma.

The heat roaring through my veins softens. It's more prickly warmth than the kick that makes me panic, and every stroke of Atlas's palm sends me deeper down the rabbit hole.

This is what they were talking about in my classes.

Why you want and need an alpha.

Kinda thought it was bullshit.

I didn't want or need *anyone*.

Now there's no going back.

"Feels better?" Atlas rubs up and down my spine.

"*Mmm*," I mutter into his pec.

"What do you want, Lilah?"

Loaded fucking question.

Because I might be limp, but Atlas is…*knot.*

The hard bundle presses my thighs in a big, bold *hello.*

Not a *hi, how you doin'*, but a busting-through-the-wall, room-and womb-destroying OH YEAH that makes me want to wave right back.

I swallow, dry and thirsty.

"Let me take care of you?" Orion hugs my ribs, gently tugging me away, and Atlas passes me to him like a plush toy.

I love being handled.

But when Orion starts to carry me to bed, Atlas stays in the living room, eyes burning as he follows our retreat.

I have a sudden vivid vision of Orion pinning me to my sheets. Atlas watching. Begging *us* to join. To touch.

But every step Orion takes throws another log on my inner bonfire. Before we cross the room, I go from cozy campfire, maybe some marshmallows, to a five-alarm, city-destroying blaze.

Pain stabs my belly and my hitched gasp stops Orion dead.

"You're too hot." He presses his forehead to mine, and his blond brows furrow. "You need…"

"Atlas." I close my eyes, knowing it's true, because just saying his name eases the pain. "*Alpha*. But…"

"Lilah," Atlas says softly.

I peek over, expecting him to charge. Lose control. Fly into a rut at my choking caramel scent.

Atlas sits in the sectional's corner, arms spread wide while he grips the sofa back. An open invitation.

His eyes flame as hot as my body, but he doesn't move. "*Come*."

Orion's breath hitches in my ear.

Fuck knows what mine does.

I'm drifting too high to feel anything but the wings in my belly and the sticky, rushing slick as my body rolls out the open house sign.

We are move-in ready.

Just waiting for the right cock to come and do a little rearranging. *Maybe some new paint?*

Orion shakes, but doesn't move.

Waiting.

I pat his shoulder. "*Go*."

The motion kickstarts him. He carries me back to the cloud of dominance and dizzying leather, setting me gently on top of Atlas's thick thighs, turning his broad chest into the back of my new throne.

"Is this okay?"

I don't know who Orion's asking, but Atlas and I gasp out a "*Yes*," mine more breathy, his more hoarse.

"I won't touch you," Atlas promises.

Not a promise I need right now, but before I can come up with a response, Orion climbs aboard.

Atlas's lap has room for two.

Orion straddles his knees, pushing my back against Atlas's chest and sandwiching me in delicious purrs.

One's softer, like fur stroking my belly. The other a deeper rumble, vibrating from behind.

"Hold on tight, koala bear." Orion hitches my arms around his shoulders and takes my lips.

I whimper into his mouth.

Orion grips my hips, but Atlas grips *Orion's* hips, crushing our bodies together and rumbling as Orion drowns me in soft kisses.

The position has me sitting on Atlas's knot while Orion's cock burns my stomach.

I bounce in the rhythm Finn taught me, trying to get friction on my clit, but with Atlas's heavy scent caressing me, friction's not going to be enough.

I need to be fucking *filled*.

Orion shifts, making room to tug down my sleep shorts and panties. Then he climbs back onto Atlas's knees, holding my pussy with the same gentle touch he uses to hold my hand.

Atlas still hasn't touched me.

Not once.

But he helps me rock, grinding me against Orion's fingers. His purr strokes my insides, and when his hot breath feathers the shell of my ear, I shake.

So wet, I must be soaking his pants.

But the trembling mini blip of an almost-climax is only half a step down, and I'm already back at the top of the rollercoaster, tense and aching to drop again.

So. Fucking. *Empty*.

"More," I gasp into Orion's mouth.

"More…" Orion's blue eyes are so deep, I'm lost. "Should I…?"

Neither of us moves, everything still—even his finger pressed to my pulsing clit.

Atlas breaks the moment in one reach, popping the button of Orion's jeans. "You'll get what you need, sweet girl."

"At…" Orion's hips jerk. He bites his lip as Atlas pulls down his zipper, and the slow *zzzzzzt* restarts my brain. "Is this what you want, Lilah?"

"Yes. Do you…?" I drop my fingers to the front of his boxers, one soft hesitant brush as the ache inside gnaws.

"Oh fuck, yes." Orion tips his head back at my touch.

"Take care of our girl," Atlas growls in my ear.

Three of us working together, we shimmy Orion out of his jeans.

When his cock pops free, I make a needy kitten gasp.

It's longer than I expected.

I've seen all the porn, but never seen a dick that pretty. Just gold and pink, not too veiny, not too red.

Lickable, suckable, fuckable perfect Goldilocks cock.

Wanna taste it.

"Lilaaaah," Orion groans.

Shit.

Out loud.

Atlas grips that perfect cock harder than I'd ever dare, drawing out a second, strangled groan that leaves Orion gripping my shoulders and me trembling.

"Use her slick," Atlas commands.

"Yes, *Alpha*," Orion breathes against my neck, flashing a smirk that tightens my belly in a new rush of heat.

Orion strokes my dripping entrance until his fingers are soaked. Lazy, teasing strokes that make my thighs twitch. He uses the wetness to rub his cock in long, slow strokes while his eyes dig into my soul.

"How does she taste?" Atlas breathes.

Orion licks a finger and his eyes roll back. "So sweet." He

reaches over my shoulder, offering a slick finger to Atlas who takes a long, lingering suck that feels like it's inside my ear.

"That's my perfect girl." His rumbling approval hits like cocaine.

"I'm n-no—"

"*Shhhhh.*" Orion silences me with a kiss.

"*Perfect. Girl.*" Atlas nips my shoulder.

My heart leaps and my vision swirls.

They want me fucking dead.

I twist in Atlas's lap, but two sets of hands hold me steady. "I need…"

"*Give her what she needs, Omega.*" Atlas says with just enough bark to leave us both moaning but perfectly able to refuse.

My head falls to rest on his wide, warm shoulder.

"Condom," Orion says, rubbing my thighs. "We can't—"

"Birth control." I yank his shirt, dragging him close. "It's safe." Been more than the week I was told to wait.

Done waiting.

Done feeling empty.

I'm protected, I'm ready, I want Orion inside.

He palms his cock and rubs his delicious tip through my slick.

"Gentle," Atlas murmurs.

"Not that gentle." I tilt my hips. "Orion…"

He kisses my nose.

Then he holds my gaze, eyes liquid sapphire as he pushes into my heat.

I haven't been a "virgin" since my first rabbit, but I tense, because everyone says your first time hurts.

What hurts is being alone.

As Orion pushes slowly and steadily inside, I've never felt so fucking *good*.

There's no hitch, no hurt.

Orion Wyvern was made for me, and his cock enters me in one careful thrust so sweet, I'm not sure if he's popping my cherry or my heart.

"Okay?" Orion thumbs my jaw, holding so still even though his fingers tremble.

"Better than okay." I test my pussy muscles, clenching on the perfect hardness of his length, tugging him up and *deeper*.

"Unh~" Orion's abs twitch like he just got punched, and gasping, he pulls out, jaw dropping as he gazes at me in a panicked kind of awe. "What the hell?"

"Omega," Atlas says, more like a sexy sports commentator than our accommodating fuck platform. "Special muscles."

"Really fucking special." Orion pushes out a breath. "Little bear. Don't try to make me come so fast. I have to take care of you."

"Sorry?"

I'm not sorry.

He knows it too, smirking. "We'll see who laughs." He thrusts back in, and my easy chuckle turns to a gasp.

"Gonna move." Orion kisses my neck. "Tell me if it's too much."

He pulls back, then thrusts deep.

Gentle.

Easy.

And every thrust bumps my ass into Atlas's bulging knot. The alpha breathes ragged in my ears.

"More." I dig into Orion's hips, trying to speed his motion.

Deeper.

Harder.

Feels so good, but there's much more room to stretch.

"Next time I'll wear a jelly knot so I can fill you up. *Or…*" He thrusts so deep, he pumps the air out of my lungs, and his smirking whisper feathers my ear. "Tell you a secret. Atlas is the biggest. But Hunter's even thicker. And Finn's so long he'll leave you screaming. But you know who has the biggest knot? The one who locks you so hard you think you'll be permanently joined. *Jett.*"

My pussy clenches.

Hard.

I don't want that information. Don't need it cluttering my brain. But now that I know, it's burned in forever.

Atlas growls. "Don't tease."

"What if she likes to be teased?" Orion rolls his hips, stroking the deepest part of me.

I clench down on him, sucking him in with all those "special" muscles and morphing his smart-ass smirk into a desperate pant.

"Then you won't mind either." Atlas reaches behind Orion, hugging us both close, and I can't see what he does with his fingers, but Orion's cock jerks inside me.

We both gasp.

"Fuck. At. *Shit*. Lilah—"

"Fuck our omega good." Atlas moves Orion's hips, grinding him into me.

Atlas still isn't touching me, but he moves Orion for me, helping him thrust in this rocking, rolling motion that makes my eyes cross and legs splay and all of the tension clench in my belly.

"You can…" I gasp, losing my mind. *Need more.* "You can touch me."

"Better, sweet girl?" Atlas keeps one hand on Orion's hips, and moves the other to my throat. Then he does the thing, digging his nails into the most sensitive spot like a dream of his bite. "Are you ready to come for us?"

"*Please*…" My voice shakes.

I don't know who or what I am right now, but I want to reach the peak that feels so close I can barely breathe.

Bathed in Atlas's energy, sheltered in his arms, I finally feel safe enough to let go.

Atlas drags Orion's hips into me for one last hard thrust.

"*Come*," he commands.

The raspy bark disintegrates us both.

Orion twitches, spreading heat in my belly, and soaking the room in apple sweetness.

I come so hard, my head hammers Atlas's shoulder, but he holds me steady while I twist.

Fuck.

So good.

Shaking, Orion kisses the column of my throat. "Perfect girl."

I shudder.

I also sense that I should be worrying, but I'm too far gone.

Orion stays inside me until our breathing slows.

Then he and Atlas do some kind of telepathy, easing me onto the couch between them while my eyelids flutter.

Atlas spoons me from behind, boulder hard while Orion can't stop kissing my throat.

Don't want him to stop.

Together, they cover me with a blanket that smells like spicy, sweet musk.

A movie plays in the background, but all I can feel is Orion's breath on my chest and Atlas's hand that protectively cups my belly.

I'm shook.

I'm broken.

I shiver so hard they jerk.

"What's wrong?" Orion scans my face.

Don't know what he sees, but I'm sure he can feel the hummingbird beat of my panicked heart. "Are we really doing this?"

"What?"

"Are you really going to fuck me and snuggle me and claim you're going to keep me forever? Because if—"

"No if." Atlas' palm tightens on my skin. *"Forever."*

Fuck my walls.

They stormed the castle. I tried flaming arrows and boiling oil, but I forgot.

Wyverns can fly.

Now they're in and there's only one soft, squishy part left in my heart. I'm offering it to them raw. If they screw me, there'll be nothing left but gnawed-up jerky. "I—"

"You don't have to decide." Orion gently nips my throat. "Just know that we're here and we're not walking away."

Atlas keeps petting my belly. "Feeling better?"

He's a wizard.

His dominance is so soothing, all I can do is nod, head pillowed on his biceps.

He didn't even fuck me and everything's fixed.

Heat gone, hormones appeased, and heart in serious fucking trouble.

I drift off, and they follow, drenching me in their soft, sleepy breaths.

But something stops me from slipping too deep.

The air stirs and my eyes crack open.

Jett stands in the shadows.

Feels like he's standing at the edge of the galaxy, he's so far away, and he watches just the same way I watched Atlas and Orion, when I thought they'd never have a spot for me.

The same way I stood in the doorway during my heat, afraid to take that step.

Just because you know you don't belong doesn't mean you stop wanting it.

Jett watches us with *longing*.

My heart scratches my chest.

He holds my gaze, and I can't help stretching out the fingers that hang over Orion's hip.

He whirls, then disappears into the darkness.

Maybe not ready.

Or maybe I'm wrong and he never wanted to belong.

What do I know about belonging?

Pressed between Atlas and Orion, it's the first time I feel like I don't need to run.

THIRTY

LILAH

I WAKE ALONE.

Someone carried me to bed, and last night feels like a dreamy bubble that'll pop into nothing but soap scum the second I set foot on the carpet.

So, I do the natural thing and grab my phone, hoping to numb out for ten minutes, maybe twelve hours or a few months.

Orion hooked my reading app to their pack card.

Big mistake.

I'm gonna download so many books that my favorite authors can all buy second homes.

Only, before I can raid the ebook store, a notification pops up with my missed messages.

Catherine called fifteen times.

I dial her back with a topsy-turvy churn in my gut.

"Lilah?"

"What's wrong?"

Catherine *tsks*. "Nothing's wrong, just urgent. The Sorensens and a handful of packs have been calling nonstop to schedule private dates."

"I didn't want to schedule any more." And freaking *yikes*. Is she paid on commission?

I definitely said no more.

"Sorensens were already on your calendar. I highly, *highly* recommend that you meet with them. They've already offered to double their bid."

Twice as much?

How romantic.

I want to say screw it and cancel, especially now, but years of shit going south stop me from torching this last flimsy getaway bridge. "I won't leave the compound. I'm not risking my life for lamb chops."

"Understandable, but can't you swing a meeting there? I'd be happy to call and see if there's a venue we can rent."

Luckily we're not on video, because my face twists.

A venue?

It's a freaking military compound.

Unless Sorensens want to take me to the shooting range, we're out of luck. "I'll ask, but don't get their hopes up."

"Wonderful. Just get back to me as soon as you can. The sooner we sign contracts, the sooner your heat partners can be at your side. It must be terrible, what you're going through alone."

Right.

So terrible.

No orgasms at all. No snuggles. *Torture.*

I cough. "I'll call you back."

Flopping into the soft pillows, I swim in the guys' scents until my nose picks something even better.

Breakfast.

I dart into the closet to grab a sweatshirt, but there are too many choices. My nose pulls me to the corner filled with guys' clothes.

Five sweatshirts hang in a row, all lightly worn and so fucking sexy, I'm not responsible for the weird purr-squeal that chokes up my throat.

I want to layer them all, but that would send the wrong signal —because at that point, I might as well get my Wyvern ass stamp.

I mean, shit.

I should check a mirror.

Might already have one.

I end up grabbing Finn's hoodie.

It has blood-orange-juicy vibes that are morning appropriate. Plus, his is sandwiched in the middle, so it carries all five Wyvern flavors.

Once the big long hoodie's over my head, my shoulders drop, my jaw unclenches, and I take the deepest breath, wrapped in their protection.

My heart beats too loud when I finally creep outside.

Atlas and Orion huddle over the stove, and it doesn't smell like burning. Hunter, Finn, and Jett have papers spread all over the island.

Now I know I'm giving off the wrong signal.

Must be a tornado siren, because the second I enter the kitchen, the guys whirl.

"Who were you on the phone with, Stargirl?" Finn sweeps me onto the island counter, smug as shit when he sees me in his sweatshirt.

I stop him from jumping me with a palm to his chest. "Catherine's been calling."

"What about?" Hunter puts an elbow on the papers.

My gut gives another churn.

I'll poison the guys with chilis or flip them on their asses if I want to take them down. What I won't do is play games.

I don't want a *who-will-I-pick* tango.

It's just that I haven't picked.

Because the more my nature roars to lock this shit down and beg my mates for their teeth in my throat, the more my nurture rebels.

I'm afraid.

I'm afraid this is all so fucking temporary. "The Sorensen Pack wants to reschedule our date."

"Is that what you want?" Hunter speaks for them, but five sets of eyes are pinned to my skin.

"I want to keep my options open." I rub my arms. "Can they come to the compound?"

I'm waiting for the Wyverns to rage and tell me no.

That I belong to them and only them and I need to stop this "other packs" bullshit.

But Wyverns never do what I expect.

"It's grudge night tonight." Atlas steps away from the stove. He and Orion are whipping off pancakes, and the sight of him with a spatula and a half apron that barely ties around his thick hips makes it hard to process what he said.

I can smell him in my hair.

"Not a bad idea." Hunter taps his chin.

"Perfect." Finn tries to worm between my thighs, but I push him out.

"What's grudge night?" I ask, holding Finn at bay so I can keep my last shred of sanity.

"A Wyvern House ritual." Hunter yanks Finn away, only instead of rescuing me, he steps into the empty spot, thighs bumping my tightly closed knees. His body heat's atomic, and his nostrils flare when he scents me drenched in his pack.

"It's fight night," Orion offers. "Anyone can challenge anyone, and we always have to be there because fucking Hunter will have thirty challengers."

"You?" He's the most normal, level-headed Wyvern. The *only* normal Wyvern.

But Hunter's feral grin reminds me his *normal's* all smoke. "Salty trainees. Supposedly, I'm the devil."

"*You?*" I repeat. Hunter's so patient and gentle when he teaches me.

But his brown eyes glow with mischief, and I swallow.

I'm getting special treatment.

"Him," Orion confirms. "He's the only one who ever gets challenged from our pack."

"Not...?" My gaze sweeps to Finn and Jett—but they both have the cold, coiled readiness of pro fighters. Even I'm tempted to see how I compare.

Jett shrugs. "I was challenged once."

Finn covers his heart and gives a wistful sigh. "Someday."

Never mind.

It wouldn't be a challenge. They'd just slit your throat. Jett would do it surgically while Finn danced in the blood.

"Can't you *give* the challenge?" I ask.

"Hypothetically," Atlas answers. "Anyone can challenge anyone, but the goal's to let the teams burn off steam. It's not for us to flex on our subordinates."

But I wanna see them flex.

I lick my lips.

A growl rumbles in Atlas's chest, quickly echoed by the other Wyverns.

Oops.

"Invite the Sorensens." Hunter clears his throat. "It'll be a party."

"I don't think they want to watch MMA."

"But you do," Orion says.

Hell yes I do.

Preferably if Wyverns are shirtless and in cages. "It sounds fun."

"Can they make it tonight?" Hunter asks.

I text Catherine.

She passes the message to the Sorensens while the Wyverns explore the mysteries of pancake batter.

It's a mess.

They tried to make blueberry happy faces and ended up with bloody-smiled nightmares that are lumpy and cute and kind of look like Finn.

So my heart's already swollen when Atlas cuts up my short stack, drenches it in syrup, and offers me the first bite direct from his thick fucking fingers.

I take the bite with an extra lick that leaves him rumbly and hot-eyed, and me questioning whether I shouldn't just borrow his knot.

You know.

Just to see if I like it?

Then my phone vibrates.

Sorensens agreed. Send details.

I slide the phone to Hunter

He nods. "I'll get them clearance. What else do you wanna do today?"

"I have boxes of data to sort. Not going anywhere else." As long as there's food, I'm not leaving my hideout.

"Good." Hunter ruffles my hair. "Stay in. Stay safe."

Jett moves to my side. "Have you found anything?"

"Still getting organized. There's a lot." It's also a lot the way his cold gaze devours me.

I chew a bite of pancake and dry swallow.

"This." Jett offers me the brown paper bag he's been hiding at his side. "For you."

Suspicious, I unfold the paper.

Inside is a chocolate-chip muffin so big I have to lift it with two hands.

And blood rushes to my heart like he just handed me a fucking diamond.

Because this is the same muffin JJ used to bring, and the scent of chocolate and cedar takes me right back to the sweet memories of *before*.

I clutch it to my chest. "Thank you."

Jett's fingers and jaw clench. "Call if you find anything. We'll jump on the smallest lead."

"I will."

I eat every bite of the muffin.

And the pancakes Atlas keeps tipping onto my plate. When they finally have to leave, Finn kisses my knuckles 'til I'm squirming and Hunter has to pull him away.

Only Hunter's worse.

He overwrites Finn's kisses with teasing nibbles until Finn pulls a knife. Laughing while he disarms him, Hunter drags Finn away.

I stick my hands in my pocket hoping they'll stop tingling.

Atlas cleans the kitchen until it sparkles. Then he crouches in front of me, cupping my face in his big hands. When he leans in, my lips part.

But he doesn't go for a kiss.

He rubs our cheeks.

Both sides, nuzzling me with freshly shaved skin, marking me in musk and leather.

Then, he pushes between my neck and shoulder, fucking painting me in his scent until I can't tell if I'm numb or on fire.

He steps back, smug and satisfied, and Orion gives him a gentle kick in the ass.

Atlas laughs.

It's a warm, rumbly sound that glues me to my stool.

"See you tonight," Atlas promises, locking the door behind him.

Orion shudders. "He smiled."

"And laughed. Shouldn't be allowed."

"Right?" Orion rucks his hand through his hair. He leans to rub the same spot that Atlas just marked, and all I do is tilt my neck, opening so he can rub *deeper*. "Gonna shower. Will you be okay?"

"I'm fine," I say breathily.

He kisses my nose, leaving me reeling.

With Atlas and Orion's clinging scents, Finn's comfy hoodie, Jett's sweet muffin, and Hunter's careful plans—all the Wyverns leave their mark.

And I'm wrecked, because I'm starting to wish those marks were permanent.

———

I SPEND the afternoon organizing papers and going through USBs of confiscated Redfang data.

It's familiar work, but it's fun to be on the good side of the con. I'm usually the one washing the cash, not the one trying to find its source.

The problem with underworld books is the shell companies.

I could sit with this data for weeks, sifting through the layers of lawyers and accountants who set up whichever front business. I could calculate Dom's entire hidden fortune if you give me enough time.

None of that puts him in cuffs.

Or an empty cell with Finn and Jett.

We need a location so we can smoke him out and get rid of the axe hanging over my scrawny neck.

"Snack break." Orion walks in with a tray and a massive sandwich, plus his laptop tucked under his arm.

He arranges the tray over my lap, like breakfast in bed, then slides in next to me, opening his laptop. "Find anything?"

"Lots. Nothing helpful." I grab a handful of chips and offer one to him.

"Like what?" He eats it from my fingers with a grin that tightens my belly until I have to shake myself to remember who I am and where we are.

"Bunch of receipts for saltwater aquariums and exotic fish. SCUBA gear. He's like a deranged Jules Verne."

"I'm not up on the investigation, but I bet they already tracked that down."

"That's what I was thinking." There aren't many fish dealers, so you'd definitely look there. No matter where Dominik's hiding, his fishies gotta eat.

"What else?"

I pull out the paper that's been bugging me. "Diamond Dolls, LLC. Does that sound familiar?"

"Never heard of it." He squints at the paper. "You?"

"I've seen it somewhere, but I don't remember."

"You will."

"I better." But I take a break to eat the sandwich Orion made me. Turkey with globs of spicy chipotle mayo.

Perfection.

When I'm done licking spicy fingers, I crawl to peek at his screen. "What are you working on?"

"Code." Orion drags me into the crook of his arm. "Still playing with my wolf game. Adding graphics and more genes."

"When are you publishing?"

"It's just for fun."

"Screw that. Publish. I'll make you a company."

"You can't make me a company."

"It's easy. Register in Panama. Get you some offshore accounts and never tell the guys you're a gaming tycoon."

He snorts. "I'd sell five copies. One to each of you."

"We'll see." I pull open my laptop, and he's so focused between his laptop and his phone, he doesn't notice me taking a break from spreadsheets.

It'll be a surprise for later.

We spend the whole day curled up in my bed, quietly working. Every so often, Orion hooks my ankle with a foot or smooths back my hair. Even more often, I nuzzle into his side.

It's the most peaceful, perfect day of my life.

I email Hunter and Jett a spreadsheet with what I've found. No smoking gun yet, but more leads to run down.

Dominik just needs to make one mistake.

Eventually, Orion closes his computer, taking a long stretch that flashes his tight stomach. "This has been the best day, but we have to get ready for tonight. Hunter's gonna pick us up."

"We didn't do anything," I mumble, disappointed when his shirt falls back in place.

"This is my everyday when they're gone. Only, I'm always so ratcheted up, I'm climbing walls. Having you is fucking heaven."

The words squeeze the softest part of my heart.

My days are the same.

Alone. Hiding and fighting, but always alone. "Won't they let you back on missions? Your hormones seem—"

"Finally not insane? Yeah. I'm much more level after that last heat. But that's not entirely why I was grounded."

"Why?"

"I've fucked up more than one mission, and there are better agents than me to take the role. Agents who want to be agents and didn't learn black ops just to fit in with their friends."

He needs a hug.

I pull his computer out of the way and climb into his lap, snuggling until our foreheads bump. "You fit in with me."

"*Lilah.*" He wraps my waist, tugging me closer.

"Orion." I stare into his blue, blue eyes, tasting apple even though our lips don't touch. My fingers find their way into his sun-kissed hair, and I scratch his scalp until he purrs.

My heart and throat tighten, but I force myself to speak. "What are we?"

"House cats."

My lips fall open. "What?"

"House cats," he insists. "Kinda cranky and cuddly and we'll fuck shit up if you leave us alone too long."

"That's not what I mean. What—"

"I know what you mean." Orion bites the tip of my nose. "You're my other half. And I'm yours."

Flutters explode in my belly.

"I..."

"This is what it's going to be like. Whether the guys are here or gone, we'll always have each other. I'll always take care of you. I'll keep learning so I always know what to do. You already take care of me so well, I can't ever let you go."

My heart pumps butterfly blood, the shiver flying through my veins.

I give up.

I'm toast, but even more baked—a fucking biscotti.

So I do the only logical thing.

Moving slowly, giving him so much time to say no, I press my teeth to Orion's throat. "Can I—"

"*Fuck, yes*," he moans.

I bite, breaking skin.

Orion's blood tastes like spiced cider.

I linger, making sure to claim my place. Then I lick the broken oval of teeth marks while he pants, fingers digging in my hair.

"Do you feel it?" he rasps.

I'm still licking blood from my lips, so it takes a second to recognize the warmth in my chest.

There's a little ball of sunshine near my heart, warming the old shadows.

"I can feel you." It's not a pack bond, but something else.

Something *ours*.

"You're mine," he growls, wiggling to the hollow of my throat. I tense, anticipating his bite, but he just drags his teeth along my skin. "Wait until your heat. Make it permanent."

I yank him back, kiss his nose, and feel the sunshine in my heart.

I have zero doubts.

Bit him. Licked him. Keeping him forever.

THIRTY-ONE

HUNTER

ADMINISTRATIVE. *Fucking. Nightmare.*

Our teams have been bagging Redfang minions left and fucking right, but Dom is a ghost, and now I'm the one who has to answer *why.*

I did not sign up for this shit.

Only, yeah. I did.

But I wanted to fix the pack, not experience the eighth circle of bureaucratic hell.

While I push papers at the office, Orion keeps the group chat rocking, texting pic after pic of his afternoon with our girl.

Their feet tangled together.

A candid with Lilah's soft brown hair spilling everywhere and an achingly sweet smile I'd fucking bet she doesn't know she's wearing.

I salivate.

The *need* to sink my teeth into Lilah's smooth throat—to mark her until she's gasping—is so fucking raw, I have to spread my knees under my desk to make room for my knot, throbbing with a second pulse.

Marking her is not the plan.

The plan is, we wait until Lilah's heat, and claim her as a pack.

We need to keep chipping away the doubts and fears that have her shuttering that gorgeous smile just before her cheeks turn pink.

This morning, she reached for me, instinctively craving her alpha's touch. She had fingers halfway to my scalp and me about to fucking *moan* over head scratches before she snatched back her hand, singed by just the idea of asking me for comfort.

She's skittish and has every reason to be afraid.

I wanna gut punch the asshole who's making us wait. Lilah needs the safety of our mate bond *now*.

But *oh fucking right*.

It's me.

I'm the asshole.

Lilah's fear is the reason for the patience plan, but it fucking hurts to watch her pull back, desperate to protect herself again and again and again.

From us.

From *me*.

That's why we have to prove we won't hurt her or let her be hurt. When Lilah *believes*, I'll claim her so fast.

But *fuuuuuuuuuuck*.

Waiting is torture.

Just want her to submit. To let me in. To let me *help*.

Orion texts a pic of Lilah's head on his shoulder, and I'm done.

Too fucking cute.

Screw work.

I'm quitting being leader, even temporarily.

Our teams will keep hunting Dom, even if I stop checking in every ten minutes. All I want to do is snuggle the omegas.

Maybe wind up Orion the way he keeps winding us up with these pics—*little shit*.

But I grin.

Bet Lilah will like watching us work Orion.

I *know* he'll like being worked for her.

Atlas is busting his ass to become the mate Orion needs. I just

want to see Orion taken care of while he takes care of our girl—
and I'll happily play any role that makes them smile.

If their heats sync—

My rumbling purr rattles the office door.

Then my phone rings, and the name on the screen euthanizes
my warm fuzzies.

Scorpio.

"Sir?" I stuff the word with scorn.

"My office." He hangs up.

So much for playing hooky.

I stand and wince.

Hard as fuck.

Hope Scorpio likes my pheromones.

I cross the building and take the elevator to the bunker of their
executive suite.

My palms sweat.

It's Atlas's job to meet with the dads.

I won't cave to their bullshit, but I'd feel stronger having him
at my back. Now he's busy grilling his new BFF, Granny Celeste,
for omega secrets.

After Jett's morning therapy session, he and Finn went radio
silent, off to hunt Secretary Stacey who thinks she can fucking run
after overseeing years of violence at the OCC.

I commanded them to bring her in alive, but I wasn't real
specific about how or when, so I expect the woman back in pieces.

I'm usually the one reigning in their antics.

Fuck with Lilah and you can get fucked.

It's a good reminder as I walk into the dads' suite, alone.

The guys can't be with me, but we're one hundred percent on
the same page.

Protect Lilah.

Especially from the scheming mercs who passed us their DNA.

The secretary waves me past, and a second atmosphere sinks
onto my shoulders. Fighting the pushback, I enter Scorpio's office
to find all four horsemen clustered in the sitting area.

Scorpio and Hikaru take up the couch, both wearing their typical *we're-businessmen-not-mercenaries* suits that fool no one when they reek of gunpowder and ash.

My dad and Kieran sit across from them in more casual camo, everyone absorbed in the stacks of reports scattered on the coffee table until their heads whip to me.

I manage not to stagger, but the dominance has my knee joints creaking.

I pound way too much collagen powder to be going arthritic this young.

They're that ridiculous.

And that used to getting exactly what they want.

I take a breath.

Much as I want to bail, much as I'll probably always want to bail, I'll step up for *her*.

"You rang?" I fall into the empty chair at their table.

Scorpio gives me the same *get-in-line* look he always gives Atlas, but I'm not his son and Max Wyvern never hit me—just dropped me in the woods for survival training any time I opened my mouth to complain.

Ah, fathers.

At least I know what not to do.

"When are you claiming her?" Scorpio asks, blunt as fuck.

A growl rattles my gut. "You don't get updates on our mate."

"Son." My dad scratches his bushy beard. He's the softest of their unholy quad, but that's like saying he's the softest brick of concrete. "We have your best int—"

"Here's the fucking thing," I bark. "You don't get to tell us how to run our pack." I'm done shoveling their shit and caring about consequences. We let problems slide with them for way too long and it almost cost us Lilah. "Disinherit us if you don't like it."

"Enough." Uncle Hikaru adjusts a cufflink. "That's not why we called."

"I'm listening." Also checking my watch. I want to take Lilah to her date, and I want to time it so the Sorensens fucking see me dropping her off.

"The board has agreed to shut down the OCC until we can appoint a new director and staff. We'd also like to liquidate the other Wyvern businesses that have been neglected. If your pack were prepared to step up, we'd hand power directly to you. But with things as they are…"

"You can bury the OCC." I stand, glad I don't have to think or even hesitate over this decision. "We're not taking any more responsibility."

All we're doing is focusing on Lilah, Orion, and nailing Redfangs.

Scorpio unfolds from the sofa. He's rocking new lines at the corners of his dark eyes—it's a toss-up if they're from stress or scowling. "This is how you're going to run the pack?"

"Yep." I don't flinch, don't shrink, don't give a fucking inch on his tyrant games. I don't give a shit how sour he is over Atlas losing his position.

Lilah and the guys are my *family*.

Not our fathers' legacy.

"Anything else?" I ask, just to wind them up.

Kieran, silent as a ghost this whole time, finally speaks. "You'll be there tonight?"

"Wouldn't miss it." I grin.

And I just had a fantastic idea.

I text the guys on my way to the garage, and they are on fucking board for my latest scheme.

Grabbing my Jeep, I book home to Lilah.

The elevator ride takes a thousand years, and I'm bouncing, I'm so juiced to see her.

When I rip open the door, Lilah hops off a kitchen stool, looking cute as shit in Orion's too-long sweatshirt.

I'm about to test my luck on a hug when I scent blood.

I stiffen.

Heart stutters. *What the—*

Orion struts to throw an arm around her shoulders. Then he stretches his neck like a smug fucking giraffe, flashing me his thick-ass bandage and the biggest *fuck you* smile.

And, yeah.

Fuck me.

Because Lilah bit him.

She fucking bit him.

I drift to them, heart humming in my throat. "Busy day?"

"Just lounged. No big deal." Orion casually scratches his bandage.

He's glowing.

Blue eyes sparkling.

All golden sunshine like I haven't seen in years.

I couldn't be happier or more fucking feral with jealousy.

Lilah shifts foot to foot, drowning me in torched sugar.

I swallow hard, *aching* for her.

A soft glow lights her cheeks, but Lilah is still hiding her smile, chewing her lower lip, eyes downcast.

Have to wait until she trusts me enough to give me everything.

I thump my chest so I can speak to her without choking. "You ready? I'll drive you to the arena."

"We're ready." Lilah lets Orion take her hand so naturally, I kind of want to choke him instead.

He knows it too, pulling her hand into his pocket. "It'll be okay. I'll stay with you."

Now I'm the one holding back a smile. "Who knows? You might even have a fun date."

I escort them to my Jeep, topside. The omegas climb into the back seat, and I'm more than happy to play chauffeur. It gives me primal fucking satisfaction peeking at their comforting touches and gentle smiles.

Orion makes her *happy.*

Can't wait to do the same.

It'll take two minutes to cross the compound, but I tilt my rearview so I can watch Lilah the whole drive.

I freeze, hand on the shifter.

Lilah shakes, and the scent that fills the car isn't the happy lust-soaked caramel she was piping out five seconds ago.

Now she's spiking anxiety so sharp, claws rip between my ribs.

Cold sweat beads on her forehead.

Complexion ghostly pale.

"Lilah?" Orion cups her jaw. "What's wrong?"

"N-nothing. Just..." Her eyes meet mine in the mirror and they yawn.

Pupils wide with need—*for me.*

I bail from the driver's seat.

Fucking run around the car and dive to get her in my arms.

Lilah trembles, taking a hitched breath against my neck.

"Killer princess," I mumble into her hair. "No one can hurt you."

"Just need..." She quivers.

"You can have anything. Take all the time you need." I pat her back while Orion and I sandwich her in calming purrs.

Lilah gulps a few times, but the pulse racing in her throat finally starts to slow. I'm bracing for her to cut me loose the second she's not freaking, so I have a mini coronary when she sighs, relaxing her cheek against my heart.

Trusting me.

Not all the way, not yet, but I'll fucking take every inch and prove she can trust me with the next.

"You want to talk about that?" I ask when her breathing settles. Don't want to press, but I need to know her triggers so I can stop them from bothering her again.

"Car." Lilah shudders. "The back seat. The crash. *Shit.*" Her fingers wring my shirt. "I can't fall apart over something that small."

"Small?" Orion snorts. "You crashed a car and saved my fucking life."

"It's not every time," she says in the tiniest voice. "I was fine when you took me to the police station."

Lilah had five Wyverns throwing elbows to sit next to her on that drive. Must've subconsciously known she was safe.

I rock her, rubbing her back. "Can't be helped. Gotta carry you."

"No. We can take the car. I'm fine. Just felt out of control." Lilah wiggles, and my heart breaks when I have to set her down.

Too soon. Too stubborn.

"Would you feel in control if you drove?" I ask, hella jealous when she grips Orion's hand instead of mine.

Unfair omega advantage.

"No!" she jumps, eyes wide with horror. "I don't even have a license."

"You want one? I can help you practice."

"You'd do that?" She tilts her head, all cute baby bird and it feels like she just pecked my soul.

Are my intentions not clear?

Shit. Gotta fix it, *stat*.

"Come here?" I offer my hand.

Orion gives her an encouraging nudge, finally playing for the team, and a sappy harp strums in the ether when Lilah Darling takes what I'm offering, setting her smooth, little fingers in my palm.

I pull her to the driver's seat and slide it all the way back.

Then, before she can run, I pluck her into the car with me, settling her between my knees. Space is tight. The position puts her a little too close—both to the wheel and my aching fucking knot—but there's nothing better than having Lilah's trust.

She grips the wheel at eleven and one, knuckles white. I'll let her go the second she twitches, but she stays with me, so I cover her hands with mine just how I've always wanted, stroking her knuckles until she relaxes.

Heaven.

When Orion climbs into the passenger seat, she lets out a breath.

"You feel okay?" I ask.

"I hate driving." She does a cute wiggle and her hair falls to the side like she's begging for my bite.

Patience, Hunter.

Ignoring the luscious vanilla sugar hijacking my nervous system, I squeeze her hands. "Well the speed limit's thirty and we only have to cross the compound, so I think you can get us there. You know which one is the gas?"

Lilah sighs. "I know. It's just… You'll see. Buckle?"

I click the seatbelt around us. It barely stretches to fit, pushing Lilah deep between my thighs. She's already so focused on the road, she must not notice my hard-ass dick saying hello. "Put us in drive?"

Lilah pushes out a breath, hits the brake, and shifts…

Then I'm coughing, trying not to laugh into her hair.

She leans over the wheel like a grandma with cataracts, squinting at the road, and at no point do we exceed a speed of nine. A confused squad of trainees jogs past, and Lilah brakes, even though they're fully on the sidewalk.

"It's okay to go a little faster." I rub her arms, trying to encourage but also not laugh at this adorable shitshow. "I can stop us if we get in trouble."

"Going fast enough." She leans until her chin damn-near touches the wheel. Eventually, we coast to a natural stop at the intersection where we need to turn.

"Take a left." I flick the signal for her.

She checks left and right four times each before zooming off at five miles per hour. Can't make eye contact with Orion or I'll lose my shit.

I need this on film.

The guys will die.

"Killer. You're the safest driver I've ever seen."

"Shut up," Lilah mutters, never taking her eyes off the empty road.

I kiss the crown of her head, and she's so distracted, she doesn't shrink away. "I'll take you out to practice. Somewhere quiet and safe."

"You don't have to—"

"You know how it is." I kiss behind her ear. "I'm going to."

Lilah shivers.

I grin.

Have to show Lilah exactly what I'm willing to do for her.

Can't wait for tonight.

THIRTY-TWO

LILAH

AS MUCH AS I hate driving, it distracts me from reality. Or maybe the real distraction is Hunter's hot breath puffing against my neck, muzzing my head with honey.

Can't stop shivering.

"Here we are." Hunter rubs my shoulders. "Park at the back. We don't want to be too close to other cars."

The combat stadium sits smack central in the Wyvern compound, behind layers and layers of security that actually make me feel secure.

I creep into the parking lot, super careful not to drive near the people streaming in for grudge night. When I coast into a spot in the back corner, I let out a breath, relaxing into Hunter.

"Was that so scary?" he murmurs, voice way too close to my ear.

Wait.

He's really close.

Like, I'm fucking *glued* between his thighs.

When did this happen?

I jerk forward, and the seatbelt snags my waist so hard I yelp.

Orion and Hunter hiss.

"Easy." Hunter unclicks us, and I scramble out of the Jeep.

Orion rushes around, hooking an arm over my shoulders. "You sure you're okay? You don't have to meet Sorensens."

I dig my nails into my palms.

Orion looks all sexy blond soldier boy in his Wyvern camo and his obscene bandage that screams what we did.

We made some kind of mini pack.

I've read every omega textbook and couldn't tell you how or what the fuck that is, but I wouldn't take it back.

The weird, warm energy of him runs through my veins like sunshine and hard cider, and for the first time in my life, I'm not alone.

I don't ever have to be alone again.

I should've said screw the stupid date. Orion and I need to talk and snuggle this out.

Hunter and I need to—

I don't know. Probably move farther apart before he gets me pregnant through two layers of clothes and an implant?

But I don't want to burn my Sorensen bridge, and I'm way too excited to watch the Wyverns fight. "I'll be good."

"I'll walk you in." Hunter waves us in front of him. His gaze is a laser on my back, but I'm glad to have him behind me when we step through the doors.

I wore leggings and Orion's hoodie. Also showered, but I'm edging so close to my heat apocalypse, I'm a walking pheromone bomb.

The building's airplane-hangar huge, with an octagon cage in the center of the stadium seating, but whether it's my sex-starved aura, my sugared perfume, or the omega leading me around like my personal golden pit bull, ready to shank anyone who steps too close, I steal every alpha's attention like the fucking queen.

Conversations cut, heads turn, and alphas *watch*.

But let them see.

I don't drop my shoulders, don't cower or give in to the waves of dominance that want me on my knees.

With Orion here, all I have to do is focus on the sunlight, and my spine stays straight. And with Hunter looming at my back, no one dares to stare for long.

"Your dates." Orion nudges me.

I'm surprised I didn't notice the Sorensens first. Dressed for a country club in nice slacks and collared shirts, they're easy to pick out from the sea of mercenaries in black tees.

Spotting me, they beeline through the crowd.

Hunter steps in, giving me a prime view of a fitted tee so tight, I can count his abs. *At least six. Maybe eight.*

"We'll be nearby. And don't miss the show. Planned a surprise for you." Hunter boops my nose, smirking, then disappears into the crowd.

I rub the spot he flicked.

Not sure I can handle another surprise.

I'm already surprised enough that I keep letting Wyverns past my walls.

"Here they come," Orion warns.

"Is it too late to cancel?" It's not their slacks that bother me. They're handsome. Nice guys. Just…

There's no spark.

I told myself from day one that I don't want, need, or deserve that connection, but I also didn't know how good it could feel.

Wyverns are breaking me.

"Lilah. Such a pleasure to see you again." Rhett's eyes crinkle behind his glasses. He reeks more of amaretto than cherry today.

I *love* almonds.

Like, hello? Ice cream?

So, I should want to *devour* this alpha and his whole foodie pack.

But they don't leave me licking my lips. They can't even cut through Hunter's lingering smoke.

Scent's the problem.

If my perfume hadn't clung to Cale's scrubs, the Sorensens wouldn't be here. They wouldn't care whether I was auctioned off or mated to the mob.

We have nothing in common, and my brain can't conjure what they'd look like naked, let alone how we'd fit together during a heat.

Could Rhett direct the other alphas to fuck me so good?

Would Cale snuggle me all day and hand-feed me chips with hot sauce?

If another pack came at me, could they even fight back?

I can picture them doing my taxes.

Maybe giving me a colonoscopy?

I shudder.

Nail in fucking coffin.

I can't keep trying to force this. I'd rather pick a random pack from Catherine's pile.

My body language must give away the sudden change of heart, because they crowd close, a hint of desperation in their stretched smiles.

"Brought these for you." Jason pushes a pastry box into my hands. "Wish I could've cooked."

"Sorry you had to come to a fight?" I hand the box to Orion.

He's my holder.

"No way. This is the greatest." Kipp bounces, absorbing the mercenary ambiance like a kid at combat camp. But his happy expression morphs into a mask when he looks over my shoulder.

Finn?

I peek back.

Not Finn.

Jett.

He stands in the shadows of the bleacher seating, black clothes, black hair, black eyes.

He is the shadow.

No one else notices him, but people make a space like they're walking past a ghost.

I'm not at the point where I want to give the guy a hug, but you know what I do know?

Jett's waiting for *me* in those shadows.

One word, one touch I don't like, and he'll stomp throats.

My favorite kind of promise.

Cale steps in to smooth over Kipp's freeze. "Glad to see you as well, Orion." He glances between us, mellow until he spots Orion's neck bandage.

Wonder if the doctor knows what we did?

"Good to see you too?" Orion answers, polite but equally wise to this bullshit development, shooting me an amused brow raise.

"It should be starting soon." Rhett offers his arm. "Join us at our seats?"

"Sure." I gingerly rest fingers on his forearm.

Rhett's dominance is there, it just doesn't do anything for me. Not a shiver, not a shudder, not a smile.

I'm much more interested in Orion, who trails behind us as Cale tries to chat him up. His answer gets drowned by the rising volume of the packed crowd, but I can read Orion's expression: *Is this guy serious?*

It's supposed to be my date.

Not their chance to steal *my* omega.

When we reach their box at the top level, Rhett steers me into my seat. His hand slips to my lower back, but he flinches when his fingers hit metal. "You're armed?"

"Always."

"Ah…" He adjusts his glasses.

"You don't carry a weapon?"

"I've never thought of it," he admits. "Never seemed necessary."

I seriously wonder what it's like to get to just *be*, never for a second worrying about being attacked.

Can't imagine.

Orion slips into the seat next to me, and Cale grabs the one next to him. The box is so high up, we have a perfect view down to the mesh-walled octagon and the stands.

The Sorensens don't stand out as much as I feared. Most of the crowd's from Wyvern House, a sea of jacked alphas in black T-shirts, but I spot families, kids, couples, and women on the prowl. Even a bunch of omegas in tight dresses who might actually be strippers.

I should ask for a business card.

I'm still peering around, trying to *Where's Waldo* the Wyverns when Scorpio climbs into the ring holding a mic. The bright lighting highlights his dark, jacked arms and the silver strands in his salt-and-pepper hair. "Settle, settle. I know you know the rules, so no bullshit. Who wants the first challenge?"

Anticipation rises in cheering and shuffling as the agents psych themselves up, eye-jousting to see who's ballsy enough to start the first fight.

They're too slow.

Atlas parts the crowd.

His Big Knot Energy strokes my spine from a ballfield away.

Finn, Hunter, and Jett appear behind him, with wrapped knuckles and gazes that are dark and out-for-blood delicious.

There's my shiver.

A good one that rolls all the way to my toes.

"I have a challenge." Atlas steps into the octagon.

And there's my fucking surprise.

"You're on leave," Scorpio says in a dismissive tone that makes me revisit my bucket list plan to kick him in the kneecap. "Next challenger."

Atlas doesn't twitch. "I challenge Scorpio Wyvern."

The crowd sucks in a breath.

Or was that me?

"Oh shit." Orion jumps to his feet.

I stand, just as shocked as Scorpio.

"On what grounds?"

"For hurting my mates."

"*Oh shit,*" I echo, heart in clammy, thumping chaos.

"Is that wise?" Scorpio's brows lift.

Atlas nods, unshakable. "Has to be done."

"*Max,*" Scorpio barks into the mic. The other three dads appear ringside on the opposite side of the cage from their sons.

No one misses the us vs. them battle lines drawn between the Wyvern generations.

"You're reffing." Scorpio tosses Max the mic. "Won't take long."

Max Wyvern is the jolly bearded dad-bod version of Hunter, who's creepily obsessed with having grandkids.

He's not smiling now. "Let's keep this clean, okay?"

"Ring the bell." Scorpio stretches, cracking his knuckles with his arms above his head. I don't know him well enough to read what he's thinking, but his body language screams.

Not his first time in the ring.

Probably not his hundredth.

I know which alphas I can take by surprise. The ones who'll underestimate me, or the ones who haven't trained or scrapped the way I had to just to survive.

Scorpio could end me in one hit.

I would run.

But Atlas takes a step.

My stomach flips. "What are the rules?"

"No hits to the face or package. Fight until submission. Everything else is fair game." Orion grips my hand. "What the hell is he thinking?"

The bell goes off like a gunshot.

Size-wise, Atlas and his father are equally matched.

Both scary fucking huge and faster than my heart can handle. They circle, wary.

Atlas hits first. Straight punch.

Scorpio ducks, then throws an uppercut. Then Atlas kicks, Scorpio twists, and my eyes glaze, following the crazy brutal back-and-forth attacks.

This isn't a cute family spar.

Atlas and Scorpio want blood, guts, and retribution.

When Atlas lands a jab in his dad's ribs, a wet grunt echoes in the pin-drop silence.

No cheers.

It's not every day your merc boss fights his son and heir.

They go blow for blow for blow.

Hit for hit for hit.

I'm shaking, Orion clinging to my hand, and I hear Rhett in my ear, but his words are mist.

All I can see is the ring.

"This is for you," Orion whispers.

"For *us*."

But when Scorpio lands a brutal face punch, ringing Atlas's head, *I wish he fucking hadn't.*

Max blows his whistle, stepping between. "DQ! Not the face. Shit, Scorp. How's he gonna get the girl if you ruin his moneymaker?"

"Ah, shit." Scorpio wipes sweat off his dripping forehead, then grabs Atlas's shoulder, peering his eyes with the first vague hint of fatherly concern I've ever seen him show. "Face punch was a mistake. You had me on the ropes, kid."

Atlas grins a bloody, split-lipped smile. "You owe them an apology."

"We'll talk. Later." Looking ten years older, and just as battered as his son, Scorpio reclaims the mic. "Next challenger."

Atlas fist-bumps Hunter, who struts into the octagon pointing straight at his father. "I challenge Max Wyvern."

"Grounds?" Scorpio asks, fully resigned to this shitshow, where Finn and Jett hover like reapers waiting for their turn to uproot the Wyvern apple tree.

"For screwing with my mate. And because she wants to watch my ass get kicked."

I taste my heart in my throat.

Hunter shoots me a wink, then strips off his shirt.

Those fucking tattoos. The patterned lines highlight every muscle, but especially the V-line that dips below his shorts.

Dreams really do come true.

When Hunter charges his dad, eating the first hit in the ribs—a hit I know he could've dodged—I realize what they're doing.

This is only half about apologies owed. "They're not trying to win."

"Not even a little." Orion squeezes my trembling fingers. "It's all for you."

When Hunter and Max are both pulped and exhausted, Hunter finally taps out of a headlock.

The cheers die when Hunter tags Finn, and my red-headed demon swings into the cage.

He finds my eyes when he peels off his shirt, flashing that obscene **LILAH** to the dads and the whole fucking crowd. "I challenge Kieran Wyvern."

No one asks his reason.

Atlas had a point to make, and Hunter took us to the rodeo. Finn just wants to fuck around.

He pulls a knife. "First blood?"

Kieran drifts into the ring, a little more spectral, but just as deadly as his son. His knife appears just as quickly and he nods. "First blood."

They move so fast I can't follow, blades glinting under the lights, and it's beautiful.

Thought I was okay with a knife.

This is a *dance*.

Have to have him teach me.

Kieran's first to lower his knife. A long slice scores his shoulder, and his grin is the weirdest display of paternal pride. "Good hit."

Finn salutes with his blade, then uses the bloody knife to blow me a kiss.

I am *dying*.

Then Jett enters the ring.

Fucking lower my body into the earth.

Hikaru doesn't need to be summoned.

He's waiting.

"Grounds?" he asks, cold as if he's staring down his enemy instead of his near-clone.

"A debt."

Hikaru nods. "Begin."

Jett rushes him. And it's…*sloppy*.

His posture's a mess, full of holes that even I could attack. So, of course Hikaru punches back.

Jett misses a dodge.

Hikaru nails a punch to his gut that sends Jett spinning into the cage. He rattles the metal mesh with his face.

"Why…" My heart seizes.

Jett shouldn't be that slow.

That easy to hit.

"Shit," Orion hisses as Jett takes a roundhouse kick that obliterates his knees. Jett eats mat.

"He's not trying." *At all*. He's just…taking the hits.

Like he wants them.

Like he deserves them.

I can't fucking watch.

"Lilah. You— Wait!" Orion tries to grab me, but I'm already thumping down the steps.

I beeline to the octagon.

A random alpha grabs for me, but before his fingers hit my shoulder, Finn's twisting his arm. I slow, expecting him or the others to stop me.

Instead, Atlas and Hunter make me a path.

I fly into the ring.

Hikaru pulls back when he spots me, his chest heaving. I spare him a quick glare before dropping to my knees at Jett's side.

"Tap out," I order.

Holding my gaze, he taps the mat.

I fold my arms to keep myself from offering him a hand up. He's sweating. There's a fleck of blood on his lip because he bit himself when he braced against a punch. "Who gave you permission?"

His eyes glitter.

His lips part.

I think he's going to say something world-endingly devastating. Something that rewrites my whole universe.

But as he climbs to his knees, Jett's gaze slips past me.

He goes corpse rigid.

Not deer in headlights, but a stag after the crash. Mangled. Staring up at the sky.

The hairs on my arms rise, and the creepy sensation sends me slowly whirling.

Lurid teal sequins flash.

Then I spot the woman in the spangled dress, with dark hair and hellish eyes, and Jett's heart isn't the only one getting embalmed.

She's older than I remember.

Faded. Black hair and olive skin.

Used to be old money. Now she's a designer bag at the thrift store, slowly crumbling under too much makeup.

A sound rumbles in my chest.

I've been making the weirdest freaking noises. Whimpers and squeaks and little kitten mewls that I didn't know I had in me until the guys touched me just right.

This is another world-debut sound, only it's not a kitten noise.

It's the warning of a predator.

A jagged growl that doesn't come from my throat. It rips from deep in my chest. The feral, protective omega snarl fierce enough to cow an alpha.

I've only heard the noise in videos because there are only two ways to really, *really* piss off an omega.

Come after their mates.

Come after their young.

Renee came for more than that.

Because of her, my childhood went off the rails and into a swamp.

And what she did to Jett—

I'm already in the ring.

It's destiny.

I point at her with a finger like a sword and lift my voice so loud they can hear it all the way to the OCC. "I challenge Renee."

THIRTY-THREE

LILAH

"THIS ISN'T A PLACE FOR CIVILIANS." Scorpio dismisses my request.

I dismiss his dismissal. "I'm challenging her for being a fucking monster."

"*Lilah*," Scorpio growls a warning.

My shoulders tingle under the weight of his command. I want to shrink, but I'm not backing down, I—

A wall bumps me from behind.

Atlas lifts me a foot off the ground to hug me under his chin. His pack leader juice flows into my veins, lending me his strength.

Suddenly, I can stand as tall as I want.

I'm *levitating*.

"*Atlas*," Scorpio barks. "*Get her out of the ring.*"

Scorpio's dominance usually grinds me into the floor. Now it rolls past. The only tingle in my body is the one from Atlas's breath on my neck.

"Why her?" Atlas whispers, not stopping me, just lending his support.

I can hardly look at the woman, so I look at Jett instead.

I don't have to say anything. All I do is tilt Atlas's chin so he sees what I'm seeing.

Jett's empty.

No one behind those eyes.

It's not the way Finn goes empty, where he's still and silent and plotting mass murder.

Jett looks like he's been erased.

But no matter how he tries to disappear, I see him because I've been there. Maybe that's why I climbed inside a barrel instead of asking for help.

Because when you hurt and you hurt and you hurt, disappearing is better than feeling.

That's why I want to hammer the banshee who started this shitshow.

Atlas's growl rumbles through me like it's my own.

"I challenge Renee," I repeat.

She tries to fade into the crowd, but Finn cuts off her path. Then Hunter appears, and her alpha escorts duck and fucking run from their blood-soaked smiles.

Hunter's growl is soul-tearing with rage that stops the woman from escaping, moving, or doing anything but shaking.

"Accept the challenge," Hunter snarls.

"Ridiculous." She clutches her purse. "I'm leaving."

"Do you want me or do you want him?" I point to Finn, who proudly holds the knife still wet with his father's blood.

Her lower lip trembles.

But Renee doesn't cave.

"Then prison?" I offer. "You know what they'll do to you in there when they find out what you—"

"I accept," her voice quavers with Hunter and Finn hovering at her shoulders like devils, but there's a flash of that old rich girl hatred in her eyes.

She glares like she's already punching the shit out of me. When she reaches the octagon, Hikaru opens the cage.

His skin-peeling sneer obliterates whatever confidence Renee gathered when she thought I was her only problem.

No one knew.

Last I heard, Renee was fired for embezzling from the center. Now her real fucking rap sheet is coming to light.

Both Wyvern packs follow her quaking motion with the murderous confidence of cats tracking a cockroach.

They will *end* her.

But I get to play first.

Jett's on his feet, but not really here. "Bring him a seat?"

Atlas sets me down and ducks out of the cage to grab a folding chair. Together, we sit Jett in my corner. Atlas moves behind the chair, putting his hands on Jett's shoulders to share the same reassurance he lent to me.

"Watch." I tug Jett's chin. "This is for both of us." I strip off Orion's hoodie and set it in his hands.

Jett hugs the fabric, and when he breathes in my scent, there's a little glitter in his eyes.

The crowd, the guys, the cage—all of it fades when I step to Renee at the center of the ring.

All the times she hit me or ordered me hit and I never once fought back. I couldn't hit a trainer. I could just barely protect myself—never attack.

Tonight, I'm paying back what she owes. "You want to change?"

"No." Renee tosses her purse and kicks off her heels. She looks like a ring girl in a teal bodycon sheath, but when she meets me center stage, her posture relaxes into a practiced stance.

She's terrified of the Wyverns, but she's not even a little afraid of me.

Gonna have fun fixing that attitude.

"No guns in the ring." Scorpio sighs, looking thirty years older than when I crashed the cage.

"Oh." I only brought three. I hand them to Atlas, expecting a lecture.

Instead, he checks that they're not loaded, tucks them away, and sets his palm on my head. "Fuck her up."

I blink. "What if I go to prison?"

"How?" Atlas softly strokes my ear, wearing a fond smile that doesn't match his crazy talk. "Police will never find her body."

Good to fucking know.

Confident I can get away with murder, I strut to the center of the ring. "Ready?"

Renee pushes a breath through her bleached teeth. "Do I have a choice?"

"Nope."

Scorpio rubs his forehead. "Fight."

The bell rings.

I lunge.

Renee ducks.

She's the typical rich girl omega, so she's spent time training self-defense.

Good.

The fight will last longer.

I fake a punch, then kick, knocking her into the cage wall.

She hisses. "Is this really necessary?"

"You screwed with my records. Why?"

Renee's gaze flicks side to side. "I did what I was paid to do."

I kick at her stomach. She catches my ankle, blocking the blow, but she's too slow when I follow up with a *crack* to her jaw.

My knuckles burn so good.

Renee stumbles, turning to Scorpio with doe eyes—only Bambi shouldn't have done so many hard drugs, because she looks more insane than ingenue.

For the first time in my life, the ref's on my side. I don't think Scorpio would step in if I cut Renee open and ate her heart.

I yank her to her feet. "Who paid you?"

"Redfangs wanted omegas groomed. I just—"

My punch cracks her nose.

She lets out a bloody wail.

"Bitch!" Renee explodes like a cornered rat. She lands a slap that rings my ears, then tries to ring her hands around my throat.

I kick and flip, landing so I'm on top, pinning her under my weight.

Groomed for the gangs.

Makes so much sense.

I'd ask her why she went after Jett, but there's no answer worth hearing. Doesn't matter.

I just want her to pay.

I let her up.

Screeching, Renee flies at me.

She lands a few crazy hits, mostly slaps, but I shove her off again and again.

Kick and punch.

Kick and punch.

My knuckles burn and her blood mixes with the sweat on my forehead.

I'm panting when I slam her back against the cage. The metal rattles and blood trickles from her lips. Her eyes glaze, and I finally let her fall.

"If they don't kill you, I will."

Renee's lashes flutter, and she passes out, otherwise I'd keep kicking.

I'm deciding if I should keep a piece as a trophy—maybe pop off an acrylic nail—when Atlas scoops me away.

He sits me in the corner of the ring, and the five of them crowd so close, they're all I can see.

Atlas moves behind me, protecting my back while Orion wipes the blood from my face with his sleeve. Finn licks my stinging knuckles in soothing tongue strokes.

Hunter keeps trying to tug him away. "Need to bandage those."

And Jett.

He kneels between my thighs, face in my lap, arms around my waist like he's never letting go.

I tug my hands free so I can stroke his hair.

He mumbles something incoherent into my skin in ticklish

breaths that feather my thighs.

"Did you see?"

Jett doesn't answer, but his grip tightens around my stomach.

As the guys shift, fussing over me, I catch glimpses of the dads directing agents to haul Renee away.

Feels like I should get in trouble?

Not that I'm going to apologize.

Kinda want Renee to wake up so I can hit her a few more times.

But my whole life, the pattern has been fight, get punished, defend myself, get punished, hurt someone, get punished.

So, I can't sink into the cocoon of the guys' coddling. "Do I have to get questioned or anything?"

Atlas rumbles. "No one questions you."

"You do what the fuck you want, Star." Finn drops next to Jett, not caring that his brother's having a moment, just worming in so I'll pet his head too.

I scratch his scalp until he purrs.

"I can do anything?" I spot a kid in the front row with saucer eyes and a tray of nachos.

Bet if I stole them, the guys would say I needed them more.

But why would I have to steal?

If I asked, they'd bring me fifty trays of chips, feed me by hand, and let me lick hot cheese from their fingers.

My head spins, so I ground myself, stroking Finn and Jett like lap animals.

I think I'm drunk.

On power and bloodlust and their touch.

Then I catch the motion in the stands—the only ones in the crowd who aren't watching the Wyverns fuss over me in open-mouthed shock.

Sorensens are walking out, showing me their backs.

I smell smoke.

Just not sure if it's Hunter or the bridge I finally fucking incinerated.

THIRTY-FOUR

JETT

I CAN'T REMEMBER what it's like to not be frozen. Keeping that icy distance is the only reason I survived.

But the ice inside me thaws at Lilah's touch.

Her warm fingers in my hair.

Lilac never changed.

She's sweet and true and loyal and fierce.

I don't deserve her, but I can't run.

Won't escape or fade away.

She took revenge.

For me.

For *me*.

After I—

I'll never deserve her, but I want to give her the same gift. Everyone who hurt her.

There are so many names on the list.

I still put myself at number one, but I'll take my punishment in servitude.

Whatever Lilac needs.

Whatever she wants.

That's why I don't let go until Atlas reminds me. "Her knuckles are bleeding. Let us take her home."

Finn and Hunter haul me to my feet.

"Told you." Finn hits my shoulder.

I finally understand his madness. How she can be the anchor we both lack.

As Atlas carries Lilah—*my Lilac*—away, head tucked against his chest, the ice creeps back, freezing me in starbursts of pain.

I'm only warm for her.

Hunter tugs me around to meet my gaze, flicking his eyes side to side. I don't care what truths he sees.

He pats my shoulder. "You want to talk to her, or you want us to take care of it?"

"I have one question." Then I'll close this chapter, stake my demons, and start chasing Lilah's instead.

"Let's go." Hunter and Finn each take an arm, supporting me down through the underground catacombs to our dungeon cells.

Smells like clay and metal.

Water and blood.

Hikaru leans against a cell door, waiting. He straightens when we near. "Do you have something to say to me?"

"No." My past is between me and Doctor Jakob.

Lilah if she wants to hear.

He nods, ending what passes as a Wyvern heart-to-heart. "She's yours."

"Always was." I should've taken her out years ago, but I liked knowing where she was. Knowing that I had her under my control the way she wanted me under hers. It kept me from digging too deep and remembering the rest of the past I couldn't bear.

"Tag team?" Finn licks his lips.

I yank him back so I can enter. "You can clean up."

He and I have a routine for breaking prisoners.

Renee's already broken.

She groans against the floor, flinching when my footsteps stop in front of her face.

I wait for the rush of memories, of pain, of shame.

Nothing comes but disgust.

Lilah obliterated the last of this woman's power over me.

I crouch, enjoying looming while she's unable to move. "Who paid you?"

"D-d-dominik." Her teeth chatter.

"Since when?"

"Since before I started at the OCC."

"To groom omegas?"

"Darlings. Lilah and her friends. Not the other girls."

"And me?"

"You were too close to her." Renee swallows hard, glancing up at me with heated, hopeful eyes. "Besides. You liked—"

Needs to die.

I pinch her chin, silencing her mouth. "Where is he?"

Her jaw quavers. "H-he sends checks. Hasn't been to Diamonds in months. I d-don't know, so… C-can I…"

"*Finn,*" I bark.

He walks in like he's been waiting with his ear pressed to the door. "Kill?"

"See if she knows anything else."

I sit in the chair on the other side of the cell and watch him work.

Finn's too out of control for fine torture, especially when the bitch admits to hurting Lilah.

If I wanted it to last, I'd work her myself.

Just want to tie up the loose end.

But Renee has nothing left of value, every scream and secret wrung out.

She shakes on the floor.

Finn offers me his gun and a psychotic smile.

I cock it to her forehead.

Feels like I should feel something when she stares with glazed, watery eyes.

Nothing.

That's probably a problem too.

I'll ask Doctor Jakob.

I pull the trigger.

The gunshot's roar is cataclysmic in the echoing cell.

I thought this moment would shake me just as much, but there's no sense of victory.

All I feel is anxious to get on with the night.

To move on.

To begin my redemption or demise.

"Do you have hair clippers?" I ask Finn as we leave the cell and Renee's body behind.

"Hunter does. For his manscaping. Why? Fresh cut for our girl?"

"Fresh cut." I nod. "You going to the office?"

"Daddy Hunter wants us back."

"I'll meet up with you later. Have a project."

Finn salutes with bloody fingers.

I stop at the condo everyone's been not-so-secretly moving out of, bringing their things underground to Lilah's. I haven't done the same, but I will, beginning now.

First, I dig the clippers out of Hunter's bathroom.

I flick them on and the *bzzzzt* makes me smile.

Fully charged.

Shoving them in a backpack, I head out.

Busy, busy night.

Appointments all over town.

Debts to repay for my Lilac.

———

IT'S deep in the night, almost morning, when I finally return to her apartment.

Atlas's soft snore rattles down the hall. He and Orion are asleep in the same bed, door open in case she calls.

I stalk to Lilah's room.

Need to see her, but the light's off.

I hesitate to knock.

Adrenaline has me shaking.

Not from killing my rapist.

Not from all the other havoc I just played.

No.

Just from standing in front of her door, terrified Lilah won't want what little I have to offer.

I drift to the bar cart in the living room and pour myself a glass.

The bourbon sears my throat.

If she doesn't accept me…

I pour another glass.

Another.

I lose count, gripping my backpack to my stomach.

When the room spins too hard to stop, I stumble into one of the bedrooms.

There's boxes everywhere. Bright orange lingerie.

Finn's room.

I fall on the bed, tipping a stack of packages to the floor.

Collars.

Big, thick, spiked collars.

I snort.

Finn's been teaching me. Telling me how Lilah's the only reason he's alive. How he inked his chest to mark himself.

So I stole one of his ideas for a gift.

But mine isn't so *tacky*.

Hope she accepts it. Hope she accepts *me*.

I drink straight from the bottle I'm still clutching.

Tomorrow, I'll be brave enough to tell her everything.

Tonight?

Bourbon.

THIRTY-FIVE

LILAH

ATLAS CARRIES me back to the apartment like a princess. Then he and Orion pin me to the couch while they bandage my knuckles.

"I'm fine," I insist, pretending they're not making me tremble with their attention.

Orion presses a bag of frozen broccoli to my cheek. "She hit you."

"I hit her harder."

"Our girl's a badass." He rubs my nose with his thumb.

"Hold still," Atlas grumbles.

He dabs ointment on my fingers, and bandages them with that crazy, single-minded focus that makes me feel like the center of the galaxy.

It's becoming a problem.

"Where are the others?" I ask, keeping it light so they don't know how deeply I'm shaken.

It's not just the bandages on my fingers.

It's the bandage on Orion's neck that no one's asked about. It's my backup pack defecting, and the Wyverns chip, chip, chipping at my determination with kisses and care and chocolate-chip muffins.

It's my growing terror that they'll do all that, and still walk.

"They're with the dads," Atlas answers. "Questioning Renee."

"Even Jett?"

"Hunter will take care of him." Atlas's shoulders dip. "If I'd known…"

"He didn't want us to know." Orion sighs. "That's been the problem. We would've done so much so differently."

I chew my lip.

I had to sit for a while before Jett would let me go. He clung like he was hanging at the edge, and the soft heat of his breath is permanently seared on my thighs.

I need to talk to him.

I need to see if he's confused, because why else would he touch me, let alone hug me like he's falling apart?

But first I have other problems. "Did you catch what she said about grooming omegas?"

"Hunter's on it." Atlas stays focused on my fingers. "He'll handle the investigation."

Orion's brows lift. "You're not going in? Don't you need to lead the charge?"

"This is where I want to be." Atlas kisses my hand, then strokes Orion's cheek.

He and I share a silent, wide-eyed *what the hell*, but before we can burst into flames, Atlas's phone vibrates with an incoming call.

I'm expecting Scorpio. Maybe some emergency that'll have him dropping all these good intentions and shipping out for a quick assassination.

Celeste flashes on screen with a picture of a cute old lady, and he answers so fast, I wonder if she's a secret agent.

There's no greeting, but the woman chatters on the other side while Atlas nods. "I already soaked the potatoes overnight. Can you walk me through? I'll put it on video."

He walks into the kitchen, propping his phone and starting to assemble bowls and knives. He lines everything with military precision, then pulls a huge bowl of potatoes from the fridge.

Orion tugs me into his lap to whisper. "He's making you homemade fries."

Fucking shit.

Just mate me now.

————

LUCKILY FOR MY SANITY, Atlas burns the first batch. The fries don't look burnt to me, but he won't let me taste. He orders us pizza while scribbling notes about what went wrong, muttering about peanut oil and prepping a new batch of potatoes for tomorrow.

After dinner, I go through more Redfang papers, but Orion snatches them and makes me take a bath.

Rough life.

It's way late, and I'm pacing my dark bedroom when I realize why I can't sleep.

The reason is a double donkey kick to the ribs.

I'm waiting for the pack to get home.

I swear it's my creeping heat hormones.

This jitter. This *need* to see the alphas.

My alphas.

To know I'll be taken care of the way they've been proving they can.

I want to throw up.

But then…

Unless I really am going crazy, I hear someone *actually* throwing up. The wracking, choking noise echoes through the pipes, and before I can even think, I'm rushing down the hall in my robe.

When Orion and I were getting dressed earlier, I realized all the guys have claimed bedrooms. Only the rooms aren't filled with *their* stuff. They're filled with the stuff they keep buying for me.

This bed's piled with tangerine lingerie that screams Finn fucking Wyvern, and my gut clenches as I hurry to the bathroom.

But instead of a red-headed mess, I find Jett on his knees.

Dark hair falling to his shoulders, shirt off, baring pale, toned, and drunk-sweaty skin.

Reeking like moonshine, he groans.

"Jett?"

His voice is a razor rasp that slices straight into my heart. "*Lilac.*"

My heart stops.

So does time.

Cheek pressed to the toilet seat, he shoots me the goofiest grin. "Finally killed her."

"Are you…okay?" Because I'm fucking not. Which of them left him on his own, so drunk off his ass he's *smiling*?

Jett *never* smiles.

JJ smiles.

JJ calls me Lilac in that sweet, little boy tone that doesn't match the merc on his knees who's made of shadows and hate.

"I…" Jett crawls away from the toilet. "Can you still look at me?"

"I'm looking at you now." The fall of his long hair and the cut back muscles that twist and bunch as he stumble-crawls.

"Disgusted?"

"No." That's not even close to what I'm feeling. A better word would be *ache*. Maybe nostalgia. Definitely some inappropriate thirst. "But you're crawling on the bathroom floor and super drunk, so you should probably take a shower."

Need to grab him some water and painkillers. "I'll go—"

Jett grabs my ankle.

His grip's a shackle, but softer.

Rabbit fur handcuffs.

"Don't leave."

I crouch to peel his fingers off my foot. He switches to gripping my hand, staring up at me with those midnight-pool eyes that aren't focusing after however much he drank to be this out of his mind.

"How come I have to stay?" I whisper, hiding the tremor in my voice. "You're the one who always leaves."

"No." He squeezes my fingers. "Not anymore. Can't."

"We can talk in the morning." When he's not wasted, and I've had a chance to recover from this half seizure, half heart attack assault on my soft omega soul.

"Give you a present." He tugs my hand to his face and rubs it like a cat.

I tear away, rescuing my fingers before they betray me and sink into his hair. "Take a shower and brush your teeth. I'll bring you water. Okay?"

"Okay." Jett stumbles to his feet, lurching toward the shower, already ripping off his pants, and I get the hell out before I have to see what's below the curve of his dimpled lower back.

I slam the door and press a hand to my pounding heart.

I think Jett finally broke.

Now he wants me broken too.

I step into Finn's closet and grab the closest handful of guys' clothes, not daring to dig after spotting his box of floggers and rope.

After setting the stack outside the bathroom door, I dash to the kitchen to grab water and pills.

I take my time coming back, hoping Jett will already be passed out. Then, tomorrow, he can pretend he doesn't remember.

I peek through the crack in his door.

Jett sits on the floor, back to the bed. He's shirtless, wearing a too-long pair of Finn's sweats that hang ultra-low on his carved hips. Long hair soaking wet and tangled, he looks more like a disoriented caveman than his usual put-together statue with a permanent scowl.

I'd duck away, but he's already watching me like he's been tracking my footsteps since I stepped into the hall.

"*Lilac.*"

Trembling, I move to crouch at his side. "Take these if you don't want a headache."

I hold out the painkillers, but instead of taking them, Jett lifts my wrist to his mouth.

He sucks the pills off my palm.

While he chugs water, I'm left with a permanent lip print on my skin.

Water drips down his shoulders.

He watches me like nothing else matters while I rummage to find a towel and a comb. I shouldn't touch him. Shouldn't let this go on, but I'm weaker for him than anyone, and his need calls to the deepest, softest part of me.

The little girl who never stopped waiting for JJ to come back.

I scoot behind him on the bed, towel him dry and gently work the comb through the drunken mess he's made of his poor hair. He's motionless until I hit a snarl.

Then he jerks, hitching my legs over his shoulders and shackling my ankles in that soft-tight grip.

"*Jett*." His shower-steamed skin sears my calves.

"Don't call me that."

Fingers in his hair, I close my eyes. "JJ."

"*Mmm*."

I keep combing long after the tangles are gone. He strokes my ankles with his thumbs.

It's so peaceful, I start to tip forward, finally getting sleepy.

Seriously have to leave.

I'm already banking on him either blacking out or claiming he blacked out when he hates me again in the morning.

"Come up." I pat the bed and start tossing the mess of clothes.

Lacy orange lingerie and the crumpled T-shirt Jett was wearing earlier. Only, when I touch it, hair sticks to my fingers.

Blonde, brown, red.

They're all mixed strands, all too long and the wrong colors to belong to the guys. "Did you rob a salon?"

"Your present."

Finally letting go of my ankles, he tugs over a backpack I didn't see in the rubble on Finn's floor.

When he tips it upside down, a wireless hair clipper *thunks* to the carpet, followed by stacks and stacks of what my brain thinks are rats.

Wait.

Not rats.

Bundles of hair bound in rubber bands.

"Are those...ponytails?" I peer over the bed and catch a hint of sharp mint.

"Juniper?" I croak.

"Juniper, Mya, Madison, Rachel."

"*Rachel?* Holy shit. JJ. You shaved their heads?"

"They hurt you. *I* hurt you." With shaking hands he grabs the clipper and flicks the switch. "One more."

He moves the clip toward his forehead, and the *buzzzzzz* fries my brain.

"No!" I grab his wrist. He doesn't fight, letting me push down his arm and turn off the machine.

"Why not?"

"That's my hair." It's thick and silky and my favorite thing to play with. If he wants to cut it to cut it, then fine. But if he wants to cut it to punish himself?

Nuh uh.

"Everything is yours." He knocks aside the hair bundles and pulls out a wide, flat box. "Here."

I want to reject on the principle that whatever's inside is guaranteed to be batshit, but the box isn't ticking, smoking, or bleeding.

Still, I hesitate.

"Open it." JJ's voice is soft, no bark, but his dark, needy eyes have me moving before I can second-guess.

I pull out a thin length of black leather mounted with a single silver O-ring.

A collar.

"If you think I'm wearing—"

"It's not for you," he says dreamily. "There's more."

Heart stuttering, too curious to stop, I dig through the tissue paper.

There's a bracelet

It's delicate black leather, with a tiny silver ring that matches the collar.

Much too small for him.

He takes my hand and buckles the leather on my wrist like he's handling fragile glass.

Gently.

Possessively.

"Now me." JJ lifts the collar, a fallen knight offering his queen her crown.

He's at my feet.

Kneeling.

So why does it feel like I'm the one being forced to submit?

His gaze *devours.*

I dry swallow. "Why?"

"Giving you my leash. Use me. Hate me. Punish me. Don't think you can love me, but I'm already yours. I've always been yours, even when I forgot. I won't forget again. Can't. There's nothing left of me but you." JJ pushes the collar into my shaking hands.

I'm drowning in cedar with that soft hit of cherry and an edge of blossoming sweetness that crawls into my brain.

So good.

His eyes are deep, glittering, galactic black.

Pupils wide with need.

This is when I tell him no.

I'm not adopting a puppy.

But then JJ starts to stroke my hands with his hot thumbs, purring so softly I wonder if he even knows he's making the sound.

Wonder if he knows he can.

It's just for me.

Only for me.

So fuck it.

I wanna see what JJ looks like wearing my collar.

His purr ratchets when I wrap the leather around his neck. His heat, his scent, his earnest insanity wash over me as I latch the band around his throat.

"Too tight?" I ask breathily, tugging him forward by the ring.

"*Fuuuck.*" His head tips back and his scent spikes so hard I taste cherries and cream. "You own me. Tell me who to kill. What you need. I'm yours, Lilac."

JJ stops my heart, sinking his teeth into the meat of my thumb.

He doesn't break the skin, but the damage is fucking done.

My panties are soaked, my willpower's roasted, and I'm just as damaged as him, because the thought of tugging him around by his throat has me ready to bend over and let him show me who owns who.

But he's drunk and I'm fucking crazy.

"Get in bed." I tear away from him.

JJ obeys, climbing between the sheets. I tuck him in *hard*, shoving the blanket tight, all the way to his chin until he's bound like a corpse and he can't come shambling after me with more of this emotional machine gun fire.

His O-ring pokes out of the blanket.

I'm going to die.

"Sleep," I command, covering his needy gaze with sweaty fingers.

His lashes flutter against my skin. "*Goodnight, Lilac.*"

I run back to my room, still feeling ticklish spider feet dancing on my palm, still wearing the bracelet JJ put on me like the softest fucking handcuff.

Still can't sleep.

Only now I'm pacing wondering if tomorrow I'll wake up to JJ, Jett, or another broken heart.

THIRTY-SIX

LILAH

IT TAKES me so long to fall asleep, it has to be almost dinner by the time I wake, feeling every ache from last night's fight.

My bed's empty.

I cock my head, expecting bickering and burning breakfast food, but everything's quiet.

A sickening feeling worms in my belly.

I grab a honeyed Hunter hoodie and walk into the hall.

It's quiet *and* dark.

"Orion?" My voice echoes.

I push into the bedrooms where they've been crashing, and their warm scents tease, but no one's home. I hesitate the hardest in front of the room where I left Jett, but when I crack the door, all that's left of last night is the pile of ponytails lining the smoothed-out bedspread like trophies.

I grip the burning bracelet on my wrist, fiddling with the silver ring, positive I'm not dreaming.

"Guys?" Tasting stomach acid, I walk the long hallway to the nest.

Empty.

Gone.

I suck in a hard breath, and my hands start to shake.

Don't panic.

Do not panic.

They just…

They just *what*?

Ran out for coffee when they promised someone would be with me at all times?

Had an emergency too dire to leave a fucking note?

My belly cramps.

I start to sweat.

No wonder I didn't spike last night.

I'm spiking *now*.

Already halfway in the nest, I trip up the steps to the big bed, burrow deep in blankets, and curl into a ball.

I rock back and forth.

Need to call Catherine. Get Juan Pablo here, stat. Review all those offers.

Instead, I hug a pillow and squeeze my eyes shut.

Knew this was coming.

Knew this would happen.

I'm not sure how long I rock.

Eventually, I hear a noise that has me peeking warily out of the blankets, cursing. Because for the first time in forever, I walked out of my room without a blade.

Thought I was safe.

"Lilah? Lilah?" Orion's voice echoes down the hall. He crashes into the nest, gripping his heart when he finally spots me, only my eyes poking from the massive pile of blankets.

I whine.

"Oh, shit." His hot whisper lifts to a frantic shout. "*Guys!*"

He vaults the steps, whipping off blankets to get to me. I ooze into his arms.

"Thought you left," I say woodenly.

"Never, little bear." He smooths my hair, pulling my head against his hammering heart. "Fucking never."

Footsteps thump the carpet.

The alphas bust in, one, two, three, four, all fighting to be first through the door. Finn throws elbows, popping out first and skips the steps, fucking high-jumping into the nest.

"Everything went dark." Finn peels me out of Orion's clinging fingers as the others pile into the nest.

Atlas strokes my back, Hunter purrs like a motorboat, and Jett hooks one finger in my bracelet and the other in the ring of the collar I can't believe he didn't rip off the second he got sober.

Under their touches and whispers and soft, stroking hands, I finally shudder, brain coming down from that high, panicked place.

"You didn't leave?" I ask, just to be sure. "Where did you go?"

Orion stops kissing my fingers, mumbling into my hand. "I'm so sorry. Just took the elevator up to grab food. The guys were all on the way back in. Didn't want to wake you when you were passed out. I texted."

"Don't know where I left my phone," I mumble into Atlas's chest. "Panicked."

"Your heat's close." Atlas drags blunt fingertips down my neck, and the reassuring stroke feels so much like teeth, I go all limp noodle. "You're going to be a little sensitive."

"A little fucking crazy," I murmur.

With all five of them rubbing me, I realize how quickly I went off.

Basically unprompted.

But my fears are my fears, and when the hormones are driving, I'm a wreck.

They stay with me for a long, long time, whispering sweet things and petting me all over. The spike evaporates as quickly as it came—even though I didn't come at all.

Feeling like a slice of melted cheddar, I finally try to wiggle out of the cuddle pile. They don't budge until I pull out the big guns. "Hungry."

Hunter grabs me first, jumping carefully down and carrying

me to the kitchen while the guys hurry behind. He sets me on the island counter.

They dropped bags of takeaway that Atlas quickly picks up, but Hunter's faster to the freezer.

He brings me a spoon and my own pint of almond cake ice cream.

"How did you know?" I reach, but he holds the treat away, pushing between my thighs.

Which I happily part.

"You robbed the kitchen." He scoops a spoonful and offers it to my lips.

I gobble sweet almond frosting with a moan.

Orion appears with a spoon and a smirk to feed me a second bite. "You'll have to eat a vegetable next."

"Almond's a nut. Super nutritious." I open my mouth like a baby bird, and Hunter feeds me another spoonful.

It's so sticky sweet, and their attention feels even better, warming my throat and making the cream go down crazy smooth.

Hunter between my legs.

Orion at my side.

Feeding me their…*cream*.

Heat creeps up my neck.

Maybe I *can* get used to this.

They trade off, feeding me bites until the collared one pushes in.

JJ holds a spoon.

But instead of feeding me, he presses the handle into my palm. "Try?"

"Mmm." I scoop a bite and offer it to his deep red lips. Just like he did with the pills, he snatches my whole wrist, locking me down while he licks the spoon and stares into my eyes.

I shudder.

Need to close my thighs.

"More." JJ doesn't blink. Doesn't break eye contact.

Hypnotized, I hold out a second spoonful.

But Finn shoulder-checks him, snapping the bite like a hyena.

He swallows, eyes burning. "Star. Aren't I your favorite?"

"Don't have a favorite."

"Then where's my collar?" Finn takes my hand, fingering my new leather bracelet.

My arm hairs lift. "You want one?"

"*Fuck yes.*"

"JJ picked his own. I just put it…" I make the mistake of turning.

Jett is fucking gone.

But JJ.

He has a finger hooked in his collar ring and a soul-stealingly soft smile that robs the air from my lungs, the room, and the entire fucking planet.

It's mass extinction.

Crops die, people suffocate, and solar systems collapse under the force of those gravity-destroying lips.

How's my heart supposed to survive?

I drop the spoon.

My chest is so heavy.

Eyes, suddenly wet.

Everyone freezes.

Atlas nudges them aside, lifting me off the counter and into his rock solid arms. I press my face into his neck and clench my jaw.

I will not cry.

I do not cry.

"Sweet girl." He rubs my back with that big palm. "We're here. We're not leaving."

His reassurance sinks into my bones.

I let out a gulping breath, muffled in his warm skin. Not a sob.

Shit.

I'm such a mess, but it feels so good.

So, so impossibly *good.*

I can't resist anymore.

Don't want to. "But…"

"We'll take care of you during your heat," Atlas promises, hand drifting to my neck so his thumb can softly stroke my collar-bone. "Wanna bite you. Make you ours. But we don't have to. It's only what you want."

The others crowd, adding their touches and scents, and all the tension melts.

My fight.

My fear.

I *submit*.

But before I can untangle all the words and things I need to say, someone's phone buzzes.

Hunter curses. "911."

The room's tension shifts, and Atlas clutches me tighter. "Answer it."

Love the way his deep voice rumbles when we're skin to skin. More vibrations pulse when Hunter spits a string of juicy curses. "Redfangs kidnapped Noelle Patrick."

My head rockets off Atlas's chest.

But…

That's not 911.

That's a reason to pop champagne.

Hunter gives a few clipped "yes, sirs" before shoving the phone back in his pocket. "Dads need us there. Now Senator Charlie and the mates are fucking frothing. Threatening to cancel our military contracts if we don't ride in and rescue their mate."

"So you're going?" My pitch rises dangerously close to a whine.

Hunter glances around. "A. Fuck Noelle. She can suffer. Also, B. Fuck the contracts. But C… It's a lead on Dom. Following might finally give us his location."

A panicked tremble rocks me.

I get it.

They have to go.

Have to hunt him down so he'll stop hunting me and Orion.

But my heat's so fucking close.

I can't be alone.

"Not going." Atlas snatches the tub of ice cream and a spoon, and gently shifts so he can feed me another bite. " Staying right here, sweet girl."

I can't stop myself from smiling around the spoon.

Atlas smiles back with a special glint in his golden-brown eyes. "Hunter will handle it."

"At. Bro. You're the leader, right?" Hunter clasps his hands in prayer. "You can—"

"I'm just a gummy bear." He pats Hunter's shoulder. "Have fun at the office."

"Guys…" Hunter glances around while Atlas carries me and the ice cream to the sofa.

"I'm omega." Orion grabs a blanket and snuggles down next to me. "Omegas don't go to the office. Too chaotic."

"Finn. Jett. We—"

"I need to lie low." Jett cuts him off. "You should be getting another call."

"What do you—" Hunter's phone rings like dark magic. Square jaw tightening, he answers. "Yeah? He *what?* No. No. I don't know. Call the fucking PR team. Fine. On my merry fucking way." He pushes out a shaking breath. "What the shit is this? Mutiny?"

"What happened?" Atlas's brow furrows, but his hand never budges from the back of my neck. His thumb rubs a slow, gentle stroke that has me wanting popcorn instead of panicking.

"Jett will have to answer that question."

JJ shrugs, icy-casual. "I shaved some heads."

"You got caught." Hunter's neck vein pops. "You teach the effing class on infiltration."

"Wanted them to see." He licks his lips, eyes boiling with shadows just for me. "Wanted them to know what happens when you touch her."

"He brought me their ponytails," I say on a happy sigh.

Who needs flowers and chocolates?

I like revenge.

Okay. Also chocolates.

But still.

Best. Gift. Ever.

"Asshole." Finn elbows him. "Why didn't you invite me?"

"It was my debt to pay."

"Fuck. Getting a collar." Finn dashes to his bondage closet, not giving a shit about Noelle's kidnapping, Jett's prosecution, or his own axing when Patricks politically cancel the Wyverns.

My heart puffs so full, my ribs can barely hold the glow. "You don't have to go…"

When Hunter turns to me, his tension melts. He scoops me out of Atlas's arms.

And holy shit.

When Atlas holds me, it's grizzly feels. Warm and soft, and yeah, muscular, but mostly big and cuddly.

Hunter's supposed to be the teddy bear.

But when he pulls me tight, hooking his arms around my waist and soaking me in smoky honey, it's a hug from a jacked statue.

Hard, cut, sculpted muscle.

Something coils inside, and my scent spikes high and wild.

My fingers twitch. I wanna flick him and see if there's give or if he's protein powder all the way down.

Hunter's chuckle strokes that coiling tickle. "Killer. They wanna make me pack leader."

"Is that okay?" I give into the urge to smooth his shoulders.

Dying, and the tattoos aren't even out.

"It is if I can bite you first. Right here." Hunter nips my throat, just below my jaw. I shudder. "Or here?" He dips to my shoulder, nibbling the soft flesh above my collarbone until my legs suction to his hard waist.

Anywhere's fine.

Or everywhere.

I want his teeth.

I want his mark.

And I can't fucking lie to myself any more.

Because I want them *all*.

I don't dare say it out loud, but I kiss his jugular, reserving the spot where I'll leave my bite.

Hunter's purr hitches under my lips. "Never let you hurt again."

I *hmm* into his pulse. "Maybe one more time."

It'll be the best kind of pain when they finally sink into my throat.

THIRTY-SEVEN

LILAH

UNEASE RATTLES me when Hunter walks away to solo-solve our gang war, but the four bodies that pile into his space quickly make up for the missing piece.

Sorry, Hunter.

They take turns feeding me takeaway french fries and chipotle ranch, Atlas muttering how he's going to perfect homemade.

I want to sink into them and this moment, but the squeak in my veins won't go away.

Maybe my heat's too close.

Maybe it's joy over Noelle's demise.

But with Wyverns absorbing me into their fold, I can't relax knowing Dom's out there, waiting to take this away before I even get to know what it's like to be happy.

I try to stand, but Finn and JJ each handcuff an ankle.

They sit at my feet, shooting each other serial killer glares that only fade when they tip their gazes up to me.

"Your nails are wet." JJ picks up my foot to breathe cold air onto my toes.

I shiver at the chill.

Hell knows where they got polish, but they made me sit so they could paint me in their colors.

One foot's neon orange, the other cherry blossom pink.

Finn grins over the spiked collar I put around his throat. His nostrils flare. "Not the only thing that's wet, Starsnatch."

I jerk my foot away, jumping onto the couch so fast, Orion tips, but he's dying laughing.

"*Banned!*"

Finn's eyes burn, emerald and mischief. "Starcun—"

"*No!*" Barf. No. *Why?* I grip my temples. "I need to look at spreadsheets."

"Why spreadsheets when we could be spreading your—"

I mush Finn's lips with my wet, orange toes.

Orion fucking roars, clutching his stomach, kicking his feet on the couch.

Even Atlas quirks a smile. "Bring your laptop? We'll sit with you. Need to be close or you might panic again."

"I'll get it. Stay." I'm tempted to yank Finn's collar as a warning, but he'll like it too much.

Instead, I hook my finger in JJ's ring and give an easy tug that sparks his purr.

I'm gentle, always checking in, afraid to push too hard, but he watches me like the moon watches the sun.

"Be good." I smooth his silky hair.

"Only for you," he murmurs.

"No. Hey. *Star...*" Finn moans, crawling after me.

Orion's still cackling.

I hurry into my bedroom, and almost do the thing where I slam the lock and fall against the door.

Instead, I smile where they can't see.

This pack is fucking chaos.

I grab my laptop and a stack of fresh Redfang papers before rejoining the mess in the living room.

I swear I've been gone thirty seconds, but JJ has Finn pinned to the carpet with a machete from who knows where and Orion flipped from maniac laughter to ragged gasping as Atlas tugs his hair and sucks his throat.

All four straighten hilariously fast—separating like they just got caught stealing my ice cream—and tug me back to my spot at the center of the pile on the couch.

Fucking.

Chaos.

And I love it.

Orion straightens his pants and goes to grab his laptop. Then he glues himself to my side to work on game code. Atlas cracks an omega behavioral textbook, highlighting like he's studying for extra credit.

He's going to get it.

JJ and Finn just pet my feet, sitting on the floor with their heads resting against my knees.

Circumstances make it crazy hard to focus on the files, but I breathe until my eyes uncross and their warm bodies read as a comfort instead of a temptation.

Have to find *something*.

I flip through pages, zoning out, trying to connect the numbers and find the one mistake the Redfangs must've made.

Finn's drooling on my leg, snoring softly when I finally jerk. "Diamond Dolls and lobsters."

"What in the what?" Orion lowers his screen.

Once upon a social, all the omegas were moaning over delicious, buttery lobster.

So I snuck a piece.

Threw up on the lawn.

But because of my long-time sea-bug hate, I remember the project I haven't thought about in years.

"Diamond Dolls, LLC. I just remembered why I know that name. I did their books a few years ago, and they kept ordering blue lobsters from this same supplier on Dom's island receipts."

I thought "blue lobster" was code for some wacko meth varietal, which is why it never clicked.

But no.

Actual live lobsters.

And shit.

I've been washing Redfang cash this whole time.

"What the—?" Orion and Atlas hover into my screen, watching me work.

JJ's grip tightens on my ankle, and his voice drops a few degrees. "Diamond Dolls is *Diamonds*. Omega strip club. Renee."

I pull the old records from my cloud, thanking the spreadsheet gods and Orion for finally giving me a keyboard because I can type one-handed while stroking JJ's hair.

I have three years of Diamonds' records.

Three years of manipulated numbers and data.

And three years of chances to pin Dominik's snaky ass.

Plus one sea bug invoice that might be the smoking gun. "Blue lobsters. Really rare. Lately, they've been shipped to Dom's island whenever they come to market. But before that, the supplier invoiced them to Diamonds and had them shipped *here*." I point to the address in my records. "Near the harbor?"

"Warehouse district," Atlas mumbles.

"I'll text Hunter." Orion whips out his phone to send a pic of the address.

I click through the other records, flagging a few more shipment locations where we can check for secret Redfang lairs.

After a while, Atlas's phone buzzes against my hip. He's careful not to jostle me when he pulls it out. "Dice?" Hunter's excited voice buzzes through the line. Atlas nods. "We'll go."

A ragged whorl twists through my stomach.

They'll go?

Now?

Atlas hangs up, then pushes my laptop to Orion so he can drag me into his lap. When he runs his nose over my forehead, the spike of panic fades. "We'll check it out. You want to sit in the tech van with Orion and J so you can follow along? They won't leave the compound."

I melt under his stroking attention and perfect handling,

because *yes*, of course I wanna stalker-follow my alphas' movements while staying perfectly protected.

But I still frown. "How many omega books did you read?"

"A few." He kisses my forehead, peeling the other guys off me so he can lift me into his arms. "Let's go. Get it taken care of now so we can focus on your heat."

I quake against his chest.

Can't believe I'm admitting it, but…

I think…

I'm finally going to trust them to take care of me.

———

ATLAS AND FINN join Hunter at the office, and my omega instincts call bullshit. They shouldn't leave when I'm needier by the second.

But I'm a big girl, so I swallow the crazy and enjoy watching them walk off in their gear. All in black, they're strapped down with holsters and harnesses and all kinds of delicious cuffs that hold their weapons and pin their clothes to their muscles.

I accept this form of leaving tax.

Orion and JJ don't gear up. Walking me between them, they take me to a panel van in the underground garage. As soon as the door slides open, I'm living secret agent fantasies I didn't know I had.

"This is where you work?" I climb in, sliding down the padded bench that takes up the side wall, facing a shallow desk and banks of monitors.

"We'd usually stay in the office or follow behind the guys in the van." Orion drops into the rolling chair and starts flicking on devices. "Buuuuut…"

"No office," JJ says coldly from the front seat. "*Nathan*."

"Wait, *what*?" Orion's feet bang the floor. "You met my brother? When? *Why?*"

I pat his knee. "He was at a social. Then I bumped into him

when JJ brought me to grab files. And I think he put in an offer for—"

Orion drags me into his lap with a fierce whisper. "Stay away from Nathan."

I shift to straddle his thighs and hug him tight. "Why would I look for him?"

"You won't. He'll look for you."

"He won't find me." I pat his hair, going gooey over his concern. "Why do you hate him so much?"

I'm clear why *I* hate him—my instincts are good like that—but they're biological brothers, so I'm curious why Orion doesn't feel the love.

"Because Wyvern Pack is the only thing he's never been able to take from me. Everything else…" Orion shudders. "I gave up fighting. He's better than m—"

I shut him up with a kiss.

It's good practice because I'm still not sure what the hell I'm doing. But when I taste his cider spice, sucking at that lush lower lip, Orion starts to purr.

It's this soft, tentative sound somewhere between encouragement and fucking bliss.

Must be doing something right.

I kiss him until we're gasping, shaking breaths, his fingers stroking my hips. When I finally try to pull away, he digs in harder. "*Lilah.*"

"He's not better than you." Won't say it out loud, but I don't think *anyone's* better than Orion. He's mine, my sunshine, and if Nathan needs reminding, I'll remind him with my knives the next time he "accidentally" bumps into me.

JJ clears his throat.

Semi-guilty, Orion and I whirl.

Forgot the rest of the world existed.

JJ slipped to the back of the van, and he strokes his collar—his new anxiety tell.

"You okay?" I slide off Orion's lap and move to him, watching for danger in his mood. "Are you uncomfortable with…"

"No." He takes my wrist and rubs with both hands, slipping his thumbs under the leather bracelet I haven't taken off and probably never will. "You're not like… You're *Lilac.*"

I smooth his hair, and he leans into my palm. "You still have to go to therapy."

"Tomorrow."

"Good."

JJ stares at me and only me until his dark brows furrow and he has to release my wrist to cup his ear. "Recon showed targets in the warehouse. They're going in now."

The dreamy bubble pops.

I scamper to the bench while Orion tunes the monitors to the Wyvern channel. The screens flicker, then pop up views from the guys' body cams.

My breathing quickens seeing Atlas, Hunter, and Finn heading a circled squad of agents. Men and women, all wearing the same black Wyvern unis.

Hunter's mouth moves, but there's no sound. I need to hear what they're saying. Need to know what's going to happen.

I clench Orion's chair. "Audio?"

"Just a sec." Orion slips on a headset, fiddling with controls.

I'm mesmerized by the silent film.

Hunter takes a deep breath, glancing at Atlas before stepping to the center. *Taking the lead.*

I smile, secretly proud. Also want to hear his leader speech, and the plan that goes with all his aggressive hand gestures.

After a few seconds with no sound, the agents start to move, cam footage jostling, but just the warehouse roof shows on screen, the monitors go dark.

The hairs on my arms lift.

"Shit. Bad reception?" Orion bangs the console.

I lean forward, heart beating way too fast. "Can you get it back?"

"We *are* underground." Orion glances to JJ. "Should we go topside?"

"We're not leaving the compound."

"Course not." Orion pets my arm, maybe trying to smooth the hairs that are still pointing like antennas. "Just park near the fence. We can—"

Tires screech.

Our heads whip to the sound of an engine gunning through the garage.

My arm hairs tingle.

Shit.

Orion and JJ pounce, driving me to the floorboards just before the siding explodes.

Tearing metal, and a world-ending *bang*.

Everything moves too fast.

And too slow.

Two desperate sets of arms cling to me, and for a breathless second, we go zero-gravity, floating just long enough for a flash of pain and—

Fuck.

The van rocks. Tips.

We land hard. We're thrown in a tangle, smashing the monitors, landing on top of the sideways desk.

My arm goes numb.

Orion groans.

Have to get out.

My left arm's wet, and the van's as black as the screens.

Can't see anything but a few confusing electrical sparks.

Something wet drips to my fingers.

Elbow went through the screen.

"Lilac." JJ moves, and my body hurts in a thousand places. He climbs to his knees, blood dripping from his scalp. "Hurt?"

"Fine." I cough. "Orion?"

"Shit. Head." He reaches for my hand. "Who the fuck—"

The sliding door—now our ceiling—bangs.

Door's stuck.

But someone's coming.

JJ pulls a gun, and I dig out the one that dented my ribs when we hit the wall.

My right arm's fine.

Only need one to fire.

Orion grabs a pistol from a busted-open drawer. Our breaths heave, and we synchro-click our safeties.

"Shoot to kill." JJ shifts, pushing me and Orion toward the back of the mangled van, shielding us with his body.

Voices echo from outside.

Muffled.

Male.

My heart trembles, but my grip is bedrock. "Shoot to kill."

"Front," Orion whispers, just as feet come into view through the spiderwebbed, sideways windshield.

A soft, vicious snarl rips from my diaphragm.

I'm this close to nesting and they want to fuck with me?

Nuh uh.

"Windshield's bulletproof," JJ murmurs.

"Bet they turned off cams." Orion shifts against me, pulling out his phone. "No signal."

"Can we wait them out?" I whisper.

No one has time to answer before the driver's door wrenches open.

My finger slips closer to the trigger, waiting for boots to drop so I can remove this asshole's kneecaps like I'm shooting targets at the range.

Instead of feet, something metal clangs into the van.

A *hisssssss* breaks the silence, then a puff of billowing smoke.

"Shit!" Orion wrenches the drawer. "Masks. Masks. Where the fuck are they? Here." He fumbles, ripping open a pouch, then clumsily jamming a gas mask over my eyes. "You have to—" he coughs, smoke growing thicker.

"Get your own!" I jam it the rest of the way on, then shove him a pouch as foggy smoke fills the van.

JJ lunges to the front, reaching for the metal can.

One arm-length away.

Fingers, reaching—

Bang!

The gunshot sounds like a cannon blast.

JJ grunts, and staggers back, clapping a hand to his forearm.

Coughing, choking.

Blood.

JJ's shot.

I fumble for my gun. Have to get out. Have to save them.

But my eyes burn, even with the full-face mask.

Lungs hurt.

Arm hurts.

While we cough, fumbling like tipped-over turtles, someone pounds our siding.

Smash!

Smash!

Smash!

Then the van rattles.

The door finally gives, sliding open.

Blind, I shoot above my head.

A sweet scream rings.

I shoot and shoot and shoot until my gun clicks. Then I toss it, reaching through the smoke, trying to find the guys' weapons.

But they were counting bullets.

Arms snag and lift, pulling me kicking through the door.

I flail, thrash, scream into the smoke.

The figure drags me out, tearing off my mask.

I choke, vision starting to spin.

For a second, I see Orion and relax.

He's safe.

But then the face smiles, sick and smug.

Not Orion.

Nathan.

"What a good girl." Nathan thumbs my cheek.

I go lethargic.

From the smoke—not his touch.

A hot coil of hate keeps me lucid even as my eyelids droop.

I let my hand drop to my pocket, just as Nathan pulls me into his chest.

Feel him relaxing.

Guard totally down because I'm fading fast.

"Get them—"

Nathan chokes.

Gurgles.

I twist the knife I just jabbed between his ribs.

He drops, and I fall, driving every pound of body weight and every muscle I have left into the knife hilt.

Nathan makes a wheezy groan.

I try to crawl away, smearing blood across the garage floor.

Voices rise.

"Shit. What do we do?"

"Nathan? Nate?"

"Do we get the others?"

"No. Fuckin'… Run. Grab her and run."

Someone yanks me into their arms.

Nathan's down.

Pool of blood.

But they're taking me away and my body can't fight.

While the masked men run me to their getaway car, my head lolls.

My vision's blurry, but I spot JJ crawling out of the van.

Hands and knees through shattered windshield glass, arm dripping, leaving a snail trail of gore.

"*Lilac!*" his voice rips.

"J…" I reach for him with numb fingers.

Then they press a rag to my mouth, and a chemical tang takes me into the dark.

THIRTY-EIGHT

HUNTER

WE BAGGED TEN REDFANG GOONS, but yet a-fucking-gain missed that snaky shit, Dom.

As our teams sweep the warehouse, double-checking we're clear, voices crackle non-stop through my earpiece, and I fucking hate being the one who has to answer.

I expected Atlas to fight.

Atlas always fights.

He was supposed to wrestle me for power.

I was going to fake cave, pretending to grudgingly hand back the reins the second he proved he could be our compassionate leader instead of our drill sergeant.

Instead, Atlas stands at my shoulder, waiting for me to give a command that sticks in my throat when his dominance is Everest to my Kilimanjaro.

Another voice crackles. "Sir! Upstairs is clear."

"On the way." I grab Finn who's dripping blood and River-dancing on a Redfang's chest, dragging him with us to Dom's converted loft.

The warehouse is stacked with crates of drugs we'll let the feds bust for brownie points. I'm more interested in what he stashed upstairs.

Finn whistles when we step inside.

Looks like King Triton's twisted fucking bachelor pad with walls of neon fish tanks, sex swings, and leather porn set furniture.

"Find anything?" I ask the squad leader.

"One desktop. Bunch of files and…" The guy looks away and swallows. "Photos."

My intuition clangs. *This is gonna be fucked.* "Photos of what?"

"Your mate."

Someone growls.

Maybe me.

Maybe all of us.

"Show me," I snarl.

He leads us through a fish tank hallway to a sleek office where agents are digging out file cabinets.

But on the desk…

Lilah.

Photos and photos and photos.

"How the hell…" A sick barb tears through my gut as I pick up a picture taken years the fuck ago.

Soft, baby Lilah, fifteen, maybe sixteen, in a ponytail, hugging her arms to her chest in a too-big sweatshirt while she scowls at something off-camera.

Candid shot.

There are dozens of them. And a ton of pictures of her with the same blonde girl who must be a friend, because they're smiling.

Also being fucking *stalked.*

Someone was taking pics of her at the OCC.

For years, long before us.

Shit.

I thought Dom wanted her because she was ours.

But Renee must've been grooming her for *him* all the fuck along.

This is wrong.

Something is—

My phone buzzes.

Jett.

Heart surging, fingers trembling, I pick up. "J?"

"Took... Took her..." His cough sounds like he's spitting blood, and the pain in his voice nails my feet to the floor.

"Where are you?"

"Garage."

"They stole her from the compound?"

Atlas and Finn go dead.

Unbreathing.

Nothing in their eyes but the same murder that rips through my veins.

"Nathan." Jett chokes. "Hurry. Have a tracker in her bracelet."

"On the way." I hit Finn and Atlas with a vicious bark that flares from the pit of my tearing soul. "*Follow.*"

We roll out.

Get Lilah back.

Have to get her fucking back.

THIRTY-NINE

LILAH

I WANT TO SLEEP FOREVER.

Head splitting, aching, *yikes*.

But I catch strains of a nightmare soundtrack so horrific, the sounds pull me back from the grave.

Sex moans.

High, fake, pornstar cries that are so irritating, pure disgust wakes me from a near coma.

I clench my jaw to keep silent, slowly peeking from crusty eyes as I come back online, aches and pains checking in one-by-one.

Arm feels chewed.

My knees burn.

I'm folded up, legs tucked under my belly, and elbows braced on jagged ground—one arm extra bloody.

Wrists bound so tight I can't feel my fingers.

Stiffness says I've been in the position for a while. But when I stealthily shift, there's nowhere to go.

I'm in a fucking cage.

A dog crate, on hands and knees.

I risk opening my eyes.

I'm eye-level with a bed frame, and the rocking mattress is the source of the ongoing squeals and thumping I don't want to know who's creating.

Have to move while they're busy.

Ignoring the instinct to panic—because this is really fucking bad—I shift my weight and try to loosen the rope binding my wrists.

The cage gives an angry creak so sharp, I freeze.

Mistake.

The bed stops rocking.

"She's awake." A familiar female voice hisses. Then a pair of legs slides down, and I taste chipotle bile.

It's not my first time bleeding, staring down these bony ankles.

Noelle rattles my cage and laughs.

Two more feet thump to the floor, but these are new.

A man's narrow, lightly hairy calves.

The room's thick with omega sex, but when he stops in front of the cage, I'm blindsided in molted snake scale leather that stops my fucking lungs.

Dominik.

"Lilah *Darling*," he purrs my name. "You're a hard omega to catch."

My heart jackhammers, but I keep my mouth shut and my eyes on the ground. Been here before.

I'll only hurt worse if I speak up.

Need to wait.

Bide my time.

Let them think I'm broken.

Then I'll show them I don't break.

Dominik clicks his forked tongue when I don't respond. "Take her out."

Noelle hops, no need for him to bark.

She's always tortured me for free.

She wrenches me by my—*oh fun, there's a fucking collar around my throat.*

But that's the least of my worries.

Freed from the tiny space, my arms and legs scream. I topple onto my side and refuse to look up. Don't want to see them staring down all victorious, especially when this picture's missing pants.

Noelle stomps my forearm. "Darling trash. Think you can steal my sister's pack?"

I bite back a scream until my jaw clicks.

I shouldn't say a word.

I should eat this, like I've eaten every other shitty thing she's done.

But…

Dominik's here, his snake scale scent clogging my throat hard enough to choke.

There's no more time to bide.

When she stomps again, I roll clumsily out of the way. "Wyverns were *never* Rachel's pack."

She kicks me in the face.

Fucking barefoot.

Toenails rip my cheek.

My head rocks back, and I catch a blurred version of the foot to scalp landscape, featuring zero clothes and Dominik's gnarly package—twig, berries and swollen purple bole.

I spit blood. "You're cheating on your mates. You're the trash."

"You—"

Dominik's warning growl cuts her off. "Enough. Noelle is mine, just as you should've been the moment you perfumed. We'll correct that mistake with your heat. Now *stay*." His bark's the last hit I can handle.

My blood freezes, and my muscles obey.

Can't move.

Can't even fucking blink.

"Feed her." Dominik grabs a red silk robe from the bed and struts from the cabin. "Then join me in the kitchen. I want a blowjob and a mimosa while I wait for her to ripen."

"Yes, *Alpha*," Noelle says, all silky and sickening.

When his bare feet pad away, she kicks me again, driving her heel into my shredded elbow.

At least Dominik's bullshit alpha command keeps me from crying out.

"He's going to rip you apart." She pads away while I try not to pass out, and I can hear her rummaging. A clinking glass. When Noelle comes back, she yanks my head back by my hair. "Open wide. It'll be good practice."

Pinching my jaw open, she pours dark liquid down my throat.

I choke.

Splutter.

But I can't move.

Shit tastes like cold pureed mushrooms. Thick, earthy sludge that coats my throat and makes me choke.

Noelle laughs. "Tick tock. Hope you're ready for his knot. But first…"

She slaps me.

A ringing smack that knocks my skull into the floor. "Don't ever fucking slap my sister."

Fuck them and their twisted sibling loyalty.

But the ringing in my ears shakes off Dominik's hold. I twitch, ready to kick out her ankles.

She kicks me first.

Ribs.

The air leaks from my lungs with an angry, popped-tire hiss.

"*Know your place.*"

Kick.

Kick.

Kick.

I curl into a ball, but Noelle keeps going, finding every soft, open spot.

When she kicks a tender one in my back, I jackknife.

Think she hit something important.

I'm limp and barely tracking. She shoves me into the cage and throws the latch.

"See you soon." Noelle finger-waves, fully fucking naked, and prances off to service her drug lord.

So, that kidnapping thing?

Total scam. Can't believe they've been banging for *years*.

Wait. Never mind.

It makes total sense.

Renee probably made the cursed introduction, long before Noelle mated. Patricks probably don't even mind pimping her out for political favors.

Don't get why they wanted Dominik's brother dead, but I need to solve my own problems. Or just wait and ask Erik Redfang *what the fuck* when we're ghost buds.

I groan, face pressed to the cage floor.

Fuck.

I swear I've had worse than this.

Like that time when…

No.

This is the worst.

My heartbeat picks up when it should be slowing, and I don't know which drugs they just fed me, but I start to sweat.

I wiggle, almost screaming in despair.

But then my fingers twitch and I make a happy gasp.

Noelle's beating loosened my wrist ropes.

I work them hard, not caring if my skin tears. Have to slither free.

Have to save myself.

It takes a long, long time.

My wrists bleed and my temperature climbs. I manage not to panic until the first cramp stabs my belly like pitchfork tines, and the room blooms with overbaked crème brûlée.

I'm full-body trembling when I finally shake off the ropes.

Bloody, battered, but free.

I have a chance.

Noelle didn't lock the cage, so even shaking, it only takes a minute to break out.

I tumble onto the floor, then stumble to my feet, crawling for the door.

I'm there by the time I remember there'll be guards.

Only, there aren't.

There's just a narrow hall.

I wrench to my feet, almost pass out from standing, and then brace against the wall as I shamble.

Can't even walk straight.

Like I'm drunk.

But then I pass a round window and *holy fucking nautical hell*.

There's nothing but waves to the horizon.

Boat.

Ocean.

Wyvern Pack had better come for me.

If they can't pull off a rescue…

I need that airplane toilet meteor and a total fucking miracle.

FORTY

ATLAS

"SHE'S *WHERE?*" I stare at the tracking app on Jett's finally-working phone, so torqued skin and muscle tear away from bone.

A blue dot blips on the map, heading out to sea.

Lilah.

Mate.

Mine.

Gone.

Haven't stopped snarling. The heinous rumble strokes the urge to rip, rend, and fucking end the ones who took her away.

Hunter lifts a gatehouse guard by the throat. "How. How the fuck did you let them take her off compound?"

"D-didn't—" the guard chokes. "Wasn't. Girl. Swear!"

"Then how—"

"Like this," Orion's shaky whisper draws us to the guard-house bench, where he sits battered and smoke-streaked, a laptop perched on his knees.

Need to comfort him but I've got nothing to give. Only possible comfort is getting Lilah back.

He tilts his screen to show the footage.

Three agents leave the underground garage that went dark.

They only knocked out the power to that floor, otherwise, they would've tripped an all-hands alert.

Nathan's crew.

They hold workout duffel bags, but one hangs lower than the rest, stuffed fat and straining the guy's shoulder.

Carried my girl in a fucking sack.

Walking fast, they cut to the guardhouse and flash badges to exit the compound.

Finn unfolds from a crouch.

He hasn't said a word.

His eyes say it all.

Pure, abyssal darkness.

Haven't seen him this goddamned dark since he came back from his own kidnapping with a body count.

"Chopper." Finn cradles a grenade.

"Now," I agree. We know what happened. Need to move.

With every flicker, the dot moves farther away.

Hunter tosses the guard. "Move out."

We barrel for the door, but it flies open.

Jett stumbles in, trailing ripped IV wires and looking like icy hell.

Eyes are worse than Finn's.

Not just death, but desolation.

Found him passed out cold and bloody next to a lump of meat that was probably Nathan.

Won't know 'til we check dental records.

Gunshot wound seeping, broken glass ground into his cheeks, he lunges for the phone. "Tracker?"

"Got it running. We're out."

"Go." He can barely fucking stand, but I'm not putting anyone on the bench.

Doesn't matter who's in charge, who gives what order. We're one heart, one mind, one soul, brotherhood finally focused on the only goal that ever fucking mattered.

Save Lilah.

FORTY-ONE

LILAH

I CREEP DOWN THE HALLWAY, hotter by the second, twisted by cramps.

Everything. Hurts.

I gag when I hear Noelle's pants and moans echoing from the kitchen.

Galley?

Yacht's so big they can probably call it whatever the hell they want. But there's still only one hallway, and I have to creep past the *ugh* to reach the deck.

Never been on a boat, but in the movies, they have life rafts up there.

Plus, maybe I looked out the wrong window. Even this wrecked, I can swim if there's a shore.

I ease to my knees and crawl.

Not going to look, but I'm praying he has her knotted. Even if they notice me, I'll have a minute to myself before he can deflate enough to pull out.

Holding my breath, I crawl past the door.

Noelle's pornstar pants don't break tempo.

I keep crawling until I'm well clear, and another, twistier cramp sinks me to my elbows.

Shit.

I'm boiling. Have to move before my scent gives me away.

I crawl up steps, hands and knees, but my arms shake.

This is worse than my last heat.

Much, much worse.

Because I know what's fucking coming.

The pain's all downhill.

Only the hill's a jagged obsidian cliff with lava veins and no bottom.

I'll fall forever, hurting and burning.

Even if I had to take the old Wyverns—the ones who weren't there when I needed them the most—I'd take them so fast.

I'd take them right now, a thousand million times.

I'd run into their arms.

Let alone the ones who feed me snacks, wrap me in blankets, and shave my bullies' heads.

Noelle needs to be bald.

I'm telling JJ.

My belly wrenches, another twist that sparks a moan. I snap my jaw shut.

Gonna save myself and pray they're on the way.

They'll come for me.

They will.

Just need to stay away from Dominik and survive until my rescue.

But it's hard to plan when my brain steams and the heat chews up my insides, that empty, gnawing ache hijacking my brain.

Like, *didn't we do this before? Thought we gave you plenty of time to lock down a thick knot.*

I shake myself.

Shut up, hormones.

Have to focus.

Plan.

Find a lifeboat, the steering wheel, or at least a freaking harpoon.

I crawl onto the deck and wrench myself up with the railing.

There's no harbor.

Open water stretches to the fuzzy horizon.

Gonna be sick.

I reel, but orange flashes at the corner of my eye. A life vest, mounted to the wall.

I rip it down and jam my arms through the holes, trying not to look too hard at the stinging gore on my left arm, or the bruises dotting every other scrap of skin.

Seriously.

What the hell did they feed me to put me in heat when I'm this beaten?

It's not sustainable.

Or survivable.

But an unfortunate flash of clarity cuts through the simmering heat brain.

They don't plan on me surviving.

Gripping the rail, I creep around the deck. I have no yardstick for boat size, but it feels pretty freaking huge.

We're moving, too.

Not anchored.

So there should be a cockpit.

A captain?

My shambles take me to the ass end, where the engine's hum drowns out my despair, and I finally find my sliver of hope.

A private submarine pod, hanging half over the water like it's just been out.

Freaking rich people.

The control panel's surprisingly easy to work. Just have to mash the arrow buttons and the pod's pushed farther out over the water.

But the mechanical *whirrrr* has my blood pumping faster.

I wrench open the hatch, but this is a two-person job, because I can't hit the button to lower it from inside.

Shit knows how I'm going to pilot a submarine, but I'd rather roll those dice than mess with Dominik's snake eyes.

Mashing buttons for my life, I will the crane to drop faster.

Smacking footsteps break my focus.

"She's here!" Noelle screeches, tearing around the corner, flying toward me with zero clothes and zero fear.

I practiced for this fight.

In my fantasies, I'm armed with twenty knives and kick her ass until she weeps.

Now I can barely stand.

But I set my jaw and brace myself.

Can't afford to lose.

Noelle comes at me like she's never taken a combat class, lifting her hand for a catty, flat-palmed slap.

I dodge, just too slow.

Her momentum carries the swat to my shoulder, but it works.

I'm not fucking playing.

I drop my weight, hug her waist for a rugby takedown, and *heave.*

Noelle squawks, losing her balance.

I throw myself, digging my heels into the deck.

Her skull rings the submarine like a gong.

When she goes limp, I release her, letting her slump into a satisfying heap.

Never mind that I'm boiling and shaking. I give Noelle one spirit-cleansing stomp that turns her lingering moan into a dead faint. Then I stumble back to the controls.

Have to get the pod into the water.

It drops agonizingly slow.

Five feet.

Four feet.

Three—

"*Omega,*" Dominik snarls.

His red silk robe billows open in the sick-humored breeze.

He *stalks* to me.

Eyes so dark, I see my death and worse.

"*Stay.*" His command locks my muscles, and my belly cramps. Hard.

He pads across the deck, giving me a full-on trench coat pervert view of what he's packing. I'm afraid my batshit instincts will tell me to jump the only alpha within nautical miles, but they finally have a sense of self-preservation, because all I feel when I see his business is a double-shot of terror and disgust.

I'm barely standing, sweaty and pained, and the only reason I could fight off Noelle was her cocky overconfidence.

Dominik isn't overconfident.

He *knows* he's already won.

And, yeah.

He'll beat me every time.

That's why I cheat.

I bite my tongue so hard I choke on blood. My body's hardly reacting, but gravity's still on my side.

All I have to do is tip, letting my weight send me sailing over the rail.

A little heave and away I—

Dominik snatches my wrist, wrenching me before I can plummet.

My feet smack the side of the boat, and my already mangled arm screams.

"You're mine, Omega. You were always mine." I feel like a bundle of twigs, being hauled back up.

No.

I don't care if this kills me.

I'd rather die than let him have me.

I'd rather drown.

And fuck it.

If this is what he wants, I'll take him down too.

When he swings me up, I use the momentum, wrapping my legs around his neck and squeezing until his eyes bulge.

He tries to hit back, but we're too tangled, and I throw myself like a porpoise, using my last strength.

Won't need it if he gets me back on this ship.

With a gurgling choke, Dominik tips.

We free-fall into the churning water.

Saltwater slaps me in the face.

Icy cold shock.

I splutter, trying to disentangle.

The life vest sends me bobbing to the surface while Dominik roars.

Distance.

Need distance, I—

He jumps me, dunking my head and using me like a buoy, fumbling, trying to get it unbuckled so I'm the one who drowns.

I kick, but the water muffles the blow.

I'm spluttering, half underwater, somehow freezing *and* sweating, twisted with pain and—

Something clicks.

I go still, letting him steal the vest, but while he's fumbling with numb fingers, I'm taking a huge, lung-filling breath.

My pulse slows.

The heat-pains simmer, but I'm weirdly calm as I sink below the waves.

The water's murkier than the pool.

Salt stings my eyes worse than chlorine.

But the hum in my ears is the same as ever. That hugging, body-glove feeling that reminds me I'm at home.

The water's mine.

I grab his ankle and pull.

Down.

He kicks out, but I'm already too far below.

Dragging him.

Deeper and deeper and deeper.

His foaming screams mix with the numb sounds of bubbles and waves.

I kick like a mermaid.

Deeper.

My ears pop.

I keep going until I realize Dominik's not thrashing.

Bubbles boil from his nose, but all he can do is make a last half-ass grab.

I look to the surface and—

Fuck.

Too far.

Too dark.

I give Dominik one last kick, using his body as a springboard, racing to get air while my heart and lungs scream.

My eyes do that blurred static flash that means I need to breathe *soon*.

Almost there!

On my last gasp, I punch through the surface.

Coughing and spluttering, I suck in sweet oxygen, trying to tread water without slipping back under.

So, so tired.

Water in all directions.

The boat fading into the distance.

But I spot a blob of orange like a beacon of hope.

I tap into the old Lilah, the one who ground laps until she passed out, and running on nothing but willpower, I kick to my only chance at survival.

Of course, the current fucks with me, trying to drag the vest away. My head keeps slipping under, and it gets harder and harder to stay afloat.

But I can't give up.

Won't.

I'm too stubborn and I finally fucking have a reason to fight.

My fingers finally bump the vest.

With an awkward dolphin roll, I force my arms through the holes and snap the buckles tight.

Then I tip my head back and take breath after wracking breath.

The spots slowly clear from my eyes.

Welp.

Managed half a rescue.

I'd do a victory dance, only now I'm stranded at sea.

But I refuse to despair.

Wyvern Pack will come for me.

They'll find me.

All I have to do is wait.

All I have to do is survive.

FORTY-TWO

JJ

I'M NOTHING WITHOUT HER.

If we can't save her—

I cut off the thought.

I'm bleeding, shedding crushed glass, but I can't feel as I haul my broken body into the chopper with my working arm.

"Finn." I drop into the seat next to him.

He gives a dead-eyed look that mirrors mine, petting his grenade like a rabbit. "Deal?"

"Deal." I nod.

Orion's eyes widen.

I'd shrug, but I can't care.

The pack must think Finn and I don't talk, but the truth is, we've never needed words.

We *understand.*

If we can't save Lilah, we'll end it for each other.

Hunter hops into the cockpit and the blades start to whir. Atlas and Orion huddle, staring at the dot on my phone.

I grip my collar and watch the horizon.

I'll destroy anything to save my Lilac.

Especially myself.

FORTY-THREE

LILAH

HEAT CRISPS MY VEINS.

Or maybe it's sunburn?

My eyelids are slits, salt-crusted and stinging after endlessly bobbing in waves and burning sun.

Even the pain hits in waves.

Heat cramps that twist me in half, gnawing with shark teeth.

Waves of hope.

They'll come for me.

Waves of despair.

They won't come for me.

Waves of muscle-melting exhaustion.

They'll be too late.

The life vest keeps my head above water, but I'm running out of grit.

As night starts to fall, my teeth start to chatter, and I have to get really fucking real about how much longer I can last.

But even when I shiver, skin freezing, it doesn't cut the heat inside.

The desperate ache.

I cackle, then choke on a chunk of seaweed. Coughing up salt-water and saliva, I tip my head back to watch the stars.

I've never trusted anyone except myself.

Maybe because I'm floating to death, trusting Wyvern Pack doesn't seem as scary.

I'd rather die believing they're on the way. Or at least that they'll scoop my pruny body out of the water and give me a pretty funeral with wreaths of those rainbow daisies.

I'd rather trust than spend my last moments crying.

I'd rather die with hope.

I just wish I'd told them sooner.

I never did admit we were mates.

I ran.

I hid.

I let myself be afraid.

They let me down, but then they lifted me up and showed me what we could have if we all stopped being so fucking terrified we aren't enough.

Orion gave up his pack.

Hunter took the lead.

Finn inked my name on his skin.

JJ handed me his collar.

Atlas quit his job.

And *fuck*.

He was gonna make me french fries.

I want to see what else they'll do to prove we belong.

I want to believe I can have more.

But the sky fades and fades and fades.

And all I see is foam and dying stars.

FORTY-FOUR

ORION

THE CHOPPER CUTS over the waves, spotlighting empty, endless water as twilight falls.

No Lilah.

I clutch my neck so hard I draw blood from her half-healed bite.

She's still with me.

Feeling her—the warm, sugary center of my heart—is the only thing keeping me from full-on collapse.

"There!" Jett points to the shape on the horizon.

It's a massive fucking superyacht I recognize from Dom's files.

My gut twists in hope and dread.

Lilah's okay. She has to be okay.

Hunter takes us down hard.

I'm still bleeding from the car crash, smoke frying my head, but all distractions burn away when the chopper touches the landing pad.

We fall on that shit like wolves.

But the yacht's empty.

I tear below deck.

Vanilla ice cream teases my nose, sharpening to burnt sugar so warped with anxiety that my heart wants to vomit out my throat.

"Lilah!" I kick down the door to a bedroom, and I don't know if the empty, sugar-choked room is the best or worst omen.

She was here.

Scent says recently.

Then I creep around the bed and gag.

Dog cage.

Blood on the floor.

The mingled scents of stale sex, roses, and snake scales.

Dominik.

Fuck.

Fuckfuckfuck.

"Guys!" Hunter screams from far away.

He found her.

Please say he found her.

I sprint, following his shout to the back of the boat where a submarine pod hangs over the water and Noelle Patrick sits against the wall with a forehead gash and a sickening smirk.

Her expression doesn't last.

Not when five of us close in, each more feral than the last.

When I catch her omega scent—that sickening floral—my hackles raise and the sound that rips out my throat is half howl.

Enemy.

"*Where. Is. Lilah.*" Atlas's bark is a punch to the liver.

Noelle curls into herself, clubbed by his dominance. But even though she's trembling, her scent sour with fear, that fucking *smirk*. "She went overboard."

"Tracker?" Hunter whirls.

Jett lifts his phone and dies, light leeching from his eyes. "Signal's gone."

"Where…" I clutch my chest, focusing on the warm little blip in my chest, that flutters, faint as a firefly.

Atlas moves behind me, pressing his chest to my back, but there's no comfort in his rumble—just the same anxious terror that has my fingers set at constant tremble.

No comfort, but…

Something else.

That firefly flicker glows a little brighter when Atlas lends me his strength.

I turn to the left.

Maybe I'm fucking crazy, but there's this needy *tug* and… "I think I can find her."

"Chopper, now!" Atlas hauls me to the pad. I jump into the cockpit while Hunter hops in the pilot's chair.

Jett and Finn vault in behind us, swinging Noelle's body like carry-on luggage. She slams to the floor with a moan just as Hunter takes us airborne, and by the time we're cutting across the waves, the sound is a lung-tearing scream.

When I glance back, Jett's tossing her sheared-off hair into the sea.

"Lose the extra weight!" Hunter yells.

Jett tosses Finn a knife.

In perfect psycho-unison, they sink blades into Noelle's chest.

She stumbles back one, two, three steps and–

With a choked-off scream drowned in engine noise, she sails into open air.

We're high enough that she hits the water like it's concrete.

And you'd better fucking believe we all enjoy the splat.

I'm only sorry Lilah didn't get to watch.

Gripping my chest, I point into the sea. "That way."

Nobody cares how or why I know—all that matters is there's hope.

We soar.

My heart pounds in time with the chopper blades, and I keep pointing Hunter on the course that feels right.

It's getting so dark.

Lilah must be freezing.

Shit.

I grip my heart until skin tears.

She's going to be okay.

We'll find her and snuggle her and spend the rest of our lives apologizing for letting her be hurt.

My skin prickles.

There's something bobbing in the waves.

"Got her." Hunter zooms so fast I almost fall out of my seat, but then I'm jumping out anyway.

Atlas, Finn, and Jett all bail, jumping the second we're low enough to leap without dying.

It's Lilah.

But she's not moving.

"*Wait*!" Hunter's frantic bark stops me from following them into the sea. "Fucking idiots. Drop the rescue basket!"

They're almost to her, churning through the waves.

I won't get there any faster.

Need to be here, ready to get Lilah warm.

So, I lower the basket and wait for the alphas to bring back my omega.

Once I have Lilah in my arms, I'm gonna latch on like a squid.

And I'll never fucking let her go.

FORTY-FIVE

FINN

MY STAR'S hair floats like seaweed.

Mermaid girl.

The brown streams are the only color in the ocean, her pale skin a flash of silver against the black-and-white waves.

I tear through the water, long arms and longer legs churning through whitecaps.

Her eyes are closed.

Lips purple.

My heart, dead motherfucker, gives a sick warning thump.

Pulled her out from the water before and she was fine.

Star has to be okay.

She's the only light.

"Starshine," I float her into my arms.

Too fucking cold.

Can't tell if she's breathing.

Can't tell if she's alive.

Fine.

I'll breathe for us both.

I pinch her nose, take her lips, and give her my air.

She can even take my life force.

Just has to breathe.

Just has to open those sweet, grey eyes.

Atlas and Jett tread water, screaming into the wind from the chopper blades, but what the fuck can they do?

I breathe into her lungs.

Again.

Again.

"*Star.*"

A wire basket drops from above.

"Get her in!" Atlas shouts.

I don't let go.

Breathing.

Breathing.

Breathing.

And finally.

Star opens her eyes.

My heart bumps—fucking golden retriever tail thumps.

Lilah took my air.

Next up?

Get her home.

Nest her hard.

Give her my bite, my knot, my leash, *my soul.*

FORTY-SIX

LILAH

I CHOKE.

So cold.

But weirdly hot.

Hurts.

But then I feel the most delicious, soothing energy. Orange-flavored air shot straight into my lungs.

A creamsicle IV.

I'm in my alphas' arms.

And something's so fucking loud it rings my head.

Helicopter.

Wyverns circle.

I feel wind, and a lift, and then I'm hit with a spike of sour apple terror as Orion drags me into his warmth.

"Got you," he whispers, already peeling off my icy clothes. "Never letting go."

They strip off the life vest, then someone hisses when they spot the collar I wasn't going to risk drowning to remove.

JJ knocks Finn and Atlas away, dropping between my knees. I've never felt anything so gentle as his fingers on my throat.

He slides off the buckle and tosses the whole fucking thing

into the sea. Then he kisses the stinging mark on my throat. "*Lilac.*"

Want to stroke his hair, but my eyelids flutter.

Orion wraps me in his sweatshirt and the alphas press my skin, dripping seawater.

They rub my arms and legs and throat, slowly bringing the feeling back to my body.

But when the cold fades, the heat returns.

I know the second the smell hits.

Their soothing, concerned purrs hitch, dropping to low, stroking rumbles.

"You're okay." Orion hugs me. "Taking you to the clinic. No heat right now. Not until you're warm and safe."

"D-d-drug…" My teeth chatter. "I—"

"*Shh.*" Atlas strokes my hip and puts the softest whip into his whisper. "*Sleep, Lilah. We'll take care of you.*"

I sink into his promise.

JJ hugs my wrist. Finn rubs my feet. Orion whispers love in my ears. Atlas pets me like he's stroking fur. And even Hunter's curses make it to my ears like the sweetest music.

My alphas.

My Wyverns.

They're warm and solid and safe, and for the first time in my life, I let go.

This is my pack.

FORTY-SEVEN

LILAH

I SLEEP on and off for days. In the hospital, then back to my cozy compound cave, in this weird, dreamy world where I'm held and petted and purred over like a soft little princess.

Holy shit.

I'm a soft little princess.

And I drowned a drug lord, but who ever earned a crown without some blood?

I smile into the sheets, roll over and—

Pillow's empty.

Panic rears, but Orion's fresh kiss lingers on my forehead, reminding me I'm not alone.

He hasn't left my side.

None of them have left my side.

Until now.

I sit up, wanting to move my hair out of my face, but instead of tangles it's all smoothly combed. And instead of empty fingers, I have a phone attached to me with hair ties.

It vibrates, screen showing a message from Orion.

My heart thumps, for once, daring to expect a *good* surprise.

Doctor Morgan says you're healed enough for the heat to hit. Should be this afternoon.

We're here. We're waiting. But we won't pressure.

Catherine sent your offers.

Read ours too.

Call if you need us.

If you need anything.

We'll give you space, but we won't run no matter what you choose.

There's a pause, filled with the happy swelling of my heart, then another message vibrates.

Waiting outside.

Miss you already, little bear.

Always thought I knew exactly what I wanted, but somewhere, my wants shifted.

Right now, I want a shower, *bad.*

Then a few answers…

Then maybe a few bites.

I scrub and shave. I'm achy, tender, and bandaged, with stitches around my elbow, so the hot water stings as much as it soothes. But even though I'm sore, I'm light in a way I never could've dreamed.

My toes bounce and my chest tingles.

Happiness.

Excitement.

Plus an itchy, scratchy sense of anticipation, and a growing need to be hidden somewhere dark and safe.

I put on leggings and Orion's apple-heaven hoodie, then grab the binders left on my bedspread and walk them to the nest.

To *my* nest.

I flick the lights from disco to a low, calming yellow, then dive into a mountain of pillows to see how much they think I'm worth.

It's a fucking *stack* of offers, and the bids aren't just cash.

Properties. Cars. *Horses?*

I toss that one to the floor.

Offers are stacked alphabetically, so I'm almost at the bottom when I spot Sorensen Pack's binder.

They're offering me a building, a multi-zeros payout, and…a *boat*.

I never need to see another ocean.

With a silent farewell to all those pastries and the hope that Atlas can follow baking instructions too, I push their binder into the growing pile on the floor.

Just wasn't meant to be.

I hope they find an omega who's a better fit for what they're offering.

Wyvern Pack's binder is last.

Catherine left sticky notes on most of them—which I ignored—but this one, I peel off, eyebrows lifting.

BAD CHOICE.

Then I crack the binder and see why.

Zero dollars.

No boats or cars or ponies.

Their offer's just an address. Deadly curious, I pull up the location on my phone.

When I find the real estate listing, my fingers start to shake.

It's a cottage so far from civilization, you have to drive in on ATVs. The place is fully off-grid with a working garden, a wood stove, and only one room with one little bed.

It's just for me.

I push the other offers to the floor and hug the Wyverns' to my chest.

When the Wyverns are bad, they're the worst, but when they're good…

Holy fuck are they *good*.

I dial Catherine, who picks up on the first ring. "Lilah? Are you alright? Have you chosen?"

Hugging the binder, I smile. "I made my choice."

———

MY NEXT PHONE call is harder.

I sweep all the binders from my nest, holding on to the winner, then regroup in the living room.

I feel itchier by the second, and my belly's starting to flutter, that achy pulse picking up between my legs. I pull up Orion's number, but my finger hovers over the call button.

My old fears rise.

Especially the one where they leave me writhing.

But now I've seen what they'll do for me—and what I'm willing to do for them.

I'm tired of being the girl who gets left.

Now I'm going to be the girl who gets *loved*.

I hit call.

Doesn't even go a full ring.

"Lilah? You okay?" Orion's instant anxiety is so cute, I can't help smiling.

"Need you."

The door whips open.

Alphas grumble from the hall, but Orion shuts them out, slamming and holding the door. He wears a soft blue sweater that matches his eyes and makes my fingers twitch to rub him… *Everywhere*.

When he spots the binder I'm clutching like my favorite child, he gives a grin so wicked, I think my birth control pops.

While he stalks to me, I touch the bump on my arm—*just in case*.

Still there.

"Koala." He wraps me in a hug, squashing the binder between us. "Did you decide?"

"Yeah. But answers first? I feel like I've been out of it for weeks."

"Anything," he murmurs into my hair.

I tug him to the couch. "Are you okay? Your bro—"

"Is dead." He twines our fingers, jaw clenching. "You don't need to think about him. Ever. What else do you want to know?"

I sigh, but let it go. *Not all family is created equal.* "Noelle?"

"Dead. Dom's missing but—"

"Nope. Also dead."

"Seriously? You?"

"We had a breath-holding contest. Which I dominated."

Orion's lips twitch. "I bet."

"Rachel?"

"Oh, this one's good." His blue eyes light. "Booked for possession and conspiracy to kidnap. Bald as a fucking hard-boiled egg in her mugshot. Jett—"

"JJ."

"J's a beast." Orion smiles softly, thumbing my palm.

"Mine though."

"Oh *hell*, yes. I'm done with all of them but Atlas. They're getting fucking crazier." He rubs his neck, and all the silver bite scars have faded but *mine*.

"Like… how done?" Because I was kind of looking forward to seeing them all…*in action*.

"Like, no more mating bites except for yours and his, but anything goes during heats. Especially if that's what you want." Orion tugs me into his lap. "Only this heat's all yours. I owe you."

"You don't—"

"*Yes*." He teases his chin into my scalp until I shudder. "Not like it's going to be a sacrifice watching them worship my omega."

"*Watching*?" I tilt my head back just in time to catch his smirk.

"Participating. Lending a helping hand."

"More than a hand." My body starts to purr, and he mirrors the sound, stroking my skin to pebbles.

House cats.

I pull his arms around me, and feeling so perfectly secure, I dial Atlas.

Insta-answer. "*Lilah?*"

"You can all come in."

The door wrenches open and Finn stumbles through. Atlas, Hunter, and JJ hurry, half a step behind.

But just before Atlas reaches the couch, he pulls back, letting Hunter reach us first.

"Lilah Darling." Hunter drops to his knees. "Will you be ours?"

"*Mine.*" Finn crawls to me.

"Mine," JJ agrees. "I'm already yours."

"Ours." Atlas covers the hand that Orion still holds. "Our mate. Our omega. Our—"

"*Everything,*" Orion purrs. "You're everything, Lilah. What we didn't even know we needed."

They stare at me so hard, my tremble ratchets.

So does my scent.

The alphas lean forward on their knees. Atlas starts to *hummmm* this gravelly rumble that's better than a magic wand.

My attention slips to my gooey center.

I'm melting by the second.

Almost time to borrow *their* magic wands.

"One thing." I climb from Orion's lap into Atlas's arms and press his neck, nuzzling his lust-spiked musk. "Stop calling me Darling."

"*Lilah Wyvern.*" Atlas smooths my back. His thumb digs between my vertebrae, making me twitch so good, I think he's melting my spine.

Hunter climbs to the couch and sandwiches me into Atlas.

Dominance and lust.

Smoke and musk.

My eyes lose focus. I make a happy pant, fingers kneading their T-shirts. "So? Who's biting me first?"

Hunter smiles against my ear. "The pack leader—"

"Is Hunter," Atlas rumbles.

"At. No. You're more dominant and—"

"And it's not a problem if I don't challenge you. Which I won't." Atlas claps his shoulder. "My omegas need my full-time attention. You can do the paperwork."

Hunter groans, but then his arms tighten around my waist. He tears me from Atlas and lifts me high, softly kissing my collarbone. "Worth it."

I squeeze his neck, more lethargic by the moment, and rub my nose against his collar. "When do I get to taste your tattoos?"

"Right the fuck now." He sprints so fast, I squeal, grabbing on as he rockets to my nest.

Our nest.

My belly warms.

It's a much more gentle heat than before. Not a snapping, clawing, scary kind of pain, but a soft…*unspooling*.

Like all the fears and doubts that kept me so wrapped up and restricted are finally falling free.

Because I'm safe.

I'm protected.

And I'm about to be fucking worshipped.

FORTY-EIGHT

LILAH

HUNTER CARRIES me into the dim, cozy nest. The pulse between my legs pounds so fast, it's like a clitoral heart attack.

He spreads me on the mattress, then crawls to straddle my thighs, draping me in dominance and blooming smoke.

When he whips off his tee, I climb to my elbows.

Been waiting for this view.

Geometric tattoos line every muscle, inked to emphasize his abs and the hard cut of his V. His bronze skin is shaved so smooth—

Can't wait.

I lick a line to his belly button, humming.

Tastes like honey.

"*Killer*." His voice strains. "You're the one who's supposed to get licked."

I push into his abs, staring up his ridiculous body. "Anyone can lick anyone in my nest."

Orion laughs, crawling to me, and when he pulls me against his chest, it feels so fucking *right*.

He's my pillow and my best support.

"There's gonna be a lot of licking." He kisses my forehead, his blond curl ticklish. Then he licks my cheek and I squeal.

"Show me," I breathe, hazier, hotter, rising into a fuzzy-warm frenzy I've never felt before, because surrounded by my alphas and my omega, the heat doesn't hurt.

It *burns*, but in the good way that leaves me tightening my thighs.

Orion moves me between his legs, putting himself in chair-back position and propping us against mounded pillows. "Let your pack leader show you."

"Lilah." Hunter kisses the joint of my thumb, then bites the pad of my hand.

My breath hitches.

He kisses and licks, slowly, slowly tracing up my arm. When he sucks the hollow of my elbow, my hips lift—but Orion presses them down.

"Sweet." Hunter slurps my skin.

Feels like I'm sweating syrup.

So.

Hot.

I gasp.

"*Finn,*" Hunter barks. "Do her other arm."

Shirtless, flashing the tattoo that proves I own him, Finn takes my hand. "Yes, *Daddy.*"

"Dude. *No.*" Hunter swats him.

Finn ignores the hit, nibble-sucking my fingers.

Um.

"Atlas would be daddy." Orion shakes with held-back laughter. "You'd be mo—"

"*Enough,*" Hunter's bark-laced growl gives me one good shiver before it stills my bones. Orion goes just as rigid.

I smirk when his cock twitches against my back.

Set your own trap, boo.

"Enough with the commentary. You want to use your mouths, use them on our girl."

"Yes, *Alpha,*" Orion purrs, still fifty percent smirk.

I have more to say, but Orion tongues my ear.

While he and Finn devour me with licks, Atlas and JJ stroke my legs with warm palms, adding their soft rumbles to the hum of the nest.

So much touch.

I'm dizzy when Hunter finally takes my lips.

He's smoke on my tongue, darting in hard and confident with a purr that vibrates my lungs and soothes me so completely, all I feel is *him*.

Hunter flattens a palm to my stomach and spreads his fingers wide. "Let me take care of you?"

"*Yes*." I shimmy. Not that I'm not enjoying every second of this, but *dude*. "Get the hell inside me."

"When you're ready." Hunter kisses my chin.

I'm ready.

Been dripping since they offered me a cabin in the woods. Their touches and scents only stroke me higher.

"*Lift your arms*," Hunter commands, his voice, this raspy, smoky scratch.

I fucking *obey*.

Elbows snapping, arms lifting high.

"That's my girl." Hunter slides off my hoodie, then pulls up my tee, but he doesn't go all the way, leaving my eyes covered, arms tangled in cloth while my chest hangs in the breeze.

Orion's hug has me double bound.

Blind and pinned.

"*Star*," Finn growls at the lacy orange bra I wore just to screw with him.

"Matching set." I smile, eyes blocked, but I don't panic. I just tense, shivering, waiting to feel what they do next.

I trust them.

So much, it shakes my heart.

Someone yanks away my leggings. Then my panties and bra fly free thanks to two or three sets of helping hands.

My heat-soaked scent sparks a roomful of growls that make my belly contract.

"Perfect girl," Atlas murmurs, suddenly closer.

"Been dreaming of this taste." Hunter's voice rumbles between my thighs. "So fucking wet for us."

Gripping hard enough to dimple my thighs, he nuzzles into my heat, dragging his nose, then his lips over my pulsing clit.

His breath hitches, a ragged inhale, then a hot, feathery exhale that leaves me wiggling.

My belly pulses.

Tension's fucking unbearable. "Hunter."

"*Relax*," he says in that rasp I'd never disobey.

I fall against my omega body pillow, caressed by hands and lips I still can't see. The darkness leaves me drowning in their scents and stroking sounds.

Like Hunter's edible fucking growl, vibrating the hollow of my inner thigh. "Show me how pretty you come, Princess. Then I'll stretch you. Right. Fucking. *Here*." Soft enough to make me go insane, he drags his teeth down my heat-slick lips, then teases my entrance with a flat-tongued lap. "Let you take my knot while I take your throat."

Yes to all of that and fucking *now*.

I arch, begging for it, but someone pins me down.

"*Alpha*." I whine and kick.

"*Shhhh*," he whispers to my clit, and I go still.

The second I relax, Hunter sucks the nub between his wet lips.

He licks and he sucks and he fucking vibrates until all I can do is flail.

Can't see.

Only feel.

Hunter flicks his tongue-tip.

Finn sinks teeth into my arm.

JJ runs his thumbs over my curling toes.

And Atlas—suddenly a fucking omega tamer—presses his wide palm over my heart, digging fingers into my bared neck.

Secret button unlocked.

I buck against Hunter's hot mouth.

He purrs against my clit, arms tightening to pin open my quaking, out-of-control thighs. His warm tongue keeps flicking and flicking, and I— "*Ah!*"

"So pretty." Orion sucks my ear.

I jerk, kicking against their hold, not because I want to be let go, but because it feels *too fucking good*.

I'm high and dripping, but my pussy gives a desperate clench. *Empty.*

"Lilah." Still can't see Hunter, but his ragged breath heats my sensitive nub. "Tell me what you want."

"Stretch. Knot. Bite." *Everything.*

"That's my girl." He smooths up my sides, fucking *finally* pulling me free of the tangled shirts.

He kneels in front of me.

Pants off.

I swallow at my first view of Hunter's cock.

So thick.

The tip strains against his ripped abs, angry purple like it's mad it's not already sheathed.

You and me both, buddy.

I rub the crown with an understanding thumb.

Spongy.

Fun.

Hunter hisses a warning. "*Lilah.*"

I stroke his shaft, exploring the ridges and smooth hardness. His purr vibrates my palm, and his knot heats under my touch, slowly filling.

It won't puff all the way until it's buried *deep*.

My fingers shake.

Stomach clenches.

Oh god.

Need it.

Need *him*.

"Hunter. *Please.*"

He palms his cock, but instead of sliding in, he strokes it

through my lips, working up and down, coating himself in my slick.

I gasp and grab for support.

Orion hugs my ribs. Atlas and Finn each snag a trembling hand and stroke my sides, while JJ handcuffs my ankles, spreading me wide for his pack brother.

Fucking soaked in my wetness, Hunter nudges his tip to my entrance.

I tense.

So big.

"He's the thickest," Orion whispers. "But you're made for him. Show your pack leader how badly you need his knot." Orion's belly-stroke melts my tension and there's magic in having my own omega at my back.

I lock Hunter's gaze, spreading my thighs and daring him to lock me right the fuck back. "*Alpha.*"

His dick twitches.

I groan, trying to grind down and force him inside.

But Hunter pins my thighs.

"Omega. *Mine.*" He thrusts.

My ass clenches, muscles shifting to make room for the slow slide that fills me so good, I think he hits my lungs.

Carefully stroking in then out, in then out, Hunter works himself deep. He's bigger than Orion. Not much longer, but so fucking *thicccccccc.*

No joke about the stretch.

My eyes cross when his knot finally knocks my gates.

Come right in, sir.

Been waiting to say hello.

Shaking, he drops to give my lips the sweetest kiss. "*Perfect.* Perfect, Lilah."

My heart oozes, omega instincts purring with primal satisfaction at his praise.

But my hips?

They just want to get to fucking *work.*

I nudge forward, bumping the hot bulb of his knot. "Gimme."

"Greedy, *Killer*." He kisses my nose, then hitches my thighs, pulling me from Orion to brace for that last push. "Always be greedy. You can have whatever you want."

Yeah, but all I want is Hunter.

He fills me so full, but there's one spot he hasn't hit.

It *aches*.

Hungry.

Fucking desperate for him.

"Easy." Atlas strokes my neck. The guys grip my hips and shoulders, steadying me while Hunter makes the last push.

The fucking stretch.

Holy shit.

He eases in and—

The air pumps from my lungs when he pops past my last ring of muscle. My body gloves him, and his knot gives a teasing pulse.

It swells and stretches, hitting spots no man, hand, or vibrator has ever touched before. *And not for lack of fucking trying!*

So.

Fucking.

Full.

Don't know what to do with my hands or legs or arms. All my attention falls to the place where we're joined. To Hunter's heat and scent and the soft, encouraging purrs of my soon-to-be-permanent mates.

The knot hooks deep inside, my muscles squeezing and trapping him inside.

"Perfect," Hunter purrs.

He rocks into me, circling his hips, driving the thick knot deeper and bumping aching new places that turn my vision to sparkles.

I gasp smoke-drenched air, slowly adjusting to the mind-numbing fullness. Still don't know what I'm doing, but my body does.

Instincts have me clamping down, pulling and stroking his length.

"*Fuck.*" Hunter's eyes roll back, and his uncontrolled tremble is just as delicious as the power trip of milking his twitching cock.

Even his abs twitch.

His release finally soothes the heat and the ache.

This is what I need.

The feel of him inside me, hot and hard and ready to fuck until we both collapse.

"*Lilah.*" He thrusts. "Make me insane. Fuck. Rut. Can't…"

His brown eyes go hazy, and his scent goes fucking crazy.

We're locked so close, his tremble feels like mine.

Desperate madness bleeds through eyes so always in control. I yank his face to mine so he can see how badly I want to feel him fall apart. "Give me *everything.*"

Hunter roars.

Pins my ankles above my head.

Then his hips go nuclear.

Pumping, pumping, *pounding* with his cock and his knot until my legs shake and my eyes cross and I claw his shoulders, praying this never fucking ends.

When my pussy clenches, a soul-deep moan has me tipping back my head, offering him my throat.

When Hunter bites, everything goes white.

Thought I was already full, but there's room for so much more.

A line of heat curls around my neck, then sinks into my heart.

It feathers like smoke.

Like Hunter.

Fucking triple penetration—body, heart, and soul.

Never be alone again.

Hunter licks his mark, washing me in glory and possessive need so deep, I keen.

Need to mark him back.

Make him fully mine.

Yanking his head exactly where I want it, I sink my teeth into Hunter's pulse.

His skin tastes like honey, but his blood tastes like smoke, and he curls into my deepest spots, filling every empty hole in my soul.

We're locked so tight, bound so full, I know he'll never let me go.

Hunter's voice hitches. "I'll never hurt you. Never let you be hurt again."

I claw his shoulders, rocking on his knot. "You can hurt me *a little*."

"*Lilah*," he growls, and I can't stir any more shit when his hips pump.

Feels like we bounce for hours, perfectly joined, but my sense of time melts.

I'm limp and lethargic when Hunter finally pulls out, looking like a smug, dried-out skeleton with good hair. He licks my neck, possessively tending the fresh bite. "Round two?"

Now?

I want a nap.

A bowl of ice cream.

But the second I'm empty, my body's all *nope*.

Need more knots.

I cramp, then groan. "*More*."

This fucking *heat*.

"Starshine." Finn looms, naked and fucking feral as he yanks me away from Hunter. "Gotta make you mine."

"How do you want—"

With a liquifying growl, he flips me onto my belly, hoists my thighs and sinks into my pussy from behind.

I'm so slick, but he's so fucking *long*.

Finn slides so deep, his knot teases my muscles at first thrust.

I am *here for it* if he wants to ride me rough.

Hunter has me *allllll* warmed up.

Instead, Finn lifts my ribs, hugging my waist so I kneel

splayed on his thighs. My head bumps his hot shoulder, resting on the pillow of my own inked name.

Breath thick with blood oranges and cream, Finn grips my throat. "*Mine. Forever.*"

Lifting his hips, he takes me with knot and teeth, in a mind-numbing, full-body claiming. He tears into me just above Hunter's sweetly stinging mark.

Cold fire lights in my heart.

Finn.

Mine.

I squeeze his thighs until he releases me. Then I twist to sink my bite into his freckled throat. "Forever."

"Star," voice wrecked, my blood on his lips, Finn fucks me until the room blurs.

When I release his throat, I tip forward.

Drunk, dizzy, dazed.

Finn's blood is orange juice and vodka.

Maybe fucking cocaine.

I want more.

Want to mark him all over, and he'll *totally* let me.

Orion comes to my rescue, supporting my front by sucking a nipple into his mouth. "Helping hand." He licks the pebbled nub and presses a thumb to my humming clit.

Finn sucks my neck and bounces me on his lap until he's moaning, "*Star,*" and I'm seeing them twinkle—whole fucking galaxies.

I work my hips and hold my belly, loving the heat that Finn pumps inside me again and again and again, satisfying the primal need to be filled.

I pant and moan while Finn sucks my neck, licking and tending my growing collection of bites.

When Finn pulls out, he doesn't let me go—just passes me to a patiently waiting Atlas who cups my cheeks, rubs our noses, and stares into my eyes. "What do you need, sweet girl?"

"More." I grip his thick, juicy thighs, finally getting to see them bare, dark and corded with muscle.

Orion lifts me into Atlas's lap, helping me sink onto his lover's cock.

My eyes roll back, but maybe because I can't feel him in my chest yet, a wisp of anxiety sneaks through the chaotic fuzz of heat. "Aren't you going to mate—"

"Not today, koala. This is all you." Orion steals my mouth, nipping my lower lip. Then he kisses up my jaw, working back to the ear he keeps sucking like candy. "Let me watch you ride my alpha. Next time, we'll both ride."

Unh. "Does it have to be next time?"

Atlas chuckles, low and stroking.

He pinches Orion's chin, yanking him for a kiss that surprises us both—especially because I don't feel the least bit jealous.

Hard to feel neglected when I'm speared on his vibrating cock.

I'm full.

Loved.

And I can't wait to see how many ways the three of us fit together.

But after stroking Orion's hair, Atlas flips his attention, feeding me an apple-flavored kiss. Then he says the magic fucking words. "After your heat, I'll make your fries."

I groan. "Unfair dirty talk."

"You're not doing heat right if you're talking." Orion presses my thighs, teasing me against Atlas's waiting knot. "Fuck my girl until she's speaking tongues."

Umm. "Yes."

Orion laughs.

He's so fucking bright, it takes my breath away, and that little jolt of shocked happiness finally seals me onto Atlas's knot.

He swells inside me.

Finn is long.

Hunter's thick.

But Atlas?

Both at the same time.

Plus, he has a partner in crime with a smirk and smart mouth that keeps licking my ear lobes and pebbled nipples.

When I moan a string of consonants, Orion laughs into my hair.

Atlas works my hips while I cling to his shoulders.

I don't even know who thumbs my clit.

When the orgasm crashes, Atlas spilling inside me, he and Orion sink dual bites, leaving me a shivering, shaking mess as two bonds sing to life.

While Atlas claims the bare side of my neck, opposite Finn and Hunter's marks, Orion goes big, biting the front of my throat.

Dead center.

Gonna have to wear his scar like a necklace.

It's unmissable.

Permanent.

Perfect.

They lick their bites in total sync, purring and rumbling, Atlas working his hips in torturously slow circles until I'm drunk on his knot and the glowing warmth of their happiness, shining next to my heart.

"Lilah," Atlas mumbles into my throat. "Give me your bite?"

I snap like a viper.

His neck's so juicy with muscle, I can barely break skin, but I work until I taste the richness of his blood.

"So lucky to have you." He rubs my head. "Perfect girl."

Atlas drops anchor in my heart.

I've never felt anything so… *solid.*

And that's saying *a lot* while I'm still clenching on his cock.

With his strokes and whispers, and Orion's instigating licks, we rock together for ages.

When Atlas finally slides me off his knot, sweaty and panting, I'm so exhausted I can't lift my arms.

But I'm ready for the cramp that forces me to go again.

Instead, my pussy gives a happy flutter.

Temporarily satisfied.

"Drink water." Orion crawls to me with a tumbler from the mini-fridge and helps hold the straw to my lips.

I chug, thirsty as hell.

I've already been knotted for hours and this is nowhere near the end.

"Sticky," I complain, turning whiny as fuck the second everything's not perfect.

Whoa.

I grip my belly, trying not to hormone rage.

Atlas kisses my forehead, and I feel his content smile in my soul. "Wash. We'll switch the sheets."

That's when my shadow reappears.

He's been here every second, at the fringes.

A stroke of my thigh. A brush of my fingers.

Now JJ scoops me away.

Barely favoring his arm with the healing gunshot wound, he carries me into the bathroom where the soaking tub waits full of steamy suds and cherry blossoms.

No one follows.

The distance is weird, but not unwelcome. As much as I crave them all against my skin, I can feel them inside and nearby. Ready if I call.

So I sink happily into JJ's embrace as he lowers me into the water.

The heat makes me moan.

JJ scrubs me while I doze, head against a tub pillow. He washes every finger and every little toe like he's polishing marble.

When his arm dips below the water, and he scrubs my belly with a soft sponge, the needy flutter returns.

But I hesitate. "JJ. If you don't want—"

"I do." He pulls my wrist from the water and kisses my bracelet with eyes so dark, my heart goes still. "Don't deserve you, but I'll work until I do."

I smile around my new favorite words. "*Show me.*"

JJ pulls me from the water, then wraps us both in a huge fuzzy towel.

The nest is empty, sheets fresh.

Guys are giving us space.

He eases me to the mattress, then pats me dry.

I watch for the smallest twitch that says this isn't right, that he's on edge, but the more JJ touches me, the more at ease he feels. He...*softens* in a way I've never seen, focused on me instead of his demons.

When I'm spread out on the bed, he crawls to lie next to me, our faces flush and our long hair mixing on the pillows.

His cedar's more cherry than blossom.

Sweet.

That nostalgic scent that reminds me of the boy I never stopped loving.

Even when we both forgot.

Even when we both stopped believing in love.

JJ moves my hand to his throat. I hook my fingers in his tight collar, and he makes the ticklish purr that's only for me.

Slowly, gently, I tug his lips to mine.

Our mouths bump.

Soft.

He doesn't close his eyes.

JJ stares scary deep, and I look back just as closely, finding sparkling galaxies instead of creeping dark.

"*Lilac*," he murmurs.

"Do you want my bite?" I run my fingers through his silky hair. "We don't—"

"*Want*." He pulls me close, inhaling my scent until I tremble, scent spiking high.

I hitch my thigh over his hip.

He shifts our weight, and his length presses my heat, drying my throat.

"Need you," I gasp.

"You have me." Agonizingly slow, he inches inside, all the while, staring into the depths of my eyes.

There's barely a stretch when his knot enters. Still feels empty when I clench.

Then JJ pulls me close and starts to roll his body.

That little bitty knot?

It starts to fill.

Then it fills and fills and *fucking fill*s until I'm so full I cling to him like I'm falling off a cliff.

The hell?

Is that thing a freaking softball?

JJ smooths my sweaty brow. "Does it hurt?"

"Not...hurt." *Holy—*

I gasp, fingers biting his shoulders and deepening his soft, special purr. The rumble vibrates *everywhere*.

I come, gasping, holding his long hair like a rope.

"I'm yours." He nips my throat, tasting my skin, savoring it with utter reverence before finally biting down.

His emotions glow into my soul.

His swelling contentment. Then his dedication to me and the pure, sweet fucking *awe* that we're here, we're together, and we're bound.

When I bite him back, the final circuit clicks.

My world flares five times brighter.

Hunter.

Finn.

Atlas.

Orion.

JJ.

My pack.

They're with me and always will be.

JJ and I move together, clinging to each other, trading orgasms and happiness until the others crowd in, stroking my arms and hips.

After JJ gives me one last, melting kiss, they pull me into a warm Wyvern pile.

I want more.

Knots and hugs and kisses and cakes.

I want it all.

And finally.

It's all mine.

TWO MONTHS LATER

LILAH

"*JUST LIKE THAT*," Orion purrs. "See how his toes are kneading the carpet? He loves it."

Atlas groans. "Been telling you I like it for a fucking *hour*. O—"

"*Shhhhhh.*" Orion pats Atlas's bare, vibrating thigh. "Don't interrupt my lesson."

I giggle around the tip of Atlas's swollen cock.

Orion's been giving me blowjob classes.

True confession?

I'm a blowjob genius—naturally talented, and a quick learner with five mates who line up to let me practice.

But we've been milking this shtick—*and Atlas*—for weeks.

It's my new favorite game, and we have plenty of time to play with Atlas on a long-term bonding leave from Wyvern House.

Orion and I crouch between his thick thighs like bandits, taking turns licking our alpha-pop. Atlas started strong, cradling my head, but now he's on his back, muffling desperate, being-murdered moans into the mountain of pillows on my bed.

I lap his shaft like a kitten, barely brushing his heated skin with the tip of my tongue. "I don't think I'm doing it right. Maybe ten more minutes and—"

"*Lilah.*" Atlas's growl dips dangerously low.

When Atlas goes growly, the game gets *really* fun.

Orion squeezes my knee, giving me the signal and a smirk that turns his eyes to sapphires.

Before our alpha can pounce, we drop in evil unison, bumping cheeks as we suck the swollen bulb of Atlas's angry knot.

Atlas flails.

Roars.

We run.

Laughing, we bolt from my bedroom, splitting off to hide.

Orion darts across the living room, while I scurry down the long hall to the nest.

Best part about this game?

No one loses.

I consider hiding in the bathtub for shock value, but it's too cold when I'm only wearing socks and tangerine panties.

Finn buys me a new pair every time he rips one off.

My need for comfy warmth wins. I dive into the nest and burrow until I'm a mole person, fully buried in soft pillows. I try to slow my panting, but even if Atlas can't hear my heated breaths, all that teasing wasn't just torturing *him*.

I'm fucking soaked and my scent is thick enough to stir.

If Atlas finds Orion first, I get to ride them both.

If he finds me…

My mouth waters.

Do I order the sandwich, the spit roast, or the full buffet?

When padding footsteps cut the silence of the nest, my pussy flutters.

Mmm.

Buffet.

The steps creak under Atlas's weight.

"*Lilah*," he rasps. "I can smell your perfume. How wet are you, sweet girl?"

I giggle.

Don't want to hide.

I love being *found*.

Atlas topples my pillows.

Then he drops, pinning me to the mattress.

I moan.

It feels so good when he covers me.

Shelters me.

His cock is tormented, molten iron, pressing my thigh. I'm so slick, he wouldn't even have to thrust. I'd slide straight onto his knot.

But Atlas doesn't take me.

Yet.

Instead, he kisses my throat, gently cupping my face with his thick fingers.

When his tongue teases the silvery scar of his mating bite, his body's the only thing that stops me from hitting the ceiling.

You read about a thing, but when you *really feel it*—

Atlas sucks my skin between his teeth, and our bond *sparkles*.

It's this ticklish, tingly feeling, deep inside.

Between the pinch and the heat and the giddy reminder that Atlas is mine—and he fucking *loves* being bound—I gasp.

Then I shudder, hooking my ankles around his hips, clawing his thick shoulders, grinding into him until—

Oops.

Atlas's chuckle vibrates my jugular. "Did you just…?"

"You *sucked* me."

He nuzzles my super-ticklish throat. "I'll suck you again. Somewhere else?"

"Mmm." I scratch his head, and the big, bad alpha leans into my touch like a wolf pup. He's still Atlas—checks our door locks fifty times and has old married couple fights with Hunter—but now he's *my* Atlas. The one who funnels his drill sergeant energy into precision-cutting ravioli and memorizing books on the omega orgasm.

His ex-military ass looks fantastic in an apron.

Try to complain about that.

"Should we find our boyfriend?" He hauls me from the

mattress, and I moan when my pussy kisses his bare abs, only one thin piece of fabric separating me from his taut skin.

"Find him fast." I'm sweating fucking bullets.

Aching.

Need them both.

One palm gripping my ass, the other cupping my neck, Atlas carries me from the nest.

Orion's cider would be easy to follow even if I couldn't feel his sunshine in my soul. Tracking him, I start to sniff.

Then choke.

Atlas misses a step.

Because the lush apple cider we know and love?

It's sharp as my favorite shiv and so desperately ragged with need that my stomach muscles scissor.

Atlas bulls into Orion's bedroom.

We find him curled in the closet, hugging his knees.

The second he spots us, he pounces, landing half in Atlas's arms and half in mine. I squeeze him tight, and his back's so sweaty hot, I think my nipples start to smoke. "Orion. *Your heat.*"

"Just a spike," he murmurs. "Hit me so fast."

Atlas and I share a look over Orion's curls, and his eyes are just as fiery as Orion's skin.

They boil with possession.

Nervous excitement bubbles in my belly.

Been waiting for this.

"Let us ease you." I kiss Orion's shoulder.

Atlas carries us to Orion's bed and I'm totally focused on helping Orion, but I can't help wiggling in his sheets. The guys spend most nights with me, but Atlas and Orion go on cute dates when I'm busy between Finn and Hunter, so the bed's a perfect mix of their mingled scents. Makes me want to go all burrowy and add my perfume to the tangle.

"*Kneel*," Atlas orders with just enough bark to curl my toes.

But it's not me he's commanding.

Orion fucking kneels.

His pink lips part, eyes glassy with need.

"*Good*." Atlas slips behind him, caging his waist and arching him back for me. He smiles with teeth, then drags the blunt edges of that smirk straight down Orion's neck. "Show him what evil shit he's been teaching you."

"Wait." Orion squirms, cheeks turning pink. "Lilah. *Koala*. Perfect, perfect, Lilah. Don't use your powers for—"

I palm his cock.

Hot.

Atlas stops Orion from shying away, one hand around his waist, the other teasing his ass. The bedroom turns full-on cider mill when Orion's slick hits the air.

"Fuck." Sweat drips down Orion's neck.

Helpful mate I am, I lick the salty drop, squeezing his cock as I tease the bite mark that won't be alone on his neck much longer.

Atlas has been waiting to make his claim.

I can't wait for Orion's heat.

I lick my omega all over.

His peaked nipples. His shaking abs. And the tip of his crown that glistens with pre-cum like applesauce.

When Atlas has Orion loose and moaning, he switches his fingers for his cock, and murmuring sweet words, slowly pushes into Orion's twitching ass.

Atlas kisses Orion's neck and rubs his stomach, adoring him the same way he adores me.

Orion's lashes flutter.

His nails dig half-moons in Atlas's forearms.

And his panting exhale makes my clit jump.

Love watching them.

But I'm done watching.

Crawling to join the fun, I flat-tongue glide Orion's shaft from base to tip while Atlas pins his hips. Then I take his head between the heat of my lips and tease his sensitive slit.

"Shit." Orion arches. "Best student."

I *hmm* as I take him deeper.

His fingers wind in my hair, and he starts to bob as Atlas gently pumps, working in his knot. Orion doesn't *actually* taste like applesauce, but my hormones are so fucking gone for him, they have me licking cinnamon.

"Ah!" He shakes as Atlas sinks his knot that last *stretch* of an inch.

They gasp as they lock together.

Before I have time to think how I'll join, they're tugging me up, into the tangle of their arms.

Atlas steals my kiss, controlling the back of my head, using his tongue to claim me the same way his body claims Orion.

I tremble, soaked in leathery warmth and heat.

Orion pushes in, tilting my face to trade Atlas's heavy, *own-you* kisses into trembling licks. Gasping, we trade air, breathing each other in and out.

Apple and caramel.

Cinnamon and sugar.

"Let me knot you?" Orion murmurs against my lips.

Um. Yes, please?

I scramble from the bed, whipping open his nightstand to grab a jelly bulb while I kick off my panties. Still locked to Orion, Atlas leans into the pillows, propping their bodies at the perfect angle for me. Atlas strokes Orion's shaft, long and slow.

Their breathing is ragged.

Muscles shaking.

But their eyes?

On me.

Always on me.

They deserve a little show.

I slide my hand down my stomach, dipping between my legs with flat-palmed strokes that leave me dizzy and slicked in burnt sugar.

When I crawl onto the bed, Atlas holds Orion ready for me.

What a gentleman.

I coat Orion's length in my slick, then squeezing, teasing him with my thumbs, I slowly drag the jelly bulb to his base.

"Oh, fuck." Orion's toes twitch. "Need you."

Atlas strokes Orion's throat. "*Come, Lilah.*"

I climb onto their laps.

Then straddling Orion, I hover over his tip.

When I sink down on his cock, I'm so ready, so wet, the stretch is all glide until I bump the girthy toy bulb.

I'll take Orion any way he'll have me, but I love fucking him with the added width.

Kind of addicted to knots.

I rock against the toy, teasing, myself and them, working it slowly, deliciously inside.

But with a helpful nudge from Atlas, the last inch sinks, with that sweet, sweet stretch that leaves me moaning. "So good."

Orion's belly is hot.

His skin so flushed.

All I want to do is make him feel better.

Cupping his face, I start to work my hips.

I've figured out this riding thing.

It's just like dance.

I rock my hips in an S-wave, swaying back and forth, driving Orion deep into me, deep onto Atlas. A little swivel in my hips. I squeeze down on Orion's cock, rubbing the jelly knot against every ticklish spot until the room disappears and Orion mutters languages I don't have to speak to understand.

When the pressure feels too good, my abs starting to clench, my rhythm falling apart, Atlas takes control.

He digs fingers in my hips, just as hard as I like, yanking me down, down, down as he pump, pump, *pumps* into Orion.

I let go.

When I go liquid in his hands, submitting and showing my throat, Atlas's ecstatic purr vibrates through Orion's ribs. Squeezing Orion between us, he sucks my neck. "Sweet, perfect girl."

His praise has my pussy tightening.

Arms shaking.

Orion's even farther gone.

Eyes blue glass.

But when I catch his gaze, he gives me this muzzy smile so perfect and sweet, it's the fucking thing that pushes me over the edge.

I come hard, twisting, arching, almost vibrating off Orion, but Atlas is there, holding me steady, keeping the rhythm going and going and—

Holy.

Fuck.

Orion jerks inside me, searing hot.

I shake.

Stroked by their purrs.

Hugged by their crazy warmth.

Orion goes limp, his forehead dropping to my shoulder as he pants. I stroke his trembling thighs. "You feel cooler."

"Better." He sighs. Then he licks my entire collar of mate marks, hitting every sensitive scar. "*Perfect.*"

With Atlas knotted, I have to ride Orion a few more times before we can pull apart.

What sacrifice.

When we finally collapse in a pile on the mattress, it's a fucking mess, but my omega instincts hum with gross satisfaction.

I'd be pregnant a thousand times if not for my implant.

So not ready.

But...

When Atlas scoops me up, propping me and Orion on his wide chest.

When we snuggle close, all three of us together.

When he strokes our hips, and rubs, and takes turns licking our throats, never stopping that gravelly *purrrrrrr*....

Everything is so fucking perfect, I can finally picture the future

I never used to let myself dream.

————

IT'S late afternoon when I wake to Orion kissing my eyelids.

"I was supposed to go to work," I groan, hugging him tight. My instincts might be smug, but I can't function as an over-glazed toaster pastry. "Need to shower."

Atlas rubs my ass, then jolts me awake with a light *smack*.

Not even hard enough to make a mark.

But my pupils blow.

More of that.

Atlas rubs deep, kneading my cheek and kissing my nose, but he doesn't miss my tremble, and the way he licks his lips says we're going to revisit that soon.

Hopefully really freaking soon.

He rolls out of bed, but I can't make myself leave the sheets.

"Sure you're okay?" I cling to Orion, probably *definitely* stalling going back to real life.

"I have a few days before the heat hits. Better go schedule leave. I want you there every second."

"I'll go," I say a little too whiny. "But tonight—"

"Need you." His voice lifts in a fake whisper. "Should we call Juan Pablo or—"

Atlas snarls from the closet.

I don't even try to bite back my crazy grin. "Are we having a threesome heat?"

"Nah. Everyone's invited." Orion licks his lips.

My greedy pussy tingles like I'm not already lying here bare and glazed. I've been plenty satisfied—love how they make me their center—but I'm *dying* to watch Orion get the same treatment.

On that note.

Have to move now or I'll climb my omega and never get out of bed.

Groaning, I stumble to the bathroom.

Cold shower.

Orion's closet is three-quarters my clothes—so are all the guys' closets—but I'm not a fan of the fancy dresses and skirts they keep buying. I change into leggings and an apple-soaked hoodie.

That's how omegas do business casual.

When I hit the kitchen, Atlas and Orion sit me between them in the breakfast nook and take turns feeding me bites of Atlas's ridiculous dozen-egg omelet.

Orion's bites come slathered in spicy Franken-sauces.

Atlas tries to stuff me with vegetables.

I don't complain.

I *purr*.

And I've fallen real, *real* far because I never want to leave them or our cozy cave.

When the door clatters, we freeze.

Finn kicks into the living room, blood spray mixed in with his freckles, and a maniacal grin that only glows crazier when his gaze snaps to me—a bloodhound who just scented his favorite quarry. "Give me my Star."

I open my arms.

He hauls me over the kitchen table and slings me over his shoulder. Then he pets my ass. "Missed you, Starbutt."

"No. Ban list."

Finn grumbles, carrying me to the door. But I'm grinning as I wave goodbye upside-down. "Call if you need the easing team."

"You're first on my list, little bear." Orion's sweet voice follows us out.

Finn hauls me into the elevator.

He flips me, flattening my back to the wall with a palm cushioning my head.

He knows exactly what feels good.

Never too hard, never too soft.

Finn's a crazy fucking psychic, and his energy rages in my veins.

Yanking my hair, he bares my throat and takes my lips.

Finn kisses like he fucks.

Spearing in his tongue, he takes over my whole mouth, letting me know who's in control.

But he teases me in the same breath that owns me.

Taking my lips, then playing with them, nipping sharp enough to make me gasp, then softly dragging his tongue over my teeth until I'm hyperventilating.

He grinds his cock against my leggings.

"Starshine." He drops his hot mouth to my neck, nipping the scar of his bite as he thrusts.

My veins crackle with red-orange fire.

I dig my fingers into his shoulder blades, trying to resist, trying not to come just from being rubbed down in a public fucking elevator that's already going to smell like sex for hours, but Finn slips his fingers into my panties.

He teases a fingertip into my ass.

Just a little circle as he grinds against my clit.

The unexpected stretch sends me spiraling.

I shake while Finn growls, proud as hell, smugness and fucking *hunger* rabid through our bond.

He gives me *the look*.

Eyes flaming green and pupils yawning black.

Not sure if he's gonna fuck me, bite me, eat me—

And I don't care which one he picks.

I punch the elevator button—the one that rings a silent alarm but stops the door from opening—and yank down Finn's shoulders.

He lets me sink him to his knees.

"Clean your mess." I pull down my leggings.

Finn hauls my legs over his shoulder, slamming my back to the wall as he burrows between my thighs.

He inhales me.

Licks every glossy, slick-dripping inch of my pussy from my outer lips to my sensitive ass to my pulsing clit.

Not just cleaning.

Lapping.

Sucking.

Fucking *devouring*.

He grinds me so hard into the wall, I don't know how he's breathing.

He never.

Stops.

Licking.

Yanking the back of his head, I pull him even deeper, and his growly, satisfied purr vibrates me to fucking madness.

I come shaking, squeezing his ears, slicking his face, tearing at his hair as my hips buck, and all Finn does is chuckle and purr, loving every fucking second of driving me insane.

After sucking me through two more mellow, aftershock orgasms, he licks me like he's cleaning his plate. When he finally has to set me down to fix my pants, I'm a baby fawn, all shaking, gangly legs.

"Thanks for lunch." He scoops me against his rumbling chest and kicks the elevator button, carrying me out.

When we reach Hunter's Jeep, idling by the curb, I realize why he didn't join us.

He's handcuffed to the steering wheel.

"*Finn*." Hunter's nostrils flare.

"Key." I elbow the troublemaker. Finn obediently presses the key into my palm.

I climb into the passenger seat to unlock Hunter's wrists.

But Hunter's frustration melts the second I'm in arm's reach. He sweeps me into his lap, turning his handcuffed arm into a pillow as he kisses me so deep, his smoke curls around my toes.

He nuzzles me with clean-shaven cheeks, mixing himself with Finn's lingering citrus.

Pack leader energy feels *goooood* on him.

I go limp in his lap, lulled almost to another lazy orgasm just from his care-soaked kiss.

He buckles me into his seat—probably super illegal—but I've never had a car panic attack when I'm safe in Hunter's arms.

Finn snags my feet and thumbs my calves.

"Have to postpone our dance night," I say reluctantly.

"No." Finn squeezes my ankles, digging in his nails just hard enough to make me squirm.

"What's up?" Hunter's brow crinkles.

"Orion's spiking." I press his wrinkle. "You're invited to the heat."

"Wouldn't miss it." Hunter's purr sends me shivering. He kisses my ear. "I'll clear my schedule."

"What's going on now?" It's been months and there's still a Redfang mess as the cartel fills its power vacuum.

"Nikolaj." Hunter pushes out a breath. "Pissed his sons are dead."

Finn scoffs. "Old Nik has fifty fucking kids. Who cares if we offed the shitty ones?"

"Nikolaj Redfang? Why do I know that name?" I've had my hands full with my new job—and all the sex—so I've been letting them deal with gang fallout.

"He's the Redfang patriarch. Dom and Erik were heavy in the fight to inherit."

"Will the new heir come for us?" I grip Hunter's shirt.

"No way." Hunter strokes my hair. "If anything they'll send a fruit basket to thank us for killing the competition."

Doubtful.

But I don't have to worry.

Hunter's ace at cleaning up a Wyvern mess.

When he pulls the car through a familiar set of iron-tipped gates and stops at the admin building, our bond gives a sad little pulse because we have to say goodbye for all of an afternoon.

Hunter opens the door. "Have fun at work, Director Wyvern."

"See you tonight." I wiggle out of his lap and onto solid ground.

I wave goodbye, then flash my badge to enter the last place I ever thought I'd agree to take over.

The OCC is still closed, pending reopening under new management.

My management.

My pack threatened to perma-quit Wyvern House if I didn't get a realllllly good apology from the dads. They sent me flowers and a portfolio of businesses to manage.

The OCC is the only one I want.

I'm starting a free scholarship program for abandoned omegas like me.

Revamping everything.

I'm going to make it a place of hope instead of a creepy, awful prison.

Already fired all the trainers except Evgenia and Eleanor.

When I walk into the remodeled office suite, now white and clean and breezy, my secretary, Alice, jumps from her desk with a big smile and an even bigger pile of mail.

Because I haven't been here in…days? Weeks?

Oops.

Oh well.

Still a better director than Hikaru.

"Miss Lilah." She passes me the huge stack of mail. "Didn't think you'd be in today."

"Have to get something accomplished before Orion's heat." I spot the huge envelope at the bottom of the pile and rip it open.

It's the finalized registration for Orion's game company.

Perfect timing for a heat gift.

"Ah. Also…" Alice's gaze drops. She blushes. "He's waiting for you."

With a flutter in my chest, I bounce into my office.

JJ waits for me on his knees.

Collar hugging his throat.

Hands behind his back.

Eyes on the door.

"*Lilac*," he purrs, lighting up when I appear.

It's not just his face and eyes that glow. I feel him coming to life. This pure, sweet, melting energy, so unlike the darkness that almost had him strangled.

I slam the door.

Alice is cool, but she doesn't get to see.

The world can have Jett.

JJ belongs to me.

When I move in front of him, JJ presses his face into my belly. I finger-comb the long hair he left untied for me.

"Missed you," he murmurs.

"How was today?"

He makes a muffled noise, nuzzling without answering.

I rub his shoulders.

His trauma is worse than just Renee. I'm giving him time to heal before asking for the other names. When he's not as fragile, the pack's going to go apeshit in his name.

But not yet.

We all need a lot of therapy before then.

"Comb?" I tug him to my desk.

JJ grabs the silver-plated comb he keeps in my top drawer, then kneels between my knees.

I spend the day stroking his head and screening OCC trainer applications until my cell phone rings.

Hikaru.

He calls a lot since he found out I'm the best candidate for his successor—Wyvern House's future CFO.

I scoff.

He can't afford me.

But today he calls back so many times, I'm curious enough to pick up.

Plus, it's fun to answer when I have his son's head pillowed between my thighs.

"Hello?"

"I'm sending you a report."

I scratch JJ's scalp, loving his purr against my fingertips. "I told you. I'm not doing Wyvern House's books. I—"

"Not that kind of report. It's urgent."

Grumbling, I click over to email. "What could possibly—"

My eyes bug at the pictures on the screen.

A gorgeous blonde with big, brown eyes. Her face is half hidden in a hooded sweatshirt, but she can't hide from me.

Tall.

Toned.

And so fucking familiar, my hitched breath has JJ jumping to grab my shoulders. "Lilac? What's wrong?"

With numb fingers, I touch her face on screen. "*Sol.*"

"We spotted your friend." Hikaru's sigh feathers my ear. "Marisol Redfang."

My fluttering heart stops dead. "Can I see her?"

JJ and Hikaru make twin grumbles.

"That would be unwise," Hikaru says.

"I want to see her." I press her face.

The girl in the photo isn't smiling.

I know that look.

Glancing slightly behind her, ducking her head.

She's being *chased*.

I don't care what her last name is.

Marisol's my ride or die.

Just want to know where she's been.

If she's okay.

If I can help.

Hikaru keeps chirping in my ear, but my vision swirls.

My forehead beads with sweat.

"Lilac." JJ sucks a breath through his teeth. "Your perfume."

My belly quivers.

I press my stomach, suddenly sweating and soaking the room in sharp, toasty caramel.

Thought I was in shock, but no.

It's a spike.

Heat.

JJ hangs up the phone and lifts me into his arms.

He carries me past a gaping Alice. Sweating, I shoot her an embarrassed wave. "Cancel my appointments?"

"Have fun." She waves me out.

JJ carries me to his car while I dial Hunter.

"Lilah? Are you—"

"Need you home." My voice is scratchy, head already full of fuzz.

"What happened?"

"Heat."

"Orion already—"

"*Mine.*"

Hunter gulps. "You're both…"

"We synced."

Finn whoops in the background.

"On our way." Hunter's brakes screech just as JJ's lowering me into his passenger seat.

He kneels to snap my buckle, placing a soft palm on my stomach. "We'll take care of you."

"I know." An unstoppable smile slips free.

I'm itching to burrow in my nest. To be safe in the dark.

But at the same time, I'm weirdly lazy.

No panic. No fear.

Because I know what happens next.

My omega.

My alphas.

My mates.

All of us together.

No matter what comes next…

Well. *It's us.*

It won't be perfect.

We'll probably make a big freaking mess.

But it'll be wild, it'll be fun, and somehow, it'll all work out in the end.

I smile. "I'm ready to go home."

ACKNOWLEDGMENTS

Extremely squishy heartfelt thanks to the mentors, Buddhist nuns, and clutch teammates who made Part Two possible:

Lisa Cron
Pema Chodron
Margie Lawson
Louise Grace Lemmon-Scott
Colette Rhodes
Sullyn Shaw
Lauren Pixley
Sam Coleman
Jenf
+ Every single member of my ROCKSTARS who said a nice thing, ever (I print a lot of them for my wall), or shared how much you were looking forward to this book. I want to write you so many more things!!

More thanks to the bookworld women who've helped me, uplifted me, or supported me (often in ways they don't know), and who continue to uplift other authors:

Alisha Williams
Willow Hadley
T.S. Snow
Mary Martel
Mary Rose PA
Flora Quincy
Kathryn Moon
Anna Fury

Rory Miles
Dreia Wells
Mila Sin
Quinn Arthurs
MJ Marstens
Grace McGinty
@s.rae.reads
Smut & Spice Podcast

ALSO BY LOLA ROCK

PACK DARLING

Part One

Part Two

+ More coming soon!

Join Lola's Facebook pack for updates:

https://www.facebook.com/groups/lolarockstars